THE RULER
OF THE RED RULER

I0607125

KUTTA

THE RULER OF THE RED RULER

Printed in the United States of America.

ISBN: 978-0-9992646-5-2

TABLE OF CONTENTS

ACKNOWLEDGEMENTS

I dedicate this book to Slim Cash, Skrew Head
and Darius gone but never forgotten...

I would like to thank Slim Cash for his vision
without his dream the motivation behind this
movement wouldn't exist. I would also like to thank
Charneese and Ace Boogie for making this
opportunity possible for me. I would like to thank
Xavier Young for his help and last but never least I
would thank my children for being the motivation
behind everything I do...

Chapter One

PRESENT DAY
NOVEMBER 19TH, 2017
12:00AM

A s the rain slammed against the windshield of his new 2018 Jaguar F-Pace Portfolio, Shah slowed down, noticing that the light was turning red at the intersection of Stoughton and Buckeye Road. Shah came to a complete stop and instantly checked his sides and rear-view mirrors. On his right he noticed a minivan approaching at a slow speed. The minivan made a brief stop at the light then turned right onto Buckeye Road. Shah was on edge as he squinted to see who was in the red Dodge Charger pulling up to the left of him. He relaxed a little when he noticed it was a white female.

Shah checked his rearview mirror again before reaching over to grab his cup of Grey Goose and Red Bull from his cup holder. He quickly took a sip and placed the cup back into the holder. Shah looked up just as the light turned green and quickly stomped on the pedal. As he made it through the intersection his phone started to vibrate in his lap. He looked down at the light from his phone that was glaring up at him and noticed it was Keisha.

"This Bitch thirsty" he thought to himself as he picked up his phone and answered it.

"What's up" Shah said.

"Shah, I hope you don't have me waiting on you and you're not coming" Keisha replied.

Shah started laughing and reached to turn the radio down so he could hear her clearly.

"I ain't on no bullshit, I'm getting off on Cottage Grove right now. Come down in like three minutes to let me in the building," Shah said.

"Alright," Keisha replied, not really convinced he was coming.

"Yep," Shah said before hanging up.

He made a left onto Cottage Grove Road then drove up to Vernon and made a left. Shah circled the area twice before pulling into Keisha's lot. As Shah pulled into the lot, he could see Keisha standing in the hall of her building. He pulled into the first parking spot he saw and parked. Shah reached into the middle console and grabbed his Glock 19 and put it in his hoodie pocket. He reached over to the passenger seat and grabbed his bottle of Grey Goose and the box of Cigarillo's and got out of the truck.

Keisha stood in the doorway to her building waiting to open the door for Shah. Keisha loved being around Shah, it was like his presence always made the stresses of her own life go away. As she opened the door Shah spoke,

"What up stranger," he said and laughed a little.

Keisha laughed, "Oh, so I'm the one that's the stranger, huh?" she replied. Shah laughed a little and made sure the building door didn't slam shut.

"Yeah! You the stranger Keisha," Shah said as he looked at her and licked his lips.

"Whatever big head," she replied. As she turned and started walking up the stairs, Keisha looked back at Shah to see if he was watching her ass bounce as she walked.

"Big head? You know what I do got a big head," Shah said, as he grabbed his manhood through his pants. "That's why you like me so much," he said. Keisha looked back from the top of the stairs and stated laughing.

"That's the only reason!" Keisha said jokingly. She then turned and walked off toward her apartment. Shah started laughing and made his way up the stairs and down the hall to Keisha's apartment. Shah walked into the apartment and noticed all the lights were off besides the light coming from Keisha's bedroom. Shah walked over to the kitchen and turned the light on. He sat the Greg Goose bottle down on one of the counter tops, then pulled his pistol from his hoodie pocket and sat it down next to the Grey Goose bottle. He took a cigarillo from the box, tossed the box on the counter, and unwrapped the cigarillo as he walked over to the trash can. As Shah broke down the cigarillo, he could hear Keisha saying something, but he couldn't make out what because her voice was being drowned out by the Jhene Aiko song "New Balance" coming from her room.

"Hold on real quick I can't hear you," Shah yelled to Keisha.

He dumped the tobacco from the cigarillo into the trash can. He looked up and was shocked to see Keisha standing in the doorway looking as if she was getting ready for a photoshoot with SHOW magazine. Keisha was a rare beauty to find. She was a beautiful Russian and Nigerian with long wavy jet-black hair. She stood 5 foot 4 inches with 34DD breasts and a 30-inch waist. Her 45inch hips gave her the perfect hourglass shape. Shah stood for a moment taking in her beauty. Her red lace pantie and bra set looked amazing on top of her caramel skin tone.

Keisha walked up to Shah and pushed him up against the refrigerator.

"I see I gotta take what I want," she said as she reached for Shah's belt buckle and squatted down in front of him to unbuckle it. Shah quickly unzipped his hoodie and tossed it on the floor next to his feet. Keisha pulled down Shah's pants with one hand and massaged his manhood through his boxer briefs with the other. She let out a soft moan while looking Shah directly in his eyes. "I missed this dick, Daddy," Keshia said.

She could feel him growing with excitement. Shah couldn't wait any longer he pulled his boxer briefs to his knees. Keisha instantly grabbed a hold of his thick shaft and stroked him up and down before twirling her tongue around the tip of his dick. Then, she slowly took him into her mouth.

"Damn Keisha!" Shah said, as she slowly took him deeper into her mouth before she slowly pulled him out. "Yeah, he missed me too," Keisha said, while running Shah's dick across her lips then shoving him back into her mouth. This time, inch by inch, she took him deeper and deeper into her mouth until he was in her throat. Keisha cupped his balls and started to play with them as she forced Shah's dick deeper into her throat. Keisha knew just what to do to drive Shah crazy. She continued to play with his balls as she sucked his dick making sure it hit the back of her throat every time, she took him all the way in. Shah grabbed a first full of her hair and helped guide her through the perfect rhythm. Within minutes Shah exploded, and without hesitation, Keisha continued sucking until Shah's dick was hard again.

"Tight," Shah said, as he pulled away from Keisha. He grabbed a hold of her arms and pulled her up onto the countertop. Shah quickly kicked off his shoes and stepped out of his pants and boxer briefs. He spread Keisha's legs apart and began kissing his inner thighs. Shah slowly and softly ran his fingertips along the outside of Keisha's thighs. Keisha moaned as she leaned back on the countertop. Shah pulled Keisha's panties off and tossed them down on the floor next to his clothes. He started rubbing his fingertips on Keisha's pussy which was already hot and moist. Shah slowly stuck his finger in and started finger fucking her as he licked and sucked on her clit. Shah continued to suck on Keisha's clit for a few minutes before she reached and put her hands on the back of his head and pulled his face closer to her pussy.

"Yes! Eat this pussy Daddy," she screamed out as she began to have an orgasm. Feeling Keisha's body stiffen up Shah began to suck harder on her clit.

"Oh fuck, Shah," Keisha screamed. She tried to push Shah's head away from her pussy, but Shah had a tight grip around her thighs and pulled her closer to him as he continued to suck on her clit. Every part of Keisha's body began to tingle as another orgasm came over her.

"Baby, baby oh my God! Sha- Shah stooooppp! Oh my God, I'm cumming again," Keisha screamed as she raised her body a little trying to get out of Shah's grip.

"Ok, ok please Shah," Keisha yelled as she pushed Shah's head away, managing to get free of his grip. Shah stood up straight and wiped Keisha's juices from his face as Keisha laid on the countertop exhausted and breathing heavily.

"I ain't done yet. I'm about to give you what you said you was finna take," Shah said as he pulled Keisha off the countertop. He turned her around and bent her over the counter, then lifted one of her legs and placed it on top of the counter. Shah reached under Keisha and started playing with her pussy. It was so wet it was literally dripping down her inner thighs.

"Daddy fuck me and fuck me hard" Keisha demanded of Shah. Without missing a beat, Shah slid the tip of his dick into Keisha's pussy. Then, he slowly began to stroke her, digging deeper every time he pushed forward. After a few minutes Shah began to pick up the pace, pounding Keisha's wet pussy harder and harder. Keisha could feel Shah exploring parts of her pussy that no man had ever reached. Keisha's legs began to tremble as multiple orgasms overcame her body. Shah grabbed ahold of her ass cheeks and began fucking her like he'd never done before. Keisha moaned louder and louder as she tried to find anything to grab ahold of as her body began to shake uncontrollably. "Shah why you doing this to me! Oh my God, Shah this pussy belong to you," Keisha screamed out as she threw her ass back at Shah, helping him go further inside of her tight pussy. Shah and Keisha went on for forty-five minutes before Shah finally exploded into Keisha's pussy. Shah leaned over and kissed Keisha on her back then slowly pulled himself out of her pussy. Shah walked to the bathroom and grabbed a towel to clean himself off. When he walked back into the kitchen, he laughed noticing Keisha was still in the same spot he left her bent over on the kitchen counter. Shah walked over and smacked her on the ass.

"Look like you got more than what you was looking for," he said as he picked the cigarillo up from the floor and pulled the weed from his pants pocket. "I did," Keisha said, sounding exhausted. She pulled her leg from on top of the counter and walked to the bathroom. As Shah stood there rolling his blunt, he could hear the shower water running, he reached down and grabbed his boxers and pants and put them on. Shah grabbed the Grey Goose bottle from the counter and opened it taking a big gulp. When he sat the bottle back down on the counter, he could feel his phone vibrating in this pocket. He pulled it out and saw that it was Audrey, so he quickly answered it.

"What up Cinderella?" Shah said as he answered the phone.

"Missing you! When you coming home?" She asked.

"I'm finna get ready to leave from down here in a little while, I'll be home soon," Shah said.

"Okay baby, I love you," Audrey replied.

"I love you too, Ima see you soon," Shah said.

"Okay," Audrey said before hanging up.

Shah put his phone back into his pocket and picked his hoodie up from off the floor. He grabbed his pistol from off the countertop and tucked it on his waistline. Shah walked to Keisha's room and sat down on the edge of the bed. He looked over at the clock on the nightstand and saw that it was 1:30am. Shah decided he was going to leave Keisha's crib after he smoked his blunt. Shah listened to Jhene Aiko's song while it played. He flamed his blunt up and coughed as he inhaled a huge cloud of smoke. Keisha walked into the room wearing a bath towel. Shah looked over at her as he exhaled the smoke.

"Damn Keisha, you sexy as hell!" he said.

Keisha laughed a little, "I am ain't I," she replied and unwrapped her towel, so Shah could get a full view of her body. Keisha walked over to her dresser and grabbed a bottle of cocoa butter lotion, then sat next to Shah on the edge of the bed and started rubbing the lotion on her body.

"Why you smoke that stuff?" Keisha asked.

"Cause I live a stressful life!" Shah answered.

"What's so stressful about it?" Keisha asked not trying to pry into his business.

"The money. I mean I would have never thought when I was broke having money would be so stressful. I gotta watch out for the police, the jack boys, the money hungry bitches, and friends that expect I give it when they ask just because I got it. Sometimes I feel like it's me against the world," Shah said.

"Well I want you to know that with or without the money I'm always on your side. I've never been controlled by the money," Keisha quickly said.

Shah took a few puffs from his blunt before he responded to what Keisha just said.

"That's not directed toward you," Shah said as he stood up and walked toward the window and peeked out the blinds to see what was outside. Keisha got up from the bed and walked over to her dresser. She opened the drawer and pulled out a T-shirt and put it on. Shah looked over at Keisha's ass cheeks as they poked out from up under the bottom of her shirt.

"Look I gotta get ready to get up out of here," Shah said.

Keisha turned around and looked at Shah.

"Alright, so when Ima see you again?" Keisha asked.

"When do you wanna see me again?" Shah asked.

"Tomorrow," Keisha said without hesitation,

"Tight, we gone make that happen," Shah replied.

"Okay good," Keisha said.

Shah walked out the room to the front door. Keisha was steps behind him as he unlocked the door.

"So, you finna leave without giving me my hug?" Keisha asked.

Shah turned around and grabbed Keisha by her waist and pulled her close to him.

"You know Ima make sure you get that," he said as he reached and grabbed ahold of her ass cheeks.

Keisha wrapped her arms around Shah and laid her head against his chest.

"Shah make sure you come and see me tomorrow," Keisha said softly.

"I will," Shah said as he gave a real big hug.

"Okay, drive safe," Keisha said as she broke away from their hug.

"Iight," Shah said as he opened the door and walked out of the apartment. Keisha closed and locked the door behind him. As Shah walked out the building, he took a few puffs from his blunt and walked toward his truck. He pulled his car keys from his pocket and pressed the unlock button as he walked closer to his truck. Just as he got in between his truck and the car parked next to him, somebody came from behind him and grabbed the back of his hoodie and put a pistol to the back of his head.

"Bitch ass nigga if you move Ima blow yo mafuckin head off yo shoulders!" the man said as he quickly patted Shah down and pulled his pistol from his hip. Another man wearing a ski mask came from in front of Shah's truck. "I been waiting to catch yo bitch ass," the second man said as he walked up on Shah.

Shah stood there speechless. He was caught completely off guard. He dropped his keys and his blunt on the ground.

4 MONTHS EARLIER

It had been a long day inside of Dejope's Casino and Shah was happy that 4 o'clock had finally arrived. Shah was itching to clock out and get as far away from his job as possible. He hated working for Dejope. He hated the lousy pay and their strict no employee gambling policy, but what he hated most of all was seeing people win thousands of dollars day in and day out while he struggled to make ends meet.

Shah stood in line behind all the rest of his co-workers that were eager to dart out the door of the casino as they began to clock out one by one.

His phone started to ring as he held it in his hand. He flipped it open and saw that it was Tammy. Tammy was Shah's childhood friend and his best friend. Shah answered the phone and could hear the music playing loudly in the background.

"Hello," Shah said as he answered.

"I'm outside," Tammy yelled over her music.

"Iight, I'm clocking out right now" Shah said as he clocked out.

"Okay," Tammy quickly said before hanging up the phone. As Shah walked toward the exit, he could see Tammy's car and that she was alone. He walked out of the building and up to her car and opened the door.

"Where Audrey at?" he asked as he got in and close the door.

"She got a late class tonight. Let me find out, she gotta be with me in order for me to come pick you up," Tammy said.

"Naw, she ain't gotta be with you. I was just asking that's all," Shah replied.

"You need to get her a phone so you could call her," Tammy said.

"Damn that's how you do me?" Shah asked.

"No, I'm just saying, it seem like ever since your brother went to prison you let yourself fall all the way off," Tammy said.

"My brother was in the streets, that ain't my lane," Shah replied.

"Shah, I'm not saying that you have to be in the streets. I'm just saying you need to do something to get yourself out of the hole you fell in. You better than your situation. Your girl ain't got no phone and you walking around with a flip phone," Tammy said.

"You don't think I know I'm fucked up, what you think I'm comfortable being broke? I'm tired of busting my ass to make sure my momma ain't living on the streets. If I hadn't been taking care of her the last three years, I'll be straight, I would have the new I-phone and a car and some more shit," Shah replied.

"That's my point! Shah, your momma grown. You gotta live your life Shah she lived hers," Tammy said. Shah hated talking about his mother. That was a real touchy subject for him, He felt he had to be her savior. "Let's just drop this whole conversation," Shah said. Tammy could tell by how Shah was acting that he took offense to what she said. "Okay Shah," Tammy said, then turned the radio back up.

Shah sat back in his seat and looked out the window as Tammy drove him home, he couldn't help but think about what Tammy just said and how much truth was in the words. Shah felt he had to make something happen. He was tired of being on the bottom. As Tammy pulled into Shah's lot, he could see Reggie leaving out of his building. Shah hated Reggie because Reggie was his mother's dealer. Reggie and Shah were the same age, so Reggie would go around bragging about the fact that his mother was spending all her money with him. When Tammy drove pass Reggie, Shah made eye contact and Reggie stopped in his tracks, he loved getting under Shah's skin. Shah got out of the car and leaned back to look at Tammy. "Thanks for the ride," Shah said. "You're welcome," Tammy replied. Shah closed the door and started walking to his building. Reggie stood in front of the doorway to the building as Shah got closer Reggie stated laughing.

"Shah yo broke ass ain't got a car yet? Yo bummy ass!" Reggie said. Shah walked up to Reggie and stopped in front of him.

"Get out my way before I give you what you looking for," Shah said.

"Yo broke ass ain't gone do shit! Make me move, pussy," Reggie replied. Shah grabbed Reggie by his shirt collar and pushed him up against the door. Reggie snatched away from Shah and pushed him and pulled out his pistol all in one motion.

"Bitch ass nigga don't ever put yo hands on me. I should kill yo pussy ass!" Reggie said as he pointed his gun at Shah.

Shah stood there hoping Reggie didn't shoot him, but he refused to let Reggie know that. He'd rather die before he bowed down to Reggie. Shah knew he could beat the hell out of Reggie. He knew he was a fraud and wasn't as hard as he portrayed to be.

"Ain't nobody ever teach you not to pull a gun and don't use it? Get the fuck out my way," Shah said as he walked past Reggie bumping him with his shoulder as he walked into the building. Shah made his way up the stairs to his apartment and opened the door. As he walked into the apartment, he could smell nothing but crack smoke in the air. Shah became instantly furious and slammed the door. He stormed toward the hall where he could see his mother's door open.

"Man, why the fuck you got the door open!" Shah said as he approached the room. He looked inside the room and saw James, his mother's Ex-boyfriend, sitting on the edge of the bed in a deep nod with his head down. James was a leach; he would use anyone he could to get his next high. When Shah's mother, Marie, first met James, he had just come home from the Afghan War. For years, James took Shawn and Shah in as if they were his own and treated their mother like the Queen she was. James worked for years in the construction field as a roofer until one summer he was one the job and lost his balance and slipped and fell from the roof breaking both his legs. During rehab James began to abuse the pain killers he was prescribed, and before anyone knew it James was addicted. He began to drink heavily on top of using many different pain killers. James quickly became very angry and mad at the world. He would beat Marie anytime she confronted him and asked him to clean his act up.

After a few months and many ass whopping's, Marie had finally had enough of James and put him out and to her surprise James didn't put up a fight. For months on end James stayed away from Marie and her kids. He started to use heroin and quickly became extremely strung out. On many occasions, Shah would see James on his way to school standing in front of gas stations asking people for change. One day while Shawn and Shah were both in Chicago for the summer, Marie ran into James outside of the gas station on her way home from work. James begged Marie to forgive him. She took James home with her and let him shower and made him something to eat. Marie made sure she locked up all her valuables and let James sleep on the couch.

The next day when she got home from work James and two of his friends were in the living room getting high. Marie got upset and told James he and his friends had to leave. James stood up and told his friends to leave so he could talk to Marie alone. His friends quickly got up and left the apartment. James begged Marie to forgive him, but she insisted that he leave and never come back. James grew into a fit of rage and flipped and started to choke Marie. "Bitch you think you better than me? Well it's time I bring you down from off that high horse!" James said as he punched Marie in the face repeatedly until he knocked her unconscious. He dragged Marie like a hostage to her bedroom and tied her to the bed. James grabbed a syringe and fixed up a hit of heroin and injected it into her arm. He watched as she nodded out, then he raped her. He held her hostage in the apartment for a week straight as he continuously beat her and forced her to use heroin and smoke crack cocaine. After a while he broke her spirit and she was now enjoying the high. He no longer had to force Marie to use, she was now begging him to go out and get more. From that moment on Marie's life went downhill and James controlled every aspect of it.

Shah walked into his mother's room looking for her, but she wasn't there. He walked out of the room and went to the kitchen hoping to find her there but still she was nowhere in sight. Shah was pissed as he walked back to his mother's room and kicked the bed causing James to jump out of his nod. "What the fuck you doing in here James?" Shah asked. James sat there for a moment looking confused. Once he finally realized where he was, he stood up and wiped his mouth.

"Damn Shah I ain't seen you in a long time," he said

"I don't know what the fuck you think this is but you gotta get the fuck up out of here," Shah replied.

"Marie must not have told you yet but we back together, how you think I got in here. She out getting us some beer," James said.

"Look James I ain't gone tell you again you gotta get the fuck up out of here!" Shah said as he stepped closer into James face.

"You gotta take that shit up with Marie, Shah. I ain't going nowhere until she tell me I gotta leave," James replied then tried to sit back down. "Ain't no nigga gone disrespect me up in my shit," Shah said as he grabbed James by his shirt collar.

"Bitch ass nigga you gotta go!" Shah said.

James yanked away from Shah and punched him in the face knocking him to the floor. Shah jumped back to his feet just as quick as he fell and rushed James. Shah picked him up and body slammed him to the floor. James had the fighting skills, but Shah had youth and power on his side. He got on top of James and started pounding him out, each blow harder than the last. Shah connected with all face shots. He stood up and started to stomp and kick James in his ribs. James knew he was no match for Shah, so he just balled up and tried to protect himself from the blows Shah was unleashing on his body. Shah grabbed James by his shirt and dragged him out the room and down the hall.

"Bitch ass nigga, I told you to leave now you made me do this shit to you," Shah said as he pulled James through the living room. Shah started to punch and kick James some more before he reached down and grabbed him by his shirt and yanked him to his feet. Shah cocked his arm back getting ready to deliver a power punch to James. Marie walked into the apartment and instantly dropped her beers once she noticed what was going on. She rushed over and pulled Shah off of James. Shah stepped back, "Now get the fuck out before I finish where Shawn left off bitch nigga," Shah said. Marie walked over to James and helped him to the couch so he could sit down.

"Shah you need to calm down," Marie said as she turned to look at Shah.

"Marie, I ain't got time for this shit I'm finna go," James said as he stood up.

"Well hurry the fuck up!" Shah said.

Marie grabbed James by his arm and stopped him, "Please, James you don't have to go," Marie begged.

"Why the fuck you begging this nigga to stay?" Shah asked furiously. James yanked his arm away from Marie and looked at her. "Marie if you want me to stay this little nigga gotta go, I'm not finna live under the same roof as a motherfucker that's trying to kill me," James said.

"Okay, Okay," Marie said as she turned and looked at Shah, "Shah you have to leave," she said.

Shah stood there shocked, he couldn't believe what he just heard. "Fuck you mean I gotta leave? I pay the bills up in this bitch!" Shah said.

Marie walked up to Shah and grabbed his shirt "Shah, don't forget who you talking to! This my damn house. It's my name on the fucking lease. I can handle it from here, now you need to go before I call the police!" Marie said.

"So, you finna choose this bitch ass nigga over me? Okay! I see where we stand. Ima get my shit and leave but when he start kicking your ass and you can't pay the rent don't come looking for me cause I ain't got shit for you!" Shah said and yanked away from Marie and walked to his bedroom.

"Okay, Shah just get your shit and leave!" Marie yelled out at him.

Shah grabbed his backpack and filled it with enough clothes to last him a few days and walked back to the living room.

"I'll be back to get the rest of my shit," Shah said as he walked out the door.

Meanwhile

Hot Boi sat in his car waiting on Big T to pull up so he could re-up. Hot Boi looked at his phone and noticed that he had been sitting there waiting on Big T for over twenty minutes. He quickly dialed Big T's number.

"My bad lil bro I'm finna pull up," Big T said as he answered the phone.

"Folks you told me that twenty minutes ago, you got me sitting right here hot as hell fool!" Hot Boi replied.

"My bad lil bro I got all types of shit going on. Just pull up to Culver's by East Towne Mall. Ima be pulling up the same time as you," Big T said.

"Tight bro, I'm coming down East Wash right now," Hot Boi said.

"Tight," Big T said and hung up. He started his car and pulled onto East Wash and headed toward the mall. As Hot Boi pulled into Culvers he could see one person getting out of Big T's minivan and another one getting in. Hot Boi parked his car a few cars away from Big T's minivan and waited until the dude that just hopped in got out and walked back to his truck. Big T was a heavy hitter in Madison. He was originally from Chicago. Big T found out about Madison a few years ago when his kids mother moved up. It wasn't too soon after, did he notice Madison was a gold mine town and had to have parts of it. Big T supplied the niggas from out East with some of the best coke they had even seen. Hot Boi and Big T met a year later through Big T's baby mother's best friend Shaneka. Big T took a liking to Hot Boi pretty fast and started fronting him work. It didn't take long for Hot Boi to show Big T that he was loyal and trustworthy. Hot Boi quickly became a true money maker.

Hot Boi got out of his 2007 Buick Lacrosse and walked over to Big T's minivan and got in the back of Big T minivan. "My bad lil bro, I had like twenty niggas online. I ain't mean to just have you sitting there you know how hectic this shit be at times," Big T said.

"Yeah, I know how this shit be, I ain't trippin'," Hot Boi said as he eyed the beautiful Hispanic chick in the driver's seat. "Man T, I see you stay with something nice," Hot Boi quickly added.

"You know me, I'm living. We only get one life," Big T replied.

"Shidd plug me, I'm definitely trying to live," Hot Boi said.

"Tight bet! Ima hit your line when I'm done taking care of the rest of this shit I gotta do," Big T replied.

"Say no more! Here go that ten bands for that last demo," Hot Boi said as he reached into his pocket and handed Big T the cash.

"Tight, this what Ima do since you running though that shit so fast. This a half of brick," Big T said as he tossed the coke on Hot Boi's lap.

"So, what you want twenty off this?" Hot Boi asked.

"Naw lil bro, just fifteen," Big T replied

"Tight I can do that! Look let me get up out of here so I can link with my people," Hot Boi said.

"Tight, drive careful lil bro," Big T said. "Bet," Hot Boi said as he stuffed the half of brick into his pants and jumped out of the minivan and walked back over to his car. As Hot Boi started driving down East Wash his phone started to ring. He reached over and turned the music down before picking his phone up from his lap. Hot Boi never saved names in his phone so he knew everyone's number by heart.

"Shah Money! What's up bro?" Hot Boi said as he answered.

"Shit! Look I need you fool it's all bad on my end," Shah replied.

"Tight, what's up?" Hot Boi asked.

"Fool why I get off work and go to the crib the nigga James in there," Shah said.

"Man, you bullshitting me!" Hot Boi replied.

"No bullshit! I told the nigga he had to leave, and he stared talking crazy. I ended up having to kick his ass!" Shah said. Hot Boi instantly stated laughing. "Man, that shit ain't funny," Shah said

"I know but I can just picture you and James tussling," Hot Boi said as he laughed.

"Tussling? Nigga it wasn't no tussling. I beat the fuck out that nigga! I ain't gone lie though the nigga punched me and put me on my back pockets before I got in his ass!" Shah said.

"Hell naw!! On what he dropped you?" Hot Boi asked as he laughed even harder.

"Yeah! Yeah, he did that. But that ain't the half of it. Why my OG come in while I was kicking his ass and chose this nigga side over mine. She even threaten to call the law on me if I didn't leave her crib," Shah said

"Her Crib? You been praying the rent in that mafucka for years!" Hot Boi said shocked.

"I know! She the main reason why I'm fucked up. Then she turn around and shit on me," Shah said.

"Yeah Shah money. She bogus, I ain't gone talk down on her cause that's your OG and no matter what we only get one of those," Hot Boi said

"Maaannnn! But look on some real shit I'm fucked up right now bro! I just used my little cash to pay the rent last week, I ain't call to ask you for no cash or nothing. I'm trying to see if you a let me rent that extra room at your spot until I get on my feet," Shah said

"Man Shah, you know damn well we better than that. You like my brother; blood couldn't make us no closer. Nigga I ain't finna charge you for that room as many times I had to crash at your crib when we was younger. Nigga you can have that room," Hot Boi quickly said.

"You know me fool I don't like handouts. I like to hold my own weight. That's the reason why I ain't go stay at my bitch crib, I can't be laid up under a bitch fucked up," Shah replied.

"Handouts?" Nigga we brothers. You better put your pride in your pocket and use that shit when it comes to those other Niggas! I'm in traffic right now where you at fool? I'm finna come get up with you," Hot Boi said

"Shit I'm walking down Allied," Shah replied.

"Walking! You trippin' bro. I'm about to pull up on you give me twenty minutes," Hot Boi said.

"Say no more," Shah said.

"Tight," Hot Boi said, then ended the call.

Thirty minutes later Hot Boi came driving down Allied and spotted Shah walking toward Cresent. He pulled up on the side of him and rolled down the window. "Shah," Hot Boi yelled out. Shah looked up then walked over to the car and got in.

"My nigga! My nigga," Hot Boi said as he pulled off.

"You need to stop somewhere before I go to the crib?" Hot Boi asked.

"Naw I'm good," Shah said

"Tight good! Cause I gotta get in this kitchen you know I gotta feed the block, my people starving they got appetites," Hot Boi said.

"Oh, you think you Jeezy now huh?" Shah asked.

"Naw, I ain't Jeezy, but at the rate I'm going niggas gone start calling me El Chapo! You need to fuck with me, fuck that job shit come get some of this real money!" Hot Boi said.

"I'm good, I'm tryna go a different route but shidd how fucked up I am I might have to get in the game," Shah replied.

"Man, you should! I'm telling you I could use the help. You know the saying two brains is always better than one and with my plug we'll be serving the whole city in no time," Hot Boi said. Shah sat there thinking and rubbing his chin, "I don't know man, you really think shit gone be that easy?" Shah asked.

"This shit far from easy bro! but if we get knee deep in this shit and grind and stack, sooner than later we'll be on top if we stay focus," Hot Boi said.

"I feel you! I gotta sit on this shit for a few days and really think about it," Shah said

"Say no more bro, I ain't gone rush you. But remember while you thinking I'm stacking," Hot Boi said and turned the music back up.

Hot Boi pulled into his parking lot and parked, then they both jumped out of the car and walked to Hot Boi's apartment. Hot Boi walked in and went straight to the kitchen while Shah closed and locked the door. Hot Boi turned the cold water on in the sink then grabbed the Pyrex from the cabinet and put it on the counter. Hot Boi walked back to the door and walked out of the apartment. He came back in a few minutes and went straight back to the kitchen. Hot Boi pulled the half of brick of coke from under his shirt and put it on the table.

"Shah Money I wanna show you something the big homie taught me. Only cause I love you like a brother. I'ma put you on game free of charge! This shit here separate the boys from the men," Hot Boi said.

Shah got up from the couch and walked over to the kitchen table. He stood there looking at the coke then he picked it up. "So, what's up?" Shah asked. "That's coke! 18 ounces of some of the finest cocaine," Hot Boi said.

"Tight, so how much it cost?" Shah asked.

"It cost $15,000 dollars," Hot Boi quickly said.

"Damn! $15,000, you playing with that kind of cash?" Shah asked.

"Yeah, but peep game. I never pay up front then the way I whip it and play with the numbers off that right there I plan to make every bit of $42,000 off that and I'll pocket $27,000 and kick back 15,000 to big homie," Hot Boi said.

"Damn you been low! I mean I knew you was doing you but I ain't know you was playing with them kind of numbers," Shah said as he sat the coke back down on the table. Hot Boi walked over to the refrigerator and pulled out a box of baking soda and put it next to the Pyrex. Shah stood there stuck. The numbers Hot Boi just told him ran through his mind over and over again. "Shah Money, you iight? You look like you just went to a whole nother world," Hot Boi said. "Shit I did, you just fucked my head up with them numbers you just threw at me. Here it is I been working my ass off for some years now and I ain't never had more than $5,000 at one time. So, how long it take you to get all that shit off?" Shah asked.

"I got two line, one I dump weight and one I dump bags. The weight line move faster but the bag line bring in the most cash. But, I'ma say the way both lines been moving I should be done with this shit in ten days only cause I plan to sell most this shit in bags," Hot Boi said

"Damn ten days? You making this shit sound too good to be true!" Shah said.

"Shah Money if I'm lying, I'm dying! you gone see bro but grab that scale and bring that coke over here. let me show you how to stretch two and a quarter to four and a half," Hot Boi said.

"Two and a quarter to four and a half? What the fuck you mean?" Shah asked.

"Bro you gotta lot of learning to do. I'm about to take 63 grams of powder and turn it to 126 grams of hard you following me?" Hot Boi asked.

"Yeah, I see what you mean now. I do the math shit well, so if you break it down to me like that, I can follow you then you can teach me what they call it later," Shah replied.

"Tight, I got you," Hot Boi said.

Hot Boi went through all the motions step by step showing Shah how to cook. He showed him what weighs what and how much it cost. Shah was fascinated with what Hot Boi just showed him. After an hour of putting Shah up on game, Hot Boi's phone stared to ring. He quickly picked it up. As Hot Boi talked on the phone Shah sat there listening. Even though he could only hear Hot Boi's response, he knew that Hot Boi had some cash on the line. Hot Boi ended his call and looked over at Shah. "It's time to put what I taught you to use. Bag up a 63 out of that real quick while I put the rest of this shit up," Hot Boi said.

"Tight I got you," Shah quickly said as he grabbed the scale.

Hot Boi grabbed the rest of the coke and left the apartment. When he came back a few minutes later Shah was sitting at the kitchen table talking to somebody on the phone.

"Bro you did that?" Hot Boi asked. "Yeah, yeah its over there," Shah said as he pointed to the counter. "You wanna run with me to make the dump?" Hot Boi asked.

"Naw I'ma catch you on the next one, I'm finna sit back and chill. Plus, I need to holla at Audrey real quick," Shah said.

"Tight bro," Hot Boi said as he picked the work up from the counter and put it on the scale to make sure Shah did it right. "Okay, Shah Money I see you catch on real fast!" Hot Boi said. "That's simple math, I do that now. All I gotta do is catch on to the cooking process," Shah said.

"After you see it a few more times you gone catch on to it but let me get to this cash though. I'm a holla at you when I get back," Hot Boi said as he put the work in his pocket and left the apartment.

Meanwhile

Audrey stood in the bathroom curling her hair while Tammy stood in the doorway giving her a word for word detail about a guy she met last weekend when she was in Milwaukee at the club with her cousin Tiffany. Tammy loved to fill Audrey in on her dating life because Audrey was a homebody and her only true friend. Tammy always tried to bring Audrey out of her shell, she wanted to add some excitement to her life and let her know that there was more to the world than little ole Madison, Wisconsin. Audrey and Tammy had been best friends since the seventh grade. Shah introduced them that year in their gym period and since that moment they have been inseparable. Despite their totally different looks they always told people they were sisters.

Audrey is an exotic blend of Cambodian and Thai, with 34D breasts, a 25-inch waist, and 38-inch hips. Her hourglass shape body was rare among many Asian women. People never seem to believe her when she tells them she is 100 percent Asian. At 5 feet tall, her ass and hips always seem to get a lot of attention.

Tammy is a mix of Native American and African American. Her light brown skin tone and long curly brown hair complement her beautiful face. Tammy has always been a beautiful bombshell who turns heads wherever she went. She was hard to miss at 5 foot 2 inches with 36 DD breasts, a 24-inch waist, 36-inch hips, and a perfectly round ass. Almost every man in Madison wanted to get to know her, but she would not give any of them the time of day.

Audrey and Tammy moved in together last year after they graduated high school. Audrey went to school during the day to become a Dental Hygienist but worked as a CNA on the NOC shift to pay for school and cover her half of the rent. Tammy worked as a phlebotomist for the UW hospital. She worked extremely hard and was well finically stable. Tammy rarely had time off but when she did have time off, she partied as hard as she worked.

"So, bitch I was standing at the bar waiting on my drink, I looked across the bar and seen this fine ass niggas staring at me. Now you know me bitch I always keep it classy, so I smiled at him and turned to talk to

Tiffany acting like I wasn't paying him no attention. So, girl he come over to me and Tiffany and introduced himself, he tells me his name is X then asked me what's mine. I paused for a second, Bitch tell me why Tiffany cut right in like my name Tiffany,"

Audrey started laughing as she stopped curling her hair and sat the curlers in the sink. "Hold on, wait a minute sis you telling me Tiffany just jumped right in? Why she be acting so thirsty?" Audrey asked.

"Yes! She did. I don't know why she be acting so thirsty. But wait girl let me finish telling you the story," Tammy said.

"Okay, I'm listening go ahead," Audrey said. "So, he looks over at Tiffany and don't even say shit, then he looked back at me and say, 'So I can't get your name?' I looked up at him and told him my name. Then he got to telling me how much he likes my name and ask me if he could buy me a drink. I told him I already ordered one but they taking all day to bring it. So, he like 'oh yeah!' Bitch tell me why he called the bartender over and made him stop doing what he was doing then asked me what I'm drinking. So, I told him patron. Bitch he made the man go get me a bottle of patron and bottle of rosé and told him if its anything else I wanted to put it on his tab!"

"Bitch his tab?" Audrey asked cutting Tammy off.

"Yes bitch but let me finish," Tammy said.

"Bitch yo story long, let's skip to the good part, did you spend the night with him?" Audrey asked.

"I ain't Tiffany bitch," Tammy quickly said. Audrey smacked her lips and looked over at Tammy.

"Tammy, don't act like you ain't never done it before!" Audrey said.

"Bitch that was different," Tammy said as they both started laughing.

"Yeah, I bet it was different" Audrey said.

"It was don't try to do me!" Tammy said. "Anyways, back to what I was saying. He told me that it was nice to meet me then walked off and went back to where his friends was. So, bitch me and Tiffany got drunk then hit the dance floor for a little while. Right when the club was about to end, he walked up to me and grabbed my hand and start telling me how beautiful he thought I was and how he wanted to get to know me, then he asked me for my number. I didn't want to seem thirsty so I told him no, but I let him know he could give me his number. So, I took it down and told him I would call him then I thanked him for the bottles, and he walked us to the car and told me to make sure I called him,"

"So bitch did you call him yet?" Audrey asked cutting her off.

"No bitch I haven't called him yet," Tammy said and frowned.

"You always do that, girl. You better call him cause I wanna know if the sex is as good as you said he looked," Audrey said and laughed.

"Stop trying to pimp me out so you can hear a story," Tammy said.

"Bitch you gone thank me latter. But right now, I need you to help me curl the back of my hair so I can get ready for work," Audrey said.

"OK, but what about you and your boring as relationship with Shah?" Tammy asked.

"Bitch my relationship ain't boring! I talked to him today and he pissed Marie is back with James," Audrey said.

"Stop it Audrey! Marie ain't got back with James after what happened with him and Shawn," Tammy said.

"Yes, she did! And Shah and James got into a big ass fight and she made Shah leave. He said she was about to call the police on him, so he packed his shit and left. Now he living with Hot Boi until he finds his own place," Audrey said.

"Girl, Marie lost her mind. She kicked her son out, the only person that really gives a fuck about her for that bum ass nigga that destroyed her life and got one of her sons 15 years in prison! Girl I feel sorry for Shah, I know that shit hurt his heart," Tammy said. "Yes, it did, but bitch you know Shah, he going to bounce back like never before now that he not taking care of her ass no more. Plus, I could hear it and his voice, he feels like he got something to prove to the world. I just hope my baby don't lose his self in the process," Audrey said.

"Yeah I hope he don't either because he one of the good guys. You know I can't stand Madison niggaz, but for him to have been around them as long as he has, he's nothing like them. And I love him because he's his own man. Damn bitch it's 10:30, you better hurry up and get dress so I can get you to work on time," Tammy said.

"Oh shit, see bitch fucking with you," Audrey said as she ran out the bathroom to her bedroom to get dressed.

Chapter Two

S hah rolled over and stretched. He pulled the blanket over his head to prevent the sun that was shining through the blinds from glaring in his eyes. He laid under the blanket for a minute before it dawned on him. Shah jumped from under the blanket and reach for his phone.

"Fuck it's 11:30am," he said to himself as he jumped out of bed. Shah looked at his phone as he rushed to the bedroom. He had five missed calls from Tammy and six missed calls and two text messages from Audrey. "Fuck!" he said to himself as he dialed his boss's number to let him know that he was on his way. As he waited for someone to answer, he ran back into his bedroom and tried to hurry and put his uniform on.

"Dejope Casino, this is the management speaking how can I help you?" Mr. Jones said as he answered.

"Mr.Jones, this is Shah Lumas. I'm extremely sorry that I'm late but I'm on my way right now!" Shah said.

"Oh, Mr. Lumas it's nice of you to finally call in. I thought that we had an understanding after you left my office last week," Mr. Jones said.

"Yeah, we do have an understanding, it won't happen again Mr. Jones," Shah replied.

"Mr. Lumas, you're a very hard-working employee, but the fact that you can't show up on time when needed has become a major problem. Last week during our meeting if you can recall, I said that if you could make it one mouth without being late, I would get off your back. But if you couldn't I would have to let you go," Mr. Jones said.

" I remember Mr. Jones, but I really need this job. If you could give me one more chance, I won't let you down," Shah said as he tried to beg for his job.

"I'm sorry Mr. Lumas, but your one more chance was the last one I gave you last week. I'm sorry but I have to let you go," Mr. Jones replied.

"Look Mr. Jones, I'm not in the business of begging but I really need this job. I can show you I can be on time if you allow me one more chance," Shah said.

"I'm sorry but the order has come from high, there's nothing I can do. There's no need to come in, your shift has already been covered," Mr. Jones replied.

"Iight then Mr. Jones. it was nice working with you," Shah said.

"Nice working with you to Mr. Lumas, and I wish you the best of luck," Mr. Jones replied.

"Yep!" Shah said and hung the phone up. Shah sat down on the edge of the bed and put his head down in disbelief that he just lost his job. He felt overwhelmed with problems, he got kicked out his crib yesterday then lost his job today. Add that on top of the fact that he already felt like a loser, Shah was really at his breaking point. As he sat there thinking, he decided to keep losing his job to himself until he found something better, he was not in the mood to have someone looking down on him and make him feel lower than he already felt.

The longer he sat there thinking, the more he started to feel that the offer Hot Boi gave him yesterday was a good idea. Shah figured if he applied his self to the dope game just as he applied his self to his job, then in no time he would be able to afford whatever he wanted. He wanted to be in a position to shit on everyone who once looked down on him. But before he could make a decision, there was one thing he had to do first. And that was to go visit his big brother Shawn to see what he thought. Shah looked up to Shawn and felt he needed his blessing before he got in the game. He picked his phone up from the bed and dialed Hot Boi's number. "Shah Money, I see you finally woke up!" Hot Boi said as he answered the phone.

"Yeah...I fucked around and overslept, My goofy ass got fired today," Shah replied.

"Damn bro. That's fucked up. You should have told me you had to be at work I would a woke you up. I been up since five this morning," Hot Boi said.

"Naw that's on me, I should've been on top of it. But fuck that shit though, I been thinking about

what we talked about yesterday,"

"So, you in?" Hot Boi asked cutting Shah off.

"Damn near, I need to go up to Green Bay and holla at big bro first then I'll be able to let you know what up," Shah said.

"Tight, so when you tryin to do that?" Hot Boi asked.

"Shit asap! I wanna get up there either today or tomorrow, I need some wheels," Shah said.

"Tight, let me call my lil bitch and see what she doing today. I fuck around get her shit and let

you take my car up there to see bro," Hot Boi replied.

"Tight bet come slide on me though I'm tryin to get in traffic wit you," Shah said.

"Say no mo, I'm finna make this dump then Ima hit you when I'm outside," Hot Boi said.

"Tight," Shah quickly said, then ended the call. He stood up and started taking his uniform off

as he reached over on the side of his bed and grabbed his book bag. Shah pulled out a pair of grey sweats, a white T-shirt, and some dingy white Air Force Ones. Shah slipped into his outfit and grabbed his toothbrush and toothpaste from his book bag and walked to the bathroom. As Shah got done brushing his teeth and washing his face he walked into the living room and sat down on the couch. He turned the T.V. on and looked through the T.V. shows on Hulu, but he stopped watching it after the first episode. His phone started to ring. He looked down and saw that it was Hot Boi.

"I'm bout to pull up, bring the rest of that move down wit you," Hot Boi said.

"Say no mo," Shah said as he stood up and turned the T.V off then ended the call.

Shah was standing in the hallway when he saw Hot Boi pulling into the lot. Shah walked out the

building and walked up to the car and got in. Pappy 2 cups mix tape poured from the speakers. Hot Boi turned the music down and tossed Shah a sack of weed and a blunt.

"Roll that shit up for me bro. What you know about this 2 cups mixtape? This nigga Pappy go hard on every song on this bitch!" Hot Boi said as he pulled out of the lot.

"Yeah he do go hard. He a make a nigga pull up and leave a nigga where he stand! Matter fact

speaking of leaving a nigga, I forgot that bitch ass nigga Reggie uped on me yesterday. That shit

wit James and my OG had me so pissed off. Ima put Reggie ass in the dirt," Shah said.

"Hold on! What you just say?" Hot Boi asked him.

"That bitch ass nigga Reggie uped on me yesterday," Shah said again.

"Yeah we gotta handle that one Shah Money. You can't let no nigga up on you and you don't do shit. After you do, he gone think you sweet. One thing about being in the streets you gotta have respect if niggas don't respect you, they gone go on you every chance they get. I'm on his ass now!" Hot Boi said.

"Naw bro, I'ma take care of it. I want him to think I ain't on shit then I'ma hit him when he least expect it," Shah said.

"Fuck that! I'm standing on this bitch ass nigga neck every chance I get from here on out! That shit got me mad as hell right now. That bitch ass nigga know not to pull that shit wit me," Hot Boi said.

"Let me handle it, you can be there wit me but let me handle it. Don't let him know we on his ass I wanna catch him off guard. Bro the element of surprise is a mother fucker trust me on this," Shah said.

"Say no mo, I'ma let you drive that car bro," Hot Boi replied.

"Ight say less," Shah said as he dried the blunt off.

"Gone flame that shit up I'm try'na get high," Hot Boi said. "Oh yeah I talked to shorty too, I'ma just let you take her shit," Hot Boi added.

"Ight, love too," Shah said.

"We gone slide on her in a minute, I got some cash on Hammersly I need to catch real quick. Did you bring that out for me?" Hot Boi asked.

"I got it right here," Shah said as he pulled it from his pocket and passed it to Hot Boi.

"Good looking!" Hot Boi said. Hot Boi turned the music back up while Shah flamed the blunt up.

6:15 pm

Shah pulled into the Green Bay Correctional Institution. He was nervous and excited at the same time. He hadn't seen Shawn in a few months and wasn't sure what Shawn was going to say about what he was there to tell him. He parked the car and made his way to the entrance of the prison. It was an eerie feeling for him as he walked into the one hundred and twenty-five-year-old prison. He couldn't help but think about how many men had died here and how many may be spending the rest of their life in this hell whole. As he walked to the desk, he was greeted by a short blonde-haired, white female guard.

"Who are you here to see?" she asked rudely.

"Shawn Lumas, ma'am," Shah replied.

"I.D?" she asked.

"Yeah!" Shah said as he handed it to her.

"Ok, I need you to take anything that you may have that's metal from your pockets and put it in this bin then walk through that metal detector. Any keys, cell phones, or other items can be placed in one of the lockers we have around that corner. The only thing allowed to go in with you is that change you have in that clear bag. You understand me?" she asked.

"Yeah! I ain't slow," Shah said. As Shah took everything from his pockets, he began to feel like he himself had just became a prisoner. He could imagine how Shawn felt and how hard it had to have been to be stripped of his freedom. The constant mockery and being talked down to by the guards was a mental game of warfare, something Shah wasn't used to, but it was something every prisoner knew all too well. Shah put his phone, car keys, and wallet inside the locker and took a seat. As he sat there his palms began to sweat. He wasn't sure what Shawn was going to say. *What if he think I shouldn't get in the game? What I'ma do then, I'm tired of breaking my back and ending up with shit,* Shah thought to himself as he sat there. After thirty minutes of waiting they finally called Shah and buzzed him through the door into the visiting room. The guard showed Shah what table he would be sitting at and told him Shawn would be out in a minute. Shah made his way over to his table and sat down. He took a moment to soak in the reality of the moment. As he looked around, he saw mothers visiting their sons, kids playing with their fathers, and wives visiting their husbands. Everyone was in for different crimes, but they all shared a moment of happiness with their family members. Shawn entered the visiting room. Shah could see him looking around trying to see who it was that came to see him. Shah stood up and waved him over to the table. Shawn's face lit up when he saw Shah. He quickly walked over to the table and shook Shah's hand and gave him a hug.

"What you been up to bro?" Shawn asked.

"I ain't been on shit, just came to see how life been treating you," Shah said.

"Man, I'm in this hell hole living bro. I'm tired of being surrounded by a bunch of goofy ass niggas. How life been treating you out there?" Shawn asked.

"Life been handling me ruff lately. I'm try'na put something in motion right now so I can make sure we both straight financially, "Shah said.

"Something like what?" Shawn asked.

"You want something from the vending machine?" Shah asked Shawn trying to avoid answering his question.

"Yeah bro, grab me some of that BBQ chicken, some flaming hots, and a blue mountain dew," Shawn said.

"Tight" Shah said as he grabbed his bag of change and walked over to the vending machine. Shah grabbed the chicken and put it in the Microwave, then grabbed a few bags of chips, some candy, and two bottles of mountain dew and took them over to the table to Shawn. Then he went and grabbed the chicken from the microwave. When Shah got back to the table Shawn wasted no time asking questions.

"What the lil bitch Mesha been on? I ain't heard from that bitch since I left the county," Shawn said.

"Man, Mesha moved to Houston, I been seeing her on Facebook every now and then," Shah said "Yeah! That used to be my lil bitch, ever since they gave me that time that lil bitch fell back from the kid. But you know what they say out of sight out of mind! What about that lil bitch Crystal?" Shawn asked.

"Shit which one you talking about?" Shah asked.

"The one wit the fat ass I used to bring over to the crib all the time," Shawn said.

"Damn, I forgot all about her. I used to want to fuck her bad ass, hell that pussy used to look so fat in them leggings she used to be wearing!" Shah said.

"That pussy was fat out of them leggings too bro. I used to be fucking the shit out of shorty," Shawn said as he smiled.

"Man, I ain't seen her since the last time you brought her to the crib. Wherever she at she been low," Shah said.

"I know you be seeing Tamika?" Shawn asked.

"Yeah, I seen her the other day. She on her shit bro! She asked me about you I gave her your info. She said she was going to write you. I got her phone number for you too. She said she was gone put some cash on the line so you could call her. I got the number in my phone, call me tomorrow and I'ma have it on standby," Shah said.

"I just had a dream about her last night! I can't lie I miss that lil pussy" Shawn said.

"Yeah! Ima make sure you get that number," Shah said.

"Say no mo! But what up wit Audrey? She still going to school for that dentist shit?" Shawn asked.

"Yeah she still in school, she super focused on getting that done," Shah said.

"That's what's up! I got a lot of respect for her. She ain't like a lot of them young chicks in Madison," Shawn said.

"I know," Shah added.

"What's up wit Tammy?" Shawn asked as he started eating his chicken.

"She doing good, she work at the UW Hospital. She a phlebotomist," Shah said.

"What the fuck is that?" Shawn asked as he took another bite from his chicken.

"Man, bro don't get me to lying. I guess it's some shit that got to do with dealing with blood or some shit like that," Shah said.

"That's what's up! I bet her little ass got thick as hell. You ain't hit it yet?" Shawn asked.

Shah started laughing, "What made you asked that?"

"Because it's obvious that y'all like each other. I been seeing it since we was younger. You better get some of that pussy!" Shawn said.

"Tight, Tight," Shah said blowing that comment off.

"What up with the G?" Shawn asked.

"Same shit still getting high," Shah answered.

"That shit crazy! She been fucking with that nigga James?" Shawn asked.

Shah paused for a moment not sure if he should be one hundred with Shawn. "If she have, I don't know nothing about it. But I don't think she is though," Shah said.

"She bet not be after that bitch ass nigga got me all this damn time!" Shawn said as he took a sip from his mountain dew.

"Fuck that nigga, mafucka gone get him out the way real soon. But look bro, I came up here to holla at you bout something!" Shah said.

"Tight, what up?" Shawn asked.

"I been thinking about jumping in the game, fucking with this coke shit, Hot Boi got going on. I wanted to know what you think before I do," Shah said.

Shawn sat up in his seat and put his hand on his chin. "Look bro, personally I think you should go the safe route, I don't wanna hear that you locked up. You better than this bro. The saddest thing in life his wasted talent and you got a lot of it bro, but at the end of the day, I ain't walking in yo shoes. I can tell you everything I know but you gotta be yo own man. I can't do that for you. So, my advice is do what's best for you bro, "Shawn said.

"I think I'ma get in the game bro. I'm tired of being broke, I don't even got a car. I got an old ass flip phone and my bitch ain't even got a phone, that shit makes me feel like I'm less of a man bro," Shah said.

"Bro, you ain't gotta explain yoself to me. I told you where I stand. At the end of the day, the decision is up to you. Either way I'm riding with you, but if you gone do it don't just do it to be doing it. You gotta use that shit as a way of getting out cause it's not a lifestyle it's an escape plan you feel me?" Shawn asked.

"Yeah, I understand what you saying," Shah responded.

"Say no more than lil bro," Shawn said.

Shah and Shawn went on talking for hours until the visit was over. They stood up and shook hands and hugged before parting ways. As Shah drove back to Madison, he felt Shawn was a voice of reasoning for him. He knew he had to do what was in his best interest at that moment. Now he was ready to get in the game and get some money.

Meanwhile

Hot Boi was at the crib getting ready. Big T had finally called and told him he had some bitches online and that it was time he showed him how he gets down. Hot Boi rarely ever spent any money on clothing. He liked to stack his money, but today he decided since he was getting up with Big T and his hoes he wanted to be prepared. Hot Boi grabbed his black Balmain jeans off the bed and put them on, then he grabbed his Gucci belt and his wife beater from the drawer and put them on. He grabbed his half of a blunt from the ash tray off his dresser and flamed it up as he walked into the living room. Hot Boi was geeked about being able to get up with the hoes Big T had online. He felt it was about time he did something other than hustle. He came a long way from bouncing house to house and sleeping on other people's couches. Hot Boi had come from a broken home, his mother and father had both been drug addicts and he was an only child.

One night, when Hot Boi was fourteen his mother and father was coming home from the bar when they got in a car accident. His mother was ejected from the car and died on the scene; his father was put in a coma but died two weeks later. Hot Boi had no other family members that were willing to take him in, so he was placed into foster care. Hot Boi ran from foster care two week before his fifteenth birthday. He bounced from spot to spot staying with different friends but spent most of his time living with Shah.

He did whatever it took to provide for his self. In the beginning, Hot Boi would rob and steal. When that wasn't working out he started hustling. When Hot Boi turned sixteen he met Big T and that's when his life made a turn for the better. When Big T first started fronting him work he would spend every dollar of his own money on weed and clothes, all he did was make sure he had enough to give Big T his money and get more work.

After his year run of blowing money, Hot Boi had enough of tricking his cash because he had nothing to show for it but a bunch of clothes. He decided it was time to stack his money up, he knew it was time to get his own crib and car. Hot Boi got focused and stayed ten toes down and after six months of going hard he reached his first hundred thousand.

Big T noticed how focused Hot Boi had become and decided to help Hot Boi get his shit all the way together. Big T had one of his female friends come up and get an apartment in her name for Hot Boi and took him to buy his first car. It'd been six months since Hot Boi moved into his apartment and his hustle game stepped all the way up. He'd been so low that no one not even Big T knew he had the hundred and fifty thousand dollars saved up.

Hot Boi grabbed his white Balmain T-shirt off the couch and put it on, then slipped his black and white Balmain sneakers on. He then walked to the long mirror in the hall to see how he looked. Hot Boi stood there checking his outfit out as he took a few puffs from his blunt.

"Yeah, I'ma boss now," he said to his self. He walked into his room and opened his safe and pulled out ten thousand, then walked back over to the mirror and took a heavy puff from his blunt as he spread the hundreds in his hand like a fan.

"I'm finna flex on these hoes tonight," he said to his self then laughed. Just then his phone started to ring. He rushed into his room and picked it up off the dresser and answered it.

"What up big bro?" Hot Boi said.

"You ready?" Big T asked.

"Yeah, I'm ready," Hot Boi quickly replied.

"Ight, I'm bout to slide on you," Big T said.

"Ight, I'm here" Hot Boi said.

"I'ma call you when I pull up," Big T said.

"Ight bet," Hot Boi said then ended the call and walked to the bathroom and grabbed his Dolce&Cabana light blue cologne and sprayed some on. As he walked out the bathroom, he dialed Shah's number.

"HB what up?" Shah said as he answered.

"Shit just checking on you. How the visit go with big bro? He straight?" Hot Boi asked.

"Yeah he good. He in that bitch working out and reading trying to get his mind right. All he wants to do is eat and talk about all the hoes he use to fuck with," Shah said.

"Yeah bro had a lot of hoes when he was out here. He put me up on game with the hoes a few times. How he looking on the cash side? I wanna send something his way. He was always a good dude," Hot Boi said.

"You know bro ain't turning down no cash. A nigga need everything you can get when he in that position," Shah said.

"You right, I'm put a band on bro books in the AM, make sure he got something to hold him over," Hot Boi said.

"That's what's up! You know bro gone appreciate that," Shah said.

"Bro my mans you already know that. But I called to just tell you to just hold the car down til tomorrow. Shorty ain't gone need it til tomorrow night. I'm finna go fuck with these bitches for the night," Hot Boi said.

"Tight, say no mo, I'ma holla at you in the morning. Oh, I'm in bro, my mind made up," Shah said.

"Shit it's on then? We gone line everything up in the AM. Fool its bout to go down, you don't even know we bout to take off," Hot Boi said.

"Bro, I'm ready to take flight," Shah said.

"Say no mo then, I'm bout to slid on these hoes. Ima get up with you in the AM," Hot Boi said.

"Yep" Shah quickly said then hung up the phone. Hot Boi put his phone in his pocket and walked over to the window and peeked out the blinds. Big T minivan pulled into the parking lot and Hot Boi phone started to ring in this pocket. He ignored the call and hurried and turn all the lights out and locked the apartment up and left the building. As he got closer to the minivan, he notice Big T was driving so he walked around to the passenger side and got in.

"Damn T I ain't never seen you driving!" Hot Boi said shocked.

"You know I wasn't gone pull up to your spot with the hoes. This where you lay your head. Its only right I respect that," Big T said.

"And that's why I fucks with you," Hot Boi quickly replied.

"I hope you ready for these bitches. I got eight bad ass hoes at the crib ready to do whatever we tell em to," Big T said as he reversed out the lot.

"Hell yeah I'm ready," Hot Boi said geeked.

"I don't know lil bro, I ain't saying that cuz you only eighteen. I'm saying that cuz these bitches boss freaks! We gone see if you really ready," Big T said.

"Bro, these hoes better be ready for me! That's all I'm saying," Hot Boi added.

"Tight, say that then little bro," Big T said as he laughed.

Hot Boi always enjoyed the long drive out to south Beloit. It always gave him time to clear his mind and think. The everyday hassle of running the streets was stressful with no time to just be at ease. Being able to get away was a blessing even if it was only for a few hours. Plus, Big T was loaded with cock sucking cash. He had a big ass mansion on six acres of land. Pulling up to Big T house always motivated him. The one mile drive up the curved driveway made him feel like he was in a movie. The three-story mansion was a site to see. He had never paid any attention to notice that Big T had an underground garage.

Big T reached up and pressed the garage door opener as he drove around the side of the house and down into the garage.

"Damn T you got an underground garage and this bitch too?" Hot Boi asked as he looked around. He couldn't believe the cars he was seeing. Most of them were worth more then what he had saved up. As long as he'd known Big T, he'd never seen him drive anything besides the mini van. He got out of the van and walked up to Big T's drop head Rolls Royce and looked inside.

"Damn T you fucked my whole understanding up with this one," Hot Boi said.

"Oh, the drop head. You ain't never seen one of them?" Big T asked.

"Hell naw'll! I seen one on TV or in a magazine but never in person," Hot Boi said. "What's the ticket on this bitch?" he quickly asked.

"I got that last year lil bro. I dropped $200,000 on it," Big T said.

"Yeah bro I need to get on yo level," Hot Boi said.

"Shit just stay focus lil bro you gone get there. You gotta remember this shit didn't happen over night. I'm putting you in on some shit that's gone help you get whatever you want. But for now, you finna party with those bitches," Big T said.

"Say no more," Hot Boi replied. As he followed Big T through the underground garage, he noticed Big T had a Mercedes Benz G wagon, a Bentley GT coupe, a four door Porsche, and some more shit. Hot Boi's mind was supposed to be on the bitches, but he couldn't help but to think about how much more he wanted out of life and how far he was behind. Big T lead him up the stairs, he could hear music playing and women speaking in Spanish. When Big T opened the door, he saw two beautiful Latina women sitting at the kitchen island. He saw one of them the other day in the car with Big T. They jumped up and screamed,"papi" and ran over to Big T and gave him a hug.

"This my mans Hot Boi. Hot Boi this is Salina and Sofia. Now I want y'all to know this my brother. I want y'all to show him the time of his life tonight," Big T said.

"OK papi," Salina said as she smiled at Hot Boi. Sofia walked up to Hot Boi and ran her finger through his dreads and whispered into his ear,"! Nostros Vamos a siéñarte un tiempo mūy bīén" then she kissed him on the cheek instantly turning Hot Boi on.

"I don't know what you just said, but you got my dick hard as hell right now," Hot Boi said. Sofia and Salina both started laughing.

"Make yoself at home bro, I got some shit I gotta handle real quick," Big T said as he walked out of the kitchen.

"Iight!" Hot Boi said.

Salina and Sofia both asked Hot Boi if he wanted something to drink.

"What y'all drinking?" Hot Boi asked as he walked over to the kitchen island.

"Wine," Salina said in a very sexy tone.

"Ain't no Grey Goose?" Hot Boi asked.

"Whatever you want Papi," Sofia said. Salina grabbed Hot Boi by the hand and walked him to the bar in the dining area and poured him a cup of Grey Goose.

"Anything else papi?" Salina asked. "Yeah, let me get some orange juice in here," Hot Boi said. Salina poured him a little orange juice in his cup.

He took a sip from his drink then he heard more female voices coming from down the hall, and he remembered Big T said he had eight hoes. Hot Boi started walking down the hall toward the voices he was hearing. As long as he had known Big T he'd never been this deep into his house. He walked further and further down the hall. As he got closer he could hear water splashing and a lot of laughter.

He made it to the end of the hall and turned the corner. He saw a long glass wall that separated the hall from the indoor pool.

He stood there shocked as he starred at four of the thickest bitches he'd ever seen sitting at the end of the pool sipping on their drinks and laughing.

He stood there for a minute. Sofia walked around the corner and saw Hot Boi stuck and mesmerized by the woman in the pool area.

She wanted to make sure she got her hands on him first, so he could experience her Latina loving.

She grabbed him by the hand and led him back up front to the living room area. She took his drink from his hand and pushed him down on the couch. She sat his drink on the coffee table and sat in his lap and started kissing on his neck. Salina walked into the room holding a black bag. She walked over and sat down on the couch next to them. Then she sat the bag on the table before opening it. She pulled out a bag of ecstasy pills, a ounce of cocaine, and a ounce of weed, and sat it all on the table.

Sofia got geeked when she saw the cocaine. She grabbed the bag and poured some on the table before making three lines.

"Papi, you go first" Sofia said.

"Naw I'm straight, I don't do coke," Hot Boi said.

"You sure you don't want to try just one-time papi?" Salina asked as she got down on her knees next to Sofia.

"Yeah I'm sure, y'all do y'all thing. I'ma fuck with one of these pills and smoke some of this weed. Ain't no blunt in the bag?" Hot Boi asked.

"No, no blunts papi," Salina quickly said. Sofia reached into the bag and pulled out a bowl and a lighter and handed it to him.

Salina wasted no time getting the coke and quickly did two lines, before reaching in the bag of pills and pulling out three of them. She put one on her tongue before standing up and kissing Sofia, pushing one into her month.

She put another one on her tongue and kissed Hot Boi pushing it into his mouth. Then she chewed the last one.

Hot Boi had Sofia grab his cup off the table and hand it to him. He took a big gulp from his drink to help him swallow the pill. Sofia leaned over and snorted the last line off the table.

Hot Boi sat there in shock. He'd never partied like this before. In a way it was kind of uncomfortable, but he just let them do them. He grabbed the bag of weed off the table and pulled out a big bud and put it and the bowl. He instantly started coughing when he inhaled a big cloud of smoke. He quickly grabbed his cup and took a big ass gulp finishing it off. Sofia got up and walked out of the living room. Hot Boi passed the bowl to Salina, she took a big hit finishing the rest, before sitting back blowing out a big cloud of smoke into the air.

He looked over at her in disbelief, "Damn these bitches don't play no games," he thought to himself.

He grabbed the bowl from her and put another bud in then hit it. This time making sure he didn't cough. He refused to let some bitches show him up. He hit the bowl two more times and blew the smoke out. The pill started to kick in full force.

He sat back on the couch as his head started to spin. Sofia walked into the room with three bottles of water, a bottle of rose and a bottle of grey goose. She put the drinks on the table and walked over to turn on some music, future March Madness began to pour though the speakers. Sofia turned it up as loud as possible and started dancing.

Salina leaned over and put her hand on Hot Boi's thigh.

"I want to see it papi," Salina said.

Hot Boi sat there stuck, he took a ecstasy pill once before, but it didn't kick in this fast,and this hard, confused he managed to lean over to Salina.

"You wanna see what?" he asked.

Salina reached and grabbed his belt buckle. Just then it hit him, and he understood what she wanted. He unbuckled his belt and sat back. Salina started kissing him on the neck. She reached and grabbed a fist full of his dreads with one hand and unzipped his pants and reached in and grabbed ahold of his dick. She was so shocked when she felt his thickness. She moaned into his ear.

Hot Boi was instantly aroused and higher than he'd ever been in his life, feeling sensations he'd never felt before. She started to stroke him as he grew with excitement in her hand. She continued to kiss him on the neck and lick his ear, breathing heavy into his ear.

"Papi put it in my mouth," she whispered in his ear. He pulled his pants down to his ankles and grabbed Salina by her hair and pushed her head down to his lap as he pulled his briefs down to his ankles.

Salina laid across the couch with her head and his lap. Sofia was high and in her own world with her back to them while dancing to the music. Salina laid her head in his lap while she stroked him with both hands.

He reached over her head to the coffee table and grabbed the Rose bottle and popped it open and took a sip.

"Iight, now go ahead and show me a good time," Hot Boi said.

"OK papi!" Salina said as she went down and took him into her mouth. She started sucking on the tip of his dick, then she went deeper as Hot Boi sat back sipping on the Rose bottle with a fist full of her hair guiding her up and down. He looked over and saw Sofia still dancing. He called her name a few times before she finally turned around.

"Come help her out" he said to her. Sofia stopped dancing and walked over to them. She started taking off Hot Boi shoes, before pulling his briefs all the way off. Sofia squatted in between Hot Boi's legs and started playing with his balls while Salina sucked his dick. After a few minutes they switched, and then went back and forth sharing him while he sat there sipping from the Rose bottle watching them take turns.

Big T came walking into the living room with the four Jamaican women that Hot Boi had seen earlier in the swimming pool area and instantly started laughing.

"I see you found out they don't waste no time," Big T said to Hot Boi.

"Yeah, they got straight to it!" Hot Boi said as he took another sip from his bottle.

"That's what's up, I know you haven't had the chance to meet these beautiful women. This is Traci, Bianca, Jade and Brianna. Ladies that's my lil brother Hot Boi and as y'all can see, we share EVERYTHING," Big T said. Hot Boi sat there with eyes on Jade. She was beautiful with nice dark chocolate skin, hazel brown eyes, and long dreads fixed up in a bun. He couldn't help but notice how thick she was.

"How you doing, Jade?" Hot Boi said and winked at her.

Salina and Sofia continued to lick and suck on Hot Boi dick as if no one had ever even entered the room.

"We finna go fuck around in this hot tub, you know where to find us when you done," Big T said as he flamed up the blunt in his hand and put his arms around Bianca and Brianna.

"Iight big bro, say no more. But before you leave let me hit that blunt. They got me smoking out this bowl and I ain't really feeling that shit," Hot Boi said.

"You should have said something, I got a few cases of blunts lil bro. You can go ahead and face his one," Big T said handing him the blunt.

"Good looking bro," Hot Boi quickly said. Big T put his arm around Brianna and turned to leave the room.

Jade couldn't help herself once she noticed the size of his dick and chose to join Salina and Sofia. "Go without me," she said to Big T and the other three girls, as she walked toward Hot Boi.

She took off her swimsuit and kneeled on the couch on the opposite side of Salina and leaned in in whispered into Hot Boi's ear.

"This what you want?" she asked. Her voice sounded so beautiful and her soft and sweet Jamaican accent made his dick grow even harder. He reached and rubbed his hand up and down her thigh and around to her ass.

"Yeah I want it! And I'ma show you what I'm gone do to it," he said and grabbed her ass cheek.

"Well, show me rude boy!" Jade said and licked around the outside or Hot Boi's ear. He stopped Salina and Sofia and stood up. He stepped over Sofia and grabbed Jade by the arm and pulled her from the couch and bent her over the arm of the couch. He licked the tip of his finger and started playing with her pussy. Jade let out a soft moan the very second his finger touched her pussy.

"Get one of them condoms from out my pocket," Hot Boi said to Sofia. She quickly reached into his pocket and tossed him the condom, as she and Salina watched in anticipation.

He quickly ripped it open and put it on all in one motion. Hot Boi gabbed ahold of Jade's ass cheeks, spread them apart, and then slowly slid into her fat pussy. Her juices quickly began to flow as she arched her back allowing him to go deeper.

After the first stroke he began to pound away at her pussy. He let go of one of her ass cheeks as he watched it bounce with waves every time, he thrust back in. Salina and Sofia both got undressed. Salina sat back on the couch and started playing with her pussy while she twirled Jade nipples through her fingertips. Sofia watched Salina as she slowly played with her clit. Sofia crawled over between Salina legs and started to kiss her inner thigh as she made her way up Salina's thigh, Salina reached and grabbed Sofia's hair and pulled her face to her pussy.

Sofia began to slowly lick her clit and Salina put her head back as Sofia ate her pussy.

Hot Boi looked over and saw them and instantly felt like a boss as he watched what was unfolding before his eyes. He switched position after position as he took turns fucking and sucking all three of them for hours.

Hot Boi was half asleep when he felt soft bare skin brush up against his own. He opened his eyes and saw Brianna. When he sat up, he saw Bianca laying behind her, everyone was ass hole naked. He rolled to the edge of the bed and sat up. His head was still spinning as he looked to the floor. He saw a pair of swim shorts and an iPhone on the side of the bed. He picked the phone up to see what time it was.

"Damn its 8:30am," he said as he stood up. He looked around the unfamiliar room confused to how the hell he got there.

The last thing he remembered was being in the living room with Jade, Salina, and Sofia.

He walked over to the door and opened it. He peeked out to see if he could see Big T or anyone. With no one in site he walked out the room and made his way down the hall. The smell of weed lingered in the air the further he walked; he could hear a woman laughing. As he made his way toward the voice, Salina came stumbling out the room at the end of the hall laughing and speaking Spanish to someone on her phone. She looked up and saw him and smiled.

"Hey papi!" she said then ended her call. Hot Boi, still a little dizzy, took a second before responding.

"How you doing?" he asked.

"Fine papi, fine. Did you have a good time last night?" she quickly asked.

"Hell yeah! Well at least what I can remember. How the hell did I end up with Brianna and Bianca? The last I remember I was with you, Sofia and Jade," he said.

"Oh papi" Salina said as she walked up on him. She ran her hand along the side of his neck.

"A lot happened after we had fun in the living room. We went to the hot tub, smoked some more weed, and after a while me and the girls talked you and papi into trying a line for the first time. Then we had a big orgy before Traci, Brianna, and Bianca kidnapped you so they could have you all to themselves," she said.

Hot Boi stood there for a moment while he processed what she said, not sure if he heard her right.

"Wait you said I did a line?" he asked.

"Oh, papi you really don't remember! You did a few lines and fucked us all like we never been fucked before. You were amazing, a whole lot better than your brother," she whispered.

"So, where bro at now?" he asked

"He out on a business's meeting. He'll be back soon. There's a bathroom down the hall. It's the last door on the left. You can shower if you'd like to and I'll go down and bring your clothes to you," Salina said.

"Tight... my phone should be where my clothes at, bring that up too," Hot Boi said.

"OK papi," she said as she grabbed his dick one last time, before turning to go get his stuff.

"You can get some more if you want! I'ma be in the shower," Hot Boi said, then started walking to the bathroom.

Chapter Three

2 WEEKS LATER

Shah sat at the kitchen table ecstatic over the amount of money in front of him. He'd never seen this much money at one time. He looked across the table at Hot Boi as he counted the last thousand and passed it over the table. It'd been two weeks since he started hustling and to Hot Boi's surprise he was a natural go getter. Hot Boi took two Puffs from the blunt hanging from his lips and shook his head. Shah sat there on the edge of his seat. He went from being excited to being worried all in one second, as he tried reading Hot Boi's facial expressions.

They both sat there for a few seconds those seconds quickly began to feel like hours to Shah. Hot Boi stood up and looked him directly in his eyes.

"Bro you went crazy! I been dumping off that line for years and that bitch ain't never did 75,000 that fast," Hot Boi said.

"Damn that 75 bands?" Shah asked.

"You ain't even count this shit?" Hot Boi asked.

"Hell naw'll! I just made sure I made 2,800 off every zip, and every time I did, I just put that shit to the side and cooked another zip," Shah said.

"You did that all off the line?" Hot Boi asked.

"Hell naw'll. I went out west last Wednesday to grab some smoke from my man's Lil Jerry on Russit. The Lil nigga had the block bussin, so I hopped out and smoked a few blunts with them niggas! While I was standing out there a few hypes pulled through looking for some work. After bro told me they was good people, I served them, then got up out of there. About thirty minutes later fool called me and told me he had two of them back over there with a band each and that I should hurry up before lil folk em rob they ass. After that I sat over there with them four days straight. I ran through 17 zips over there alone," Shah said.

"You ain't put none of them on the line?" Hot Boi asked.

"I put six new ones on the line, the ones who came through every time with the big money!"

"Shit you ain't wrong. You went crazy tho bro! This weight line been slow. I ain't made shit but nine bands this week. Altogether it's 84,000 on the table. After we take off 30 for big homie, we both gone have 27 each," Hot Boi said.

"Tight, take off that 5 you gave me to get that car," Shah said

"You sure?" Hot Boi asked.

"Yeah bro. I gotta carry my own weight from here on out fool!" Shah replied.

"Tight, say no mo. We on our way to the top," Hot Boi said.

"I'm ready," Shah replied

"I know, the hunger is real. I can see it in your eye!" Hot Boi said.

"You know that!" Shah replied.

"I'm bout to go link up with the big homie, so we can get back to this cash!" Hot Boi said.

Tight, say no mo, I need to link up with Audrey. I think she mad at me cause I ain't been spending no time with her since I lost my job," Shah said.

"Oh yeah! Go ahead and spend the day with her. Take her out somewhere and let her know it's a good reason why you haven't spent much time with her lately," Hot Boi replied.

"I been fucked up for a minute now. I really don't know no nice spot to take her out too," Shah said.

"I got you! As a matter of fact, you should take her to Ruth Chris out in Middleton. Take her out to buy something nice to wear. I'ma call and make a reservation for you. Oh yeah you gotta take her over to hotel Red, grab a suite, and chill with her for the night," Hot Boi said.

"Where the fuck hotel Red at?" Shah asked.

"Damn Shah money, you ain't never been to the red spot? I gotta boss yo life up a little. Its over on the corner on Regent and Monroe. I'ma book the room for you too. Just make sure you give me my cash back," Hot Boi said.

"How much is it?" Shah asked.

"400 but---"

"Hold on! $400 for a hotel?" Shah said cutting Hot Boi off.

"Yeah, but you ain't paying $400 for a hotel, you paying for that experience. Showing Audrey, a night she will never forget is priceless! I'ma put you up on game, don't worry I got you bro," Hot Boi said.

"Game nigga I got that. It's just the money I ain't use to yet. Knowing what the bitches like run in my blood," Shah said. Hot Boi started to laugh. He and Shah both knew the only female Shah ever been with was Andrey, and that he was far from a player. He handed Shah 22,000 and separated his 32,000 from Big T's 30,000. He grabbed his money and walked to the room and put it directly into is safe. He came out of the room and heard Shah on the phone talking to Audrey. He grabbed Big T's money off the table and put it into a brown paper bag.

"Shah let me see that other line, I'ma take care of business today. You can go ahead and enjoy yourself for the day. I'ma have them leave a key at the front desk for you bro," Hot Boi said.

"Tight, good looking," Shah said and tossed the phone to him. Hot Boi put the bag in the front of his pants and left the apartment.

Meanwhile

Tammy sat on the living room sofa wrapped in a blanket with a bowl of popcorn on her lap as she watched a movie. She could barely focus on her movie because she could hear Audrey in the back talking on the phone with Shah. She could hear how excited she was and she was dying for her to get off so she could find out what was going on.

Audrey got off the phone and came running into the front room. She instantly started twerking. Tammy started laughing as she watched her twerk like a dancer at the strip club.

"What got you so happy? Fill me in bitch?"

Audrey stopped twerking and put her hands on her knees out of breath. "It's Shah bitch, he finna take me out shopping. He on his way over right now!" she said as she tossed Tammy her phone back.

Tammy sat her popcorn bowl on the table and took the blanket off as she sat all the way up.

"Where he get some money from?" She quickly asked.

"Bitch who care! I ain't been shopping in a long time. I need some new shit. Girl I gotta get ready," she said, then turned and ran from the living room back into her room.

Tammy covered herself back up with the blanket and started back watching her movie. She heard her phone chime with a text massage, so she reached and picked it up. She looked at it and saw that it was a text from Shah telling her he wanted to take her shopping as well to thank her for always being there for him when he needed her. She quickly jumped up.

"Audrey, bitch Shah must really got some money. He want me to come shopping with y'all," she said.

"Throw something on then girl let's go fuck this mall up," Audrey replied.

"Bitch you ain't gotta tell me twice," Tammy said as she ran into her room and slipped into some sweatpants and threw her hair in a ponytail.

"I hope Shah don't be rushing cause bitch I like to take my time!" Tammy yelled to Audrey.

3 Hour Later

Shah sat on the bench in the middle of the mall flipping through his new iPhone. He bought one for him and Audrey. As he sat there, he started to realize he made a big mistake taking Tammy and Audrey to the mall. He should have let them go alone cause he'd been in the mall with them for over two hour, and they still hadn't found everything they wanted. Shah sat there, legs aching, and body tried as he tried to figure out how to work his iPhone. His other phone beeped with a text massage. He flipped it open and saw it was Hot Boi and quickly read it.

"A fool, the reservations for Ruth Chris is in Audrey's name and the key at the front desk for you, whenever you ready,"

Shah quickly texted back, "Good looking bro,"

Shah looked up from his phone and saw Reggie and three of his homies headed his way. Shah and Reggie locked eyes on each other. Shah quickly stood up. Reggie started tapping his homies letting them know he was on bullshit.

"What up broke boy!" Reggie said as he approached Shah.

"Move around with that bullshit Reggie," Shah said.

"Bitch ass nigga don't say my name like we cool!" Reggie said as he stepped closer to Shah.

Shah took a moment to size up the situation. He knew it was four on one, so he didn't have no win coming his way plus he didn't wanna fuck the night up with Audrey, so he kept it cool.

"Look you got that! I'm on something. Catch me another day and I'll give you what you looking for," Shah said.

"You a pussy, you keep saying that but ain't did shit yet!" Reggie said. Shah's blood began to boil, and his heart started to pound. His first thought was to just show Reggie right now that he could beat the hell out of him. Shah walked through Reggie and his homies crowd and walked away. He figured it was in his best interest to move around. He walked over to the Rogers and Holland Jewelry store. He browsed around the store for a minute looking at a few rings and watches and chains until a diamond encrusted bracelet caught his attention.

"Yeah that bitch a look nice one Audrey," he mumbled to himself.

"Hi sir, is there anything I can help you with?" a woman asked from behind him.

"Yeah I like this bracelet," Shah said turning toward her.

He was caught completely off guard by her beauty. He stood there for a moment just staring.

"OK, I can help you with that. Which one were you looking at?" she asked as she came from behind the counter.

As she walked past Shah and over toward the other counter, he couldn't believe what he was seeing. Her slacks hugged her thick ass and thighs tightly.

"Damn!" Shah said unable to keep his thought to himself. She instantly knew what he was talking about but turned to ask anyways.

"You OK sir?" she asked as she smiled

"Yeah, yeah I'm fine," he answered, embarrassed.

"OK then," she said and turned and walked behind the counter. "So, which one did you have in mind?" she asked.

"This one right here," he said pointing to the bracelet as he avoided eye contact.

"Nice, out of all the jewelry in the shop this is my favorite," she said reaching in and pulling it out.

She handed him the bracelet for him to inspect it for himself.

"Sound like we got the same taste," Shah said as he checked the price tag. He quickly thought about putting it back when he noticed it was $2,500.

"Yeah, I'll take it," he said trying not to look like he wasn't used to money.

"OK, wonderful," the clerk said as he handed her the bracelet back. She walked from behind the counter and back over to the counter with the cash register to ring him up.

"Would you like insurance or maybe pay for the 60-day warranty?" she asked as she scanned the price tag on the bracelet.

"Na, I think it'll be in good hands," he responded.

"You sure? For this amount of money, I would get it insured," she said.

"Oh, it ain't nothing," he said trying to be cocky.

"OK! Your total is $2600 dollars," she said. Shah deliberately pulled all his money from his pocket to show off. He counted off $2,600 and handed it to her. She quickly boxed and bagged the bracelet and handed it to him with the receipt.

"Thanks for the help I really hope you enjoy the rest of the day," Shah said.

"Thank you, and you enjoy the rest of your day as well. Also, thanks for shopping with Rogers and Holland," she said smiling. He walked out of the store and back over the the bench in the middle of the mall and sat back down.

"Man let me see if they ass ready," he said to himself. He pulled his iPhone from this pocket and called Audrey.

"Heyy baby," she answered.

"Man y'all done yet? I'm tired as hell!" Shah said.

"Yeah we done, we in the food court," she replied.

"Oh, iight I'm on my way over there," Shah said

"OK," Audrey replied.

Shah hung the phone up and made his way to the food court and saw Audrey and Tammy on the opposite side eating, so he walked over.

"Man, I ain't know we was finna be in here this long. My damn legs and shoulders hurt. Next time I'll let y'all do this by y'all self," he said as he sat down next to Audrey.

"Boy stop! We didn't take that long," Tammy said, then looked at Audrey and they both started laughing.

"Oh, y'all think this shit funny! Iight," Shah said, then put the Rogers and Holland bag one the table.

"What you get from Roger and Holland? "Audrey asked.

"Nothing much," Shah said as he reached into the bag and pulled out the bracelet box and handed it to Audrey.

"It's for me?" she asked.

"Just open it," Shah quickly said.

She opened the box and smiled. "Oh my god Shah, its beautiful," Audrey said, then turned and gave him a hug and kiss.

"Thank you, baby!" she said

"Your welcome," Shah said.

He felt good being able to buy her some nice shit and being able to watch her smile.

"But on some real shit lets get up out of here, I got some shit to take care of and I need you to get ready so we can go out on a date tonight," Shah said.

"OK, where y'all going?" Tammy asked.

"Ruth Chris, then to a suite so I can put this mafucka all in her stomach," Shah said and laughed.

"Boy I don't want to hear that shit," Tammy replied with a look of disgust on her face.

"Bitch don't do my man! You know I was gone fill you in any ways," Audrey quickly said.

"You filling me in and him filling me in is two different things," Tammy said.

"Look y'all can finish y'all discussing at the crib. Let's get up out of here!" Shah said and started walking toward the exit.

Later that Evening

Shah and Audrey pulled into Ruth Chris parking lot. He parked the car and got out and walked around the car to open the door for Audrey. As she got out the car, Shah caught a quick glimps of her pink panties.

"Damn that mafucka fat!" Shah said as she got out of the car.

"Boy stop! You know little mama got a fat cat!" she said. She knew Shah loved her alterego lil mama.

Shah started laughing and closed the door. "Damn lil mama huh?" he asked.

"Yeah its lil mama tonight," she replied.

"OK! I like lil mama, she be busting it open," Shah said and laughed a little.

"Boy stop," she said slapping Shah on the shoulder. They both started laughing as he opened the door to the restaurant for her to walk in. They were greeted by the hostess who confirmed their reservation and showed them to their table.

They sat there for a moment looking at the menus, then placed their orders. As they waited on their meals to arrive, they filled each other in on whats been going on in their lives since the last time they saw one another. For Audrey, it seemed just as fast as they ordered their food arrived and was gone.

She knew time flies when your having fun, but time was moving too fast for her. She wanted to soak in every minute with Shah. She wasn't happy about his decision to start selling drugs, but she could tell by the look in his eyes that there was nothing that she or anyone else could say to stop him. She finished her drink and Shah paid their bill and they left.

As they pulled out of Ruth Chris parking lot, she pulled her iPhone from her purse and plugged it into the Aux cord and turned on Cardi B and started dancing in her seat.

Shah really didn't care for Cardi B's music, but he noticed she was tipsy and enjoying herself, so he just sat back and continued to drive. Halfway to the hotel he turned the music down. "Did you think about what I asked you?" he asked her.

"I don't remember what you asked me!" Audrey said, tipsy and confused.

"I asked what do you think about us getting our own apartment?" Shah asked. Audrey sat there for a moment trying to remember if he really asked her that. She knew if he had she would've never skipped over the conversation.

"Now I know I'm tipsy but you ain't ask me about moving into an apartment together," Audrey said.

"Iight you got me!" he said and started laughing. "I didn't ask you but I'm asking you now. What you think? he asked.

"Baby I love you more then anything in this world and would love for us to move in together, but I can't just up and leave Tammy."

"I dont want you to just up and leave her but I do want you to think about eventually moving in with me," he replied

"When are you talking about moving in together?"

"I dont know maybe in the next couple of months. It was just something I was thinking of and just wanted to see what you thought," he said.

"OK well I'm gone talk to Tammy and see if she will be able to handle all the bills on her own, if I move out. That's my girl and I want to make sure she gone be OK," Audrey said.

"I understand and respect that Cinderella," Shah said as they pulled into the hotel parking lot. Then parked in the underground parking.

"Oh my god Shah, I been waiting to see how this hotel looks inside for a while now. I been hearing its real nice. Hold on! Wait a minute, what bitch brought you here?" she asked seriously.

He started laughing at the question as he got out of the car, but quickly realized she wasn't joking when he noticed the look on her face.

"You serious?" he asked.

"Yes! Shah don't bring me to where you take your little hoes,"

"Man knock it the fuck off. I ain't know shit about his hotel until today. Plus, lil mama my only hoe and I know this better be her first time here," he said.

"Lil mama ain't no hoe, and she ain't never been here before!"

"Man get yo ass out this damn car," Shah said as he laughed. Audrey got out the car laughing, before closing the door. She walked up to him grabbing ahold of his hand as they made their way into the hotel, and to the front desk

"Excuse me ma'am there should be a key here for Shah Lumas," he said.

"OK, may I see your I.d?" She asked.

"OK!" Shah said pulling his I.d from his pocket and handed it to her. She looked at it, then reached under the desk and handed him the key card.

"Thank you," he said.

"You're welcome,"

Shah and Audrey made their way to the elevator and pushed their floor. Shah led the way to their room and opened the door for her to enter.

"Oh, my god! This room is like a apartment, "Audrey quickly said, as she walked into the room.

"Yeah, this bitch nice," Shah said as he looked around. They both walked through the room admiring how big and nice the room was. He looked and noticed a bottle of Rose Moet sitting on ice in a bucket on a table. "Man, folks a good nigga," he thought to his self. Audrey sat her purse on the couch and took her heels off and walked over to the balcony and opened the door.

"Shah thank you! I needed a day away from my crazy life of school and work," Audrey said.

"You ain't gotta thank me, you deserve it and so much more," he said and walked up to her pulling her close, then kissed her on the back of the neck.

"I love you," he whispered into her ear. She turned and faced him,"I love you too," she quickly said, then kissed him and walked away.

"OK, now let's get drunk and enjoy the night," she added.

"OK, I see lil mama finna show up," Shah said. Audrey started laughing as she popped the bottle of Rose and poured two cups.

"She ain't here yet, but when she get here you better be ready!" she said winking at him.

"She need to hurry up and get here cause I'm ready right now! As a matter of fact, come here," Shah said.

Audrey slowly and seductively walked toward him swaying her hips side to side as she sipped on her drink. She reached and rubbed her hands across his chest.

"So, tell me how you finna take a look at me?" she asked.

"Oh, I can show you better than I can tell you," Shah said, turning her around and unzipping her dress, before peeling the straps from her shoulders. He watched as it fell from her body and on to the floor. He picked her up and carried her to one of the bedrooms and sat her on the edge of the bed. He spread her legs open, got down on his knees, and began to kiss her inner thighs. She watched as he worked his way up. She reached over and put her cup on the nightstand. It had been a while since they had sex, so every touch of his warm hand sent chills up her spine. Shah pulled her panties off, then stood up and kissed her, forcing her to lay all the way back.

He put both legs in the air, then bent over and begin kissing her pussy.

"Oh, my god baby!" she said once he started to suck on her clit.

"Yes baby yes!" she screamed as he worked his tongue. Within minutes she was beginning to have an orgasm. Shah was shocked and turned on by how fast she came.

8:30am

Shah woke up feeling refreshed after a night of passionate sex. It had been well over three weeks since they last had sex, so last night was much needed for them both. Audrey laid next to him still sleeping, her hair was wild and covered her face.

Shah rolled over and looked at her. He moved the hair from her face and kissed her on the forehead. He got out of bed and walked to the living room area and grabbed his iPhone off the desk, before turning on the t.v. Shah decided to check his Facebook since he hadn't been on in a long time. When he logged in his account, he had four new friend request, three new massages and fifteen new notifications. He went straight to his inbox to see who left massages, because he rarely got on Facebook, so he wondered how long ago they were sent. Shah opened the first one from Lisa, she was his childhood friend who had a crush on him for years and always tried to have sex with him. Lisa knew a relationship would never happen being that Shah was in one with Audrey since seventh grade. But that never stopped her from trying to fuck him.

-Lisa Stone

"Heyy handsome, I was just stopping by to say hello since I hardly see you anymore. I hope all is well with you and hope to hear from you soon..,"

Shah looked at the last message and noticed she sent it at 6am. Not sure if he should reply right now or not, he decided not to. Instead, he clicked on the next massage. It was from Terri; they never met in person but they've been friends on Facebook for years. She was from Houston,

Texas and just so happened to see his profile picture one day and decided to send him a friend request because she thought he was handsome. Overtime they became really close, going back in forth flirting through messages.

-TerriSweet_AsBerries

"OMG! You are so fucking sexy Shah. I hope you dont mind me stealing this picture of you and make you my MCM?"

Shah looked at the bottom of the massage and noticed she sent it a week ago. He enjoyed the back and forth flirting with her so he responded to her massage.

-Shah_Money

"Hey beautiful, I know I'm late as fuck responding to your message, that's only cause I haven't logged back on since I uploaded that picture. You know I wouldn't have a problem with you making me you MCM. Hopefully one of these days I'll be able to make my way down to Houston and give you what you looking for!"

After sending that message to her, he checked his last one, and saw that it was from his cousin in Chicago. He hadn't talked to or seen his cousin Lil Ant in three years and was shocked to even see that he had a message from him.

-GetRich_Ant

"Cuzzo what up? I ain't seen you in a minute skud! When you get this message hit my line. (773-319-2110) Make sure you hit me up and accept my friend request too skud,"

Shah checked the bottom of the message and noticed lil Ant sent it a week ago, so he quickly replied.

-Shah_Money

"Cuz what's up? I'm glad you found me cause I ain't seen you in a long ass time. I got yo number. I'm gone hit you so you can have mine cause I hardly be on the book."

He went back to Terri's message to see if she wrote back yet. But she didn't, so he went to his friend request and quickly accepted all four friend requests.

He clicked on his notifications and noticed most of them were from Lisa liking a bunch of his old pictures and statuses. He logged off the book and called lil Ant. As Shah waited for him to answer, he grabbed the remote and started flipping through the channels.

"Hello?" lil Ant answered.

"What up cuz? This Shah"

"Shah! Damn skud it's been a minute," Lil Ant said shocked to hear from him.

"I know! Fuck you been on down there?" Shah asked.

"Shit skud tryna get some bread and stay out the way! What you been on out there?" Lil Ant asked.

"Man cuz, I'm trying to get my shit together right now. I was working but lost my job. So now I'm trying to figure some shit out!" Shah replied.

"What that nigga Shawn been up to? I tried to find cuz on the book too, he must ain't got a Facebook?"

"Bro locked up!" Shah replied.

"Damn for what?"

"For attempted homicide," Shah said.

"Damn cuz," lil Ant said.

"I know! You remember my O. G's boyfriend James?" Shah asked.

"Yeah,"

"Bro got into it one day with him, and when James came outside bro shot him six times. But he ended up seeing that it was Shawn, so when the ambulance got there, he told them Shawn shot him," Shah said.

"Damn skud cuz was supposed to make sure he hit that nigga in the head. That's a for sure kill," lil Ant said.

"I know! They ended up giving bro fifteen years for that shit,"

"Damn skud! Yeah that's fucked up cuz a good nigga. It's crazy how all the good nigga's end up in fucked up situations. So, what's up with Auntie Marie?" Lil Ant asked.

"Man cuz, that shit a whole nother story! She back fucking with dude,"

"NEVER! You bullshiting!" Lil Ant said shocked.

"No bullshit cuz, she living with the nigga right now as we speak!" Shah said.

"Damn! Auntie bogus. Do cuz know?" Lil Ant asked.

"Naw, bro don't know. You know I can't tell him about that shit. I can't put no stress on him at all. That shit foul cause the only reason he was arguing with James was because of my O.G!" Shah said.

"Man, skud I might have to slide up there in lay dude down cause he fucked Auntie up and got cuz all that damn time," Lil Ant said.

"That's gone get done, when the time right cuz, trust me,"

"But look my other phone over here ringing. I'ma hit you back later on cuz!" Shah added.

"Tight, do yo thang skud," lil Ant said.

"Tight, love cuz," Shah said, before getting up from the couch and grabbing his other phone off the desk. He looked in the room to see if Audrey was waking yet.

Meanwhile

Tammy laid in bed talking on the phone with X. She had finally decided to call him last night and was surprised at how smart he was. He had a good since of humor and could hold a good conversation.

She enjoyed talking to him and was happy when he called just to tell her good morning. She managed to keep him talking a little bit longer.

"OK, so since you don't want me to come visit you in Madison, when you coming back to the mil to see me?" X asked.

"It's not that I don't want you to come see me, I just want to take time to get to know you before I bring you around my people cause they over protective of me. Plus, I want to be sure about us!" she said

"I understand where you coming from and I respect it but in order for you to be sure about me we gone have to spend some time together face to face. So again, when we gone do that?" he asked.

"Honestly, I'm not sure, I gotta check my work schedule when I go in. Then I'll be able to let you know," she replied.

"OK, that'll work. How bout you call me later tonight when you get off so we can talk more. I got some business I need to take care of real quick. I want you to make sure you have a nice day at work too iight," X said.

"OK, I will talk to you when I get off and make sure you have a nice day as well,"

"I will," X said.

"OK," Tammy said ending the call.

Chapter Four

H ot Boi was sitting in his car at the BP gas station on Verona Rd waiting for Almundo to call and let him know that he was on Britta. He had never met Almundo before, he was one of Shah people and according to Shah he was good people. So, he wanted to meet him his self to fill him out. He started rolling a blunt when he noticed Reggie pull into the station. He quickly put the blunt down and reached under his seat and grabbed his 9mm before putting it on his waistline.

Reggie parked at the pump next to him and got out of his car and walked into the gas station. Hot Boi's blood began to boil as he thought about what Shah told him. After a few seconds, he jumped out of the car and stood in front of his car and waited on Reggie to come out the store.

As he stood there waiting, a blue Cadillac truck pulled in and parked in front of the door blocking his view. A dude jumped out the truck who looked real familiar to Hot Boi and caught his attention.

"Aye Cass," Hot Boi called out to see if he was who he thought he was. Cass turned and looked real hard at him, before walking toward Hot Boi.

"Damn bro you look different as hell," Cass said as he got closer.

"D-boy I ain't seen you since we was twelve. Where the hell you been at?" Hot Boi asked as he shook Cass's hand.

"I been down in Atlanta getting to it, what you been up to?" Cass asked.

"Shit I finally got that chance we was trying to get back when we was shorties. I been low running it up," Hot Boi said.

"Oh, that's whats up! I been in the A, getting to it on so many different levels. I fucked around on the hustling tip for a minute, but once I got on that real estate shit, I had to let the game go," Cass said.

"That real estate shit cra---, hold on real quick," Hot Boi said once he saw Reggie come from around Cass's trunk.

"Aye bitch ass nigga," Hot Boi said. Cass turned around and saw that he was talking to Reggie. Cass didn't know what was going on cause he hadn't been in Madison in years, but whatever it was he ain't have time for. Reggie looked back to see who Hot Boi was talking to. When he didn't see nobody else around, he stopped.

"Who you talking to?" Reggie asked. Cass automatically knew some bull shit was about to jump off, so he walked over to his trunk. Before he was able to get in, he heard a loud crack and looked back and saw Reggie on the pavement and Hot Boi standing over him with a pistol. Hot Boi kicked Reggie as he laid on the ground. "Oh, bitch ass nigga you got a burner," Hot Boi said as he reached down and took it off Reggie hip. Hot Boi laughed when he noticed Reggie was knocked out cold. A few different cars pulled into the gas station and people from inside the store came out and watched.

Cass started his truck and pulled off. Hot Boi looked up and noticed there was a crowd of people watching him, so he rushed over to his car and peeled out the gas station.

Almundo became frustrated when he dialed the number for the fourth time and got no answer. "Fuck," he said and banged his fist up against the middle console. Alice sat next to him quiet as a church mouse. She knew better than to say anything when he was frustrated about getting high. His phone started to ring, and he noticed it was Hot Boi. His attitude quickly changed as he answered the phone

"Brother, I sat here and waited. Where are you?" he asked.

"My bad, what kind of car you in?" Hot Boi asked.

"A blue Oldsmobile, "Almundo quickly said.

" iight, iight I see you, I'm finna pull up next to you. Just follow me," Hot Boi said.

"OK migo," Almundo responded.

Hot Boi ended the call as he pulled up next to them, he gave him a head nod then pulled off. They pulled off after him and followed him for a few blocks until Hot Boi pulled over on a side street and parked. Almundo got out of his car and walked up to Hot Boi car and jumped in.

"Where is my main man Shah? he asked.

"He busy right now. But I'm here to make sure you get straight, " Hot Boi said.

"This the same thing, right? Cause I don't want no garbage,"

"This the same shit. I don't do garbage. As a matter of fact, you can hit this shit right now to make sure it's straight," Hot Boi said.

"No, no I'll take your word," Almundo said and handed him five hundred dollars.

"Tight," Hot Boi said, then reached into his baggie and pulled out ten fifties and gave them to him.

"Call you tonight brother, when this bitch makes more money," Almundo said.

Hot Boi started laughing and looked through his rearview mirror and saw a white lady sitting in the passenger seat of Almundo car.

"Tight," Hot Boi said.

Almundo got out of the car and Hot Boi pulled off.

Meanwhile

Shah and Audrey pulled in front of her apartment building. They both had a wonderful time last night and wished it could last forever. Audrey was late for school and Shah had to get back to business, he leaned over and kissed her.

"I'll see you later," Shah said.

"OK, I love you and be safe," Audrey responded getting out the car.

"Love you, call me later," Shah said.

"OK," she said closing the door. Shah watched as she ran into her building and until the building door closed, before pulling off. As Shah drove down the street, he dialed Hot Boi number but got no answer. Hot Boi was always on point and never missed a call, so Shah was worried.

"Maybe he sleep," he thought to himself, before heading straight to the crib.

He pulled into their parking lot fifteen minutes later and didn't see Hot Boi car, so he called him again. Hot Boi still didn't answer. He got out the car in walked into the building. He put the key into the lock and unlocked the door. As he opened it, his phone started ringing. He flipped it open in saw Hot Boi's number before answering.

"You good bro? I been blowing yo line up!" Shah said worried.

"My bad bro, I left the phone in the car. I was fucking the shit out this lil bitch Erika, we went to school with," Hot Boi said proudly.

"You talking bout the one that used to be wit the lil red bone bitch Tasha?" Shah asked.

"Hell Yeah! I been wanting to fuck Erika for some years now!" Hot Boi said.

"That bitch got some good pussy?" Shah curiously asked.

"On the D she do, I can't even stunt. But that lil bitch can suck a watermelon thru a coffee straw! She gave me some of the best neck I ever had," Hot Boi said geeked.

"And that ass super soft! She be throwing that mafucka back at a nigga hard to bro! For her to be so short she can take some dick," Hot Boi quickly added.

"Man, you making me want some of that pussy!"

"I'm sliding back through there TONIGHT!" Hot Boi said.

Shah started laughing, "Man let me find out she put that pussy on you like that fool!" Shah said.

"Na, Na you know me I ain't on none of that. But how shit go with Audrey last night? Did she like the spot?" Hot Boi asked, trying to get Shah off his line.

"You know she did! But low-key that room fucked my head up. I fucked the shit out of her all over. I had to get my money worth," Shah said.

"Man, yo cheap ass a fool. But that's good shit she enjoyed herself though,"

"Yeah she did, good looking on getting that bottle, that shit came in handy," Shah said.

"Oh, yeah you know I was on some playa shit. I told you I was gone put you up on game!"

"Here we go!" Shah quickly said as they both started laughing.

"But check it out, I need you to meet me at East Town Mall real quick," Hot Boi said.

"Say no mo, I'ma be there in like ten minutes," Shah replied.

"Bet," Hot Boi said and ended the call.

Shah locked the crib up then went and got in his car and headed out east. He never liked being out east because it always made him feel out of place. He would rather be out south or on the westside. He pulled into East Town Mall and luckily found a parking stop by Barnes and Noble. He pulled out his iPhone and called Hot Boi.

"What up?" Hot Boi said once he answered.

"You here?" Shah asked.

"Yeah, I'm in the food court!"

"Tight I'm on my way in," Shah said and hung up. He got out the car and walked in the mall thru the food court door. He looked around and spotted Hot Boi sitting at a table by Taco Bell eating. Shah walked over and sat across from him. "Man Shah, you came walking in here like a new man, Audrey must of put that pussy on you last night," Hot Boi said, try'na get him back for earlier.

"Man knock it off. I'm the same nigga I was last night," Shah said.

"Yeah iight nigga yo face glowing like you just got out the joint," Hot Boi said. Shah instantly started laughing.

"Yeah, you on some bullshit," he said while laughing.

"Na, I'm just fucking with ya... But on some real shit, I linked up with Almundo he seemed like a good dude," Hot Boi said.

"Yeah he good people," Shah added. Hot Boi slid the phone across the table to Shah.

"Ain't nobody but Almundo hit the line so far," Hot Boi said.

"Tight," Shah replied.

Hot Boi pulled the baggie from his pocket and put it under a napkin and slid it over to Shah.

Shah quickly grabbed it and put it in his pocket.

"The reason I wanted you to meet me up here is because I talked to big homie yesterday and he was putting me up on game about some credit shit, he got going on," Hot Boi said.

"And?" Shah asked, confused to what he was getting at.

"He got somebody that can take our credit score and get it up to a 750-800. That way we can get different kinds of loans for a house a car or a business. You know this hustling shit is only a steppingstone," Hot Boi said.

"Oh, OK so when he gone turn us onto this shit?" Shah asked.

"Well my shit in play already! You know you my mans and I wanted you to be able to get right too, so I told him about you. I told him you my partner in his shit now, so he wants to meet you. He only fucks around out east, that's why we here. Shit he should be here any minute," Hot Boi said.

"Tight, well shidd let me grab something to eat real quick then. Oh yeah! I saw this bad as bitch yesterday at west town Mall," Shah said

"Nigga you ain't try to get at her?" Hot Boi asked.

"Hell naw'll. But I'ma get her watch what I tell you!" Shah said before standing up and walking toward Toco Bell.

Minutes later, Big T walked into the food court. Hot Boi stood and waved him over to the table. Big T walked over with Sofia and Salina. Hot Boi greeted him then gave the ladies a hug. Big T sat down reaching into his pocket and pulled out a stack of cash and peeled off a thousand for Sofia and Salina each before telling them to go shopping for a little while. They took the money and left without hesitation.

"So, where yo mans at?" Big T asked.

"Oh, that's him over at the cash register in front of Taco Bell," Hot Boi replied.

"We gotta boss his life up, he eating Taco Bell," Big T said with his face frowned up.

"No bull shit T I just got done eating it too," Hot Boi said. "I like to remember where I came from. It keeps me humble," he added.

"See that's why I fucks with you. You speak yo mind and you smart lil nigga. But me personally I ain't eating no Taco Bell. Its other ways to remember where you came from," Big T said.

"I feel you! But you gone like bro too. He a good dude," Hot Boi said.

Shah turned around with his tray in his hand and saw Hot Boi sitting at the table with someone. *That must be Big T,* he thought to his self as he walked toward them.

Hot Boi and Big T both stood up when Shah got to the table.

"Big T this my man's Shah, Shah this my man's Big T," Hot Boi said. Shah sat his tray on the table and extended this hand to greet Big T. Big T reached and grabbed Shah's hand and gave it a firm grip. He was shocked when he was met with a grip to match his own.

"What up Big T?" Shah said.

"What's up Sha-Shah right?" Big T asked.

"Yeah, it's Shah," Shah quickly replied.

"Tight, nice to me you,"

"Same here," Shah said.

They all sat down at the table and started off with small talk as Big T felt Shah out. The longer they talked, the more comfortable Big T felt and quickly grew a liking to Shah. They talked about Shah's family for a while then the conversation finally made it around to business.

"So, I hear you got some hustle to yoself, pulling in 75,000 your second week in the game, that's major no bullshit. I wanna personally welcome you to the team. The only thing I need you to understand is that we keep it real with each other and we maintain a low profile. You gotta fly under the radar in order to last in this game," Big T said looking at Shah.

"I feel you, keeping it real is what I do. Y'all welcome me into this and gave me the opportunity to provide for myself and that's real. Also, I don't have a problem keeping a low profile," Shah said.

"Big T, I was telling bro about the credit demo. He like a brother to me, and I want what's best for him like I want what's best for myself. Right now he staying with me, but I know as a man he gone want his own spot so if it's cool with you I was wondering if you could plug him in on the credit shit, and maybe help him get a spot when he ready," Hot Boi said.

"Oh yeah without a doubt. I got him Just give me yo info and I'll get that shit rolling. And for the meantime I'ma get on top of the crib situation," Big T said

"Tight, I can get that info to you tonight," Shah said, as his phone started to ring. He stood and walked away from the table. Hot Boi and Big T finished talking until Big T stood up and walked off. He looked over at Shah and signaled for him to make sure he called him later. Shah nodded his head letting him know he would.

Meanwhile

Reggie was getting ready to leave ST. Mary's Hospital after Hot Boi split his forehead open. He had to get thirty stitches to close it. He was pissed and had every intention to make Hot Boi pay for fucking his face up. He had met with the police earlier, and they insisted he tell them what happened. Reggie acted like he couldn't recall anything that happened. The officers didn't believe him but had no choice but to take his word.

After he got discharged, he got on the phone and called his cousin Rasheed.

"You good?" Rasheed asked when he answered the phone.

"Damn, how you know already?"

"Cuz the streets talk!" Rasheed said. Reggie paused hearing that the streets was already talking, was a blow to his pride. He felt like a clown and automatically knew he had to redeem his self.

"Pull up on me cuz this nigga gotta die," he finally said.

"Iight where you at?" Rasheed asked.

"St. Mary's Hospital," Reggie said shamefully.

"Say no more, I'm on my way," Rasheed said. Reggie ended the call. "This nigga gotta die, if not niggas gone think I'm sweet. I can't have none of that," he thought before going to sit down in the waiting room," I gotta get this nigga myself. If I let somebody else do it, it won't mean shit," Reggie thought to himself. Ten minutes later his phone started to ring. He looked at it and saw his cousin Khalil number, so he answered.

"What up?" Reggie said.

"We outside," Khalil said.

"Iight I'm on my way out," Reggie said and got up and walked outside. His head was down as he walked up to the car and got in the back seat. Rasheed looked thru the rearview mirror at his head all bandaged up. He pulled off wasting no time making his motive clear.

"Cuz I'm killing this nigga where ever I catch him, then I'm going back to the crib. These nigga don't know I do this shit," Rasheed said.

Reggie looked up at him,"Folks look at my face. I gotta be the one to kill this nigga. All I need you to do is drive. I'ma handle the rest," he said.

Khalil cut into the conversation. "Man fuck that shit! Reggie, you know I ain't going on no drill to sit in the car, so that shit you talking is dead," he said.

"Look folks take me to the crib so I can change my cloths," Reggie said to Rasheed.

"Iight," he answered and continued to drive.

Meanwhile

Shah had been making non-stop moves since he left the mall. He was driving down Gammon Rd when his phone began to ring. He quickly answered it.

"Hey migo, what up?" Almundo asked.

"What up?" Shah replied.

"Can you come meet me at the Extended stay in Middleton? I wanna show you something," Almundo said.

"Iight, give me like twenty minutes. I'ma call you when I'm outside," Shah said.

"Ok," Almundo responded.

Shah hung the phone up and made a right turn onto Schroder Road. He made a quick stop in Willow Point, before heading toward the Extended stay. Fifteen minutes after he got of the phone with Almundo he pulled into the hotel parking lot and called him.

"Hello," Almundo said as he answered.

"I'm outside in the back,"

"Ok, I'm on my way down," Almundo replied. Shah ended the call and sat there for a few minutes before Almundo came walking out. Almundo stood there looking around for a second before he spotted Shah's car. He walked over and got in smelling like beer and crack smoke. Shah quickly rolled down his window to get some air flowing through the car.

"My main man Shah. What up?" Almundo said.

"Same shit, what's going on?" Shah asked.

"I got five hundred and I wanted to know if you would trade me something for this?" Almundo asked tossing twenty-five grams of heroin into Shah's lap.

"What the fuck is this?" Shah asked looking at it.

"That's 25 grams," Almundo said.

"25 grams of what? I don't know what the fuck this is," Shah said.

"This is some of Mexico's finest heroin. My family got it by the tons. But due to the fact I get high, they spoon feed me every now and again. I usually trade it to my other guy for $750. But your stuffs a lot better, so I wanted to see if you wanted it," Almundo said.

"Man, I don't know shit bout no heroin," Shah quickly said.

"Shah just do it for me this one time. You can take it to someone who knows what to do with it, they'll tell you it's worth it. If you can't do nothing with it, I'll buy it back and let you keep it. Trust me it's worth it," he bragged.

"I don't know! Look just cuz I like you, I'ma grab it and take your word for it," Shah said.

"Thank you! This might be one of the best decisions of your life,"

"We gone see," Shah said as he slowly counted off 25 fifties and handed them to Almundo, who handed Shah the five hundred dollars before quickly getting out the car. Shah sat there looking at the heroin hoping he didn't let Almundo get over on him. Shah figured he'd take the $750 out of his cash and put it in place of what he gave Almundo, so he didn't throw the count off.

As he got back on the beltline, he thought of who he knew that fucked with heroin. The only people he knew was his mother and James. The thought quickly went from his mind. "That shit dead, I ain't fucking with them on no level," he thought to himself. Shah sat back and turned the radio up and nodded his head to NBA Youngboi's mix tape. He pulled through Russit and the whole block was packed. There were niggas and bitches everywhere. He hurried and pulled to Cameron and parked his car and got out. He walked up the block to the building Lil Jerry and his mans be in. Lil Jerry was standing in the doorway when Shah walked up.

"Shah what you on?" Lil Jerry asked.

"Shit bro, tryna grab some bag and get some of this cash over here," Shah replied.

"You know I keep that bag on deck," lil Jerry said letting Shah into the building. When he walked in the lobby it was filled with smoke. He noticed three bad white bitch and two bad red bones standing at the bottom of the stairs. Shah heard some niggas upstairs shooting dice. Russit was busy how Allied use to be back in the day, when Shah was young. It was like anybody and everybody was over there.

"Let me get a dub real quick," Shah said and went in his pocket pulling out a dub and handing it to Lil Jerry.

"Iight," Lil Jerry said and handed Shah a sack.

"Oh yeah! I damn near forgot, let me holla at you outside real quick," Shah said.

"Iight, hold on," Lil Jerry said, as he went upstairs and came back down within seconds with a 9mm glock in his hands. Shah watched as he put one in the chamber before tucking it on his waistline. When he pulled his shirt down the 30-clip was poking out.

"I'm into it with the T's I can't let them catch me lacking," Lil Jerry said.

"Shit I feel you, but we ain't gotta go far from the building," Shah said.

"I hear you but anytime I step outside I gotta have it on me. I'd rather get caught with it then get caught without it,"

"Iight," Shah said as he walked out of the building, with Lil Jerry a step behind him. "What you know about heroin?" Shah asked.

"I know a lil something, why what you trying to find out?"

"I'm tryna find out the price on this shit," Shah said.

"It all depends, my cousin be fucking with that shit, he be grabbing it for 80 sometimes 100 a gram depend on who they get it from. But they be dumping that shit for like 200 a gram to they people," Lil Jerry said.

"Damn 200 a gram?"

"Hell yeah! I don't fuck with it cause if it's too potent they could die from that shit, and I ain't tryna catch that case," Lil Jerry said.

"So, it's sold by the gram?" Shah asked.

"Yeah, they sale by the gram. You can get 100 for each one from a nigga on the streets, and that's to a hustler. To a mafucka that use, you can get 250 at the most," Jerry said.

"You don't know nobody who fucks with it?" Shah asked.

"You talking about somebody that use it?"

"Yeah," Shah said.

"I know a few, its one that stay right up the street," Lil Jerry said.

"I got some of that shit, I need somebody to tell me what's to it. You should take me down there and introduce me to them so I can try to start me a line," Shah asked.

"Oh, you trying to get yo feet wet huh? Say know mo I got you. I'ma take you down there," Lil Jerry said.

"Say no mo," Shah happily said. They started walking up the street, when Lil Jerry looked up and saw a black impala turn off Cameron onto Russit.

"Keep walking bro," Lil Jerry said as he ducked behind a car and pulled out his 9mm. He was ready to shoot at first sight of anything suspicious. As the car got closer, he noticed it wasn't the people he was into it with. He saw Reggie in the back seat with a hoodie on looking back at Shah real hard.

"You got into it with Reggie? He looked like he was on bullshit once he saw you," Lil Jerry said as he walked from behind the car.

"We get into it every time we see each other. He ain't on shit," Shah said.

"Tight, just be on point, cause he had a real grimy look on his face," Lil Jerry warned.

"Tight, say no mo," Shah said as they continued up the block until they made it to the last building on the corner of Russit and Cameron. Lil Jerry buzzed the doorbell then stood there for a moment until a real fralie black dude poked his head out one of the windows on the second floor.

"Hustle Man, come open the door. I need to holla at you!" Lil Jerry said as he looked up.

"Tight now Lil Jerry dont be wasting my time," Hustle Man said.

"Man bring yo ass down stairs, before I knock you out when I catch you," Lil Jerry said.

"Lil nigga I ain't worried about you!" Hustle Man said then closed the window.

"He good people we just be talking shit to each other," Lil Jerry said to Shah.

"Tight, I thought you was serious," Shah said as Hustle Man opened the door.

"Lil Jerry what the hell you want?" he asked letting them into the building. "Man move the fuck out the way before I knock yo old ass out," Lil Jerry joked.

"Lil nigga it ain't gone be the first time I been knocked out. Keep talking shit and I'ma introduce you to your first knock out," Hustle Man said and put his fist up like the fighting Irish dude. Shah started laughing and looked over at Lil Jerry.

"All bullshit aside Hustle Man this my mans Shah, he be fucking around with he boy. I brought him over here so y'all could link up, he got something he want you to test and tell him what's to it," Lil Jerry said getting down to business.

"Alright, let's go up stairs and see what's to it then," Hustle Man said geeked. They followed him up the stairs to his apartment. Shah was shocked when he walked in Hustle Man apartment. Judging solely off the way Hustle Man looked Shah assumed he had a dirty ass crib. But it was actually clean with red leather furniture, black glass coffee end tables, along with a 60inch flat screen mounted on the wall. He had all kinds of different black and white African art and pictures on the wall, with plants everywhere.

"Alright, Lil Jerry you know the rules, take them damn shoe's off in my house!" Hustle Man quickly said.

Shah and Lil Jerry both stopped at the door.

"Man I ain't taking shit off old ass nigga, I just brought fool over here so y'all could meet. I'm finna get up out of here!" Lil Jerry said.

"Well get yo black ass out then," Hustle Man replied.

"Keep talking shit I'ma catch yo old ass outside and knock you out yo shoe's!" Lil Jerry said.

"Try me and you gone find out you can't fight," Hustle Man shot right back. Lil Jerry started laughing before walking out the door. Shah took his shoes off as Hustle Man closed and locked the door. "You can follow me to the kitchen young blood. So what they call you again?" Hustle Man asked. "Call me Shah."

"Tight, Shah, let's get to business. What you got?" Hustle Man asked.

"Some of Mexico's finest" Shah said as he pulled it from his pocket. Hustle Man noticed it was in a brick, so he walked over to the counter and opened the drawer and pulled out a hammer and handed it to Shah.

"Use that to break it up," he said.

"Tight," Shah said walking over to the counter, as Hustle Man handed him a towel.

"Put this over it," Hustle Man said. Shah had no clue what the hell he was doing but didn't want Hustle Man to know this. He put the towel over the grams and hit it with the hammer lightly until he heard it crack, then he took the towel and pinched a pieces off the crumbs and gave it to Hustle Man. Hustle Man grabbed a plate and a spoon and walked over to the table. Shah followed him over to the table.

"This looks like some good shit! How much you charging?" Hustle Man asked.

"200 a gram," Shah quickly said.

"200 damn? That's the Price the white folks pay ain't nobody around here gone pay that. Right now I get them for 150," Hustle Man said.

"That's cause what you getting ain't this," Shah said.

"That's what they always say young blood and it end up being trash."

"Trust me, this the best shit in Wisconsin," Shah said.

"Well we finna find out right now!" Hustle Man said using the spoon to crush the boy up into dust. He pulled a card from his pocket and scrapped all the dust up into two piles. He pulled a dollar from his pocket and rolled it up. He leaned down to the plate and quickly snorted a line in one nostril then put his head back.

"Damn," he said loudly which instantly made Shah nervous. "This some good shit! It give me an instant drain which is really good!" Hustle Man said. Shah stood there and watched as he wasted no time snorting the other line into his other nostril and quickly put his head back again.

"Yeah, yeah Shah, this the best shit I had in years!" Hustle Man said.

"I already know," Shah said as if he really knew. Hustle Man got real quite as he entered into a stage of Bliss. His eyes started rolling in his head as he whipped his face. Within seconds, Hustle Man was in a complete nod, his upper body started to lean away from the table and out of his chair.

Shah heart dropped in his stomach as he thought about what Lil Jerry said, "If it's too strong they could die," he sat Hustle Man back up straight.

"Hustle Man you good?" Shah asked.

When he didn't respond, Shah ran over to the kitchen counter and used his shirt to wipe his fingerprints off the hammer. He ran over to the door and quickly put his shoes on then used the bottom of his shirt to open and close the door behind him. He ran down the stairs and looked out the building window to see if anyone was outside before he left out. Then ran around the corner to Cameron jumped in his car and sped away from the area.

For the next three days, Shah stayed as far away from Russit as possible. He was nervous because he wasn't sure if Hustle Man died.

Lil Jerry had been blowing his phone up, but he was sending him to voicemail. He wasn't ready to hear he killed Hustle Man. He felt it was best to stay away and only come out to catch his cash.

Shah sat in the house smoking a blunt and watching Paid in Full when Hot Boi walked in.

"Shah money, it's nice as hell outside, why you sitting in the crib?" he asked.

"I just been chilling, tryna be low that's all bro," Shah said.

"Oh, ok," Hot Boi said.

"That's how I'ma stay under the radar."

"Ok I see you catching on fast. I been real low over at Erika crib," Hot Boi said.

"I know I see she put the pussy on you. I ain't seen you in two days," Shah said. Hot Boi started laughing.

"Bro that pussy so good, I been tryna put a baby in that bitch!" Hot Boi said. Shah jumped off the couch and ran into the kitchen then back into the living room laughing.

"Man, you ain't never just say that shit out yo mouth!" Shah said.

"On The D," Hot Boi quickly said.

"Man, you tripping!" Shah said laughing.

"Naw I ain't trippin, this shit chess not checkers. I been pushing these pawns now it's time I get me a Queen!" Hot Boi said.

"Yeah she put that pussy on you! Erika done sucked the soul out my nigga!" Shah added shaking his head.

"Stop playing with me man!" Hot Boi jokingly said.

"You know I'm gone let you make it this time," Shah said.

"This time? So you telling me it's cool for you to cuff Audrey, but I'm wrong if I cuff something?" Hot Boi asked.

"Naw, I'm fucking with ya! You know you my mans no matter what!" Shah answered. His phone started to ring on the coffee table. He walked around the couch and picked it up. "Damn Jerry fool, what you want?" he thought to himself before deciding to answer.

"What up?" Shah asked calmly.

"Shit you tell me what up? I been blowing yo line up. The nigga Hustle Man been running around like a chicken with his head cut off looking for you," Jerry said.

"Man, I been laying low because of Hustle Man. I thought that nigga was dead," Shah said, relieved he wasn't.

"This old ass nigga ain't dead. He been around here getting on my nerves looking for you bro. This ugly ass nigga standing right here. He said slide through ASAP! He want you to bring 10," Lil Jerry said.

Shah paused for a minute, debating if he wanted to fuck with that shit because that last situation scared the hell out of him.

"You know what tell him to give me 30 minutes. I'm finna be on my way," Shah said.

"Tight, hurry up bro so this nigga can leave me the fuck alone."

"I got you," Shah said, then started laughing. He ended the call and left the apartment. He went to the basement and grabbed the grams from his stash spot then ran back up to the apartment. Shah walked in the kitchen where Hot Boi was and opened the drawer and pulled out the hammer and scale.

"Damn, Shah money. Where you get that shit from?" Hot Boi asked as he watched Shah break it into pieces.

"Man, bro I stumbled on this shit a few days ago. I gave a mafucka $750 for 25 grams. I found out I can sell each gram for a $100 to $200 dollars depending on who I sell it to," Shah said.

"So, if you sell them all for $100 dollars each you gone triple yo money? That's a good investment!" Hot Boi said.

"I know and I think this shit might go super-fast. I got somebody that want 10 right now."

"Just one?" Hot Boi asked.

"Yeah and I'm bout to charge him $200 a gram," Shah answered.

"That's a stain, I heard they could overdose off that shit. So, I be scared to fuck with it," Hot Boi said.

"I know, that's why once this shit gone, I'm done. But I gotta make this profit real quick."

"You ain't wrong bro, get that money!"

Shah phone started to ring again. "Fuck I hope they ain't change they mind," Shah said out loud when he noticed it was Lil Jerry again.

"Hello" Shah said.

"A fool, he say bring thirty now!" Lil Jerry said.

"Damn thirty?" Shah questioned.

"Yeah fool,"

"Tight, tell him I got 25 left. I'ma bring them," Shah said.

"Hold on!" Lil Jerry said then took the phone away from his mouth for a few seconds. Shah could hear him talking to someone in the background but couldn't make out what he was saying.

"Fool, he say bring them, they over here waiting on you," Lil Jerry said.

"Tight," Shah said.

"Bet," Lil Jerry said then ended the call. Shah quickly tied the baggie back up and put the grams in his pocket. He made sure he had the coke in all three phones before leaving the crib.

He was geeked the whole ride to Russit. All he could do was think about how easy and fast this shit was about to sell. "I might have to get some mo of this shit," he thought to himself.

Twenty-five minutes later he was turning off Verona Rd onto Raymond Rd. He pulled his iPhone out and called Lil Jerry.

"Yo," Lil Jerry said as he answered.

"I'm coming down Raymond Rd now I'm bout to pull up," Shah said. "Tight cause this nigga sitting right here like a dog waiting on his master!" Lil Jerry said and started laughing.

"You stunting!" Shah quickly said.

"On BD bro, I ain't seen this shit since I left the city!"

"Say no mo, I'm pulling up now," Shah said.

"Tight," Lil Jerry said laughing.

Shah ended the call with Jerry and his phone started ringing as soon as he hung up. He looked and saw it was Almundo and quickly answered.

"What up?" Shah said.

"How my main man doing," Almundo asked.

"You know me, same shit different day!" Shah said.

"Ok, well meet me at the room," Almundo said.

"Tight give me twenty minutes," Shah said.

"Ok," Almundo replied.

Shah quickly ended the call and made a right onto Whitney Way then made a left on Russit. He rode past the building; Lil Jerry be in and saw a group of females standing in front of the building. Lil Jerry had his head sticking out of the building door and Hustle Man was sitting on the crate on the porch. Shah drove down Russit and made a right on the Cameron then pulled over and parked. He got out the car and walked around to Russit. Lil Jerry and Hustle Man were walking up the block, so Shah stopped in front of Hustle Man building.

"Nephew let me get yo number cuz the Lil skinny ass nigga ain't wanna give it to me!" Hustle Man said as he walked up to Shah.

"Old ass nigga I wasn't gone give it to you cause he ain't tell me to!" Lil Jerry said with some aggression in his voice. Shah stood there quite not sure if Jerry was about to fuck Hustle Man up or not. Hustle Man unlocked the building door and walked in. Shah and Lil Jerry followed him in and up the stairs to his apartment.

"Y'all know the deal, shoes off," Hustle Man said as he kicked off his shoes and walked over to the kitchen. They took their shoes off and followed him. Hustle Man sat down at the table and started counting off a roll of money, he pulled from his pocket.

"It's the same shit you gave me last time, right?" he asked.

"Yeah it's the same shit," Shah answered, as he pulled the boy from his pocket and tossed it on the table. "That's 24.8," Shah said.

"Damn that's all you got? I got a few white boys who want some too. When you gone have some more?" Hustle Man asked.

"I don't know, but as soon as I do I'll call you, you might as well take my number right now," Shah said.

"Alright, what's the number?" Hustle Man asked.

"312-436-2211"

"Alright, I got it. Here go 5,000. Nephew you gotta bring that price down some for me if I keep coming like this," Hustle Man said.

"I got you if you keep coming like this."

Shah said counting the money, making sure it was 5,000 dollars. Shah turned and gave Lil Jerry 1,000 dollars.

"Good looking," Shah said.

"Love," Lil Jerry said counting the money to see how much Shah gave him. They both walked back over to the door and put their shoes back on.

"Lock the door old ugly ass nigga!" Lil Jerry said before walking into the hallway. "Yeah get yo black ass out, " Hustle Man said as he walked toward the door.

"Be careful with that shit!" Shah said as he thought about the last time.

"Trust me I got this nephew," Hustle Man responded.

"Tight," Shah said walking out the apartment. Hustle Man closed the door and locked it.

Shah and Lil Jerry stepped out of the building before Shah looked over at him.

"Good looking out too," Shah said.

"You know it's love fool," Lil Jerry quickly replied.

"Tight, I'ma bend back on you later," Shah said.

"Tight fool," Lil Jerry said before walking off. Shah walked around the corner and jumped in his car before pulling off.

Meanwhile

Shah dialed Almundo number as he was turning into the extended stay parking lot. Almundo wasted no time answering the call.

"You outside?" he asked.

"Yeah I'm out here," Shah said.

"Ok, I'm on my way down now."

"Tight," Shah said, then hung up. A minute later Almundo came walking out the building, he came to the car and jumped in.

"I got $500" he said closing the door. Almundo was fidgeting and moving fast.

"You iight?" Shah asked.

"Oh, yeah I'm good"

"Tight. You remember that shit I got from you last time?" Shah asked handing him the work.

"Yeah, what you still got it?"

"Naw that shit gone I'm tryna see if you can get me some more."

"My cousin only give me 25 grams every now and then so I don't do no dumb shit that could land me in jail. He don't like doing business with me cause I get high," Almundo said.

"You should talk to him and see if you can get him to do business with me," Shah said.

"I don't think you want to go into business with them cause once you in there's no way out! Trust me I know how they operate. You gone have to give up your family information and all kind of extra shit just for them to trust you," Almundo said.

"I ain't got no problem with that! As long as the price right I'm in. Trust me Almundo I need this chance," Shah pleaded.

"This aint no game, this the cartel you trying to get involved with. If the money ain't where it needs to be when they want it, if they start to believe they no longer can trust you or if you fuck up ONCE you and your family dead," Almundo said seriously.

"I want in Almundo, put the word in for me I can handle it," Shah said.

Almundo sat there for a moment looking off into space thinking. He knew this was some deep shit Shah was trying to get involved with and he didn't want to put the boy's life on the line if he fucked up.

"Trust me Almundo, and once I get in and get my money right, I'm gone make sure you benefit too," Shah added.

"Man, man man, alright! I can put the word in for you but please don't fuck up cause I'm putting my life on the line if I go in there in vouch for you," Almundo said.

"My word, I won't fuck this up!"

"Alright we got a deal! How much money you think you can scrap up?" Almundo asked.

"I don't know it depends," Shah said.

"Well scrap up as much as you can cause he might decided to fuck with you, and if he do, he gone want you to show you can produce some cash,"

"Say no mo," Shah said.

"When I talk to him, I'll let you know," Almundo said as he opened the car door and got out.

"Tight," Shah said as Almundo closed the door. Almundo quickly ran back into the hotel. Shah slowly pulled out of the lot feeling geeked. He knew if he got connected with the cartel the sky was the limit.

Chapter Five

*I*t was 10:30pm on a Monday night. Reggie and Rasheed were driving down Worthington looking for Hot Boi. Reggie got word from Tasha that her best friend Erika was fucking Hot Boi. Tasha told him she saw Hot Boi over Erika's house last night and the night before. She told Reggie she was sure he would be over there tonight because Erika said he was coming to pick her up to go out for drinks.

She took Reggie and Rasheed through Darbo earlier and showed them where Erika stayed. They drove past Erika crib looking for his car, but he wasn't there yet. They planned on catching him getting out before he made it to the crib.

"Call that lil bitch Tasha and have her call shorty and ask did she leave out yet," Rasheed directed Reggie.

"Tight, I'm finna see right now," Reggie said.

"Tell her don't make it seem suspicious. Naw hold on," Rasheed quickly said as he looked through his rearview mirror. "Folks on the G, the nigga behind us right now!" Rasheed said.

"Yeah?" Reggie asked with excitement in his voice. He quickly dropped his phone and picked up his 9mm.

"When we get to this stop sign make sure it's him. I'ma jump out and blow his ass down," Reggie said.

"On the G that's him, so as soon as I stop jump out," Rasheed said. He started to pump on the brakes as he approached the stop sign. Reggie had one hand on the door handle with his 9mm in his other hand. He was ready to jump out the moment they stopped. Rasheed hit the brakes hard and Reggie instantly popped out shooting at a rapid pace.

The shell casing quickly ejected from the chamber sounding like change hitting the concrete. Hot Boi ducked down in the car and threw it in reverse. He stomped on the gas unable to see where he was going. The car veered to the opposite side of the road crashing into a parked car. Reggie continued to fire shots into the car. Glass shattered everywhere as bullets hit the windows and penetrated the driver side doors. Hot Boi grabbed his gun from under his seat and fired two rounds back at Reggie. He climbed across the passenger seat and out the door. Reggie stopped shooting and creeped closer to the car as Hot Boi crawled on the other side of the car he crashed into. Hot Boi peeked from the other side and saw Reggie walking toward the crash.

"Hurry up!" Rasheed yelled out. Reggie looked into Hot Boi's car and was shocked when he didn't see him. He was sure he'd hit Hot Boi a few times. He noticed the passenger side door open. So, he turn to run around to the other side. Hot Boi popped out and fired three shots at Reggie hitting him once in the chest dropping him instantly. Hot Boi quickly ran around the car and fired two more shots as he stood over Reggie hitting him once in the neck and once in the head killing him immediately. He turned and fired a few shots at Rasheed's car before jumping into his and pulling off in the opposite direction.

Rasheed jumped out his car and fired some shots at the fleeing car. He ran over to Reggie and his heart dropped when he saw blood gushing from his head and neck. He heard sirens getting closer, so he turned and ran back to his car. He knew there was no saving Reggie, so he left him.

Meanwhile

At 10:12am, Almundo pulled into his cousin's auto body shop on Keeler and Park in Beloit. He parked the car and got out before walking through the side door of the shop. Almundo found his cousin Alberto helping an employee strip the paint off a car that needed repainting. He walked up to Alberto who had his back to the door, putting a hand on his shoulder. Alberto turned around shocked to see him. He'd just given Almundo a package and assumed he was there to beg for more.

Almundo quickly spoke when he noticed the look of disgust on Alberto's face.

"Can I speak with you in your office?" he asked.

"Let's make it fast cause I have to finish the car today!"Alberto said before leading the way to his office while Almundo followed closely behind him on his heels Alberto walked into his office and over to his desk, Almundo walked in and closed the door behind him. Alberto had every intent to make this conversation short, so he spoke.

"So, what is it cousin?" he asked.

"I didn't come for what you think. I came to talk business," Almundo said to clear the air. Alberto laughed," Almundo I'm not doing business with you until your clean. Right now, your high risk!" he said.

"I know, I know just hear me out cousin. As you already know, Wisconsin is the land of opportunity. I know someone who can accumulate a lot of cash and unload a lot of product. The problem is he not connected with the right people. His demand is high, but his supply is low. I'm here to see if you would be willing to supply him," Almundo said.

"How long have you known this person you speak of Almundo?" Alberto asked with concern.

"I've known him for a year now. Alberto, listen, he check out clean as a whistle. He's trustworthy, reliable, and has honor. Not to mention he can unload a lot of product."

"How do you know he's not DEA of FBI?" Alberto asked.

"Because I've known him since he was 17 years old. He just turned 18. I used to do business with his big brother before he went to prison. He checks out Alberto, you can check him and his family out yourself. I wouldn't come to you unless I was sure trust me cousin," Almundo begged.

"You know what, I want the name of his mother, father, and that brother of his you did business with and any other immediate family members. If they all check out, I will consider doing business with him. You know the rules, this is your guy, so if he not right you're responsible for him. Get me their information by tonight and I'll have them checked out. I'll call you to let you know what's next!" Alberto said.

"Trust me cousin you won't regret this!"

"For your sake, you better hope not," Alberto said getting up from his desk and walking out his office. Almundo stood there for a moment, he couldn't believe he'd just lied to Alberto. He turned and walked out of the office and left the shop, before getting into his car. He pulled his phone from his pocket and called Shah.

"What up," Shah answered.

"My main man, how you been?"

"You know me, same shit different day! How bout you?" Shah asked.

"Fine, fine. I'm on my way back to Madison. I need to see you when I get back it's important."

"Tight, just call me when you make it," Shah said.

"Ok."

"See you then," Shah said.

"OK," Almundo added before hanging up the phone. He started his car and pulled out the lot.

Meanwhile

Tammy and Audrey sat at the kitchen table eating breakfast. They sat across from each other enjoying the meal Tammy made.

Tammy was excited that X was coming to Madison to meet her Best friends Audrey and Shah. The fact that they both had so much going on with school and work it was rare that they were able to sit down and have a meal together. Tammy looked up and noticed Audrey stuffing her mouth full of food.

"Bitch you aint gotta eat that fast!" Tammy said.

"Girl let me eat!" Audrey said after chewing and swallowing her food.

"I know its good bitch but damn!" Tammy replied.

"Ok now don't do me!"

"Whatever! Did you call Shah and ask him if he gone be able to go out to eat with us tonight?" Tammy asked.

"Bitch I forgot! I'm bout to call him now."

"You ain't no good, I'll call him myself!" Tammy said with an attitude.

"Don't start acting like that!" Audrey replied.

Tammy got up from the table and walked to her room and grabbed her phone off the nightstand before walking into the living room and sat on the couch.

She looked over at Audrey and flipped her middle finger at her. Audrey started laughing.

"I don't care cause you mad," she said, spreading jelly on her toast. Tammy dialed Shah's number and waited on him to answer.

"What up," Shah said as he answered.

"How you been? I haven't heard from you in a few days, Mr. Busy body!" Tammy said.

"I'm straight. My bad I haven't called, I been busy getting my shit together," Shah said.

"I understand get yo shit together. But in the meantime, don't forget about us over here, we love you and want to see you too!" Tammy added.

"I love y'all too! You know I could never forget about y'all," Shah said.

"That's good cause I want you to meet my friend and let me know what you think about him," Tammy asked.

"Yo friend?" Shah quickly asked.

"Yeah, my friend," Tammy said before laughing.

"Ain't shit funny, who is yo friend?" Shah questioned.

Shah you know you not my daddy, right?" Tammy asked.

"Man, who the fuck is yo friend?" Shas asked again.

"You don't know him. His name Xavier he from Milwaukee and he coming down here tonight, so I want you to meet him," Tammy said.

"You know I'm coming to meet him! When he coming?" Shah asked.

"He'll be here around six, I told him I wanted to go on a double date so he could meet y'all," Tammy replied.

"A double date?" Shah asked.

"Yes! Me, you, Audrey, and him tonight for dinner. And don't embarrass me either!" Tammy said.

"Tight, I got you. Where y'all tryna go out to?"

"I want to go to the melting pot,"

"I'm with it. But look my other phone ringing. I'ma see you later!" Shah said.

"Ok see you later," Tammy said before ending the call. Audrey sat at the kitchen table hanging onto Tammy every word. Tammy put her phone down on the coffee table then got up and walked into the kitchen.

"You know what you wearing tonight?" Audrey asked Tammy as she emptied her plate into the trash can.

"Girl you know I had my mind made up a few days ago. I'm finna look so fye bitch he gone want to eat me as soon as he see me!" Tammy said, and they started laughing.

"Not eat you!" Audrey said.

"Yes, bitch eat me," Tammy quickly said as they walked back to the living room, she picks her phone up and checked her Facebook app and started scrolling down her timeline. "So, do you know what you're wearing tonight?" Tammy asked.

"Yes, I thought about it last night. I'm wearing that red dress I bought that makes my ass look super fat with my black blazer and some black heel. I----"

Tammy cut her off when she shouted, "Oh my god! Bitch do you remember Reggie the dude Shah use to always get into it with?"

"Yes, I hate his ass," Audrey quickly responded.

"Girl somebody killed him last night. They found him over by Darbo," Tammy said.

"Somebody got tired of his disrespectful ass. Oh well," Audrey said before switching the subject. "But anyways bitch like I was saying before you rudely interrupted me. I got this cute ass red clutch that's gone make my outfit pop!"

"Bitch you cold hearted," Tammy said laughing at Audrey.

"No, I ain't " Audrey responded cleaning under her fingernails. "Why waste my time and energy on a nigga that's always giving my man a hard time. Plus, he was a disrespectful bitch," she added.

"I didn't like him either, but I still feel bad for him. My sensitive ass don't wish death on nobody!" Tammy said.

"Me neither, but if it happens it is what it is," Audrey said.

Meanwhile

Khalil sat and comforted Reggie's mother Denise as she cried out. She had just made it home from the county morg identifying Reggie's body. She asked Khalil over and over did he know why this happen to her baby. He couldn't tell his aunt he knew, so he kept saying he had no idea who would want to kill Reggie.

Rasheed told him what happened last night. Rasheed also made calls back home to Chicago and let their other cousins know what happened. Their family in Chicago was pissed and planned to come to Madison to take care of the situation. Rasheed was on his way to Denise house; he had just left Reggie's Apartment gabbing the rest of his work and money to plan his funeral. He pulled up to Denise house twenty minutes later and made his way in. As soon as he walked through the door, he hugged her.

"I'm sorry Auntie," Rasheed said as he hugged her. "I promise I'ma find whoever did this and make them pay for it," he said.

"Thank you, Rasheed, but that ain't gone bring my son back," she cried.

"I know Auntie but it's what he would want me to do. I owe him that much!" Rasheed replied. He broke away from their hug and went into his pocket and pulled out thirty thousand dollars in all hundred dollars bills and handed it to Denise.

"This will cover his funeral and whatever else you might need to take care of," Rasheed said. "Thank you," Denise said as she took the money and sat it on the coffee table. Khalil walked up and pulled Rasheed to the side.

"Man, why the fuck you call cuz nem, them niggas calling my phone talking bout they up here. We don't need them niggas to handle shit," Khalil said pissed.

"I wanted to let them niggas know Reggie was dead. I ain't ask them niggas to come up here, they did that on they own!" Rasheed said.

"Well them niggas bout to meet us at my bitch crib in fifteen minutes. Since you called them niggas I need you to make sure they stay the fuck out my way."

"Man, let's get outta here," Rasheed said blowing him off. He knew Khalil was a hot head who wanted to do all the killing. They walked over to Denise before giving her a hug.

"Auntie we gotta go take care of something but we'll be back later," Rasheed said.

"Ok, y'all be safe out there," Denise said.

"We will," they said as they walked out the door.

Meanwhile

Almundo pulled back into Town and called Shah as he passed Stoughton Rd. "Hello," Almundo said as he turned his radio down.

"What's the word?" Shah asked excited. He knew if Almundo really had cartel connections he'd be rich in no time. Even though Shah had only been hustling a few weeks, he was a fast learner. Shah already had plans as to how he would unload the shit if he got connected.

"I'm passing Stoughton Rd," Almundo said.

"Shit I'm right here on Monona Rd right now, just meet me at the Buffalo Wild Wings on Monona," Shah said.

"Ok, be there in one minute," Almundo said getting off on the Monona Rd exit. He pulled into the parking lot and drove though until he found Shah car and parked next to it. Shah got out of his car before getting in the car with Almundo. When he closed the door, Almundo got straight to the point. "I talked to my cousin today and he want me to get your information. I need your full name, birthday, and social security number. I need your mother's, father's, and brother's information as well. If everything checks out, he might decide to do business with you," Almundo said.

Shah looked over at him shocked, as all kinds of different thoughts ran thru is mind.

"My social security number? What kind of shit is that?" Shah asked in a confused tone.

"That's what he need to have his people check you out."

"How I know they ain't gone do know bogus shit with my social?"

"Just trust me! If any bullshit happens with your social you can have my life, that how sure I am nothing will happen," Almundo said.

"Ok, Almundo I'ma trust you," Shah said

"Good! I need the information in a few hours, he want it by tonight. I really hope you can unload a lot of product, because he's going to flood you with it and want his money by the deadline not a day later," Almundo said.

"What? Watch how I work Almundo we gone be straight trust me!" Shah replied.

"I trust you. I put my life on the line for you by doing this," Almundo said.

"But I need to get back to his hotel and check up on this bitch. I need you to front me until tonight," Almundo quickly added.

"Tight, I got you," Shah said, then reached into his pocket pulling out his bundle. He opened the baggie before reaching in and counting out 10 fifties and handed them to Almundo.

"Just hit me later, I'ma text you that info in a little while," Shah said. He jumped out of the car and walked back to his car and pulled off.

Meanwhile

Hot Boi and Big T sat at Perez Autobody shop. Big T was close friend with Perez, so Perez had his crew get straight to work on Hot Boi's car. Big T wasn't happy with Hot Boi but he understood the situation. Perez pulled in front of the shop in a black Chevy Tahoe and parked. Big T and Hot Boi got out the minivan and walked over to him.

"I got this one right here. I just put a new engine and trans in it and I did the paint job last week. I wanted twenty thousand, but for you I'll do fifteen!" Perez said speaking to big T.

"What you think bro you want it?" Big T asked Hot Boi.

"Yeah! What year is it?" Hot Boi asked.

"It's a 2015" Perez said opening the hood so they could look at the engine. Hot Boi opened the driver door and got in so he could check out the black leather interior. "Yeah this bitch nice," Hot Boi said. Big T looked over at Perez. "We gone take it," he said.

"I'll have Salina pull back up on you later with the cash," Big T added.

"You know you good for it, come to my office so we could get this paperwork done," Perez said. Hot Boi jumped out and followed them to the office. Perez went straight to his file cabinet and pulled out the title and sat it on the desk. Hot Boi took a seat next to the door while Big T took one in the chair in front of the desk. Big T turned around and told Hot Boi to step out the room so he could talk to Perez. He got up and went back to the van. Once inside, he called Shah.

"Man, bro I see Erika got you missing in action," Shah said as he answered.

"Naw bro it ain't that. Look I need to link up with you so I can holla at you. It's important too," Hot Boi said.

"Tight, you good?" Shah asked.

"Yeah bro, I'm straight right now. I'ma finna get ready to leave this car shop in a minute, I need you to meet me at the crib," Hot Boi said.

"Say no more! How long til you there," Shah asked.

"Meet me in 30 minutes bro!" Hot Boi said.

"Yep!"

"Love bro," Hot Boi said, then hung the phone up. He turned and looked to make sure no one was creeping up on him while he sat in the car. His nerves were bad after what happen last night. He was happy he was able to get his car in the shop before the police was able to find it and link it to him and to Reggie murder. He knew there was one more thing he had to do and that was get Rasheed out the way. He looked Rasheed directly in the eyes as they passed each other in traffic a week ago. Rasheed was driving the same kind of car Reggie jumped out of when they stopped at the stop sign. It didn't take long to put two and two together. Rasheed and Reggie were cousins, so it had to have been Rasheed in the driver seat. The fact that Rasheed fired shots at him had him out for blood.

Hot Boi sat there thinking about his next move. He needed to catch Rasheed before Rasheed caught him. Hot Boi looked up and saw Big T coming out of the shop. He got out the van as Big T got closer. Big T handed him the keys and the title to the truck.

"I need to holla at you before you leave. Hop back in real quick," Big T said. Hot Boi got back into the passenger seat and closed the door. "Listen lil bro, you been doing good and headed in the right direction. Now you know my motto and that's stay under the radar. You can't beef and get money the two don't mix. We in a position where we can't afford to be kicking up dust in this small as town. I understand what happen last night wasn't your fault and I'm glad you made it out of that situation. I need you to lay low for a few days until the heat blow over. If you know who the other nigga is I'll have him taking care of while we on the beach in Miami somewhere that way they can't tie nothing to us, so do me that solid lil bro and lay low for bout a week," Big T said.

"I got you bro, I can go lay low with my people in Beloit for a week. I'm gone have Shah hold shit down while I'm gone," Hot Boi said.

"You sure he gone be good up here while you're gone?" Big T asked.

"Yeah, he straight, we ain't known to hang out together, so he good!" Hot Boi said.

"Tight, let him know that the card shit went through. Y'all got 750s now so y'all can start putting shit in yo name. When you in Beloit go open up a bank account, put two thousand into a saving and three into checking. When you get back I'ma show y'all how to clean up that money y'all making," Big T said.

"Tight I'm with it, good lookin too bro," Hot Boi said as he got ready to get out of the car before big T stopped him.

"Make sure you go down there and chill with yo people. Trust me it's gone get handled," Big T said.

"I'm finna go there today. I know your word valid that's why I fucks with you," Hot Boi replied.

"Tight lil bro," Big T said.

"Love" Hot Boi said as he got out the van and walked over to his new Tahoe truck. One of the shop workers was putting temp plates on the trucks.

"We good to go?" Hot Boi asked.

"Yeah, yeah you good," the worker said.

Hot Boi jumped in and started it before pulling out the lot.

Twenty minutes later he pulled into his lot and saw Shah car was already there. He parked and put his pistol on his hip. He quickly jumped out the truck and hurried to his building trying to avoid anyone seeing him and identifying where he lived. When he opened the apartment door, he saw Shah sitting on the couch watching TV.

"What's the word?" Hot Boi said as he closed the door and locked it.

"Shit I just been getting to it," Shah said with a big ass Kool-Aid smile on his face.

"That's what up! Last night I missed so much cash it's a damn shame!" Hot Boi said.

"Why? What happened?"

"Man, the nigga Reggie and Rasheed tried to get down on me last night. I put the nigga Reggie in the dirt," Hot Boi said.

"Damn! I heard a nigga got bodied last night. Fuck that nigga tho," Shah quickly said.

"Hell yeah! That bitch as nigga dumped like 30 shots at me. Made me crash the whip and some more shit," Hot Boi said.

"NEVER!" Shah said.

"Bro on BD, this shit real life. Big T got my shit put in the shop, and I just grabbed a Tahoe truck," Hot Boi said.

"What up with the nigga Rasheed then?" Shah asked.

"I couldn't get his ass, I had to hurry up and get out of that jam. But he gone get his, trust me! But I need you to work both lines. The nigga Big T want me to lay low for a little while until the heat from this shit blow over," Hot Boi said.

"I got you. It's damn near time to re-up anyways. It ain't shit but two zips of soft left. I got three fifty's left, I was finna whip one of those up for this line," Shah said.

"Damn bro, you be going crazy I ain't dump shit but eight zips in baskets and I still got a whole zip in baskets. You ran through twenty-five zips!" Hot Boi said shocked at how fast Shah was still moving the work.

"Yeah, I got a lil bit over sixty-nine bands in the room right now. I gotta pick up some cash from Almundo in a minute so let's just say I got an even seventy bands," Shah said

"Tight I made eight bands so that's seventy-eight. This what we gone do, we gone take that thirty and re-up. Then we can bust that forty-eight down the middle and what you make off them three zips is all you," Hot Boi said.

"Tight bet,"

"Hit Big T up when you can and bust that move. I'm finna get up out of here. Oh, that credit shit official too. Big T just put me up on game he said open a bank account and put three bands into checking and two into savings. He gone tell us the next step after this shit blow over," Hot Boi said.

"Yeah that's what up. Shit falling into place," Shah said.

"Check it out. I'ma keep this eight bands just give me sixteen. I'm finna go fuck with cuz in Beloit," Hot Boi said.

"Tight say no mo!" Shah said as he got up from the couch and walked into the room. Hot Boi walked to his room and opened the closet before opening his safe. He pulled out ten bands putting it into his pocket. Then walked over to the dresser and grabbed his ID, Shah walked into the room and tossed sixteen thousand dollars on the bed. "Man, you aint finna go down there and fuck no hoes" Shah joked and laughed.

"You got me fucked up. I'm finna go down there in the big boy Tahoe truck with bands to blow. You know a bitch gone bust it open for the kid" Hot Boi quickly shot back at Shah.

"Man, you ain't on shit!"

"You know what, just cause you said that on BD I'm fucking two bitches tonight. I'ma send you a video and show you boss shit," Hot Boi said picking up the sixteen band on the bed. He looked in the closet and made sure his safe was closed before walking out the room. Shah followed him into the living room.

"Bro keep your eyes open out there and watch out for the nigga Rasheed. Hit my line if you see him" Hot Boi said.

"Tight, bro I got you. I'ma hold shit down while you gone," Shah said.

"Love bro," Hot Boi said before leaving the apartment.

Shah sat back on the couch and started back watching TV before he remembered to get in the kitchen to whip them other two zips, so he'd be ready when the line started ringing again. He got up and ran down to the basement and grabbed the scale and two zips then ran back up to the apartment got down to business.

At 3:00pm, he pulled into his mother parking lot on Allied. He had to talk her into giving him her social security number. He hadn't seen her since they got into it a few weeks back. Shah parked the car and stepped out before walking up to the building and ranging the doorbell, "Who is it?" Marie yelled from her window. Shah stepped back so she could see him. "It's yo son, I need to talk to you," he said looking up at the window.

"Ok give me a second."

Shah stood there for a moment before the door came flying open. He jumped back to avoid it hitting him. Marie stood in the doorway she looked like she lost a lot of weight since the last time Shah saw her. His heart dropped into his stomach, he could barely recognize his mother, who was once a beautiful sight on the eyes.

"You alright?" he asked as his voice cracked from fighting back tears.

"I'm ok," Marie said scratching her neck.

"Where James at?" Shah angerly asked.

"Shah please don't come over here starting shit. I'm not in the mood."

"You right! I didn't come over here to start nothing, I need to get my social security card and I need Shawn social security number too," Shah said.

Marie stood there for a moment before she turned and walked back up the stairs. Shah followed her to the second floor before she turned and stopped him.

"Shah please don't start with James when we go in here," she pleaded with him.

"Man, I ain't on that. I'ma respect the fact that you got you own life and the right to live it how you choose," Shah said.

Marie turned and open the door before walking into the apartment, Shah came in behind her and instantly got upset with how the crib looked. There was trash everywhere and the house smelled like nothing but beer and crack smoke. James was laid on the couch watching TV. Marie made it to the hallway before she turned and looked at Shah.

"Come on Shah," she said making sure not to leave him alone with James. He followed her to the bedroom. She lifted that mattress and pulled out a folder filled with papers. She reached inside and grabbed his social security card and handed it to him.

"I need Shawn's too," Shah said reaching into his pocket and pulling out his wallet. She flipped through the papers in the folder and found Shawn social security card. She told him Shawn's number and he quickly put it in his phone.

"Ma I need one more thing," he said as she stood there with the folder in her hand, "What else you need Shah?"

"I need yours and dad's number too."

"Boy what is you trying to do?" she asked.

"I got some shit I need to get done. I really can't tell you right now."

"Boy no! I'm not giving you my social," Marie said.

"Come on ma, I need it! I'm trying to take care of something important that's why I need it. Trust me, you gone benefit from it in the long run. Look how bout I give you a hundred dollars," Shah said.

"Shah, I'm not finna---" she quickly stopped speaking once she notice the roll of money in Shah hands.

"Alright boy! Don't do nothing you not supposed to do with my shit!" she said as she quickly gave him her social security number and his father's as well. He put them in his phone before peeling off five twenties and handing them to her.

"Can I get twenty more Shah?" Marie quickly asked before he put the money back into his pocket. He handed her twenty more before turning and walked out the room. She followed him to the door. Shah turned and gave her a hug. Then told her to be careful before walking out the door. When he got in his car, he quickly text Almundo the information. He started the car before pulling out the lot.

Meanwhile

Rasheed and Khalil sat in the back seat of their cousin minivan. Their oldest cousin Jimmy was driving, and their cousin Twin sat in the passenger seat. They drove down Allied looking for Hot Boi or anyone who would know where to find him. Rasheed leaned over and told Jimmy to pull over at the gas station. Khalil sat next to him smoking a blunt, he had a glock 40 with a 50-round drum on it sitting in his lap. All he could think of was Reggie, he couldn't believe he was gone. Khalil had been a demon since he was 11 years old. All he wanted to do was kill, he got high off smoking shit. The only reason he carried a drum was cause of the way it looked. But back home they called him one shot shorty because he was sneaky and wouldn't shoot unless he was right up on you. He had well over twenty bodies under his belt and was itching to add Hot Boi and anyone riding with him to his count.

Jimmy pulled into bp gas station, Rasheed and Khalil sat up to see the cars in the station hoping to see Hot Boi.

"He ain't up here!" Rasheed said disappointed.

"Ride through the south, I saw that nigga over by Post Road one time," Khalil calmly said.

"Take this street straight down then get on the beltline. You gotta get off on the first Fitch Hatchery exit" Rasheed explained to Jimmy. As they rolled Khalil continued to take puffs from the blunt. He was a lil pissed that Jimmy and Twin came to Madison, because it made him look bad. Jimmy and Twin was both real life demons, they'd been killing shit since the early 90's. They had bodies in over fifteen states. He looked up to them when he was growing up but when he made his first kill, he made it his business to outdo them both.

They drove through almost every block in Madison more than once, looking for Hot Boi. Khalil wanted his head bad.

Meanwhile

At 5:00pm, X turned on East Pass Rd. His GPS kept saying he made it to his destination, but he couldn't find Tammy's building. After circling the block a few times, he finally decided to pull over and give her a call.

"Hello," Tammy said, sounding like she had ten different things going on all at once.

"I'm on East Pass, but I can't find your building," X said looking around.

"How far down are you?" Tammy asked.

"I'm not sure, I used my GPS and stopped when it said I reached my destination, so I think I'm outside."

"Alright, well I'm still getting dress so I'm finna send my brother down to see if he see you. What kind of car you in?"

"I'm in a red Cadillac truck," X said.

"Ok I'm finna send him out there. He got on a red polo shirt," Tammy said.

"Tight" X said. He began to wonder if Tammy was on some bullshit tryna get him robbed. Everyone he grew up around was cutthroat, so he trusted no one and being that this was his first time kicking it with Tammy he wasn't sure what to expect. X looked around outside and still didn't see anyone. He pulled his glock 40 from the center console and sat it on his lap. He looked into his rearview mirror and saw a dude a few buildings down the street with a red shirt on. He put the car in drive and made a u-turn pulling up to where dude stood before rolling his window down.

"You Tammy brother?" X said.

"Yeah," Shah quickly responded.

"Tight," X said before pulling over to park. He put his pistol on his hip, cause he wasn't feeling the vibe of the situation. He jumped out his truck and walked over to Shah.

"What up, I'm X," he said to Shah.

"What's up X, I'm Shah," he responded.

"Tight," X said.

"So how long you been fucking with Tammy?" Shah asked as they started walking toward the building.

"We been talking for about three weeks," X answered, sensing that Shah was sizing him up on his intentions with Tammy.

"That's what up! Where you from?" Shah asked.

"I'm from Milwaukee."

"Ok," Shah said as they walked into the building and up the stairs to Tammy apartment. Shah opened the door and let him walk in first then he entered and closed the door and locked it. X stood by the door looking around the apartment. It was nice and clean which made him a lil more comfortable.

He could hear Tammy's and another female's voice coming the back of the apartment.

Shah sat down on the couch and looked at X and noticed he was uncomfortable.

"A bro you can sit down if you want too, it ain't no telling how long they finna be," Shah said.

X walked over and took a seat on the other couch. He like the way the crib was decorated with the white leather couch and the black and gold pillows, the glass end tables, and the coffee table with gold trim. There were gold elephant statues in different places throughout the living room with black and white drapes over the windows. A 75-inch flat screen mounted on the wall. He could tell by the way the apartment was put together that Tammy was on her shit, and that was a major plus in his book.

Shah got up from the couch and went to the kitchen and grabbed his four phones off the table and his blunt he had rolled. He walked back to the couch and sat back down, he put his phone on the table and flamed up the blunt.

"You smoke bro?" Shah asked.

"Yeah, I smoke!"

"Shah, I know you not smoking in here," Tammy yelled from the bathroom. Audrey came walking into the living room wearing a red dress that hugged her hourglass frame. X couldn't help but to stare at her thick thighs. He could tell from the front that she had a fat ass. He was shocked cause he never saw an Asian woman that strapped.

"Baby you know we don't let nobody smoke in here, so can you please put that out," she asked, as she walked over to the couch he was sitting on.

"light I got you," he said before taking two more puffs from the blunt. Audrey turned and started walking back to the bathroom to help Tammy finished getting dressed. Shah quickly stood up and walked behind her grabbing her around the waist and kissed her on the back on the neck. She started laughing before turning to kiss him.

"How long y'all finna be?" Shah asked as he held her close to him.

"About ten minutes," Audrey said when she walked off, he smacked her on the ass. She turned and winked as she walked away swaying her hips to tease him.

"Damn you wearing that?" he said and sat back down.

Twenty minutes later Tammy came walking from the back room wearing a yellow long sleeve fitted dress that hugged every curve on her body. She had on some red Gucci heel with tassels hanging from the straps that covered the top of her feet. Her straight blonde hair hung over her shoulder. X stood up when he noticed her.

"Damn you sexy as hell," X said as he looked her up and down.

Shah sat there; eyes wide with shock that Tammy came out looking good enough to eat. He'd never looked at her like this before, but that dress and hair had her looking like someone he never saw before.

Tammy laughed at what X said.

"Thank you," she said walking over and giving him a hug. "I'm sorry I had you waiting so long," she added breaking their hug.

"Shit the wait was well worth it," he replied.

"Audrey came walking for the back this time with a black blazer over her red fitted dress, along with some black red bottom heels. Her jet-black hair was shining. It was pinned up in a bun. She had Tammy red clutch in one hand and hers in the other.

"Damn lil moma bring yo sexy ass over here," Shah said. Audrey handed Tammy her clutch before walking over giving Shah a hug and kiss.

"Ok, let's go before we miss our reservation," Tammy said. She started turning the light out as Audrey, Shah, and X left out the apartment. She closed and locked the doors, as they made it out the building, Tammy asked if they were all riding in the same car or taking different ones. Shah insisted that him and Audrey take his car and Tammy and X ride together.

Twenty minutes later they all walked into the melting pot and was shown to their table

After ordering a few drinks they ate and talked for hours before deciding to leave.

They made a quick stop at the liquor store before heading back to Tammy's and Audrey's place.

At 11:15pm, Tammy and X sat at the kitchen table talking. She already had a few drinks in her system and was feeling herself. Audrey and Shah sat in the living room with music playing softly in the background. Shah knew she was tipsy when she reached her hand inside his pants and grabbed his dick. She started playing with it while Tammy and X sat no more than 30-feet away from them in the kitchen.

Tammy leaned closed to X and whispered in his ear, "How about you come help me get out this dress," she said before standing up and grabbing ahold of his hand and pulling him to her room, before closing the door.

Once in the room, X wasted no time turning her around and moving her hair to the side of one of her shoulders. He unzipped the back of her dress then started kissing down her neck. She pulled her arms out the sleeves and pulled her dress down over her thick hips and ass letting it hit the floor. X instantly became aroused at the sight of Tammy in her panties and bra. He reached around and slowly ran his hands down her stomach until he reached her thighs. Her skin was so soft and silky smooth. He turned her around and laid her onto the bed. He took his shirt, pants, and shoes off, then walked up to her and started kiss her stomach. She started breathing heavily then arched her back and reached back grabbing ahold of the comforter. He started to work his way lower to her hips then her inner thighs. Tammy tried to work her feet out of her heels, but X stopped her.

"No keep them on," he said before pulling her panties off. Her pussy was shaved bold just the way he liked. Ever since the day he met her there was nothing he didn't like about her. He went in for the kill and started kissing and licking on Tammy's pussy. He brought her to climax twice before he got up and pulled a condom from his pocket. She laid there out of breath while he pulled down his boxers before putting the condom on, he pulled her to the edge of the bed and spread her legs and slowly guided his self-inside her. She moaned softly while X slowly stroked in and out of her. He quickly began to pick up pace with each stroke he pounded harder and harder.

"Oh my god Xavier!" she yelled out.

Shah and Audrey were still sitting on the couch. They could hear Tammy over the music screaming, which turned Audrey on more than she already was. She unbuckled Shah's belt and unzipped his pants before pulling his boxers briefs down to his knees. She laid on her stomach on the couch next to him and slowly took his already hard dick into her mouth. She quickly started going crazy. She took him from her mouth and spit on it then she took him back in her mouth. He sat back and grabbed her bun and guided her further down until he felt his self in her throat. Audrey quickly came up for air then hurried and went back down, deep throating every inch of him. She continued going crazy as she held him with both hands. He sat there shocked as she continued deep throating him until he bust. Audrey kept going as he came in her mouth swallowing every drop of his cum. Within seconds, Shah was back hard. He could hear Tammy screaming, "Oh my god, oh my god" in a sexy ass voice, which made him want to fuck her. Audrey got up and took Shah into her bedroom where he fucked her for hours until they both fell asleep.

Chapter Six

Shah sat at the bar with Lil Jerry talking shit and taking shots. He felt good about where he as at in life. He'd come a long way in a little over a month. He had a hundred thousand dollars of his own money in the safe and a little over ten thousand dollars in the bank. Shah took another shot of patron. He looked up when he saw a group of females walk into the bar. He overlooked the first few that came through because they were white, but the last two caught his attention when he recognized one of them.

"Damn that's ole girl that works at Rogers and Holland's," he said to Jerry.

"Damn on BD she thick as hell, "Lil Jerry said as the group of women walked past them.

"As soon as they get settled in, I'm on shorty line, I need that!" Shah said as he took another shot.

"Shit I like the white bitch standing next to her, she got a fat ass in them leggings," Lil Jerry said.

"That pussy fat as hell too," Shah said.

"Yeah, we on them," Lil Jerry said taking another shot.

Fifteen minutes later, Shah noticed she was standing by the wall near the dance floor sipping her drink and watching her friends dance. He knew this was the opportunity to approach her, so he got up from the bar and walked over to where she stood.

"Excuse me, my name is Shah. I don't mean to bother you but I couldn't help but notice how beautiful you are. I had to come over and ask what's your name?" he said.

She smiled and stood there for a moment before speaking.

"My name Keisha, I'm sorry what did you say your name was again?" Keisha asked.

"My name Shah!"

"Hi Shah, nice to meet you," Keisha said reaching her hand out to shake his hand. He grabbed ahold of her hand and shook it.

"Nice to meet you to Keisha," Shah said as he held her hand.

"I take it you don't like to dance?" Shah asked.

"Why you say that?"

"Because your friends on the dance floor and you standing over here,"

"Oh no, I like to dance I just don't wanna go on the dance floor with my drink in my hand. There's too many people out there. I don't want to spill it on myself."

"Oh well that's understandable."

"So, what about you? Do you like to dance?" Keisha asked.

"When I was younger, I couldn't dance. So now I'm the type to hold the wall in the club and make sure the building don't fall down on everybody "Shah said.

Keisha started laughing," I see you funny I like that" she said as she looked over to him for a second look.

"I'm glad I can make you laugh. I would like to make you laugh more often, how bout you give me your number so I could arrange that," Shah said. Keisha started laughing again then took the last sip of her drink and sat it down on the table.

"How bout I make a deal with you. If you come out on the dance floor and dance with me, I'll think about giving you my number," she said before walking on the dance floor. Shah stood there for a moment then took her up on her offer. She looked back and noticed Shah was right behind her. She grabbed ahold of his hand and led him through the crowd to the middle of the dance floor. She started dancing to the beat of the song. Shah stood there stunned at how good she could move her hips. He hadn't dance in years, so he followed her lead and moved to her rhythm as he held on to her waist. She felt he could keep up, so she started throwing her ass back forcing him to plant his feet firmly and put some strength in his stances. Shah looked across the dance floor and saw Lil Jerry dancing with Keisha's friend.

Keisha and Shah danced through a few songs before they left the dance floor and went back over to the bar. Shah bought a long island for Keisha and a triple shot of patron for his self. They sat at the bar getting to know more about each other. Keisha was really feeling the vibe between them. She took his phone and put her number in it.

"There now you have my number. You better use it," she whispered in his ear.

"Trust me, I'ma use it," Shah said smiling.

"I hope so," she said as her friend walked up to her grabbing her hand telling her they were getting ready to leave. Shah stood up and gave her a hug before telling her he'd call her soon. Lil Jerry walked up to Shah and started laughing.

"Did you get the number?" Lil Jerry asked.

"Hell yeah! What bout you?"

"You know that. I'm finna link with shorty tonight."

"Oh yeah? She going like that?" Shah asked.

"Naw, I just got it like that," Lil Jerry said then started laughing.

"OK then! Let's get up out of here," Shah said laughing as well. They got up and walked out to their cars. Shah looked at his phone checking the time, it was 2:30am.

"Tight folks," he said as he got in his car.

"Yup," Lil Jerry said.

Shah started the car and pulled off heading home. He had business to attended to in the morning.

Meanwhile

Hot Boi and his cousin Quantay were riding in his truck trailing two bitches they met at the bar. They finally pulled over on Gerald Ave. Alesha and Kayla got out of their car drunk and stumbled up the sidewalk talking loud. Quantay and Hot Boi jumped out and walked up to the house the girl's stayed in. When they got to the door their roommate opened it and let them in. Quantay and Hot Boi followed the ladies into the living room and sat down on the couch. Hot Boi started breaking down a cigarillo when Alesha and Kayla walked out the living room and up the stairs. He could hear them talking and laughing he leaned over to Quantay, "Cuz them hoes lit," he whispered and Quantay laughed.

"What you whispering for? These hoes going one of us damn near finna fuck two of them if we don't end up fucking all three of them together. Trust me!" Quantay said. Hot Boi stood up and started laughing as he walked toward the kitchen to dump his tobacco from his cigarillo. Alesha came stumbling down the stairs then walked into the kitchen with Hot Boi. She knew Kayla was feeling him but she was too, so she wanted to beat her to him. Alesha grabbed him by the hand and pushed him in the bathroom next to the kitchen closing the door. She got down on her knees and pushed him by his waist up against the wall before unbuckling his belt and pulling his pants and briefs down all at once. She grabbed ahold of his dick licking and kissing it. "Damn this bitch thirsty," he thought to his self as he looked down on her.

She was a sight to see. She was mixed, black and white, with long curly hair, hazel and green eyes with a nice petite body frame with a fat ass. Within seconds, she had his dick balls deep in her mouth while she played with his balls. He put his head back and closed his eyes as she cupped his balls and took him all the way in and all the way out of her mouth with ease.

"I gotta record this bitch," he thought. He reached down to his pocket and pulled out his phone and started recording. She looked up at him and started performing for the camera. She took the dick from her mouth and stuck her tongue out then started smacking his dick on her tongue. She spit on the tip and slowly ran it across her lips as she stared into the camera.

"You like how I suck this dick?" Alesha asked.

"You know that! Now gone show me something," Hot Boi said then reached and grabbed a fist full of her hair. She started sucking his ball as she stroked him with on hand still looking into the camera. He moved the camera to the side for a different view. Alesha's other friend Terry knocked on the bathroom door.

"Alesha, bitch you in here?" she asked. Alesha started making loud gagging sounds then took his dick from her mouth and looked directly into the camera.

"Bitch I got a mouth full right now," she said stuffing him back in her mouth. He stood there shocked at her boldness. Terry wanted to be nosey, so she opened the door. Alesha looked over at her but kept sucking his dick.

"Bitch you really in here sucking dick!" Terry said standing in the doorway. Alesha stopped. "Yes bitch. You can come over here and help if you want to," Alesha said rubbing his dick over her lips.

"No, I'm good, you can finish, but bitch is it a big one?" Terry asked as she looked him directly in the face.

"Well how bout you come see it up close in person" Hot Boi quickly said.

"No, I'm good!" Terry said and laughed before closing the door.

Quantay sat in the living room on the couch next to Kayla he had her skirt pulled up to her waist. He used one hand to play with her pussy and the other to smoke his blunt. Terry walked in the living room and stood there.

"Y'all bitches some sluts," she quickly said to Kayla then started walking toward the stairs.

"Damn, where you going?" Quantay asked.

"I'm finna go upstairs," Terry said in a sassy tone.

"Naw come here real quick," Quantay said.

Terry stood at the bottom of the stairs for a moment debating if she wanted to be involved with what was going on. Quantay knew she would go cause he already had all three of them just never at the same time. She was the type to put up a fight and play hard to get so she didn't seem easy. But by nature, she was more of a slut than Alesha and Kayla put together.

"Man stop playing in bring yo sexy ass over here," he said.

"Boy!" Terry quickly shot back.

"Bitch don't act brand new," Kayla said, standing up and taking her skirt all the way off before sitting back on the couch. Quantay stood up and faced Kayla, she reached and unbuckled his belt, then pulled out his dick and started sucking it. He looked back over his shoulder at Terry who still stood there.

"So, you really finna just stand there?" he asked. She smacked her lips then walked over and sat next to Kayla. She pulled his pants all the way down while Kayla sucked his dick. She grabbed the back of Kayla head with one hand to control her rhythm while she played with his ball with the other.

Meanwhile

It was 8:30am. Almundo sat in his hotel room pissed at his girl Lisa. She lost a thousand dollars when she went to the store to buy some cigarettes. He sat by the window smoking a cigarette when his phone started to ring. He was too pissed to get up and answer it, so he let it ring until it stopped. It started to ring again, so he got up and picked it up from the dresser. He looked at his phone but didn't recognize the number so he debated if he should answer. "Fuck it," he said to his self and picked up.

"Hello?" he said.

"Come by my office, I have a mission for him and if he completes it I'll go into business with him," Alberto said before ending the call. Almundo wasted no time calling Shah.

"Hello," Almundo said geeked.

"What up?" Shah asked clearing his throat.

"I gotta go meet with him today, he got a mission for you to complete. If you do it right he'll do business with you," Almundo said.

"What kind of mission?"

"I'm not sure, but I'll find out and let you know," Almundo said.

"Tight, just let me know."

"OK," Almundo said ending the call. His whole mood had changed, he knew after this mission money was about to come pouring in.

Meanwhile

Shah rolled out of bed and walked over to the bathroom to take a piss. He washed his hands then brushed his teeth and washed his face. He walked back in the bedroom and picked up his phone. Shah texted "good morning beautiful" to Audrey and Keisha.

He put the phone down on the bed then walked to the kitchen and grabbed his box of cigarillos off the table. He took one out and broke it down and dumped the tobacco in the trash can. He grabbed the weed off the table and walked into the living room and sat down on the couch and started rolling his blunt.

He wondered what kind of mission he would have to do in order to get plugged. His mind started to race with many different thoughts. He finished rolling the blunt and turned on the news. He knew in the back of his mind whatever the mission was he was gone complete it cause he needed this connection. His phone chimed with text message, so he got up and walked to his room, he grabbed all four phones before flaming up his blunt as he walked back to the living room. Shah sat down and checked his message from Keisha.

"Who is this?"

Shah quickly texted back, "This Shah."

"Oh, I'm sorry I didn't have your number. Good morning to you to handsome," Keisha replied. Shah took a hit from his blunt when something on the news caught his attention.

"A woman was found dead in her apartment on Madison's east side. Officials have ruled this investigation a homicide. Police have not released many details and haven't named any suspects. They say this is an isolated incident and that the public is not in danger," the news anchor said.

Keisha texted him back again. "I see you up early."

"You know it's late nights early morning, plus I got a business to run, I can't sleep all day," Shah replied.

"What business you run?" Keisha asked.

"A t-shirt company I started last month. I'm still building my brand so I have to put in as many hours as I can. The say the early bird catch's the worm," Shah replied.

"That's nice I like that," she replied.

"You should let me know when you free. I would like to take you out on a date," Shah replied.

"I enjoyed talking to you last night and wouldn't mind seeing you again. I'm actually off today so tonight would be perfect for me," Keisha replied.

"OK, how bout we go out to eat at seven," Shah replied.

"That'll work. So, where do you plan on going?" Keisha asked.

"How bout long horn steak house?" Shah replied.

"OK. I'll see you there at seven "

"I'll see you later," Shah replied. Keisha replied with thumbs up emoji and two hearts eyed emoji. Shah sat his phone down and finished smoking his blunt.

Meanwhile

Rasheed and Khalil sat in the living room at Khalil's girl crib watching the news. Rasheed was pissed at Khalil for killing Tasha.

"Cuz the bitch was gone tell, I saw it in her eyes," Khalil said to Rasheed trying to plead his case.

"If she was gone tell she would have told when they asked about Reggie," Rasheed said.

"Man look Rasheed, I don't know about you, but I follow my gut feeling and my gut told me to get her out the way," Khalil said.

"You could have waited. The lady downstairs saw us go in the crib," Rasheed said.

"Man, fuck that! You acting like a bitch right now, fuck that old lady. We been down here for five months she don't know us!" Khalil said.

"I aint acting like no bitch. It's about being smart fool as nigga!" Rasheed said. Khalil sat there for a minute trying his hardest to control his tongue, but he couldn't, so he let his true feeling out.

"Nigga you been acting like a bitch, you let Reggie get killed and let that nigga get away!" Khalil said. Rasheed jumped up from the couch and walked up on Khalil pulling out his pistol. Khalil quickly stood up.

"Number one rule, never up it if you ain't gone use it," Khalil said looking him directly in the eyes.

"If you ever disrespect me again I'ma knock yo head off yo shoulders," Rasheed said as he gritted his teeth.

"And if you ever pull a pistol on me again I'ma leave you in the dirt like I did the last nigga that uped on me and didn't use it," Khalil said. Rasheed tucked his pistol back on his waist and walked over to the door and left.

Meanwhile

Hot Boi pulled up on Porter Ave and parked his truck. Quantay and a group of niggas was shooting dice on the side of an abandoned house. Quantay looked up and saw Hot Boi walking up the driveway.

"What up cuz?" Hot Boi asked as he approached the dice game.

"Shit cuz tryna get this money," Quantay said.

"What they shooting?" Hot Boi asked.

"Yeah nigga, bet back, bet back," Quantay said as he turned and stood in the middle of the dice game. Everyone stood there hollering and shouting bets.

"Police, police," somebody yelled from across the street. Hot Boi looked toward the street and saw three police officers running up the driveway. Everyone took off running so Hot Boi ran with the crowd. He didn't know anyone but Quantay, so he followed him. He saw him in front of the crowd running through the backyard headed toward a fence. A few dudes ran to the left toward another backyard and some ran to the right and around the building. Hot Boi jumped the gate behind Quantay and ran through another backyard and around the house onto Prairie. He looked back to see if the police was close behind him, Quantay was two house ahead of him, he quickly cut across the street and ran behind a house and into the back door. Hot Boi was right on his heels. He quickly pushed the door open before Quantay could close it.

"It's me cuz, it's me," Hot Boi said before Quantay stopped trying to push it close. He let Hot Boi in and quickly closed and locked the door.

Jamie came running from the living room to see what the hell was going on at her door. She turned the corner and saw Hot Boi and Quantay standing at the bottom of the stairs.

"Quantay what the hell you doing just busting in here like that?" Jamie asked.

"My bad Jamie, you know if it wasn't serious, I would've never came through here like that," Quantay said. Hot Boi stood there nervous, and hoping she wasn't about to put them out. Quantay started walking up the stairs.

"Boy you lucky cause if you was anyone else, I would've put yo ass out," Jamie said. Quantay gave her a hug and grabbed her ass.

"That's why I love you!" he said as he held her in his arms.

"Yeah, tell me anything Quantay," Jamie said. Quantay looked back at Hot Boi. "Come on cuz we finna chill here for a few hours," he said. Hot Boi walked up the stairs and into the kitchen.

"How you doing?" he asked Jamie as she walked pass him headed to the living room.

"I'm fine how you doing?"

"My bad Jamie this my cousin Hot Boi, cuz this my boo Jamie," Quantay said. She turned and looked at Quantay, "Oh now I'm yo boo huh? Quantay you funny!" Jamie said.

Quantay started laughing, "You always my boo, don't try to embarrass me in front of company," Quantay said. Jamie started laughing. "Boy you always joking, " she said then turned and walked in the living room. Hot Boi followed Quantay in the living room and sat on the couch across from him and Jamie. Quantay sat there talking shit to Jamie while Hot Boi watched t.v.

"You got some bag?" Quantay asked Hot Boi.

"Hell yeah, I still got some from last night" he said reaching in his pocket and pulling it out. "I ain't got know rellos," he said as he tossed the weed to Quantay.

"Damn," Quantay said. He looked over at Jamie. "You got some blunts in here?" he asked her.

"Yeah, I do, they in the room on the dresser,"

Quantay go up and went up the stairs to grab the blunts. Jamie got up and walked toward the kitchen before she stopped and turned around. "You want something to drink?" she asked Hot Boi.

"Yeah," he said.

"I got water and Gatorade," she said as she pulled her leggings up and fixed her shirt. He stared at her pussy print then looked at her. She was smiling at him while they locked eyes for a minute.

"I'll take a Gatorade," he said. He could tell she was feeling him by the way she looked at him. She turned and walked toward the kitchen. He couldn't help but look at her ass. Jamie was mixed with black and white; her mom was black, and her father was white. She had light brown skin with a little weight on her but was far from being out of shape.

Her thighs were thick, and she had a big ass with nice titties. He could clearly see she had no parties on cause her leggings cupped her ass cheeks perfectly. Quantay came back downstairs breaking down one of the blunts. "Man, cuz yo ass ain't never stayed in Beloit this long. You good?" he asked Hot Boi.

Jamie came walking in the living room with a Gatorade and two bottles of water. She handed Quantay a water then gave Hot Boi the Gatorade. Hot Boi gave Quantay a look letting him know he didn't want to talk about it in from of Jamie.

"Damn Jamie what you got us in here watching?" Quantay asked.

"Boy this the hateful eight, it's a good as movie," she said.

"This shit look like an old ass western," Quantay said grabbing the remote.

"Naw, cuz this a decent movie you just gotta watch it. I saw this shit before it's funny as hell too," Hot Boi said before Quantay could change the channel.

Quantay grabbed the ashtray and sat the remote down. He dumped the tobacco in the ashtray and started rolling up. As they sat there watching the movie he felt Jamie starring at him so he looked at her. She didn't look away she sat there starring him directly in the eyes.

"Hot Boi where you from?" she asked trying to spark up a conversation with him.

"Why you all in cuz business?" Quantay asked before Hot Boi could answer.

"He can speak for his self Quantay he grown" Jamie shot back. Hot Boi sat there feeling awkward cause he knew she was on him, but he really didn't know where Quantay stood on the situation.

"Cuz Jamie want to give you some of that pussy, that's why she all in yo business," Quantay said as he flamed up the weed. Jamie looked at Quantay shocked at what came out his mouth.

"How you gone tell me what I wanna do with my pussy?" Jamie said as she slapped Quantay on the shoulder. "Cause I know you. But it's cool cause we share everything but underwear. Ain't that right cuz?" Quantay asked.

"Hell yeah! We share everything but underwear," Hot Boi said looking at her. She started laughing before getting up from the couch. "Yeah, y'all ass crazy! I gotta get ready for work," she said then walked up the stairs to her bedroom.

"You want me to send cuz up there to get you right before work?" Quantay asked her.

"No! But he can come get me right when I get off work since you offering," Jamie yelled back down the stairs before closing her room door. Quantay took a few hits from the blunt and passed it to Hot Boi.

"She got a big ole ass" Hot Boi said as he hit the blunt. Quantay started laughing. "Yo ass a fool," he said. "You know she was serious about you getting her right when she get off," Quantay added.

"On BD, I wouldn't waste no time getting behind them big cheeks and fuck the shit out of her," Hot Boi said.

"Well when she come down ask her what time she get off," Quantay said.

"Say know more," Hot Boi said as he passed the blunt.

"What you be fucking with?" Hot Boi asked Quantay. "As far as what?" Quantay asked.

"On the hustling side," Hot Boi said.

" I be fucking with the coke,"

"Oh, you be fucking with the soft?" Hot Boi asked.

"Naw I be fucking with the hard"

"You got a line or you be on the block?" Hot Boi said.

"I got a line but it ain't consistent cause the work these niggas be selling is some bullshit," Quantay said. Jamie walked down the stairs, "Quantay let me hit that weed," she asked.

"Tight" he said passing her he blunt. She took a hit and walked over to the door and grabbed her shoes.

"Jamie what time you get off, so I know what time to come through and get you right?" Hot Boi asked

Jamie started laughing as she stood there for a moment smiling ear to ear.

"I can tell y'all related cause both y'all ass crazy!" she said

"I ain't joking though! I really wanna come put this mafucka in yo life," Hot Boi said

"I get off at seven, now I hope you got enough to put in my life!" Jamie said and smile

"Tight!" Hot Boi quickly said before Jamie handed him the blunt and grabbed her purse.

"Quantay lock the bottom lock when y'all leave out!" Jamie said as she opened the door to leave out.

"Tight," Quantay said as she walked out and closed the door.

"Tight cuz she gone now. What's up? Yo ass ain't never stayed this long you straight?" Quantay asked.

"Oh yeah cuz I'm good! Some shit happened up there, so I just gotta lay low til that shit blow over," Hot Boi said.

"Nigga what happened?" Quantay asked

"A nigga and his cousin tried to get down on me, so I had to lay his ass down. My big home told me to lay low til we catch his cousin," Hot Boi said

"You know where they be at?" Quantay asked

"I do but fool want me to lay low for a while," Hot Boi said.

"Man fuck that shit! Look cuz on the Mighty let's go up there you know that shit right up my alley I'ma get rid of every mafucka in the crib and we can slide back down here asap yo mans ain't even gotta know," Quantay said.

Hot Boi sat there thinking he knew Quantay was wit the shits, but he wasn't sure if he wanted to take the risk.

"So what up cuz?" Quantay quickly asked

"Tight man fuck it we on it!" Hot Boi said

Meanwhile

Almundo pulled into Alberto's shop at 11:45 am and pulled into the first spot he seen. Almundo got out the car and quickly walked to the shop and walked in, he looked around for Alberto and when he didn't see him, he walked to his office. Alberto was sitting behind his desk looking through some paper when Almundo walked into his office.

"Cousin!" Almundo said as he walked over and took a seat in front of Alberto's desk.

"Let's get straight to the point!" Alberto said.

"Ok," Almundo quickly replied.

"Here is a list of instructions and a plane ticket. Make sure he follows the instructions and don't deviate from the plan if he makes it back have him come see me. If anything goes wrong, you're going to be held accountable," Alberto said.

"Ok and I'll make sure he follows the instructions," Almundo quickly said.

"Good his plane leaves tomorrow. Now I have work to get back to I'll give you a call," Alberto said.

"Ok" Almundo said as he grabbed the plane ticket and instructions off Alberto's desk and left the office just as fast as he entered.

Almundo walked outside and got into his car and pulled out the lot. He wasted no time calling Shah as he drove down Keeler.

"Hello?" Almundo said as Shah answered.

"Shit! So, what's up?" he asked.

"I need to meet with you when I get back," Almundo said.

"Iight just call me when you get here," Shah said.

"Ok," Almundo said then ended the call.

Meanwhile

Shah got off the beltline on Simonole Hwy Exit and got caught at the red light. He looked down to his phone then back up then back to his phone again. The sound of a car horn startled Shah, causing him to jump. He looked up and noticed the light was green and the cars in front of him were all gone. The light quickly turned red again so he slowly pulled to the crossing lines, looking into his rearview mirror he could see the guy behind him cursing him out. Shah started laughing as he looked closer and noticed it was Rasheed, then hurried and picked up his phone to call Hot Boi. The light turned green again and Shah made a slow left turn as Rasheed was on his bumper. Rasheed sped around Shah then turned right onto Verona Rd. Shah quickly dialed Hot Boi's number as he trailed behind Rasheed on Verona Rd.

"Shah Money! What's the word?" Hot Boi asked as he answered the phone.

"Check it out I'm behind this nigga Rasheed right now," Shah said.

"Yeah? is he still driving that blue impala?" Hot Boi asked.

"Hell yeah! He driving down Verona Rd right now," Shah said.

"He by his self?" Hot Boi asked.

"Yeah, he just pulled into BP," Shah said as he drove past the gas station.

"Tight say no more. Be easy up their bro," Hot Boi said.

"Oh, I'm good!" Shah quickly said.

"Tight love bro!" Hot Boi said.

"Love," Shah said.

Just as Shah ended the call, his phone started to ring he looked down and saw it was Almundo, so he quickly answered.

"What up?" Shah asked.

"I'm back in town where do you wanna meet?" Almundo asked.

"Meet me on Russit," Shah said.

"Ok good I'm on Raymond Road right now," Almundo said.

"Tight," Shah said then ended the call.

Shah pulled onto Cameron and parked his car he got out and walked around the corner to Russit. As Shah walked up the block, he could see Almundo's car coming up the block, He stepped closer to the curb and waved to Almundo as he got closer. Almundo pulled up next to Shah and unlocked the door. Shah walked up to the car and got in and Almundo quickly pulled off.

"So, what's the word?" Shah immediately asked.

"I just got back from seeing my cousin and he wants you to take a test run to Laredo Texas. You got to pick up a package and drive it back. You fly out tomorrow," Almundo said as he handed Shah the plane ticket and instructions.

"Now you need to make sure you follow the instructions down to the letter because our asses is on the line if you don't," Almundo said to Shah as Shah looked at the plane ticket and instructions.

"Tight I can do that!" Shah said as he looked at the instructions. "So, this all I gotta do?" Shah asked.

"Yeah. Just do whatever those instructions say then when you get back, I'll give you his address so you can go and talk business with him yourself," Almundo said.

"Tight!" Shah quickly said as he thought about how connected he would be once this mission was complete.

"Now that we got that out the way I need you to front me until later," Almundo said.

"Tight!" Shah said as he immediately pulled his work from his pocket and handed Almundo ten fifties. "Just call me, you can let me out right here," Shah said.

"Alright," Almundo said as he pulled over on Cameron so Shah could get out.

Meanwhile

Khalil walked into the back bedroom to wake Brittany up. Reggie hooked Khalil and Brittany up when Rasheed and Khalil first came to Madison. Brittany was a neighborhood thot, but Khalil didn't give a fuck he only cuffed her up to have a spot to hustle out of until he got on his feet.

Reggie was the real money maker of the group. He was fronting Khalil and Rasheed work and he set them both up with a nice clientele. Khalil had no problem getting rid of the work he got from Reggie, but he had a hard time saving his portion of the money. He would have enough money to pay Reggie his money so that he could get another front.

Khalil wasn't known as a hustler. Back home in Chicago, he was a known jack boy and shooter. Now that Reggie was dead Khalil needed to find a way to bring in some cash, Khalil knew Brittany was in love with him and would do anything for him just to keep him around. He had every intention to use that to his benefit. He walked into the bedroom and leaned over Brittany as she slept then he shook her.

"Aye Shorty wake up!" Khalil said. Brittany quickly jumped up from her sleep scared and confused as she looked at Khalil half asleep.

"Damn Khalil you scared the shit out me!" Brittany said as she wiped her face.

"Man get yo ass up!" Khalil said.

"Why?" Brittany asked.

"Call the dude you used to fuck wit and tell him you got somebody tryna buy a pound," Khalil said.

"Okay Khalil damn!" Brittany said as she got up and grabbed her phone off the dresser. Khalil walked back into the living room and sat down on the couch, he flipped through his phone and started taking selfies. Khalil took his dreads out of his ponytail and laid them over his face as he grabbed his 9mm with the fifty-round drum on it and flipped it upside down. He took a picture of his self-holding it by the drum then logged into Facebook and uploaded it with the caption "#OT #OppHuntin!"

Minutes later his Facebook started going crazy with likes and comments. He sat there going back and forth commenting on his picture with his friends from his hood. Brittany came out the room thirty minutes after Khalil woke her up.

"Khalil, he downstairs," she said.

"Tight," Khalil quickly said as he jumped up and walked out the door. He walked downstairs and looked out the building door and saw dudes black Tahoe truck parked in the lot. Khalil walked out to the truck and jumped in the back seat when he seen a female sitting in the passenger seat.

"It's right there in that bag on the floor," Cory said as he looked back at Khalil.

Khalil grabbed the bag and opened it and looked in it.

"Tight this look good," Khalil said then quickly upped his 9mm and pointed it at Cory.

"Now bitch ass nigga put yo hands on the steering wheel. Bitch reach over and grab everything from his pockets and hand it to me. If you do anything stupid I'ma kill both y'all!" Khalil said to the woman in the passenger seat. She instantly complied and reached over and pulled all the money from his pockets and handed it to Khalil.

"Bitch grab that phone too," Khalil said.

She quickly grabbed the phone and handed it to Khalil without saying a word.

"Damn fool this what you on?" Cory asked as he held his head down and kept his hands on the steering wheel. Khalil reached up and smacked him in the back of his head with the butt of the gun.

"Bitch ass nigga shut the fuck up!" Khalil said, then looked over to the bitch in the passenger seat. "Bitch hand me that purse too!" he said as he pointed the gun in her direction. She grabbed the purse and handed it to him.

"Where yo phone at bitch?" Khalil asked.

"It's in my purse," she quickly said.

Khalil opened the middle console and found a stack of cash wrapped in rubber bands. "Oh, y'all was tryna hold out on me huh?" he asked as he quickly pulled it out and stuffed it in the bag with the weed. He reached over and patted Cory's waist to make sure he didn't have a gun.

"Shorty you sexy as hell, you need to stop fucking wit bitch ass niggas!" Khalil said as he opened his door.

"Now bitch ass nigga hurry up and get out my lot before I shoot this bitch up!" Khalil said then jumped out the truck. Cory hurried and pulled out of the lot. Khalil walked back into the building and went back to Brittany's apartment, he emptied out the purse and didn't find shit worth keeping.

"Yeah that was sweet!" Khalil said as he laughed then started thumbing through the cash.

"Aye Brittany I got you a Gucci purse!" Khalil yelled out to Brittany as he continued to count the cash.

Meanwhile

Shah walked into the building and saw Lil Jerry standing at the top of the stairs smoking a blunt.

"What's up boa?" Lil Jerry asked as Shah walked up the stairs.

"Shit bro I'm tryna get rich!" Shah said.

"I see! It's been nonstop traffic through his bitch looking for that shit you got!" Lil Jerry said.

"Damn I know I missed all kinds of cash today. But I ain't trippin it's gone come back," Shah said with confidence. Lil Jerry and Shah both jumped and damn near took off running when the building door flew open. Lil Jerry's cousin Cory came running into the building.

"Folks on Bd this bitch ass nigga Khalil just poked me! He hit me for fourteen bands and a pound," Cory said out of breath.

"When?" Lil Jerry asked as he came running down the stairs.

"Bout ten minutes ago! I need a pole I'm finna kill this nigga," Cory said.

"Bro how you let a nigga poke you?" Lil Jerry said, pissed.

"I been selling the nigga weed through the lil bitch Brittany. This bitch called me and asked me to slide through wit a pound, so I slid on the bitch and this nigga jumped in as always but this time he upped on me!" Cory quickly said.

"Come on, Let's go find this nigga!" Lil Jerry said as he walked out the building. Cory and Lil Jerry walked to Cory's truck and hopped in and quickly pulled out the lot. Shah stood in front of the building and watched as Cory and Lil Jerry drove down the block. His phone chimed in his pocket with a text message, so he quickly pulled it out and seen that it was from Keisha.

"I'm sorry Shah I really wanted to see you tonight, but I have to cancel. I have something very important I have to do and I can't put it off. Maybe we can do lunch tomorrow?"

"Damn!" Shah said to himself. He was a little salty cause he wanted to chill with Keisha, but he figured as long as he had her online, he would get his chance.

"Damn, Tomorrow won't work for me I gotta go out of town. But maybe we can make plans when I get back," Shah replied.

"Oh, that sucks! but we can make plans when you get back," Keisha replied.

"Tight, well you enjoy the rest of your day beautiful," Shah replied.

"Aww thank you! You enjoy the rest of your day too handsome!" Keisha replied.

"Thanks, I will!" Shah replied then looked up and seen two hypes walking toward him. He quickly put his phone in his pocket and walked them into the building. Shah quickly sold them what they wanted and let them out of the building and three more was walking up to the door. Shah was flooded with nonstop traffic for hours on end. He sold his last bag at 9:30pm and decided to leave and call it a night cause he had important business to attend to in the morning.

Meanwhile

Quantay and Hot Boi were hiding in the bushes for almost three hours outside of Alexis's crib. Hot Boi wasnt used to lurking so he started to grow tired of waiting. Quantay was used to it he had popped two ecstasy pills and was alert and itching to unload every bullet in his clip.

"Cuz we been out here for a long ass time I don't think the nigga coming over here tonight," Hot Boi whispered to Quantay.

Quantay wasn't ready to leave just yet. He looked down at his watch and saw that it was 3:06am. "Look cuz if they don't pull up by 3:30 we gone," Quantay said.

Hot Boi sat there quiet, he really wasn't feeling the situation. His legs started to go numb from squatting for so long, so he sat all the way down to stretch his legs a little.

"Somebody coming, get ready!" Quantay said as he noticed some head lights coming from the side of the building. Hot Boi quickly bounced back up into a squatting position and got ready.

He could see a car pulling into a parking space three cars from the bushes he was hiding in.

"Is that him? is it him?" Quantay quickly asked.

"Naw, but that's his bitch," Hot Boi said.

"Another car coming," Quantay whispered. Hot Boi squinted real hard to look past the head light that was turning into the lot trying to see what kind of car it was. He noticed it was Rasheed when he turned in a parking space in front of the building door.

"Go left and I'ma go right! That's him!" Hot Boi quickly said. No sooner than the words fell from Hot Boi's mouth, Quantay was out the bushes and up on the driver side door. He let off three quick shots, hitting Rasheed in the back of the head leaving him slumped on the steering wheel. Shots quickly erupted from the passenger seat Hot Boi instantly brought those shots to an end as he emptied his clip into the passenger window. He opened the passenger door and pulled Khalil from the car and shot him two more times, then looked over into the driver seat to make sure that was Rasheed. Hot Boi ran around to the driver side and saw Quantay stumbling off in a panic to get away from the scene. He grabbed Quantay's arm and put it over his shoulder and helped him hurry back to their car.

"That bitch ass nigga shot me!" Quantay said as Hot Boi drove down the street.

"Where you hit at?" Hot Boi asked.

"He got me in the shoulder. It ain't bleeding yet, but it's burning like a bitch! Get me to a hospital," Quantay yelled.

"Damn, we finna have to go to Rockford. We can't go to a hospital in Wisconsin," Hot Boi said.

"Tight well get me to Rockford!" Quantay said in pain.

"I got you!" Hot Boi said as he sped to the beltline.

Chapter Seven

NEXT DAY

S hah was woke up by both trap phones ringing off the chain. He quickly jumped out of bed as if he was in a life or death situation. He rushed over to the dresser and grabbed one of the phones and answered it.

"Yo!" Shah said as he answered the phone.

"Aye bro you up?" Leroy asked.

"Yeah what up?" Shah asked.

"I need you to pull up on me," Leroy said

"Tight give me twenty minutes," Shah quickly replied.

"Tight!" Leroy said then ended the call.

Shah picked up the other phone and dialed the last number that called back.

"Yo" Shah said as they answered.

"You ready for me yet?" The man on the other end of the phone said. Shah pulled the phone away from his ear and looked at the number cause he didn't recognize the voice.

"Who the fuck is this?" Shah asked aggressively.

"Damn nephew it's me Hustle Man!" he said.

"Oh, damn I thought you was somebody playing on my phone. But naw I ain't ready for you yet but as soon as I am I'm going to call you," Shah said.

"Damn nephew I need you," Hustle Man said disappointed.

"I got you as soon as I can!" Shah said.

"Alright nephew make sure you do cause they been knocking my door down. You missing out," Hustle Man said.

"Tight I'm on it," Shah said.

"Ok just call me nephew," Hustle Man said.

"Tight," Shah said then ended the call. Shah sat the phone down on the dresser and walked into the living room. A cold breeze ran over his body giving him chills.

"Damn it's cold as a bitch in here," he said to his self as he walked over to the window to make sure they were shut. Shah noticed all the windows were shut, but it was still a cold breeze creeping through the window seal.

"Damn it feel like winter!" Shah thought to his self as he walked away from the window and went back to the room. He picked up his phone and looked at the time.

"Damn it's only 7am," Shah said then grabbed a pair of jeans and put them on then he opened his closet door and grabbed his wheat timberland boots and put them on. Shah picked up the jeans he had on yesterday from the floor and emptied the pockets on the bed. He looked down and noticed his plane ticket on the floor.

"Fuck I didn't even check my boarding time," he said as he quickly picked his ticket up to check and see what time he leaves.

"Ok, Ok I'm good," he said after he noticed his flight don't leave until 4pm. Shah sat his plane ticket down and grabbed his hoodie and put it on. He grabbed all four phones from the dresser and left the room. He walked out of the apartment and locked the doors and rushed to the basement and grabbed an ounce from the stash spot and went back upstairs.

"God damn!" Shah said as he opened the door and the wind smacked him in the face feeling like a thousand needles piercing his skin. Shah instantly took off running to his car. There was only one thing Shah hated and that was the cold. It wasn't winter yet, but it sure as hell felt like it. Shah jumped into his car and started it and turned the heat on full blast, but he was met with nothing but cold air. He turned the heat off just as fast as he turned it on then pulled out the lot.

Meanwhile

Lil Jerry and Cory were chilling at Cory's crib on Mansion Hill. Cory's grandfather set up a trust fund for him when he was born so when he turned 21 last year, he was given five hundred thousand dollars. Cory and Lil Jerry quickly jumped in the game and started flooding Madison with kush straight from California. Within no time they had Madison locked down on the weed tip and nine times out of ten everybody who smoked weed got it from them.

Cory was known to be soft, so he was robbed on multiple occasions. Lil Jerry quickly gained a reputation that he was one not to be fucked with and if you fucked with Cory then you had to answer to him. Over time every jack boy in the city started to give Cory a pass off the strength of Lil Jerry.

Lil Jerry was sitting on a recliner in the living room across from Cory smoking a backwood as he flipped through Facebook. He strolled past a news article someone on his timeline shared. He double backed and read the headline.

"Two men found murdered," he quickly clicked on the article and started to read it.

"At approximately 3:20am Madison police responded to multiple reports of shots fired on Madison's westside. Officers discovered two unknown males shot multiple times. The department is not releasing many details at this moment but urge anyone who might have information regarding this incident to please come forward. There are no known suspects at this time and the department believes this to be an isolated incident and ensures the public is not in danger. If anyone has information regarding this, please call 1-800-251-1881."

"Damn two niggas got they ass bodied on the west!" Lil Jerry said as he sat up in his recliner.

"Yeah? What they say happened?" Cory asked.

"They ain't really say. They just said they found two niggas on the west," Lil Jerry said as he stood up.

"Look we need to slide back on that bitch Brittany I know she know where that nigga at. She tried to act like she ain't know the nigga was finna get down on you," Lil Jerry said.

"On Bd that bitch knew that shit. I wanted to kill that bitch," Cory said.

Lil Jerry looked over with a side eye cause he knew damn well Cory wasn't gone do shit that's why he pulled up on him. Lil Jerry laughed off Cory's comment and switched subjects because he knew Cory was a bitch and hated when Cory tried to act like he was with the shits.

"When that batch gone touchdown?" Lil Jerry asked Cory who was sitting there looking stupid cause he caught on to what Lil Jerry was on.

"That shit should touch down tonight," Cory said.

"Good cause I ain't got shit left but a half a pound and I know I'ma run through this shit tonight," Lil Jerry said.

"If you run through it before that shit touch I still got two pounds," Cory said.

"Tight say no more I'm finna slide to the block. Hit my line when you come outside," Lil Jerry said.

"Tight!" Cory quickly said as Lil Jerry walked toward the door.

Meanwhile

Shah slowly started to reduce his speed as he exited the beltline on to Midvale rd. He hit his left turning signal as he approached the intersection and made a left on Midvale. His phone started to ring and rattled the change it was sitting on top of in his cup holder. Shah turned down his radio and answered the phone. "I'm bout to pull up I'm down the street," Shah said as he answered the phone.

"Naw don't pull over here bro it's hot. Just meet me on Loreen," Leroy said.

"How long til you there cause I'm damn near on Raymond right now," Shah asked.

"Give me five minutes," Leroy replied.

"Tight bet!" Shah said and ended the call. He tossed his phone back in the cup holder as he hit his right turning signal and made a right onto Raymond Rd. Shah made a quick left into the speedway gas station, he hated when somebody switched the meeting place at the last minute, it made him nervous. Shah pulled to the very last pump and parked, he picked his phone up and called Leroy back.

"What up?" Leroy asked as he answered the phone.

"Just pull to speedway," Shah said.

"Tight shidd I'ma be there in two minutes," Leroy said.

"Tight!" Shah said then ended the call. He opened his car door and despite the sun being out and shinning down on him he was quickly reminded of how cold it was when the breeze blew past him. Shah pulled his hoodie over his head and ran into the store. He looked up and saw Tia standing behind the cash register. He hadn't seen Tia since she moved out of his mother building last year. Shah had been wanting to fuck Tia since the moment he first laid eyes on her. No matter how many times he tried she wouldn't give him no play cause he was too young.

"Damn Tia!" Shah said as he walked up to the cash register.

"How you been Shah?" Tia asked as she laughed a little.

"Oh, I'm livin, how you been? I see you getting sexier and sexier as each year pass by," Shah said.

Tia started laughing "Thank you! I see you never give up," Tia said in a seductive tone teasing Shah. Shah leaned in closer to Tia as the door opened and more customers walked in. "I'm grown now!" Shah whispered.

Tia started laughing but quickly realized she had more customers.

"How can I help you?" Tia asked Shah as she gave him a look letting him know this wasn't a good time.

"Oh yeah! let me get thirty on pump ten and a box of cigarellos," Shah said as he reached into his pocket and pulled out a fifty-dollar bill and handed it to her. Tia quickly rung up Shah's order and handed him a box of cigarellos and his change.

"Have a nice day!" Shah said as he gave Tia a look letting her know he wanted her bad.

"You too," Tia said as she laughed a little. She thought Shah was handsome, she just wasn't sure if he was old enough. Shah looked out the store window and saw Leroy park at the pump next to his car. He hurried out the store and walked over to Leroy's car and got in.

"Man, it's hot as fuck over here!" Leroy said as Shah closed the door. Shah reached into his hoodie pocket and pulled out the ounce and handed it to Leroy.

"What happened over there?" Shah asked as he looked around outside of the car to make sure everything was good around him. Leroy looked at the ounce and sat it in the cup holder. He reached into his pocket and pulled out a roll of cash and handed it to Shah.

"Man, they say two niggas got killed on Thurston early this morning. I don't know if you knew Rasheed and Khalil, but they saying it was them!" Leroy said.

Shah looked over at Leroy shocked "You bull shittin?" Shah asked tryna get more information out of him. "Who told you that?" Shah asked as he counted the money Leroy just gave him.

"My bitch cool with one of them niggas bitch and shorty called this morning and told her," Leroy said.

"Damn that's fucked up!" Shah said nonchalantly.

"Let me get up out of here I got a few of my people waiting on me," Leroy said.

"Iight bro be careful" Shah said as he opened the door and jumped out of the car. He quickly walked over to his car and started pumping his gas, Shah jumped in his car and started breaking down a blunt while he waited on the gas to finish pumping. He was too cold to break the weed down, so he just lined the inside of the blunt with buds and licked it closed. Shah heard the pump handle click letting him know the gas was done pumping, he jumped out and snatched the pump from the tank and twisted the tank cap back on then jumped back into the car. Shah turned the heat on full blast then flamed his blunt up and pulled out of the gas station.

Meanwhile

Tammy stood over the stove making herself some waffles and eggs for breakfast. She poured her eggs into the frying pan and started cooking them. She paused for a second when she heard her phone ringing. She quickly ran to her bedroom and grabbed her phone and rushed back to the kitchen. Tammy answered the phone and put it on speaker then sat it on the counter.

"Hello" Tammy said as she answered.

"How you doing over there?" Shah asked.

"Oh, I'm doing fine. I'm just making me some breakfast right now. How you doing?" Tammy asked.

"I'm good but I would be a lot better if you made me some breakfast too!" Shah said.

"I'll make enough for you if you really want some," Tammy said.

"Ok good cause I do want some. I'm right around the corner I'm finna pull up. Where Audrey at? I just tried calling her she ain't answer," Shah said.

"Boy you know Audrey don't answer that phone while she in class!" Tammy quickly said.

"Damn it is Friday, I thought today was Saturday," Shah said.

"Yeah well slow down cause you a day ahead of the rest of us," Tammy said.

"I was born a day ahead of the world!" Shah said being funny.

"Boy stop! I know you better not make me cook this food and you don't come eat it," Tammy said.

"You think I'm playing. I told you I'm right around the corner I'm at the light by Walgreen's right now I'm finna pull up in like two minutes," Shah said.

"Ok I'll see you when you get here," Tammy said.

"Iight!" Shah quickly said

Tammy pressed the end button on her phone and pulled out some more eggs and bacon. She knew Shah loved turkey bacon, so she quickly put a few pieces on a cookie tray and put them in the oven. A few minutes later the doorbell started to ring, Tammy walked over to the door and unlocked it then buzzed Shah into the building.

Shah walked into the apartment and the aroma of Turkey bacon lingered in the air.

"Damn that bacon smell good!" Shah said as he walked to the kitchen.

He was caught completely off guard when he saw Tammy standing at the stove wearing a black blouse and a pair of black shorts so small, he could see the bottom of her ass cheeks out. Her hair was pinned up in a messy bun, Shah stood there staring at Tammy's ass cheeks as his dick grew harder and harder.

"Why you outside so early?" Tammy asked as she bent over and pulled the bacon from the oven.

"I had some shit I had to take care of," Shah said as he turned away and walked over to the table and sat down.

"So, it is true huh?" Tammy asked.

"What's that?" Shah quickly asked.

"Audrey told me you started hustling, but I thought she was just messing around," Tammy said.

"Naw, it's true I been fucking around for damn near two months," Shah said.

"If you don't mind me asking you. Is this a permanent thing or something you doing until you find another job?" Tammy asked as she walked to the table and handed Shah his plate.

"To be real wit you Tammy this shit might be long term until I get enough money to start my own business," Shah said.

"You grown and I know I can't tell you what to do so just be careful," Tammy said as she looked at Shah with a look of disappointment.

"Oh, I will!" Shah answered with a mouth full of food.

"You know the plate not going to run away from you Shah!" Tammy said as she watched him stuff his mouth full of more food.

"You already know ever since we was kids I loved your cooking," Shah said.

"Yeah I know! I remember that one time I came over and cooked for y'all yo momma fucked that food up! She tried to get me over there to cook every day after that," Tammy said as she laughed. Shah started laughing as he took another bite.

"Hell yeah! I remember that shit too. She used to try to get me to trick you over to the crib so you could cook for her," Shah said.

"Marie ass crazy. How she doing? I haven't seen her in a long time," Tammy asked.

"Not to good!" Shah sadly said.

"Why you say that?" Tammy asked.

"Cause last time I went over there she looked strung out. She lost a lot of weight and that bitch ass nigga James over there like he a king or some shit," Shah said.

"Damn that's sad! Marie used to be on top of her shit before James. Do Shawn know she back wit him?" Tammy asked.

"Naw I can't tell bro that shit. I don't want to add stress on top of the shit he already got to worry about," Shah said.

"Yeah that's probably a good idea," Tammy said.

"She grown I can't control her life I just gotta let her live it," Shah said then got up and put his plate in the sink then opened the fridge and pulled out the orange juice.

"You want some of this juice?" Shah asked.

"Yeah!" Tammy said.

Shah went into the cabinet and grabbed two cups and filled them both with juice then walked back to the table and gave her one. He walked into the living room and sat down on the couch.

"What up wit buddy you fucking wit?" Shah asked.

"What you mean by that?" Tammy asked.

"I mean what's to him? What he be on in Milwaukee?" Shah said.

"He doing the same shit you do. He doing pretty good down there, well at least that's the way he make it look," Tammy said as she got up from the table and walked into the living room and sat on the couch next to Shah.

Shah tried his hardest not to look at Tammy in those shorts she was wearing but he couldn't help his self. Shah started eyeing Tammy's thigh out the corner of his eye. Tammy looked over at him and caught him staring at her thighs. Her body temperature started to rise as she became aroused at the thought of Shah being interested in her. The stories she once heard from Audrey about how big his dick was now at the front of her thoughts; she could feel her pussy getting wet as she sat there thinking. Shah waved his hands in front of her face bringing her back to reality.

"You straight? You ain't hear shit I just said huh?" Shah asked.

"I'm sorry I zoned out thinking about some shit I forgot to do at work. What you say?" Tammy asked as she looked over at him.

"I asked was you off today?" Shah said as he laughed a little.

"Yeah I'm off today and tomorrow," Tammy said as she got up from the couch and walked to the kitchen and grabbed her phone. She walked back into the living room and sat back down on the couch next to Shah.

Shah had been knowing Tammy since they were eight years old and for the first time, he could sense a vibe from her that he'd never felt before. Tammy sat with one leg on the couch and the other on the floor, Shah felt tempted to look in between her legs being that she had them spread open. He looked then quickly looked away, but her pussy print was so fat he couldn't not look again. Shah looked again but this time he stared at it when he looked Tammy was looking him directly in his eyes, he knew she caught him.

"My bad! I couldn't help it, that mafucka fat I damn near wanted to touch it!" Shah said jokingly just to see what she would say.

Tammy started laughing but didn't say anything or she didn't close her legs so he couldn't look. Shah finally realized that what Shawn said to him was true, Tammy was just as into him as he was into her. The more thoughts that raced through his mind, the more he couldn't fight back the urge. They sat there for a few minutes in an awkward silence before Shah reached over and ran his hand along her thigh.

"Damn your skin soft as hell!" Shah said in a real low tone. The touch of Shah's hand caught her off guard but sent a tingly sensation through her body. Shah looked up at Tammy when she didn't respond, and her facial expression showed him that she wanted him. Shah leaned a little closer and started rubbing her pussy through her shorts, Tammy quickly looked over at Shah as she bit her bottom lip. Shah leaned closer and started kissing her, they kissed for a moment before Tammy broke away from their kiss.

"We shouldn't be doing this!" Tammy said, but for Shah there was no turning back he wanted her and couldn't help but go after what he wanted. He pulled her leg from under her ass and spread them both apart, he got up from the couched and kneeled down between her legs and started kissing her thighs.

Tammy was fighting within her self as to why this was a bad idea but if it was such a bad idea why it feel so good. He gripped her thighs as he kissed and licked closer and closer to her pussy. Shah reached for the waist band on her shorts, in her mind she kept telling her self to stop him but her body wouldn't let her. Tammy lifted up a little allowing Shah to pull them off. Shah pulled her hips closer to the edge of the couch and started playing with her clit with one hand while he finger fucked her with the other one. Shah's dick grew harder and harder the more Tammy's pussy became wet. He instantly started sucking on her clit while he finger fucked her. Tammy moaned heavily as she laid back in ecstasy enjoying every second. After a few minutes Tammy came to a climax as Shah continued to suck on her clit, her body began to shake uncontrollably as another orgasm overcame her.

"Shah!" Tammy yelled out as she pushed Shah's head away from her pussy! Shah stood up and unbuckled his belt and pulled his pants down. Tammy looked up and saw Shah standing there naked.

"Shah, I don't think we should fuck this is so wrong!" Tammy said as she stood up and grabbed her shorts from the floor.

"Audrey will kill us if she found out about this, this gotta stay between us Shah!" Tammy said as she panicked and ran to the bathroom.

"Damn!" Shah said as he stood there looking crazy with his dick in his hand. He thought he was about to get the pussy. He was a little embarrassed so he pulled up his pants and left the apartment before Tammy could come out the bathroom.

(O'Hare Airport Later That Evening)

Shah put his wallet, phone, belt, and keys into a bin then kicked off his shoes and put them in a bin as well. The man in front of him pushed his bin through the x-ray machine then walked through the metal detector. Shah pushed his bin through the x-ray machine then walked through the metal detector. This was about to be his first flight, so he didn't know what to expect or what to do. He grabbed his bin from the other side of the x-ray machine and put his stuff back in his pockets and put his shoes and belt back on.

Shah had thirty minutes before his flight was scheduled to depart. He got on the escalator and looked at his plane ticket.

"Terminal thirty," he said to his self as he made it to the top of the escalator and got off. He stood there for a moment trying to figure out where the hell he should go.

"Excuse me, I don't mean to bother you but this my first time in an airport. Can you point me in the direction of terminal thirty?" Shah asked a random guy.

"Yeah I can help you. If you go that way, you'll find terminal thirty. Those signs up there are the number to which terminal it is keep going till you reach thirty," the guy said.

"Ok, thanks" Shah said

"No problem" the guy said as he walked off.

Shah headed in the direction he was sent until he found terminal thirty. He took a seat in the waiting area and pulled his phone from his pocket to text Audrey. "I know you sleep right now but I just wanted to text and let you know I love you," Shah sent the text then quickly started texting Keisha.

"How's your day going beautiful?"

Before Shah could press send his phone chimed with a text from Audrey. Shah quickly pressed send on the text to Keisha then opened the message from Audrey.

"I love you too baby. I'm off tomorrow and I wanna see you!" Audrey replied.

"I been trying to get in touch wit you to let you know I'm on my way to Texas. I'll be back in town Sunday," Shah replied.

His phone chimed with another text but from Keisha, Shah quickly opened the message.

"I'm doing fine! How's the trip going?" Keisha replied.

"It's good. But I can't wait to get back so I can hang out wit you!" Shah replied then his phone chimed with a text from Audrey.

"I'm sorry baby this schedule I'm on leaves me with no time. I want to see you when you get back cause I miss you," Audrey replied.

His phone chimed again with a text from Keisha.

"I already know you be busy. I'ma make sure I come see you as soon as I get back because I miss you too!" Shah replied to Audrey then clicked over to read Keisha's text.

"I enjoyed hanging out with you and I look forward to seeing you, so call me when you get back in town," Keisha replied.

Just as Shah got done reading Keisha's message his phone chimed with another message from Audrey.

"It'll be the first thing I do as soon as I get into town. You enjoy the rest of your day beautiful," Shah replied to Keisha.

"Now boarding terminal thirty" the woman over the intercom announced. Shah stood up and made his way to board the flight. Shah checked his ticket with the flight attendant and walked through the terminal and boarded his flight.

Shah walked through the aisle and found his seat. It was between two older white women. The woman in the aisle seat stood up and let Shah into his seat then she sat back down.

"At this time, we ask that you buckle your seat belts and put all cellular devices on airplane mode as we prepare to take off. We thank you for choosing North Western Airlines and hope you enjoy your flight," the flight attendant announced.

Shah quickly buckled his seat belt and put his phone on airplane mode. He looked around and watched as everyone buckled their seat belts. His heart started to beat fast as the plane began to move. He was nervous, so he closed his eyes.

"God please don't let this plane crash while I'm on it," he whispered to his self as the plane started to pick up speed. The plane started to shake a little as it began to take flight. Shah grabbed both arm rest and held them tightly as the plane started to ascend. Shah kept his eyes closed until the plane was smooth sailing.

"Fuck this shit I'm finna go to sleep!" he said as he reclined his seat back what little space he did have and closed his eyes until he fell asleep. Two hours into the flight the plane hit an air pocket and descended a little. Shah woke up in a panic.

"Oh shit!" Shah screamed as he grabbed a hold of the arm rest. His sudden outburst startled the two women he was sitting in between. Shah looked around and noticed he was the only one in a panic.

"It's Ok young man," the woman sitting by the window said quickly ensuring Shah that everything was ok.

"It's just an air pocket," the second woman added.

Shah was sweating profusely as he wiped his face and tried to catch his breath.

"I thought we was going down. I didn't mean to scare y'all this my first flight," Shah said.

Both women started laughing then informed him that they understood. They each took turns telling stories of their first flight. After while, Shah looked up and noticed they was already landing. As they pulled up to the terminal, Shah thanked both women for their help and let them know he enjoyed their stories. Shah exited the plane and walked through the terminal, once in the airport Shah became a little nervous as he looked around the almost empty airport. He walked to the escalator and made his way down to the lower level. He had no idea who he hell he was looking for, so he made his way outside the airport.

He stood there looking around when a black Jeep Cherokee pulled in front of him and the back window rolled down.

"Hey, Migo, get in!" a young Mexican dude said from the back seat. Shah slowly walked up to the Jeep and got in, nobody said a word as they pulled off. Shah had no idea what to say cause he was so uncomfortable. Twenty minutes into the ride they pulled over in front of a small house that looked like a shed, the guy sitting next to Shah in the back seat handed him some car keys.

"That's your ride!" he said as he pointed at a black Dodge RAM pickup truck.

Shah grabbed ahold of the keys and jumped out of the Jeep. He looked around the neighborhood nervous as he walked to the pickup truck and got in. Shah started the truck, then pulled his phone and his instructions from his pocket.

"2360 Sanders road Conway Arkansas," Shah said out loud as he types the address into his GPS then pulled off.

(Meanwhile)

Quantay sat on his living room sofa barely able to keep his eyes open as he tried to watch Tv. Quantay wasn't sure if he was tripping off the pain killers or if his girl was really talking to someone at the front door.

"Who dat?" Quantay yelled out to her.

"It's Hot Boi's ass!" Nicole said as she walked into the living room. Hot Boi walked in behind her and sat on the couch next to Quantay and started laughing.

"Ain't shit funny Hot Boi you let my baby get shot!" Nicole said giving Hot Boi a look that could kill.

"Man, I ain't have nothing to do wit him getting shot I just drove him to the hospital. Cuz let her know," Hot Boi quickly said. He knew Nicole was Quantay's ride or die. She was down to do the shooting and driving if need be.

"He ain't have nothing to do wit it. I told him to call you and have you come pick me up from the hospital," Quantay said getting Nicole off Hot Boi's heels.

"Alright cause I was finna fuck you up Hot Boi, you know I don't play about my man," Nicole said Hot Boi started laughing

"Shit I see you was ready to kill me like I was the nigga that shot him," Hot Boi said.

"Hell yeah!" Nicole said and started laughing.

Hot Boi laughed a little but he knew she was serious, so he quickly made a mental note of that. Nicole got up and left out the living room.

"Good lookin on that!" Hot Boi said.

"Man, that's just Nicole being Nicole, you know how she is," Quantay said.

"I ain't talking about Nicole. I'm talking bout goofy nem," Hot Boi said.

"Cuz we share the same blood I would take a bullet for you!" Quantay said then started laughing "Shit look at me I did that already!" he quickly added.

Hot Boi sat there staring at the floor then he looked up at Quantay as Quantay struggled to keep his eyes open. Hot Boi tapped him on his leg.

"Cuz wake up!" Hot Boi said.

"Shit I am woke, them pills got me feeling like I'm off the drank!" Quantay said.

"Let me ask you something on some serious shit," Hot Boi said.

"Tight what up?" Quantay said

"You got some cash put up?" Hot Boi asked.

Quantay opened his eyes and looked over at Hot Boi then sat up straight as he fixed his arm in his sling.

"Between me and you right now I'm fucked up cuz. I can't seem to get over the hump. It seem like when I get some good coke and run through it I can't get no more when it's time to re-up. I always end up getting some bull shit and end up sitting on the shit for too long. When I finally get it off I gotta pay rent and shit, sometimes I feel like I'm doing this shit for nothing," Quantay said seriously.

Hot Boi could see the frustration in his face.

"Check it out cuz, I can get some good coke for you. It's always top of the line, I'ma slide back to Madison in the morning and holla at my mans. I'ma grab a brick from him for thirty bands and I'ma front it to you, just pay me the thirty I paid for it when you make it. After that I'll take your extras and re-up for you that way you always got some good coke online.

I'ma give you thirty bands too that way you got some cash already and you can sit back and stack," Hot Boi said.

"On the mighty that's good looking cuz," Quantay quickly said.

"Don't trip, we blood remember! You know how to whip?" Hot Boi asked.

"Hell, naw'll I been getting that shit on the hard side" Quantay said.

"Man!!! Look cuz I'ma show you how to straight drop this shit. I'ma monster in that kitchen watch how the feens flock to you like flies on shit," Hot Boi said.

"I need to learn that! You don't know how hungry I am. On my daughter, as long as I got a steady connect it ain't no looking back," Quantay said.

Hot Boi looked over at Quantay he could hear it in his voice that he was ready to take off.

"The coke gone be there as long as you stay focused. Take some of that cash I'm finna give you and pay the rent for a whole year, that way you ain't gotta worry about it. Then all you gotta do is sit back and stack that cash up cause as sure as shit stank once this coke hit the streets it's gone be rolling in," Hot Boi said.

Quantay sat there nodding his head because he knew if Hot Boi was true to his word shit was about to get real.

"Yeah that's the plan! Quantay said Hot Boi stood up and shook Quantay's hand. "Look cuz I got a date wit chunky butt over on Prairie. I'm finna go fuck the shit out of her I'ma pull up on you with that tomorrow so we can get to business," Hot Boi said.

Quantay started laughing then followed Hot Boi to the door. "Tight cuz," Hot Boi said as he opened the door and walked out.

"Love!" Quantay said and closed the door. He stumbled up the stairs and went into the bedroom with Nicole.

Meanwhile

In her pitch-black room Alexis laid in her bed in the fetal position with one pillow between her legs and another one under her head. Tears flowed down her face as she thought about Rasheed. She couldn't believe he was gone. It seemed like just minutes ago she was in his arms laughing and smiling. Now he's laying in the county morg in a freezer box. Alexis rocked back and forth thinking about their last conversation. Her stomach started to cringe as she replayed the images of Rasheed laid over on the steering wheel with glass and blood everywhere. Alexis quickly jumped up and grabbed the trash can that was next to her bed and started throwing up.

Alexis sat the trash can back down, then reached over to her nightstand and grabbed the bottle of Hennessey and took a big gulp from it then sat it back down. She sat up at the head of the bed with her knees to her chest as she rocked side to side. The light from her phone lit the room up as it started to ring. She was in no mood to talk to no one, so she let it ring until it stopped. Alexis continued to cry as she rocked side to side trying her hardest to think of who would want to kill Rasheed.

The doorbell started to ring and startled Alexis. She jumped and ran over to the closet and grabbed the glock 19 that Rasheed had given her. She wondered if Rasheed and Khalil's killer was now there to get her. Alexis slowly opened her room door and crept through the hall and to the living room window. She put her back against the wall and pulled the curtain back enough so she could peek out the window. The doorbell rang again so she rushed to the door and looked out the peep hole to see if anyone was in the hall. Alexis peeked out the window again and noticed Brittany walking back to her car, so she opened the window.

"Brittany? Girl you scared the hell out of me," Alexis yelled out.

Brittany turned around and walked back to the building.

"Buzz me in girl I really need to talk to you," Brittany said.

Alexis figured Brittany had to have been hurting as bad as she was because Khalil was the love of her life. Even though they wasn't the best of friends, Alexis often seen Brittany posting pictures of Khalil on

Facebook and Snap Chat. Alexis walked over to the door and buzzed Brittany into the building. She unlocked the door and opened it when she heard Brittany get close to the door.

Brittany walked in and stood by the door. The apartment was pitch black after she closed the door. The kitchen light came on and Alexis stood there holding her gun at her side with her hair all over the place and tear tracks on her face. Brittany could see that the Alexis standing in front of her right now looked nothing like the Alexis she always saw, happy and well maintained.

"Girl put the gun down!" Brittany said.

Alexis looked down at the gun in her hand and started laughing as she looked back up at Brittany.

"I told you, you scared the hell out of me girl. I was ready to shoot if I had to," Alexis said as she set the gun down on the table and walked into the living room and turned on the light.

"You can sit down," Alexis said as she pointed to one of the couches. Brittany walked over to the couch and sat down.

"I was about to ask you how you doing, but I can see this shit killing you just as much as it's killing me. I'm sorry for just showing up, I tried calling but when you didn't answer I got worried and just wanted to check on you," Brittany said as Alexis sat there, wiping tears from her face.

"It's Ok, I haven't answered the phone because it's been ringing all day with people trying to ask me if I'm ok. I know their intentions is to just be nosey, it's been so much fake love sent my way today it's driving me crazy girl. I know you loved Khalil! How you holding up?" Alexis asked.

"When I got the news this morning that Khalil was killed, I almost died myself. I haven't been able to eat or do shit all day. I put his shirt on and laid on the couch and cried for hours. The more I thought about him not being here the more my sadness turned into anger now all I want is revenge," Brittany said.

"Revenge on who? No one knows who killed them," Alexis said cutting Brittany off.

Brittany sat there for a moment not sure if she should share what she knew with Alexis. Brittany didn't want Alexis to get mad and think it was Khalil's fault that Rasheed got killed.

"You must know something I don't know. If you do please tell me Brittany," Alexis asked.

"I'm not one hundred percent sure who did it, but I have a good idea of who might have wanted to do it," Brittany said.

Alexis sat there quite as her heart dropped into her stomach.

"Who?" Alexis asked as she looked Brittany directly into her eyes.

"I think it was Cory and Lil Jerry. Yesterday Khalil robbed Cory, then around 6:30 Cory and Lil Jerry came to my house asking me where Khalil was at. I'm pretty sure Lil Jerry did it because he had a gun on him. I called Khalil and told him they came by looking for him, he said he was going to handle it," Brittany started crying. "That was the last time I talked to my baby!" Brittany said as she put her hands over her face and her head into her lap. Alexis sat their thinking as she soaked up the information Brittany just gave her. She planned to use this information to her advantage.

Meanwhile

Hot Boi sat in the middle of Jamie's bed with his legs open as Jamie laid on her stomach in between his legs giving him head while he smoked a blunt. He reached down with one hand and grabbed Jamie by her hair and pushed her head down further onto his dick. She wasn't even halfway down and she started choking and gagging.

He didn't want to fuck up the mood but the fact that she couldn't suck dick the way he liked his dick sucked was frustrating him.

"Iight that's good!" Hot Boi said as he pulled his dick from Jamie's mouth and got out the bed.

amie rolled over on her back in anticipation of Hot Boi eating her pussy. Her hopes was quickly shot down when Hot Boi got in between her legs unwrapping a condom. Hot Boi put the condom on and reached down to play with her pussy he was shocked to find that her shit was already dripping wet. He grabbed both legs and put them on his shoulders then slowly slid into her pussy. Jamie instantly started backing up further into the bed but Hot Boi pinned her against the headboard, so she had nowhere to run and dug deep into her pussy.

"Fuck!" Jamie screamed as she turned her head to the side and bit down on her bottom lip. Hot Boi wasted no time pounding her pussy and Jamie's screams grew louder and louder with each thrust.

After a few minutes Hot Boi let go of her hands and slowed his pace down. Jamie laid there enjoying every stroke as she grabbed ahold of the sheets.

"Don't stop! Don't stop Hot Boi! I'm cumming!" She screamed out. Hot Boi continued to slow stroke her in the same position for twenty minutes straight.

"Ok ok let me get on top!" Jamie said

Instead of stopping Hot Boi started to pound her harder and harder he wanted to leave his imprint just in case he decided not to come back. Jamie started running trying her hardest to get away until her whole upper body was

hanging from the bed.

Hot Boi let go of her legs and stared laughing.

"Tight now you can get on top!" Hot Boi said as Jamie got up and got back into the bed.

"Oh my god!" Jamie said as she pulled her hair up into a ponytail. Hot Boi laid there as Jamie got on top of him reverse cowgirl and started riding him. He watched as her ass cheeks bounced up and down as she rode him.

Jamie leaned her upper body forward putting her forearms on his legs and started bouncing her ass harder on top of his dick.

"Yeah throw that ass like that!" Hot Boi said as he grabbed both ass cheeks helping her bounce it harder.

"Oh, shit baby I'm cumming!" Jamie yelled out and stopped bouncing her ass and laid there shaking.

"Oh, shit I can't stop shaking!" Jamie said

Hot Boi could feel every time her muscle tightened up cause her pussy grabbed a hold of his dick tighter every time it did. Jamie started to slowly rock back and forth on his dick. Hot Boi didn't like her head but he was loving her pussy.

"Damn I'm bout to ---" Hot Boi's body stiffened up before he could finish his sentence. Jamie started grinding harder while Hot Boi gripped both ass cheeks. "Fuck!" Hot Boi said out loud then smacked one of Jamie's ass cheeks.

Meanwhile

"Your destination is on your left," the GPS said. Shah looked up at the Candlewood Suits Conway sign and turned into the parking lot. He was happy he finally made it, it was 7:15am and he'd been driving for ten hours. He pulled his instructions from his pocket.

"There's a reservation in your name. Check in and rest for a while, you'll need to be back on the road by 12pm," Shah read out loud. He put the instructions back in his pocket and got out of the pickup truck and walked to the lobby of the hotel. Shah walked up to the front desk where an old white lady stood.

"How can I help you sweetie?" the woman asked with a real strong southern accent.

"Reservation for Shah Lumas?" he asked as he pulled his wallet from his pocket.

"Shah Lumas!" the woman said out loud as she typed his name into the computer.

"Yes, there is a reservation for Shah Lumas. May I see your I.D," she asked.

Shah pulled his I.D from his wallet and handed it to her. The woman looked at the I.D and handed it back to him. She quickly made two key cards and handed them to him.

"Room 122, Thanks for choosing Candle Woods," the woman said.

"Thank you," Shah said then walked away. He walked through the hall until he found his room. He quickly unlocked the door and walked into his room, happy that he was finally able to rest. Shah set his alarm for 10:30am then quickly laid down.

Chapter Eight

H ot Boi woke up and got an early start to his day. He drove back up to Madison and made a quick stop at his crib. He grabbed the cash he owed Big T for the truck, the cash for Quantay, and the cash for the coke. As Hot Boi drove down Evan Acres road he wondered where the hell Shah was. He had called his personal phone and both trap phones a few times but got no answer.

Hot Boi made a right onto Millpond road and drove to the Magnuson Grand Hotel and pulled into the parking lot. He pulled next to Big T's minivan and parked. He jumped out of his truck and looked around for a second before he walked up to Big T's minivan and got into the back with Big T. Hot Boi loved seeing Sofia and Salina, and he knew Big T rarely went anywhere without at least one of them with him.

"What up ladies?" Hot Boi asked Salina and Sofia as he shook Big T's hand.

"Hello papi," Sofia and Salina both said.

"How you been?" Big T asked.

"Man, I'm well! how bout you?" Hot Boi asked.

"You know me I'm livin lil bro!" Big T said and smiled.

"That's always good bro! Aye did Shah ever get up wit you?" Hot Boi asked.

"Yeah he got up wit me twice since you left. He been doing his thang lil bro no bullshit," Big T said.

"Yeah that's what's up he do go crazy that shit shocked me too," Hot Boi said.

"As a matter of a fact, here go this $45,000. $15,000 for the truck and $30,000 for that book I need. I'm tryna open up shop down in Beloit," Hot Boi quickly said as he handed Big T the cash.

"Ain't nothing wrong wit that just be careful down there lil bro!" Big T said as he handed Hot Boi the coke. Hot Boi quickly grabbed the brick and stuffed it in the front of his pants and pulled his shirt over it.

"Yeah bro I'ma be careful. I ain't finna work it I'ma let my people handle that. But let me get up out of here so I can get that shit rolling down there," Hot Boi said.

"Tight lil bro drive safe" Big T said as he shook Hot Boi's hand.

"I will bro," Hot Boi said and jumped out the van. But before he closed the door, he put his head into the van.

"Salina and Sofia I'ma need y'all to show me a good time again when the time is right," he said looking at Sofia. Salina started laughing and looked at Sofia as she smiled. "Sure, anytime Papi!" Sofia said and winked at him.

"We gone make it happen again lil bro!" Big T said and laughed cause he knew Hot Boi was serious.

"Tight, Y'all be smooth," Hot Boi said and closed the door. He jumped back into his truck and trailed Big T's minivan out of the parking lot.

Meanwhile

Tay G and X sat on the couch in their honeycomb hide out on 77th and Bender playing Maden on Xbox One. Tay G jumped up off the couch and ran over to the front door laughing.

"Snatched it out of his mouth! Nigga you can't fuck wit me, pay me my money!" he yelled out to X as he laughed. X tossed his controller on the coffee table and reached into his pocket and pulled out a roll of hundreds and tossed one on the table.

"Nigga you got that bet it back!" X said as he put his money into his pocket. Tay G stood there laughing. "Naw I'm good. I'ma let you cool off for a while," Tay G said.

X looked over his shoulder at Tay G with a look that could kill. "So yo weak ass tryna quit wit my cheese?" he asked.

"Trying? Nigga I ain't trying I quit!" Tay G said and started laughing. He knew he was pissing X off plus he wanted to get him back for quitting on him last week. X sat there pissed cause he knew exactly what Tay G was on.

"Broke ass nigga won a hunnit dollars and quit," X said to his self but loud enough for Tay G to hear him. He got off the couch and started walking to the kitchen but stopped when he heard somebody knock on the door.

"It's on me" X said as Tay G opened the door.

"What up Wayne?" Tay G said as he let him into the apartment and closed the door. Wayne was the building Manager and a good spender he would stop by on occasions and grab some work. Tay G and X would take turns catching the action when he came through.

"Man can I get a wake up until this money come through?" Wayne asked.

Tay G stepped back and started laughing "Yeah this one on you!" he said. X started laughing cause he knew he was going to have to bite the bullet.

"Tight I got you," X said and reached into his pocket and pulled out a plastic bag full of rocks and handed him two dubs. "You know I'll be back later," Wayne said and quickly turned to the door. X unlocked the door and opened it for Wayne as Wayne stepped into the hall Kendall was walking up to the door.

Kendall, Tay G, and X all grew up together and was very close friends until Kendall started getting money with some of his cousins off Dime Bag. Kendall would only come around when X and Tay G were ready to re-up so he could over tax them on the coke they were buying.

He knew they ain't have nobody else to get quality coke from so this was his way to handle them rough and stunt on them.

"What's hannin, everything good?" he asked as he walked up to the door and looked at X wit a big ass smile on his face making sure X could see that his mouth was full of gold.

"What's hannin?" X said as he let him into the apartment and closed the door.

"Let me see dat lil money real quick," Kendall quickly threw out there. X looked over at Tay G instantly letting him know he wasn't feeling the way Kendall just came at them.

"Let's go in the kitchen," X said and turned and walked to the kitchen.

"Iight," Kendall said. Tay G and Kendall followed X into the kitchen, X opened the freezer and grabbed a waffle box and pulled it out. He opened it and pulled out a roll of hundreds and put the box back into the freezer.

"Damn you niggas can't afford a safe," Kendall said and started laughing as X handed him the cash. "If niggas come snatch this light as cheese from you niggas, you niggas gone really be fucked up. Don't trip doe I got a line and a trapper for you niggas," Kendall said.

He finished counting the rest of the bread and pulled a half of brick from his waistline and tossed it on the kitchen table. The whole time X stood there pissed thinking to his self "Its like this nigga done went and threw on his freshest shit and emptied out the jewelry box just to flex on us. He got that!"

"What you niggas finna do?" Kendall asked.

"Shit we gotta get in this pot!" Tay G said as he grabbed the half of book off the table.

"You niggas wanna blow some of this gas? It's free" Kendall said then laughed.

"Naw we good. good lookin doe!" X quickly said, trying his hardest not to get on that wit Kendall.

"Come on man we ain't chopped it up in a lil minute," Kendall said.

"Hell yeah! But shit waiting on you we been missing plenty lil ack we gotta get our people straight. We a catch-up wit you some other time. Ain't no pressure on this shit it's all love my nigga," X said.

"Love bro!" Tay G quickly threw out there.

"Iight, iight I can respect that. Y'all gotta stay down if y'all wanna get like me!" Kendall said then started laughing.

"You forcing it now fool, be smooth out their doe," Tay G said.

"I'ma gone get up out of here somebody come lock the door," Kendall said.

Tay G followed Kendall to the door and let him out.

"Man, I hate dealing wit dawg, that shit dead I gotta find another plug asap!" X said to his self and sat down at the table. Tay G came walking back into the kitchen.

"Bro I already know what you finna say. The nigga had the nerve to ask me did I want to flex the yays and the rollie for a lil bit. Dawg trippin," Tay G said.

"I told you bro be tryna flex on us. But fuck dude we got a whole line of heads to knock down," X said.

"Say no more" Tay G said

X's I-phone chimed with a text message, He pulled it from his pocket and looked at it.

"OK Tammy!" he said to his self as he opened the message.

"Come get me, I wanna kick it tonight," Tammy texted.

"Who dat?" Tay G asked being nosey.

"A lil hoe bitch I been fucking wit from Madison," X said.

"You talking bout shorty from the club?" Tay G asked.

"Hell yeah!" X said.

"What up wit shorty that was wit her? She looked familiar," Tay G said.

"Shit I don't know, and I don't care!" X said as he texted Tammy back.

"Tight I'ma be up there around 7:30pm," X replied.

"Okay see you then," Tammy replied.

"Tight" X replied and put this phone down on the table.

"Whip that shit up Dawg it's yo turn!" X said to Tay G.

"Say no more!" Tay G said as he stood up and got to work.

Meanwhile

Hot Boi pulled into Quantay's driveway and saw Quantay standing in the doorway waiting on him. Hot Boi grabbed the plastic bag off the passenger seat and jumped out of his truck and walked up to the door.

"What up cuz?" Hot Boi asked.

"Shit cuz! My shoulder hurting bad as hell" Quantay said as he let him into the house. Hot Boi walked past Quantay and went straight to the kitchen. He sat the Walmart bag down on the counter as Quantay walked in behind him. Hot Boi pulled the brick from his pants and set it on the table. Quantay had never seen a whole brick so he walked over to the table and picked it up.

"Damn cuz you plugged like that?" Quantay asked.

"Man cause this shit light if you ready we can get some real money!" Hot Boi said.

"I'm starving cuz trust me!" Quantay said.

"Oh yeah, before I forget this the $30,000, I said I was going to give you," Hot Boi said as he reached into his pocket and pulled out the cash and handed it to Quantay. Quantay stood there in disbelief, it was hard for him to believe his lil cousin was getting money like this. He held the thirty thousand in all hundreds in his hands just staring at it. It's been a while since he held this much cash in his hands at once.

"Man, cuz this love" he said as he looked at Hot Boi.

"It's light we blood!" Hot Boi said.

"Now let's get in this pot. Once yo people get some of this they gone be all over you like flies on shit!" Hot Boi added. He pulled the pyrex, scale, and a box of baking soda from out the bag and sat it on the countertop.

"I'ma put this shit together this time so just watch me. Next time you can put it together and I'll watch. I wanna make sure you learn this shit fast. Do me a favor and turn that water on," Hot Boi said as he grabbed a small pot. Quantay turned the water on and Hot Boi walked over and put some water in the pot and went to work. Twenty minutes later Hot Boi pulled the pyrex from the freezer and flipped it over and tapped on the bottom of the pyrex until a chunk of crack in a cookie shape fell out onto a plate looking like popcorn pieces.

"Call yo people and tell them you got a sample for them to test out. Once they get a hit of this shit it's over!" Hot Boi said.

Quantay stood there looking at the move Hot Boi had just put together, He still couldn't believe his lil cousin was doing what he was doing. He knew it was time for him to get paid cause his lil cousin was opening up doors that's been closed for years. Quantay pulled out his phone and started calling his people one by one.

Meanwhile

It was 9:30pm when Shah pulled into the parking ramp on 320 South Canal Street in Chicago. He was drained, but happy he had finally made it to Chicago. Shah wondered what was in the back of the pickup truck, but quickly decided against looking to see cause it could be a part of his test. He promised Almundo he would follow the directions and checking to see what was in the truck wasn't part of the instructions.

Shah drove to the top of the ramp and parked next to a black Jeep Wrangler as instructed. He took the keys out of the ignition and put them under the driver seat. He got out of the pickup truck and walked over to the driver side of the Wrangler and got in. He reached under the driver seat and grabbed the keys and quickly started the Jeep and pulled off.

As Shah turned out of the parking ramp on Canal Street, he was happy the mission was complete. He looked around at the scenery and soaked in the bright lights and fast pace of Chicago's night life. Shah loved being in Chicago even though he hadn't been for years it felt like he was there yesterday. He thought about calling his cousin Lil Ant and staying for the night as he drove. He pulled his phone from his pocket and started dialing his number but before the phone could ring, he decided against it and ended the call. He clicked on to Audrey's number and called her instead.

"Heyy Baby!" Audrey said as she answered the phone.

"What yo sexy ass doing?" Shah asked.

"Nothing, laying here bored watching a movie. Tammy left me home alone tonight. she went to Milwaukee so I'm just home alone watching a movie until I fall asleep. when you coming back?" Audrey asked.

"I'm on my way to see you now give me two hours. And when I get there, I want a massage and some head just cause I miss you so much," Shah said.

"Awww I miss you too baby! And you got that coming when you get here cause you miss me so much. You better be ready for lil mama cause she gone be here tonight," Audrey said and started laughing.

"Oh yeah? I love lil mama tell her I'm on my way," Shah said and laughed a little.

"OK see you when you get here, I love you baby," Audrey said.

"I love you too!" Shah said and ended the call.

Monday Morning

It had been an extremely long weekend for Shah. His body was tired from the long drive back from Laredo Texas. Not only that, but both trap phones had been off the chain all day Sunday. Shah wasn't going to let nothing get in the way of this opportunity. He wasted no time getting to Beloit, He pulled into Alberto's auto body shop at 7:15 am. He looked over and saw a short grey-haired Mexican guy grabbing some tools from his truck as he parked next to him. Alberto put his tools down and walked over to Shah's car before he could get out and opened the door for him.

"My brother how was the vacation?" Alberto asked as he extended his hand to Shah. Shah grabbed ahold of his hand and gave him a firm handshake.

"No disrespect but who are you?" Shah asked.

"I'm the guy your here to meet. You can call me Berto," Alberto said.

"Oh ok, well its nice to meet you Berto!" Shah said as he got out of his car.

"Like wise. You mind grabbing those tools and bringing them inside for me? Alberto asked.

"Oh yeah I can do that," Shah said then walked over to Alberto's truck and grabbed both toolboxes and followed Alberto into the building. Alberto's crew was working hard early taking the doors off a Lexus when Shah and Alberto walked into the shop.

"You can put the tools over there" Alberto said as he pointed to a cart in the hall. Shah walked over and placed both boxes on the cart.

"What they about to do, re-paint it?" Shah asked as he walked past them. Alberto stopped and looked at the Lexus. "Oh no, they're just changing the hinges, so the doors open up like Lamborghini doors do," Alberto said,

"Oh, ok I got you!" Shah said. He continued to follow Alberto to this office. Alberto opened his office door for Shah to walk in and he followed behind him.

"You can have a seat right there," Alberto said as he pointed to a chair in front of his desk.

"You did excellent brother. That drive was just a show of good faith and you showed me you can be trusted. So now I'm going to do a show of good faith and trust you. There's ten kilos of Mexico's finest heroin in your car right now. I want forty thousand per kilo. Come see me in two weeks with four hundred thousand dollars not a day late or a dollar short! You understand?" Alberto asked.

"I understand!" Shah quickly said.

"Great. Now I got work to get to, so I'll see you back here in two weeks," Alberto said.

"Tight," Shah said and stood up.

He followed Alberto out of his office and to the buildings exit and left the building. Shah walked back to his car and got in, he looked back and noticed a black duffle bag sitting on his back seat. He reached back and pulled the duffle bag into the passenger seat and unzipped it.

"Damn! Yeah it's time to get this money!" he said out loud when he seen the ten kilos of dookie brown heroin. Shah quickly zipped the bag up and put his seat belt on then started the car and pulled out of the parking lot. Shah made his way to I-94 north headed straight to Madison. Shah started piecing his plan together as he drove.

"Damn I need somebody I can trust to keep this shit at they spot," he thought to his self. "Oh Tammy! Hell yeah," he said out loud. She was the first and only person he trusted outside of Audrey. He hadn't talked to her since Friday and really wasn't sure where they stood, but regardless of what happened between them, he knew he could trust her. Shah picked up his phone and called her. He quickly put his phone on speaker and sat it on his lap as he waited for her to answer.

"Hello," Tammy said as she answered.

"What up? How you doing?" Shah asked trying to break the ice he knew the whole situation was awkward, but it was money on the line, so she was going to have to get past what happened.

"I'm doing fine. how you doing?" Tammy asked.

"I'm good but I need to talk to you, you at home?" Shah asked.

"If it's about what happened I think we should put it behind us and make sure it never happens again," Tammy quickly said.

"I agree we need to put that behind us. I'll make sure it never happens again. But that ain't what I wanna talk to you about," Shah said.

"Alright! Well I'm at home but I gotta leave out for work in two hours," Tammy said.

"Tight good I'ma be there in an hour," Shah said.

"OK Shah," Tammy responded.

"Tight," Shah said and hit the end button on his phone. He looked into his rearview mirror and his heart instantly dropped into his stomach when he saw a state trooper driving behind him. He quickly looked at his odometer to check his speed. His heart was still pounding when he realized he was only going 65mph. He could hardly breathe. Shah started to panic as he thought about what would happen if he got pulled over.

"God please don't let this nigga pull me over," he prayed out loud as he slowly reached and turned the music off.

"Fuck this shit, let me get over," he said to his self and hit his left turning signal and switched lanes. The state trooper switched lanes with him, and he really started to panic as he looked in his rearview mirror and saw that the state trooper was so close on his bumper, he could see the little badge on his hat. Shah worried that at any second it could all be over wit for him.

"God please don't let him pull me over," Shah prayed as he put the car on cruise control. His legs started to shake uncontrollably as he passed a car that was in the center lane.

"Switch lanes Shah," he thought to his self, then hit his right turning signal and switched lanes, so that the car was now behind him. The state trooper picked up speed and passed by him. Shah let out a huge sigh of relief and started laughing.

"Yo bitch ass damn near shitted on yoself!" he said to his self. Shah sat back and drove the rest of the way back in silence.

Shah pulled into Tammy's parking lot at 8:15am and parked he grabbed his duffle bag off the passenger seat and got out the car. He walked to the building and buzzed the doorbell. Tammy buzzed Shah into the building and Shah made his way up to her apartment. He opened the apartment door and seen Tammy sitting on the couch wearing her red scrubs.

"Damn she sexy ass fuck!" Shah thought to his self as he closed the door.

"Why you got that big ass bag?" Tammy asked as Shah sat the duffle bag on the couch.

"This what I wanted to talk to you about," Shah said and unzipped the bag and pulled out a kilo. "Tammy you the only person outside of Audrey that I truly trust, and I need some where to keep this shit," Shah said.

"What the hell is that Shah?" Tammy asked as she got off the couch and walked closer to get a good look.

"This heroin," Shah said trying to sound like he was an expert. "This worth $100,000 dollars at the least. Now I'm here cause I trust you and I need you as a partner. All you gotta do is keep this shit here and don't let nobody know it's here and I'ma give you $10,000 a month," Shah said.

"$10,000 a month Shah, you sure?" Tammy quickly asked not sure if she heard him right.

"Yeah but you can't have no niggas or nobody but Audrey over here," Shah said.

"Okay we got a deal!" Tammy said.

"Tight," Shah said as he put the brick back in the bag and zipped it up.

"I'ma put this under yo bed. What time you get off work tonight?" Shah asked.

"I get off at 5:30pm" Tammy responded.

"When you get off I'ma need you to go get me a key made. I'm finna leave nine of these here and take one wit me. I'm telling you so you know how many in here. I'ma see you when you get off," Shah said He reached into his pocket and pulled out a roll of hundreds and handed Tammy one.

"Okay Shah. I like this, you really stepping yo shit up," Tammy said.

"This only the beginning, we bout to be rich!" Shah said as he picked the bag up and started walking toward Tammy's room. He tossed the bag on the floor next to the bed and unzipped it and pulled out a brick and sat it on the bed then zipped the bag back up and pushed it under the bed.

"Tammy come here real quick" Shah said.

"Yeah?" Tammy asked as she walked into the room. "You got a bag I can put this in?" Shah asked.

"Yeah its a McM book bag on my shelf in the closet. Shah you better bring my bag back cause if you don't you gone be buying me a new one," Tammy said. Shah opened the closet door and looked around then grabbed the bag off the shelf and tossed the brick in it. Tammy turned and walked out of the room and Shah followed right behind her. He looked down at her ass as they walked into the living room, but before he even realized it, he reached and grabbed her ass. Tammy turned around fast "Shah I thought we---" But before she could finish what she was about to say Shah pulled her close to him and kissed her. Tammy didn't even try to fight him off. She knew what they were doing was wrong, but it felt so good, plus she had a weak spot in her heart for Shah. Shah broke their kiss and looked Tammy in her eyes as they stood their chest to chest.

"I had to do that for the last time," Shah said and walked over to the door and opened it. He looked back at Tammy who just stood there looking at him still in shock.

"Make sure you call me when you get off," Shah said.

"OK I will," Tammy said softly.

Shah closed the door and walked downstairs and to his car. He jumped into his car and tossed the book bag on his passenger seat. Shah knew it was time to get to work and he needed to build his clientele fast because if he didn't get rid of this shit fast, he was a dead man. He pulled his phone from his pocket and called Lil Jerry.

"What up?" Lil Jerry asked as he answered the phone.

"I need to holla at you," Shah said.

"Iight slide on me I'm on the block," Lil Jerry said.

"Say no more I'm around the corner," Shah said.

"Yep," Lil Jerry said then ended the call.

Shah looked up and seen Tammy coming out the building, so he rolled his window down and stuck his head out the window.

"Don't forget that key!" Shah yelled to her.

"Boy I won't! Tammy said as she walked toward her car. Shah started laughing and rolled his window back up and pulled out of the parking lot. Shah pulled onto Cameron and parked near the corner. He grabbed his bookbag off the passenger seat and jumped out of the car. Shah walked around the corner to Russit and made his way up the block to the building Lil Jerry be in. Shah walked into the building the hall was packed as usual.

"Let's slide in one of these cribs I need to holla at you real quick," Shah said to Lil Jerry.

"Tight we upstairs," Lil Jerry said and walked up the stairs. Shah and Lil Jerry walked through the middle of the dice game outside of Lil Jerry's cousin Tamara crib and went in.

"We good ain't nobody here," Lil Jerry said and closed the door. "Tight," Shah said as he took his book bag off and opened it and pulled out the brick. Lil Jerry's eye got buck wide like a deer caught in the head lights.

"Damn bro why you riding wit that?" Lil Jerry asked shocked.

"I just got this shit. I'm tryna see if you could call yo cousins and let them know I got grams for the eighty," Shah said.

"Tight I got you. I'm finna call them niggas right now," Lil Jerry said as he pulled out his phone and called his cousin TJ.

"What up?" TJ asked as he answered the phone.

"Cuz my mans got some shit on yo side I think you might wanna come check this shit out asap!" Lil Jerry said.

"I'm glad you just called me. Where you at?" TJ asked.

"We at Tamara's crib," Lil Jerry said.

"Tight, I'm around the corner," TJ said.

"Tight" Lil Jerry said then ended the call. "Cuz around the corner he bout to pull up" Lil Jerry said. "You got a scale?" Shah asked.

"Yeah it's in that drawer," Lil Jerry said as he pointed to the counter in the kitchen. "What about a hammer and some baggies?" Shah asked.

"I don't know about a hammer but its some baggies in that cabinet over the fridge," Lil Jerry said.

Shah walked into the kitchen and grabbed the baggies from the cabinet and the scale from the drawer. He wanted to be sure he only showed Lil Jerry's cousin a small amount just in case he tried to get on some bull shit. Shah grabbed a pot from under the sink and used it to break a chunk off the brick. Then, he grabbed a knife and used it to cut open the vacuum sealed plastic the brick was wrapped in. He pulled out a chunk and sat it on the scale. "33.2 grams," Shah said as he pulled it off the scale and tossed it in the baggie. He grabbed a plastic store bag from one of the drawers and put the rest of the brick in it and put it back in his book bag.

"Do me a favor and watch them grams for me," Shah said as he walked to the door.

"Tight. You know cuz finna pull up," Lil Jerry said.

"Yeah I know I ain't finna go far," Shah said and walked out the door. Shah ran out the building and down Russit and around the corner to Cameron. He opened the trunk to his car and tossed the book bag into the trunk and closed it. Shah quickly ran back around the corner to Russit and stopped at Hustle Man's building and rang the doorbell three times. Hustle Man popped his head out the window and seen that it was Shah.

"Nephew you ready?" Hustle Man asked.

"Look, come down to the building I need you to check something out again," Shah quickly said then ran off before Hustle Man could say anything. Shah walked back into Tamara's apartment breathing heavy. "Shah bro yo ass been on one since the last time I seen you. You dumping on both sides I see yo weak ass tryna check a bag for real!" Lil Jerry said as he twisted up his cigarello.

"Bro I'm tryna see a Million!" Shah said as he turned and looked at Lil Jerry.

"I see bro! I'm just scared to fuck wit that shit," Lil Jerry said.

"I don't know why! Look bro think about it like this. You can ride down on a nigga and blow his brains out over some small shit and take the risk of getting jammed up. So why not take a risk and get some cash out the deal," Shah said.

Lil Jerry flamed up his blunt and took a few puffs as he thought about what Shah just said cause it made a lot of sense. He risked his freedom everyday why not try getting rich doing it. Shah walked into the kitchen and grabbed a towel and put it over the grams and used the pot to break the chunk into smaller pieces. Shah's phone started to ring at the same time somebody knocked on the front door. He looked back at Lil Jerry "I think that's cuz right there!" Lil Jerry said as he walked to the door.

"What up?" Shah said as he answered the phone.

"My main man! How you been? Almundo asked.

"I'm good you know same shit different day," Shah said.

"I'm trying to come see you," Almundo said.

"Tight meet me on Russit," Shah said.

"OK be there in twenty minutes," Almundo said. "Cool," Shah said and ended the call.

Shah turned around and seen Lil Jerry his cousin TJ and Hustle Man walking into the kitchen.

"What up," Shah said to TJ.

"What up," TJ said.

"This my mans I was telling you about!" Lil Jerry said.

"Oh OK," TJ said.

"I want you to check this out," Shah said and turned around and grabbed a small piece of the boy off the counter and handed it to Hustle Man. Hustle Man walked over to the table and sat down.

"Let me get a spoon and a plate," Hustle Man said to Shah.

TJ and Lil Jerry stood there and watched as Shah handed Hustle Man a spoon and a plate. Hustle Man wasted no time getting to business as he used the spoon to crush the boy into dust then pulled his ID from his pocket and used it to separate the dust up in two line and quickly snorted one into each nostril.

"You wanna hit this shit?" Lil Jerry asked TJ as he tried to pass him the blunt.

"Naw cuz I stop smoking a few weeks ago," TJ said as he stood there looking at Hustle Man.

"Let me hit that shit," Shah said to Lil Jerry.

"Not wit that shit on yo hands," Lil Jerry said. Shah quickly washed his hands and grabbed the blunt from Lil Jerry. TJ stood there watching Hustle Man's every move.

"So, what you think?" TJ asked Hustle Man. Hustle Man looked up at TJ sniffling and rubbing his nose.

"It's a bomb, the best shit around here," Hustle Man said as he kept rubbing his nose.

"Tight let me see what that shit look like?" TJ asked Shah as he walked over to the counter. Shah turned around and grabbed the grams and handed them to TJ. TJ quickly inspected the grams.

"What's the ticket?" TJ asked.

Lil Jerry started laughing so TJ and Shah turned around to see what was funny.

"This nigga bout to fall off the chair!" Lil Jerry said as he pointed at Hustle Man.

"Yeah lil bro this that move! I ain't seen nobody nod out that fast in a long time," TJ said.

"So, what's the ticket," TJ asked Shah again.

"I ain't gone lie I damn near want a hunnit a grit but depending on how many you grab I can do eighty," Shah said.

"Tight how many can you sell me?" TJ asked.

"I got whatever you need, but I only got 33 on me and I need to keep 3 so I can sell you this 30 right now," Shah said.

"Tight let me get that 30-real quick. If my people like this shit I'ma need 2 hunnit," TJ said.

"Tight I can make that happen," Shah quickly said. "Just give me eighty a move for this thirty and we gone do eight bands for each hunnit if yo people like it," Shah said.

"Tight," TJ said without a second thought. He knew this shit was ten times better than the shit he normally be getting. TJ was a beast at the re-rock game, he was turning ten to twenty-five easy with the shit he was getting, and his people was eating it up. He knew he wasn't gone have a problem getting this shit off. TJ pulled his money from his pocket and counted off twenty-four hunnit and handed it to Shah. Shah weighed up three grams on the scale and gave the rest to TJ.

"What's the number?" TJ asked Shah.

"I'm bout to go get a new line right now. Just give me your number and I'ma hit yo line as soon as I get mine," Shah said.

"Tight, 227-1302," TJ said.

"Tight I got you," Shah said. TJ turned around and shook Lil Jerry's hand.

"Good looking cuz, that was perfect timing I just ran out I was finna get on the road," TJ said. "You know it ain't shit!" Lil Jerry said.

TJ walked to the door and left out the apartment. "Wake yo ugly ass up!" Lil Jerry shouted as he shook Hustle Man. Hustle Man sat up and wiped the slob from his mouth and Lil Jerry started laughing.

"On God, that nigga wouldn't fall from that chair for shit. I was watching and waiting on his ass to fall the whole time," Lil Jerry said to Shah as he laughed. Shah looked back and started laughing.

"You good?" Shah asked Hustle Man.

"Yeah," Hustle Man managed to say. "Well good cause I gotta buss a move yo ugly ass gotta go," Lil Jerry said.

"Fuck you! You lil skinny bastard," Hustle Man said as he stood up. "Nephew I'm about to make some calls I know my people gone want some more of this shit," Hustle Man said.

"Tight," Shah quickly said. His phone started to ring again so picked it up and seen that it was Almundo's number. "You over there?" Shah asked as he answered. "Yeah," Almundo said.

"Tight here I come," Shah said and ended the call. Shah reached into his pocket and pulled out a baggie full of crack and counted off ten fifties for Almundo. He quickly bagged up the three grams and put them into his pocket. Lil Jerry let Hustle Man out and told Shah to make sure he closed the door when he leave out. Shah left the apartment right behind Lil Jerry and walked downstairs.

"I thought you had to buss a move?" Shah asked Lil Jerry as he walked past him.

"I just ain't want dude sitting in cuz crib. You know I play the hall I'm a lobby loiter!" Lil Jerry said. Shah looked around the hall for a second. "Aye where Cory at?" he asked.

"He in traffic or at the crib. Damn, I ain't tell you somebody got down on that nigga that robbed cuz huh?" Lil Jerry asked.

"Hell naw'll" Shah said.

"Man, somebody laid him and some other nigga name Rasheed down," Lil Jerry said.

"Damn that's crazy! I heard about that shit on Friday but I ain't know Khalil was the one who robbed bro," Shah said.

"Hell yeah! But fuck him he dead now," Lil Jerry said and laughed.

"Fuck him!" Shah said as he opened the building door and ran outside and jumped in the car with Almundo

"What up?" Shah asked as Almundo pulled to the back of the building. "I got five hundred and I want to see how everything went with the trip," Almundo said.

"Oh yeah! Shit went good, we in business. When I get this shit up and running I'ma hit you and make sure you straight for putting me in," Shah said as he handed Almundo the work. Almundo pulled the five hundred from his shirt pocket and handed it to Shah.

"OK that's good! I'll be calling you," Almundo said.

"Tight just hit my line," Shah said and jumped out of the car and quickly ran back into the building. Shah stood in the packed hallway thinking while he smoked on a blunt Lil Jerry passed him. "Damn I forgot all about big bro!" Shah said to his self then pulled out his old phone and dialed his big brother Shawn best friend number.

"What up lil nigga?" Blue Dini said as he answered the phone.

"I ain't on shit big bro! I called cause I got a lil situation and I know you the perfect person to help me out wit it," Shah said.

"Tight what up?" Blue Dini asked.

"I don't wanna talk on the phone this a face to face situation," Shah said.

"Oh OK! where you at? Blue Dini asked.

"I'm out west on Russit," Shah said.

"OK, I'm finna pull up on you I'm coming down Raymond right now. Matter of a fact come outside," Blue Dini said.

"Tight," Shah quickly said. Shah ended the call and walked out to the sidewalk in front of the building. Shah hadn't seen Blue in a few months, so he had no idea what kind of car he was looking for. Shah stood there looking back and forth up Russit until he saw a rose gold Porsche truck on some rose gold rims turning off Whitney way on to Russit.

"If this fool, he went nuts with this one!" Shah thought to his self as he waited for the truck to get closer. The truck slowly drove down the block and stopped in front of him, Shah stood there for a moment looking cause he couldn't see through the tint. The window slowly rolled down and Blue Dini popped up from his seat so Shah could see him.

"What up lil nigga?" Blue Dini said as he looked over at Shah. Shah walked up to the truck and opened the door. "Damn this bitch go hard!" he said as he got in and closed the door. Shah looked over at Blue in the driver seat shinning like new money.

"How much this tax you?" Shah asked as he looked around the truck.

"A lil bit of nothing," Blue Dini quickly replied. "I just got off the phone wit Shawn about ten minutes before you called me," Blue Dini added.

"Yeah? That nigga ain't called me in a minute," Shah said.

"Yeah I know. He told me in so many words that you out here getting to it and he wanted to give you time to get your shit together before he hit you up," Blue Dini said.

"I gotta slide up there and visit bro or hit him wit some cash sometime soon," Shah said.

"I'm finna send bro a band, so just focus on getting yo cash straight then hit him," Blue Dini said. "Yeah you right, but I called cause I need some help moving this shit I got. I'm tryna build my clientele," Shah said.

"Tight what you got?" Blue Dini asked.

"I got some dog food!" Shah said looking over at Blue Dini.

"Well I can tell you, you jumped in the right lane lil bro. You can run it up fast and be straight for life if you stay focus. How much you got?" Blue Dini asked.

"I got like 970 grams," Shah replied Blue Dini looked over at Shah not sure if he heard him right.

" lil bro you sure you got 970 grams? You sure you working the scale right?" Blue Dini asked.

"Yeah bro I'm sure! it's 969.8 grams bro," Shah said. Blue Dini pulled the car over to the side of the road and put the car in park giving Shah his full attention. He thought Shah was small timing, but after hearing them numbers he knew this shit was worth his attention.

"What, you hit a stain on that shit?" Blue Dini asked tryna get some more information on the situation. "Naw I know somebody that know somebody else," Shah said as he sensed Blue was fishing.

"I need to dump this shit so I can hit a mafucka wit they cash," Shah said.

"Tight I can help you lil bro. I got a few niggas I be taxing a hunnit a grit and they be grabbing a hunnit at a time. I'ma make a few calls for you. But what's to it?" Blue Dini asked.

"I let somebody check it out and they said it was the best shit they had in a long time. And no sooner then two minutes later he was in a deep nod!" Shah said. Shah reached into his pocket and pulled out the three grams he had and handed them to Blue Dini so he could check it out. Blue Dini looked at the grams real close then smelled them through the plastic.

"Oh yeah lil bro, this shit that move. You can hit this and still sell it for a hunnit a gram," Blue Dini said.

"What you mean hit it?" Shah quickly asked.

"You can turn that shit into double what it is, and it'll still be good. Only cause I love you I'ma show you how to do it," Blue Dini said.

"Tight I'm wit it. I need to hurry up and dump this shit so I can get them out my way. If you can dump these for a hunnit a move you can just give me eighty a move," Shah said.

"Tight I'm finna line some shit up for you then I'ma call you so just make sure you on standby," Blue Dini said as he pulled off and headed back toward Russit.

Chapter Nine

S hah sat in his car outside the Madison Area Technical College east campus waiting on Audrey to come out. Shah had his plan mapped out in his head and Audrey was to play a major role in it, so it was important that he got her on board. Shah looked to the entrance of the building as a group of people exited the building. Audrey walked out and stood there for a moment looking around trying to see if Shah was out there yet. Shah noticed Audrey was looking around, so he got out of the car and waved to her catching her attention. Audrey started walking toward Shah so he decided to meet her half way and gave her a hug and a kiss.

"I missed you baby," Audrey said as she grabbed ahold of Shah's hand and held it.

"I missed you too," Shah said as they walked back to the car.

"So how was school?" Shah asked.

"It was alright, but for some reason it felt like it was longer than normal," Audrey said. Shah walked Audrey over to the passenger side and opened the door for her. Audrey got in and Shah closed the door behind her. She watched as Shah walked around to the driver side and got in the car.

"Well I'm proud of you for staying focused and chasing your dreams. It's gone pay off in the long run," Shah said as he started the car and pulled out of the parking lot.

"Aww thank you baby! That's means a lot, cause some days I be wanting to just quit and do something else," Audrey said. Shah looked over at Audrey and put his hand on her thigh. "Naw don't do that you on the right path just keep going," Shah said.

"No, I'm not going to quit, but it do be a thought sometimes mainly when I gotta go straight from work to school that shit be kicking my ass," Audrey said as she ran her finger through her hair.

"You know you can quit working whenever you want too, I'll pay your tuition for you that way you can just focus on school," Shah said.

"I don't know Shah, I don't want you to spend your money on putting me through school," Audrey said as she looked out the window.

"Audrey I wanna do this cause I love you! I want what's best for you. This money don't mean shit if I can't use it to help the people I love. Plus, I want you to quit so I can see you more than once a week," Shah said.

Audrey sat there for a moment quite before Shah spoke again. "Did you think about moving in with me?" Shah asked.

"Yeah, I thought about it and I talked to Tammy and she said she can handle the rent on her own," Audrey said.

"Tight that's good. We should start looking for something," Shah quickly said.

"It's this girl in my class that I'm cool with and she stay out in Beaver Dam. Her mom and dad own a few houses and apartment complexes out there. I talked to her and she said she could help me get one," Audrey said. Shah quickly looked over at Audrey. He couldn't believe what she just said. He was shocked that she was on top of it, plus this was perfect timing. He knew he wouldn't run into anyone he knew out there and his money would be far away from his product just like he needed.

"Talk to her and see when she could get you in. Tell her you can pay the rent up a year in advance and you would like to move in as soon as possible," Shah said.

"Ok I'll call and talk to her tonight," Audrey said.

Shah pulled into his parking lot and parked. Audrey looked around the parking lot wondering why they stopped here. "Is this where you stay?" she asked.

"Yeah why you say it like that?" Shah asked.

"Oh no real reason. I think it's a nice neighborhood. I wouldn't have pictured Hot Boi living over here," Audrey said.

"That's why they say believe half of what you see and none of what you hear!" Shah said.

"What you mean by that?" Audrey asked.

"I'm saying you never know what's to a person based off their outward appearance," Shah said.

Shah popped the trunk and got out the car he looked back in at Audrey when he noticed she didn't move. "Come on, we finna go up here for a lil while," Shah said and closed his door. He walked around to the back of the car and grabbed the book bag from the trunk and put it on his shoulder. Audrey came from around the passenger side of the car and stood next to Shah as he closed the trunk. Shah led the way to his building and Audrey followed him into the building and up to his apartment. "This nice!" Audrey said, shocked as she walked into the apartment. "I know y'all be having all kinds of lil bitches up in here," Audrey said as she looked around the apartment. Shah started laughing at Audrey's comment. "Hell Yeah! We make them bitches walk around ass hole naked too," Shah said jokingly.

Audrey stopped in her tracks and looked over at Shah as he stood there laughing. "Don't get fucked up, ain't shit funny!" Audrey said.

"Man, I'm fucking wit you! Don't nobody come over here. Shit you the first person that I've seen here besides HB since I been living here," Shah said. "I better be!" Audrey said as she took a seat on the couch. Shah tossed his book bag on the couch and walked to the door.

"I'll be right back," Shah said as he opened the door and left out the apartment. Audrey grabbed the remote and turned the Tv on and flipped through a few channels before her phone started to ring in her bag. She reached in her bag and pulled out her phone and looked at it. "Bestie," Audrey said before answering.

"Girl aren't you suppose to be working?" Audrey asked as she answered.

"Yes, but my shift ended early. What you doing, cause I'm hungry I wanna go get something to eat," Tammy said.

"I wouldn't mind going out to eat right now, but I'm wit Shah and I'm tryna get me some dick," Audrey said and laughed.

Shah walked in on the ass end of Audrey's comment and started laughing.

"Ok lil mama!" Shah said as he grabbed the book bag next to Audrey and walked to the kitchen.

"Ok, well I'll see you later then," Tammy said.

"Ok gir---" before Audrey could finish what she was saying Tammy ended the call.

"Well Ok then!" Audrey said as she looked at the phone then put it back in her purse. Audrey got up and walked into the kitchen and sat at the table with Shah. Shah sat there breaking the boy down into hundred-gram portions.

"So, what's that Shah?" Audrey asked Shah stood up and wiped the sweat from his forehead. "This heroin," Shah said as he walked over to the sink and grabbed a towel then walked back to the table and sat down. Audrey grabbed a baggie with a hundred grams in it and looked at it closely.

"Why it's so dark?" Audrey asked.

"I don't know I guess that's how it comes," Shah said as he put more chunks onto the scale trying to get it at exactly a hundred.

"So much this cost?" Audrey asked.

"It depends. See I'm paying four thousand for it but I'm selling it for eight thousand just to get rid of it fast. But if I broke it down and sold it in smaller pieces, I could make twenty thousand off what's in yo hands," Shah said.

"Damn baby, twenty thousand? That'll be four times more than what you paid for it," Audrey said. Shah started laughing as he emptied what he had on the scale into a baggie and tied it.

"You catch on fast," Shah said.

"Not really, it's just basic math," Audrey said trying not to sound too smart. "Simple math huh? That's good cause I need a partner that view math as being simple. So, what you think about quitting your job and taking a job with my business?" Shah asked.

Audrey started laughing "Your business! I like that one. So, if I decided to work at your establishment what would be my job title?" Audrey asked.

"Yo job gone be to safeguard the cash. So, your title would be Chief of Finance. You would also have to invest some of the funds into something legit," Shah said.

"Ok Ok so what would my pay rate be?" Audrey said in a real flirtatious voice.

"You wouldn't have a pay rate as long as the books straight you spend what you want!" Shah responded. "Ok I like that! I might have to put my two weeks' notice in at my job and take you up on your offer then baby!" Audrey said.

"Ok well I'ma let my assistant know to go ahead and process your application then," Shah said. Audrey started laughing and put the grams back on the table. Shah's phone started to ring so he reached into his pocket and pulled out his phone and answered it.

"What up Big Bro?" Shah said.

"Shit, I got something lined up for you," Blue Dini said.

"Iight where you at?" Shah asked.

"I'm over east but I can pull up on you if you need me to," Blue Dini said.

"Naw I can pull up what's the word?" Shah asked. "Four Hunnit lil bro," Blue Dini quickly said.

"Tight where to?" Shah asked.

"Just hit me when you get to Milwaukee street," Blue Dini said.

"Tight say no more," Shah said and ended the call. He got up from the table and walked to his room. Audrey got up and followed Shah to his room.

"So, this where you bring your lil bitches to?" Audrey asked as she sat on the bed. Shah started laughing and went in his closet and opened his safe and pulled out a hundred thousand dollars and tossed it on the bed next to Audrey.

"I only fuck wit dead niggas! No homo!" Shah said as he bent back down and pulled more cash from the safe and stood up holding it in both hands. Audrey's jaw dropped at the site of the bundles of hundred-dollar bills that laid on the bed next to her.

"Oh my God! Shah all this your money?" Audrey asked as she picked up the bundles of cash.

"Yeah that's all me," Shah said.

Audrey looked over at Shah shocked, cause she had never seen so much cash in her life. Shah turned around and put the cash he had in his hands back in the safe. Audrey stood up and walked to the closet and handed Shah the money back one bundle at a time until he had it all put back in the safe.

"This what I been up to. I'm trying to never go broke again but I need you on my side and I need you to trust my vision cause this for both of us and our future kids," Shah said. Audrey stood there; pussy completely wet she was turned on by Shah's confidence.

"I'm always on your side baby. I'm ready to do whatever you need me to do in order to help you reach your goal," Audrey said.

"Tight that's what I wanna hear!" Shah said as he walked out of the closet and walked back to the living room. Shah went into the kitchen and grabbed the four hundred grams and set them to the side. The other five hundred and sixty-nine grams he grabbed and took them to the basement and hid them. He ran back upstairs and put the four hundred grams in his book bag and hurried and left the apartment to go meet Blue Dini. As Audrey got close to Milwaukee street, Shah pulled out his phone and called Blue Dini. The phone rang and rang then went to the voice mail. Shah hung up and called back this time it went straight to the voice mail.

"These niggas be faking!" Shah said to his self as he put his phone down in his lap.

"Where we going?" Audrey asked as she made a left turn onto Milwaukee street.

"Just drive to your crib, these niggas be faking now he ain't answering the phone!" Shah said, frustrated cause he was counting on catching that cash.

Audrey made a U-turn and headed back toward East Washington. She made it to the intersection of Milwaukee and East Washington when Shah's phone started to ring. Shah looked down and seen that it was Blue Dini he hurried and answered the phone.

"What up?" Shah asked.

"My bad my phone was just trippin pull up to the Woodman's," Blue Dini said.

"Tight," Shah said and pulled the phone from his ear.

"Pull up to the Woodman's on Milwaukee," Shah whispered to Audrey.

"Tight bro" Blue Dini said and hung up.

Audrey made a left onto East Washington, then quickly made a U-turn and turned back onto Milwaukee street.

"Look baby when you get to the Woodman's don't pull in, I want you to park on the side street I'ma walk over to the wood mans," Shah said.

"Ok," Audrey quickly replied. A few minutes later Audrey made a right turn onto Dempsey Road and pulled past Woodman's and parked in front of an apartment complex. Shah got out the car and walked up the street to Woodman's. He stood there and scanned the parking lot looking for Blue Dini's truck but couldn't find it. He instantly started to get a bad feeling that Blue Dini was on some bull shit. Shah pulled out his phone and called him.

"What up bro?" Blue Dini said as he answered the phone.

"Shit where you at?" Shah asked.

"Look over to your right! That's me in the black car," Blue Dini said. Shah looked to his right and seen a beat up Dodge Neon and started laughing.

"Tight bro I see you," Shah said and ended the call. He made his way over to the Neon and got in the passenger seat.

"I was looking for the Porsche truck," Shah said.

Blue Dini started laughing as he looked at Shah. "I can't be riding in that truck wit four hundred grams on me. I might as well just pull up to Dane County jail with the shit," Blue Dini said.

"You right!" Shah said as he sat the book bag on the floor in between his legs. Blue Dini went into the middle console and pulled out a stack of cash and tossed it in Shah's lap.

"That's $32,000" Blue Dini said and looked out the car to make sure nobody was watching them. Shah grabbed the cash and looked at it.

"This the whole 32?" Shah asked.

"Come on lil bro! My money gone be correct every time," Blue Dini said, disappointed Shah even asked him that.

"Nothing personal big bro but I gotta make sure," Shah said as he reached into his book bag and pulled out the four individual hundred gram bundles and handed them to Blue Dini.

"That's the whole four hundred bro" Shah said as he put the cash into his book bag.

"Good looking lil bro. Now that I see you ain't small timing, don't forget to send some cash bro way. It's our duty to make sure we look out for each other," Blue Dini said.

"I can't forget about bro!" Shah quickly said. He jumped out the car and closed the door and quickly made his way through the parking lot. He looked over his shoulder the whole way back to the car. He got in the car and instantly started counting the money.

"Where to now?" Audrey asked quickly glancing in Shah's direction as she pulled off.

"Slide back to my crib real quick," Shah said never taking his eyes away from the cash.

Meanwhile

"Damn cuz you wasn't lying about this shit running like water. I went through a nine piece already and it's six o'clock," Quantay said as he sat at the table. His left arm was still in a sling and he had a fist full of cash in both hands as he counted the money he made so far. Hot Boi stood over the stove working his wrist whipping up another batch for Quantay.

"I know! I told you I'm a monster in this kitchen I'm The Ruler of The Red Ruler! Matter of fact, I just wrote some shit I want you to tell me what you think about it," Hot Boi said as he walked over to the sink and sat the pyrex in a bowl of ice and grabbed a towel and wiped his hands off.

"Damn I forgot you used to be fucking around wit the Rap shit. Let me hear that shit," Quantay said.

"Iight," Hot Boi said then started making a beat on the countertop.

"Bitch I'm the ruler of the red ruler/dope boy dreams cause I want it all/Never had shit so I can't lose/tryna score a point so I could win it all/Cause I'm the ruler of the red ruler, ruler of the red ruler, ruler of the red ruler/Gang and ain't a nigga gone take shit/ I gotta bunch of hittas on speed dial/Tryna put a hunnit on my right wrist finna take flight niggas like how/ Cause I'm the ruler of the red ruler, ruler of the red ruler, ruler of the red ruler gang/ I swear to God I'm Kobe/ 5 rings on my hand and I'm balling out the ass and they think they could hold me/ Swervin in traffic pull up at bp and hop out of something it's foreign/ yo bitch she boring she give me top and I drop that bitch off on the corner/ roll up this loud and get gone on her/ I got some money to chase/ this ain't a race niggas be plotting and lurking so I play it safe/ Plus they the Jakes I got some money put up so if I catch a case nigga/ I'ma be straight I keep some chickens and turkeys on top of my plate/ I could put you on today/ This shit ain't nothing to me zip after zip man ain't nobody fuckin wit me/ While yo pockets be broke ass a bitch I be working my wrist and copping whatever I see/ bitch I got a hustlers degree loving my money my money be talking to me/ cause I came up from nothing my pockets was empty and broke and wasn't nobody fucking wit me/ so don't tell me how hard it could be/ they show me love on these streets/ I show my love to the heat/ try me if you think that its sweet I got 50's and 30's fuck boy you don't want no beef/ I can front you a zip shit I can front you a split/ get it right back in a flip/ ruler that ruler that ruler that ruler that ruler it don't get no better than this!"

"Then I'ma come through with that chorus again and drop another verse to that shit!" Hot Boi said.

Quantay sat there still nodding his head. "Cuz on the mighty you went nuts on that shit. You should stop playing wit that shit and drop some tracks you could fuck around and catch a deal!" he said.

"I ain't thinking bout no deal cuz I'ma get it regardless!" Hot Boi said and he walked back to the sink. Quantay continued to count the money in his hands.

"Man, I wish I could rap like that. I would be out here going crazy wit that shit," Quantay said.

"If you run through this shit tonight, I hope you ready to get in this kitchen cause I'm going back to Madison tonight. I got a business to get back to I been gone too long," Hot Boi said switching subjects as he walked over to the table and sat across from Quantay.

"I'm ready. I might not be as cold as you but I'm ready. I'ma be straight. I see you been lamped out at Jamie crib a lot lately don't tell me you fell in love," Quantay said as he stood up and sat his money down on the table.

"Nigga I ain't been lamped out at her shit!" Hot Boi quickly said. Quantay started laughing as he pointed at Hot Boi.

"Yeah she put the pussy on you cuz! I see you ain't say shit about not being in love wit her," Quantay said as he continued to laugh.

"She ain't put no pussy on me either nigga and I don't love the bitch," Hot Boi said with a lot of aggression in his voice. Quantay started laughing harder and louder as he jumped up and down then ran into the living room. He turned back toward Hot Boi and pointed at him.

"Dude mad!" Quantay said.

Hot Boi jumped out of his chair and ran toward Quantay. Quantay ran around the couch making sure to keep some distance between him and Hot Boi. Hot Boi started laughing.

"On bd cuz don't make me fuck you up!" Hot Boi said. Quantay held his side with his right hand as he tried to catch his breath.

"Fuck I can't breathe! Cuz you funny as hell but she good people though," Quantay said.

"Yeah you on some bull shit! I run through these hoes at will!" Hot Boi said.

Quantay came from behind the couch and sat down. "All bullshit aside I'm fucking wit you. I knew you was going to get mad about that one," Quantay said.

"Yeah you got that one. But I'm finna go slide on Alesha before I leave, I need some more of that top," Hot Boi said.

"You ain't wrong," Quantay quickly said before his phone started to ring. He hurried and jumped up and rushed to the kitchen and picked it up and looked at it.

"Yeah cuz they eating this shit up!" Quantay said before he answered it. Hot Boi walked back into the kitchen and pulled the pyrex from the bowl and used his finger to check and see if it was dry. He grabbed a plate from the dish rack and sat it on the counter. He flipped the pyrex over and hit the bottom a few times until the cookie fell on the plate. Quantay got off the phone and walked over and stood next to Hot Boi. "I'm a beast!" Hot Boi said stoking his own ego.

"Yeah you did that!" Quantay said, not aware that he was boosting Hot Boi's ego up even further.

"I'm finna slide over here on Gerald and get some top from this bitch Alesha real quick before I get on this road," Hot Boi said and walked out the kitchen.

"Damn cuz you ain't finna help me bag this shit up?" Quantay yelled out to Hot Boi.

"No sir! What you gone do when I leave! Lock the door fool," Hot Boi said as he closed the door.

Meanwhile

"14,15,16 thousand," Shah counted out loud as he sat on Audrey's bed. The room door opened, and Tammy stuck her head in.

"Your keys in my room on my dresser I'll be back tomorrow," Tammy said.

Shah sat the money down on the bed and got up. "Where you finna go?" Shah asked.

"Shah yo girl in the bathroom in the shower right now. why you all in my business?" Tammy said with a smerk on her face trying to hold back the fact that she found it attractive that Shah was all in her business.

"Cause I'm nosey that's why I'm all in yo business. So, where you finna go?" Shah asked again.

Tammy started laughing then pushed the door all the way open and stood in the doorway.

"Boy yo ass crazy! Since you so nosey I'm finna go with X, and I need some money so let me get two hundred dollars," Tammy said as she extended her hand in Shah's direction.

Shah started laughing, then reached into his pocket and pulled out a roll of hundreds and peeled off five hundred and gave it to her. Tammy folded the money and tucked it into her purse.

"Thank you! Now if its Ok with you I gotta go cause he waiting down stairs for me," she said

"Call me when you get back," Shah said. Tammy started laughing then turned around and walked away. Shah walked out of Audrey's room and over to Tammy's room and grabbed the keys off her dresser and put them on his key ring. Shah walked to the bathroom and opened the door. Audrey popped her head from behind the shower curtain when she heard the door open.

"Damn you been in here for a minute," Shah said as he walked into the bathroom and sat down on the toilet.

"Aww you missed me already?" Audrey asked as she looked at Shah then to the door. "Did Tammy leave out?" she asked before giving him a chance to answer the first question she asked him.

"Yeah, she just left," Shah said.

"Ok good! Come get in the shower with me," Audrey said. Shah stood up and quickly kicked his shoes off and unbuckled his belt and pulled his pants off. "Shit you ain't gotta ask me twice," he said as he snatched the rest of his clothes off and jumped into the shower. Audrey started laughing when Shah almost slipped and fell.

"Ok now thirsty!" she said as she turned to face him.

"You know I'm thirsty!" Shah said as he pulled her close to him and started kissing her. He grabbed her ass cheeks in both hands, and she let of a soft moan then broke away from Shah's kiss and his grip and turned around.

"Shah fuck me and fuck me hard!" Audrey demanded as she leaned forward and put both hands on the wall and poked her ass out at him. Shah looked down at her ass as the water ran down her back. He grabbed one of her legs and lifted it up and put it on the edge of the tub. Audrey reached back and pulled him closer "Shah fuck me!" she demanded again.

"Ok now thirsty," Shah said as they both started laughing. Shah grabbed her ass cheeks then slowly slid inside of her wet pussy.

"Oh, shit Shah!" Audrey said as she reached back with one hand and pulled him closer helping him go deeper. Shah started with slow strokes then slowly began to pick up his pace.

"Yes, just like that," Audrey yelled out as Shah started to pound her harder. Shah was enjoying the moment, but he could hear his trap phones ringing in his head. He laughed to his self-cause he thought he had been trapping so hard he was imaging his phones ringing in his mind. But as he kept going, he could hear it clearer and clearer. He slowed down a little to make sure, then he completely stopped.

"What the fuck Shah! Why you stop?" Audrey asked frustrated.

"My phones ringing," Shah said then jumped out the shower.

"Fuck them damn phones Shah!" Audrey yelled out to him as he ran to her room to answer them. Audrey took her foot off the edge of the tub and started washing up. She couldn't believe Shah stopped fucking her just to answer his phone. She was quickly starting to realize that fucking with a dope boy has its negatives and its positives. She hoped there was more positives than negatives. Three minutes later Shah turned to walk back into the bathroom, but Audrey was on her way out.

"Move!" Audrey said as she used her arm to push Shah to the side.

"Damn! My bad lil mama I had to answer that!" Shah said as he walked into the bathroom and picked up his clothes. He quickly turned and walked back to Audrey's room.

"So, you mad at me now?" Shah asked as he looked at Audrey who was sitting on the bed.

"Oh no I'm fine," Audrey said, but Shah could clearly see she was pissed off at him. He walked over to the bed and leaned forward to kiss her on the neck, but Audrey moved away from him. Shah grabbed her by the arm and snatched her towel off and pushed her on the bed. He grabbed her legs and pinned her thighs to her chest and started eating her pussy. Still mad, Audrey tried to push his head away but quickly gave in.

"Hold your legs" Shah directed, and Audrey quickly grabbed ahold of her legs and held them in the air. Shah got down on his knees and started playing with her clit with his thumb as he licked her asshole.

"OH MY GOD!" Audrey yelled out, as the sensation sent chills through her body. She quickly moved Shah's hand and started rubbing her clit hard and fast as Shah continued to lick her ass.

"oh shit!" Audrey said as she started to have an orgasm. Shah continued to lick her ass until she stopped shaking. He stood up and slid inside of her pussy with force cause he had every intention to fuck the the hell out of her.

"This how you want it?" he asked as he held her thighs to her chest and fucked her hard.

"Yes Shah! Now shut up and fuck me!" Audrey yelled as she moaned. Shah wasted no time giving her what she wanted. He took his time and fucked her through multiple orgasms then he finally came. Shah pulled out and walked to the bathroom and washed off, then walked back in the room with a towel for Audrey. He stared laughing when he saw that Audrey was knocked out asleep. Shah quietly put on his clothes, then put his money up and left to go meet up with Hot Boi.

Meanwhile

Shah pulled into Zimmer's liquor store parking lot and parked. The lot was full of cars and people was rushing into the store before it closed. Shah looked around to the side of the building and saw Hot Boi in his truck with two bitches leaning into his window talking to him.

Shah got out of his car and walked over to Hot Boi's truck and jumped into the passenger seat.

"Heyy Shah!" Amira said to Shah letting him know she still wanted him.

"What up Amira," Shah said as he looked down at his phone.

"Girl you know Shah be trying to act brand new!" Net said to Amira.

Hot Boi looked over at Shah who was still flipping through his phone, then back to Net and Amira. "Man, bro ain't acting brand new. Y'all got on some bull shit with Audrey on Facebook the last time we kicked it wit y'all. Bro ain't got time for that shit he ain't fucking wit y'all," Hot Boi said.

"Fuck him and Audrey!" Net said as she stuck her head farther into the truck so Shah could hear her clearly. Shah started laughing but continued to flip through his phone never looking up.

"Bitch you trippin! Stupid ass bitch just spit on me," Hot Boi said as he pushed Net's head back away from the window. Amira instantly grabbed Net and pulled her away from the truck. Amira grew up around Hot Boi and Shah and she knew Hot Boi would get out and kick Net's ass.

"Bitch ass nigga don't put yo hands on me!" Net yelled out causing a scene as Amira pulled her away.

"Who put they hands on you?" a man yelled from in front of the store.

"This bitch ass nigga right here in this truck!" Net said as she pointed at Hot Boi's truck.

Hot Boi instantly reached under his seat and grabbed his 9mm and put it in his hoodie pocket and jumped out the truck. Shah quickly jumped out behind him as three dudes came running from in front of the store.

"This who you talking bout?" a big prison swoll ass nigga asked Net as he walked toward Hot Boi. Hot Boi quickly pulled out his pistol and pointed it at him.

"On Bd I will leave yo big ass out here in this parking lot!" Hot Boi said as he walked toward the big dude who stopped in his tracks. The other two ducked and ran back to the front of the store.

"Look fam just keep yo hands off my lil cousin," big dude said as he held his hands up.

"Well tell that bitch to keep her spit in her mouth then nigga!" Hot Boi said.

"Bro this shit aint gotta go this far!" big dude said as he slowly backed up.

"Bitch ass nigga you aint my brother! Don't let that swoll shit get you filled up with this hot shit!" Hot Boi said.

"Bitch ass niggas always pulling guns out!" Net yelled out as Amira pulled her back. Hot Boi started laughing "Shah jump in yo whip we up out of here," Hot Boi said to Shah and stood there until Shah got into his car. Hot Boi walked back to his truck and pulled off. Shah and Hot Boi pulled over on Britta. Shah parked his car and jumped in the truck with Hot Boi.

"Bro yo ass crazy!" Shah said as he closed the truck door. Hot Boi pulled off as if nothing ever even happened.

"Grab that bottle and them cups from back there I need a drink after that shit!" Hot Boi said. Shah reached into the back seat and grabbed the box of patron and opened it. He popped open the bottle and poured them both a cup. Hot Boi started laughing as he drove down Allied.

"That big ass nigga was finna try and kick my ass. That iron got his mind right quick!" Hot Boi said.

"His whole tone switched up! He was like 'Aye bro this ain't even gotta go this far' He bitched up quick!" Shah said and started laughing.

"I ain't been in town for a whole hour and I'm in some bullshit. That drunk ass bitch spit in my face. You think I was bogus?" Hot Boi asked.

"Naw, I would have did the same shit!" Shah said.

"That bitch lucky I ain't punch her ass in the mouth cause that shit hit my lip!" Hot Boi said Shah started laughing.

"Nooooo, not on yo lip!" Shah said.

"Get off that before you have me knock her ass out the next time, I see her," Hot Boi said.

"Iight, iight," Shah said laughing.

"But on some real shit how shit been going since I been gone?" Hot Boi asked.

"It's been iight. The weight line been slow, but the bag line been going nuts. I got $68,500 put up in the safe for you and the $30,000 for Big T. I was going to link with him in the Am to re-up but shit you can handle that now," Shah said.

"Iight, iight that's good shit. I'ma take over from here and let you chill for a while since you been holding shit down. I'ma make sure you still get yo cut," Hot Boi said.

"Say no more!" Shah said and quickly put both trap phones in the cup holder. This was right up his alley cause he'd rather focus on getting rid of the bricks he got from Alberto. They drove around the town for hours smoking and drinking. Shah debated on telling Hot Boi about the bricks but quickly decided to keep it to his self.

Eight Days Later

Shah and Audrey had moved into their three-bedroom house in Beaver Dam three days ago. Audrey's friend Melissa talked her parents into doing a rent to own lease for Audrey on the house. Melissa's parents had been struggling to sell the house so they were more than willing to help Audrey out, plus they would be making money off of it instead of having it sitting their empty.

Audrey loved her new place and she wasted no time on her plans to decorate and furnish their new home. Audrey and Tammy were out shopping for more decorations for the living room and the bathroom. Shah sat on the floor in the bedroom he planned to make his office in front of his safe. He counted over $500,000 dollars so far as he waited on their living room furniture to be delivered. His clientele had shot through the roof thanks to Blue Dini, everybody who was somebody was hitting his line. With eighty-dollar grams that could be hit five times and still have the feens coming back for more Shah had niggas knocking his door down. Shah opened up a spot at Hustle Man's crib letting him sell grams to his people for a hundred and twenty a grit. Hustle Man had Russit knocking off the meter. Shah counted the last thousand dollars and sat it on top of the pile of cash in front of him then stood up.

"Damn $710,000 dollars and I still got a brick left! This shit crazy!" Shah said to his self as he looked down at the cash on the floor. His train of thought was interrupted by the doorbell. He walked over to the window and peeked out the blinds and saw the Ashley's furniture delivery truck outside. Shah walked out the room and closed the door then walked downstairs to answer the door.

"Hi sir, I have a delivery here for you," A tall red-haired white man said as he handed Shah the paperwork.

"Ok!" Shah said and grabbed the papers and looked at them. Then, he looked past the man at the door and saw the delivery crew ready to unload. The delivery man at the door looked back at the crew and gave them the ok to start unloading the furniture. As the crew unloaded the furniture and brought it to the house Shah stood there directing traffic.

"You can put the couches and shit for the living room in there," Shah said as he pointed to the living room. He walked to the top of the stairs and stood there making sure no one went into his office as he directed them to the bedroom with the bedroom set. After they were all done placing the furniture where it needed to be, he gave them all a fifty-dollar tip and showed them out.

Meanwhile

Hot Boi stood in the shower while the water ran over his head. He had made it home last night after a long crazy night with Erika. Ever since the moment he woke up this morning, he couldn't stop thinking about what Blue Dini said to him last night at the club.

"My people going crazy off that D you and Shah got." Hot Boi thought about it over and over again. He was confused, and he thought maybe Blue Dini was fishing for some type of information because he wasn't fucking with the boy. He was almost certain that if Shah was, he would have told him. The more he thought about it, the more it bothered him. And the more it bothered him, the more he wanted to know. Hot Boi finished showering then went to his room to get dressed.

Meanwhile

Cory was sitting at the light at the intersection on Badger Rd and Park St. He'd just dropped Cortez off at a bitch's crib in Saddle Ridge. Lil Jerry was laying across the back seat knocked out. Cortez and Lil Jerry both had popped a zan and drop an eight in a two liter earlier. Cory hated fucking with that shit, but he slid on them anyway to smoke them out. The light turned green and Cory made a left onto Park St. Lil Jerry slid across the leather seats from one side to the other hitting his head on the door. Cory quickly looked back as he got on the beltline and turned the radio down.

"Bro you good?" he asked, but Lil Jerry was knocked out. His dreads cover his face and he was sweating like somebody poured a bottle of water on him. Cory started laughing as he drove, he continued to drive until he made it to the Seminole Hwy exit and got off. He made a left turn then a quick right onto Verona Rd. Lil Jerry slid back and forth across the back seat. Cory's phone started to ring, and when he looked down at his phone, he didn't recognize the number. Cory let it ring until it stopped. Then it started to ring again with the same number.

"Who the fuck is this!" he thought to his self before deciding to answer it.

"Who dis?" he asked as he answered.

"This Alexis, you gave me your number on Facebook last night," Alexis said.

"Oh yeah! I thought you was going to call me last night?" Cory asked.

"I was, but I ended up drinking too much and fell asleep," Alexis said and laughed a little.

"Oh, ok so what's going on wit you right now?" Cory asked.

"I wanted to see if you wanted to come over and match," Alexis said.

"I'm wit it. Let me drop my man's off real quick. Where I'm coming to?" Cory asked.

"I live on Thurston," Alexis said.

"Iight give me like thirty minutes and I'ma call you when I get on Thurston," Cory said.

"Ok. Don't send me off," Alexis said.

"I won't!" Cory responded.

"Ok. See you in thirty minutes," Alexis said.

"Yep," Cory said and ended the call. Cory was geeked Alexis had finally called him. He accepted her friend request on Facebook a week ago and immediately jumped in her inbox. The first few days Alexis wouldn't respond to his messages but would like every status and picture he posted. This made him want her even more, plus she was beautiful, and he felt like he had to have her on his team. One day, Cory took a picture in his living room with a hundred thousand dollars to his ear like a cell phone and sent it to Alexis with the caption "When you gone let me take you out?" Alexis responded right back saying, "Nice picture! But that's not how you're going to get me to go out with you. I hope that's not how you get women cause it's a bad look." The fact that Alexis replied gave Cory satisfaction and hope, so he continued to message her for days and now his persistence was finally about to pay off. Cory pulled into Tamara's parking lot on Russit and reached in the back seat and shook Lil Jerry, but he was dead to the world. Cory jumped out of his truck and walked to the building and looked through the window. Juice opened the door for him.

"What up bro?" Juice said.

"Help me get this nigga Lil Jerry upstairs," Cory said.

"Shit what's wrong wit him?" Juice asked.

"He off the Zans," Cory said.

Juice started laughing and walked out the building. Cory walked to the driver side rear door and pulled it open. He lifted Lil Jerry up and pulled him out the truck. Juice grabbed his legs and helped Cory carry him up to Tamara's apartment.

"When that nigga wake up tell him to hit my line," Cory said.

"I got you," Juice said as they walked out the apartment.

10:15pm

Hot Boi pulled into the Bennett's bar parking lot and parked. Hot Boi couldn't focus all day the only thing he could think of was Shah and if he was making moves on the side without him. He got out of the car and walked into the bar. He stood there looking around until he spotted Shah sitting at a table with a female he had never seen before.

"What up bro?" Hot Boi said as he walked up to the table.

"Coolin," Shah said as he extended his hand to shake Hot Boi's hand.

"Keisha this HB, HB this Keisha," Shah quickly said.

"Nice to meet you," Keisha said shyly as she looked up at Hot Boi then looked away.

"Nice to meet you Keisha. I don't mean to interrupt y'all date, but I need to holla at Shah real quick," Hot Boi said.

Shah looked over at Keisha then pulled out a roll of cash. "Grab you another drink and grab me a double shot of Hennessey," Shah said as he handed her a fifty-dollar bill.

"You bought the last round, this one on me," Keisha said as she stood up and put the money back down on the table. "I'll be at the bar," Keisha said and walked away.

"What up bro?" Shah asked Hot Boi as he sat down.

"I hear you been going crazy with the boy," Hot Boi said.

"I been iight. Who told you that tho?" Shah asked.

"The streets talking. But I thought we was on the same team and we was gone get this paper together. Why you aint bring me in on that shit like I did wit you?" Hot Boi asked.

"Look bro I ain't yo bitch I ain't gotta tell you everything I do and when I do it. And you can take me out the fold of that shit, I'm good on that small cash," Shah said then took a sip from his drink. Hot Boi was shocked and didn't know what else to do but laugh.

"You know what bro I see you drunk right now so I'ma give you a pass," Hot Boi said then stood up.

"Give me a pass? So, what you saying?" Shah asked and stood up.

"We ain't finna do this right here. I'ma catch you when you sober. I see you geeked right now," Hot Boi said and walked away.

I got something for his bitch ass," Hot Boi said as he walked out to his car. Hot Boi was pissed and he felt like Shah used him to get where he needed to be then switched up on him.

Meanwhile

Alexis opened the door for Brittany and let her into the apartment. "Damn bitch it took you all day to get here," Alexis said as she closed the door.

"Girl I was doing something I couldn't just drop it and rush over here. This better be important cause you been blowing my phone up," Brittany said.

"It is! Come here," Alexis said as she motioned for Brittany to follow her. Brittany was a little leery because the hall was dark, so she slowly walked behind Alexis. Alexis opened the room door and cut the light on. Brittany peeked into the room then quickly backed away from the door and rushed into the living room.

"Bitch is you crazy?" Brittany asked as she paced back and forth through the living room.

"Am I crazy? This was your idea!" Alexis said.

"We was drunk and I was joking Alexis!" Brittany said as she continued to pace the living room.

"Well I didn't take it as a joke. I did what you said I should do so it's too late to turn back now," Alexis said.

"I don't want nothing to do with that!" Brittany said.

"We in this together, so you got everything to do with it Brittany!" Alexis said as she reached and pulled her pistol from her waistline and looked at Brittany. Brittany stood there and quickly realized what was going on. She understood that she had no choice but to go along with whatever Alexis had planned. Brittany knew if she didn't go along with it, she would become a part of the plan.

"Ok girl I'm in," Brittany said.

"Good! Now let's go in there and get some answers," Alexis said. Brittany slowly started to walk toward the room. Alexis walked behind her with pistol in hand. Brittany walked into the room and stood next to Cory who laid there, duct tapped, and hog tied on the floor.

"Is he dead?" Brittany asked as she looked down at Cory who laid there motionless.

"No, he's alive. Watch!" Alexis said as she pulled a stun gun from her back pocket and stuck it to Cory's leg. Cory started to shake and flop around the floor like a fish fresh out the water. Alexis started laughing as she watched him flop around. "You see? He woke now girl!" she said. Brittany stood there terrified, she always saw Alexis as a sweet innocent pretty girl, but now she looked as if she had been doing this type of shit for years.

"This what happens when you think wit yo dick and don't watch what you drinking," Alexis said, and snatched the duct tape from Cory's eyes. Cory laid there on his stomach trying his hardest to look around, but everything was blurry as the room was spinning it was hard for him to make out who was who. Alexis pushed him over to his side.

"Look at me bitch nigga!" Alexis demanded.

"I'ma ask you two questions and you better get straight to the point with your answer. Cause what you say will determine if you live or die. Do you understand?" Alexis asked. Cory nodded his head yes. His eyes were buck wide and he was petrified, not sure if he was going to live or die. Alexis snatched the duct tape from his mouth and pointed her gun to his face.

"So, it was you and Lil Jerry that killed Rasheed and Khalil huh?" Alexis asked.

"I swear to God we didn't! I wanted to catch Khalil cause he robbed me but I couldn't find him. I ain't have no problem with no Rasheed," Cory said without delay. Brittany swiftly rushed over and kicked him in the stomach.

"Bitch you did kill him! Who else was with you?" she asked. Cory laid there in pain from Brittany's kick.

"I swear to God I didn't kill them niggas!" Cory managed to force out as he attempted to catch his breath.

"Well maybe this will help you remember!" Alexis said as she pressed the stun gun to his nuts and held it there for a few seconds.

"Now I'ma give you a chance to be honest!" Alexis said.

"Look I swear I didn't -----" before Cory could finish what he was about to say Alexis hit him with a volatile shock. Cory's body instantly became tauten as saliva fell from his mouth.

"He not going to tell us!" Brittany said.

"I know, that's why we're just going to get it over with and kill him!" Alexis said. Brittany looked down at the floor momentarily scared to speak her mind. She didn't want to kill Cory, but she knew there was no way she was going to be able to talk Alexis out of doing it. Alexis was set on revenge and was willing to go through any and every measure to achieve her goal.

Chapter Ten

S hah opened his eyes and smiled when he saw Keisha's face. Keisha was a natural beauty and Shah couldn't help but love her personality. He knew he couldn't commit to her because his heart belonged to Audrey. Shah sat up and scanned Keisha's body, He couldn't remember what happened last night, so he took a moment to appreciate the site before him. Shah considered himself a boss in his own right and felt like he shot to the moon over night. He was ready to take over and shit on any and everybody who once looked down on him. He reached over and smacked Keisha's ass and watched as it jiggled.

"Damn that ass fat!" he said.

Keisha woke up perturb and slapped Shah on the shoulder.

"Shah that shit hurts!" Keisha said. Shah laughed while he reached over and rubbed on her ass.

"My bad I couldn't help it, it was looking too good," Shah said.

"It's not funny!" Keisha said. Shah leaned over and kissed Keisha on the back. "I'm sorry.... You forgive me?" Shah asked as he slowly kissed down Keisha's back.

"Mmmm yeah I forgive you," Keisha said softly. Shah stood up from the bed and grabbed his pants and put them on. Keisha rolled over and looked up at Shah.

"So, you just gone tease me?" Keisha asked.

"My bad I ain't tryna tease you, I got some business I gotta take care of real quick. But I'm free tonight if you wanna go out again," Shah said as he continued to get dressed. Keisha laid there looking disappointed, but she understood he was chasing his dreams and she didn't want to try to get in the say of that.

"Yeah that's fine. I'm free tonight, just call me when you done taking care of your business," Keisha said while she pulled the sheets over her body.

"Tight I'ma call you when I'm done. Maybe tonight we can go bowling or something," Shah said as he walked toward the room door. Keisha swiftly pulled the sheets from over her body and got out of bed.

"Yeah that's fine," she said as she followed Shah through the hall and to the front door. Shah turned around and gave Keisha a hug.

"I'll see you later," he said while he held her in his arms.

"Ok, see you later," Keisha quickly replied. Shah turned and unlocked the door and left out the apartment. The sun was shining brightly, and it was a lot warmer than what Shah had expected when he stepped outside. He stood there and took a deep breath. It was a beautiful October day and just perfect for him to put the rest of his plan together. Shah had plans to take the city by storm, but first he needed to meet up with Alberto. He pulled out his phone and flipped through his contacts while he walked to his car. He found Lil Ant's number as he got into his car and called him. Shah pulled out of Keisha's lot as he waited on Lil Ant to answer.

"Who dis?" Lil Ant asked when he answered.

"This Shah," Shah quickly said.

"Damn, what up skud? I ain't heard from you in a minute," Lil Ant said.

"I aint on shit cuz, fuck you been up to down there?" Shah asked.

"Shit skud it's been slow motion I'm tryna get my cash right. It's a little hard cause we steady beefing with these niggas over here cause we on their block. I can't really focus cause I gotta worry about not getting caught lackin!" Lil Ant said.

"Shit cuz you might as well slide up this way, I got some shit in play and I need some help and somebody I could trust!" Shah said.

"Skud you know I hate Wisconsin. Them crackers be tryna hang a nigga out there," Lil Ant said. Shah started laughing "Man cuz you ain't been up here in a long ass time. This shit aint like it used to be trust me plus it's a whole lot better than dodging bullets. Plus, you got a chance to get yo cash right!" Shah said in an attempt to get Lil Ant to change his mind and see shit from his point of view.

"I don't know about that shit skud I love my city," Lil Ant said.

"You gotta think outside the box cuz. You ain't gotta stay here forever this shit all about checking a bag. trust me if you slide up here you gone love it! So, you tryna get some real money or not?" Shah asked. Lil Ant weighed his options before he spoke.

"You know what I might as well see what's to it I ain't got shit but fifty dollars to my name right now," Lil Ant said.

"Tight can you get a ride to the bus station downtown?" Shah asked.

"When today?" Lil Ant asked.

"Yeah today! I'ma text you the info to the Van Galder bus schedule. Just let me know what bus you getting on so I know what time to pick you up from the bus station," Shah said.

"Tight skud do that, I'm finna find me a ride. I'ma let you know what time I'ma make it down there," Lil Ant said.

"Say no more I'm finna get on it right now," Shah quickly said.

"Tight skud," Lil Ant said.

"Yep," Shah said and ended the call.

Meanwhile

Hot Boi and Big T sat behind the tint of Big T's minivan talking as they drove through the streets of Madison. Hot Boi hit the blunt and passed it to Big T.

"Man, bro I can't believe this nigga played me like that. I thought he was my mans, I put money in his pockets and just as soon as he got right, he switched up on me!" Hot Boi said. Big T hit the blunt and turned the radio down some.

"Lil bro I fucks wit you so I'ma give it to you in the raw. This a cold game and it ain't fair, sometimes a dog a bite the hand that feeds him cause he knows no better. You can't expect him to do for you what you would do for him cause he ain't you. Just stay focus and get yo paper," Big T said. Hot Boi sat back rubbing his chin as he soaked up the game Big T was giving him. He felt what Big T was saying, but the way Shah acted last night hit a nerve and dug deep under his skin. He wanted to hit Shah where it hurt to bring him back down to reality. Hot Boi reached over and grabbed the blunt back from Big T.

"Man, big bro I aint gone lie to you it ain't that easy for me to let that shit go," Hot Boi said.

"I ain't saying let that shit go, I'm saying stay focused on your cash. Don't let that throw you off cause you came a long way keep yo eyes on the prize!" Big T said.

"You right big bro I been focused and I'm finna stay focused and get this money," Hot Boi said then turned the radio back up.

Meanwhile

Quantay had been to every gas station in Janesville and Beloit dropping off flyers for a concert he had been promoting. Quantay was smart. He wanted to put his money into something that would give him a legit face. Promoting parties and concerts would be the perfect front for him since he enjoyed going out. Quantay pulled into the citgo gas station on Prairie and parked at the pump. This was his last stop before he got back to meeting his people. He jumped out of the car and walked into the gas station, the store was packed so Quantay stood at the door and looked around then made his way to the counter.

"I'm finna put these flyers right here," he said to the clerk as he set the flyers on the counter. He turned around and started passing out flyers.

"Come kick it wit me and Cardi B at club Addictions on November 17th," Quantay said as he passed each person in the store a flyer. Quantay looked up and noticed Trouble G in the back of the store by the coolers. He hadn't seen Trouble G in months.

"Troub what yo weak ass been on?" Quantay asked as he walked up to Trouble G. Trouble G looked over his shoulder at Quantay and started laughing as he turned all the way around. "Damn bro, you cut yo shit bald! Just three months ago you had a fro," Trouble G said.

"Oh, you tryna ride me? Nigga you up in here looking like a bird. Get yo Big Bird lookin ass yo Tucan Sam looking ass up out of here!" Quantay said in the attempt to shoot his shot back at Trouble G.

"Man, if you don't get yo common looking ass, yo Derek fisher looking ass, yo it took three razors to do the job looking ass up out of here," Trouble G said as they both started laughing.

"You got that, you got that!" Quantay said trying to get Trouble G off his heels.

"I ain't seen you in a minute, you must have been out of town?" Quantay asked switching subjects.

"Hell, naw'll I been around I just been low. I gotta focus on my music I be in the studio all day every day," Trouble G said.

"Damn I forgot you do go crazy on that rap shit. I got Cardi B coming thru in November and I got a few local acts opening up for her. I can make room for you if you wanna get in," Quantay said.

"Hell, yeah I wanna get in. How much time you gone give me?" Trouble G asked.

"I'ma let you be the last one right before she come out so you gotta make sure you turn that bitch up!" Quantay said.

"You know I'ma turn that bitch up. Just give me ten minutes and I'ma give you ten minutes of straight heat!" Trouble G said. He was geeked to be able to have the opportunity.

"Tight I got you! Just give me the tracks by next week so I can make sure the DJ on point. I don't wanna have to deal with no last-minute shit!" Quantay said as he passed Trouble G a flyer and gave him his new phone number.

"Just hit my line," Quantay said then walked off.

"Come fuck wit me and Cardi B November 17th," Quantay said to a female as she came into the store. He passed her a flyer and walked out of the store.

Meanwhile

Shah got out of his car at Alberto's auto body shop. He stood there for a moment looking at a short Hispanic chick. Her ass caught his full attention as she stood in front of a Cadillac truck with two of Alberto's employees.

"Damn she got a nice ass!" Shah thought to his self as he walked to the building entrance. Alberto was standing at the front desk with two of his employees, he looked up when he heard the bell on the door ring when it opened.

"Brother it's always good to see you!" Alberto said and smiled.

"It's always good to see you too brother!" Shah said and extended his hand to shake Alberto's hand. Shah was there on official business. He needed to re-up and see if Alberto could supply him with some quality cocaine. He had plans to lock Madison down with both the girl and boy. He wanted to make sure he was second to none and show the whole town he was a boss in his own right.

"Early huh?" Alberto asked.

"Yeah, I'm early," Shah said quickly. Those words were like music to Alberto's ears. He was shocked that Shah had got rid of the ten kilos in eight days, but he was happy cause he knew he just added a real money maker to his team.

"Come, come to my office so we can talk," Alberto said as he put his arm around Shah and started walking to his office. Shah walked into Alberto's office and took a seat. Alberto closed the door and shut the blinds.

"I wasn't expecting you so soon brother," Alberto said as he walked over to his desk.

"Yeah I know. It's about to get a lot better. I got the money in the car," Shah said. Alberto sat back in his chair smiling with his left hand on his chin. I like that! My money man Shah. I can be ready for you in an hour, you can wait here, or I can give you a call and tell you where to pick up at," Alberto said.

"I can wait the hour. I wanna check Beloit out and see what's down here anyway. But before I forget, I wanted to see if you could get me some top of the line cocaine. I have a nice clientele, but I need a reliable connection," Shah said. Alberto nodded his head as he looked at Shah.

"Ok, Ok I can help you out with that brother. I'll give you ten kilos for twenty thousand each. ninety five percent pure. Do you think you can handle that?" Alberto asked. Shah sat there for a moment doing the math in his head before he spoke.

"Honestly, I'd rather just pay up front. If you can do fifteen for me, I got the money in the car for it right now," Shah said. Shah knew twenty a key was better than what Big T was letting them go for. He was almost sure that the ninety five percent purity was better than Big T's coke. His heart started to race as the profit margin ran through his mind.

"Yes, I can do that. Is your car unlocked?" Alberto asked.

"Yeah, the money is in the trunk," Shah said. Alberto stood up from his desk and walked over to the door and opened it. He called out to Hector. Hector hurried and walked to the office and stood in the doorway.

"Recoje la bolsa negra de el carrgo Azul y polo en tu troca," Alberto said in his native language. Hector nodded his head then left the office. Alberto closed the door and walked back to his desk. In one hour, I want you to go to the 8th street store to make the pickup. This time I'm giving you twenty kilos at our regular price. Your fifteen kilos will be there as well. Bring me $800,000 no later than one month from today," Alberto said as he looked at Shah.

"Ok I can do that," Shah said, then stood up and shook Alberto's hand.

"8th street store in one hour, tell him Berto sent you," he said.

"Got it!" Shah said.

"Ok brother I'll see you in a month or sooner if you need me," Alberto said.

"Tight brother," Shah said then left Alberto's office. When Shah stepped outside, he immediately looked to see if he could see the Hispanic chick. He was glad to see she was still standing in front of her truck.

"Damn I would fuck the shit out of her!" he thought as he slowly walked back to his car. Shah jumped in his car and sat there flipping through his phone before he pulled out of his parking spot. He looked through his rearview mirror to catch one more glimpse of her ass before he pulled out the lot. Shah made his way to Prairie and pulled into the citgo gas station to fill up his tank. He jumped out of his car and walked into the gas station.

"How you doing?" Shah said as he approached the counter.

"I'm fine, and you?" the clerk asked.

"I'm good, can I get $30 on pump 3," Shah asked as he handed her two twenty-dollar bills.

"Ok, $30 on pump 3," she repeated. Shah stood there waiting for his change when he noticed a flyer with a picture of Cardi B on it.

"You have a nice day," the clerk said as she handed him his change.

"You too," Shah said as he picked up a flyer then walked out the store. Shah walked over to his car and put the pump into his tank and started pumping his gas.

"Oh yeah I gotta check this shit out," he said to his self as he read the flyer. "$50 regular admission and $100 V.I.P tickets available call (608-

213-3321)," Shah read out loud. He instantly went into his pocket and pulled out his cash and counted it.

"I gotta grab a few of these tickets right now," he thought to his self as he walked to his car door and opened it. He reached in and grabbed his phone from his cup holder and quickly dialed the number.

"Hello," Shah said as he heard the phone being answered.

"Hello," Quantay said.

"Yeah I'm calling bout the Cardi B tickets. I wanna grab ten V.I.P tickets," Shah said.

"Iight you in Beloit or Janesville?" Quantay asked.

"I'm in Beloit at the citgo gas station right now," Shah said.

"You on Prairie?" Quantay asked.

"Yeah," Shah quickly responded.

"Iight give me five minutes and I'll be there," Quantay said.

"Iight cool," Shah said then ended the call.

Chapter Eleven

B ro make a left at the second stop sign up there," X said as he pointed up the street.

"Tight bro," Tae G said. X pulled out his phone and called Andy back.

"Hello," Andy said as he answered the phone.

"Come outside and walk down to the corner I'ma pick you up there," X said.

"Dude you sure you don't wanna meet my people? Andy asked.

"Hell naw, just do what I told you!" X shouted then hung up.

"Dawg stay doing some dumb shit," Tae G said as he laughed. He knew X got pissed off every time he dealt with Andy.

"I know, but I ain't finna play wit dude today," X said. Tae G hit the stop sign then made a left. Andy was already standing on the corner. Tae G stopped in front of Andy. He ran up to the passenger side window and X quickly cracked it open.

"Man get in!" X shouted. Andy hurried and jumped into the back seat and immediately started talking.

"Man, bro my family from up north is down here. Dude they're like fuckin rich! Our fuckin grandfather just passed and left them fuckers with a lot of cash!" Andy said.

"Slow down! Let me see that cheese first," X said cutting Andy off.

"Oh, oh ok, here you go," Andy said quickly passing X the money. X started counting the money and Andy went right back to rambling off again.

"Dude I wanted to tell you they're into that heroin shit heavy and their looking for some right now," he said. X ignored him and quickly handed him a couple bags of work.

"Man take this shit I gotta go I got shit to do," X said loudly.

"Alright," Andy said as he opened the door to get out of the car. "But dude that's where the real money at, if you get any let me know I got you dude!" Andy said as he closed the door.

"Yeah, yeah," X said knowing he would never discuss his business ventures with a hype.

"I ain't gone lie, niggas out here eating fucking wit that boy. We should check him out no bull shit," Tae G said as he drove up the block. X looked over and gave him a crazy look.

"Dawg where we gone get some from? Kendall? If he selling us this bullshit work, what make you think Dawg gone sell us some boy worth selling?" X asked. Tae G sat there with a dumb look on his face cause he knew X was right but he also knew it was a lot of real money in the boy.

"Dawg that look like that Audi that followed me the other day," X said and grabbed his pistol as he looked out the passenger side mirror, He watched as the car turned off.

"Dawg you paranoid as fuck fall back!" Tae G said.

"Naw I'm on point, you better start getting on point," X said as he put his pistol back in the door panel.

Meanwhile

Shah sat outside the 8th street store in his car posting a picture of the ten V.I.P tickets he just bought. He looked at the time and noticed it was time to make the pickup. He jumped out of his car and walked into the store. Shah instantly smelled nothing but cigarette smoke. The smell reminded him of when he was younger and used to peek in his mother room while she was getting high with James and their friends. He walked up to the front of the store and noticed an old Armenian sitting behind the counter smoking a cigarette with a super long ash hanging from it.

"What you need?" the old man rudely asked in a broken English accent.

"Berto sent me," Shah said. The long ash fell from the cigarette to the floor. The old man took a long drag from the cigarette and stood up and put it out in the ash tray that sat on the counter.

"Berto huh?" the old man asked as he looked Shah up and down.

"Yeah Berto!" Shah said with a little aggression in his voice. The old man smiled then laughed. "Ok follow me," he said and walked from behind the counter and headed toward the back.

"This old nigga weird" Shah thought to himself as he followed him to the back of the store. The old man walked to a freezer and dragged out a big ass black duffle bag. Shah noticed the old man was struggling to get the bag out the door, so he helped him. The old man stood holding his lower back. "It's all there, twenty and fifteen," the old man said. Shah unzipped the bag and looked in the bag then quickly zipped it back up.

"Good," Shah said as he put the strap on his shoulder and stood up.

"Take that door," the old man said as he pointed to the door in the back of the store.

"Tight," Shah said and made his way to the door and out the store.

(Back on Russit)

Lil Jerry, Cortez, and Juice stood in the lobby of Tamara's building. Juice pulled out a bag of yellow school bus zans from his pocket and tossed them back and forth from hand to hand as he leaned against the wall.

"On Bd we need some of them!" Cortez said to Juice as soon as he seen the zans in his hand.

"Boa y'all dead! Goofy nem on they way to grab all these," Juice said and stuffed them back in his pocket.

"Man fuck goofy nem! sell us four of them bitches" Lil Jerry said. He knew juice was finna hit them other niggas over the head and tax them for the zans, so he had room to sell four.

"Hell, naw'll fool nem want all these. Y'all ain't tryna pay what I'm finna tax them," Juice said.

"Fuck that nigga!" Cortez said to Lil Jerry.

"Don't trip my mans on his way up here wit a whole jar," Lil Jerry said.

"Good! Cause I wasn't finna sell y'all none anyway especially not after I had to carry Lil Jerry up these stairs," Juice said. Lil Jerry started laughing as he walked to the door and looked outside. He quickly opened it when he seen Katrice two building down.

"Katrice bring yo ass over here!" Lil Jerry yelled out.

"Boy don't be calling me like you own me!" Katrice yelled back but quickly started walking over to Lil Jerry.

"I'm bout to make this bitch suck my dick!" Lil Jerry said to Juice and Cortez as he closed the building door.

"Bro yo ass crazy!" Cortez said and started laughing. Katrice walked up to the building door and stood there while Juice opened the door for her. She walked into the building and stood by the door.

"Whhaaatt Lil Jerry?" Katrice asked as she stood there looking up to Lil Jerry at the top of the stairs.

"Man stop playing. Bring yo ass up here!" Lil Jerry said. Katrice smacked her lips cause she knew just what Lil Jerry wanted. Her first mind told her to turn around and leave but she didn't. She walked her way over to the stairs and made her way to where Lil Jerry was standing.

"Why you be on bullshit?" Lil Jerry asked.

"I ain't on bullshit, that's you! You always on bullshit Jerry," Katrice responded. She really liked Lil Jerry, but she hated the way he treated her like he didn't give two fucks about her.

"On Bd this mafucka getting fat!" Lil Jerry said as he reached and grabbed Katrice's ass.

"It ain't getting fat, it's been fat!" Katrice said smiling. Lil Jerry started laughing then pulled down his sweatpants and boxer briefs and stood there with his dick in his hands.

"Gone head and hit this mafucka for me," he said looking down at his dick then back up to Katrice. Katrice smacked her lips and rolled her eyes.

"I knew that was all you wanted," Katrice said, then grabbed a hold of his dick and bent over and started sucking it. Lil Jerry couldn't see Cortez and Juice, but he could hear them downstairs snickering.

"Aye Juice" Lil Jerry yelled out.

"What up bro?" Juice asked.

"You ain't seen Cory?" Lil Jerry asked as he reached down and grabbed a handful of Katrice's hair and pushed her head down shoving his dick deeper into her mouth.

"I ain't seen bro since he dropped you off yesterday," Juice said before him and Cortez walked out of the building. Lil Jerry stood there thinking while Katrice continued to go crazy.

"Something ain't right this nigga Cory always answer the phone. That's his lifeline," he thought to his self.

"Yeah hit that mafucka like that! Play wit my balls too," Lil Jerry said as Katrice went crazy nonstop for fifteen minutes before he bust in her mouth.

(Shah)

Sitting in Tammy's apartment at the kitchen table, Shah calculated how much he would pull in off the heroin. He had twenty-one bricks of boy in front of him.

"Ok I owe Berto $800,000. If I sell 17 of these bitches for $80,000 a piece that's what?" Shah quickly calculated the numbers on his phone.

"Damn that's $1,360,000 minus Berto $800,000. That leaves me wit $560,000 and 4 more bricks... I'ma dump them bitches to Hustle Man's people for a buck twenty a grit. Shit that's $480,000 dollars," Shah said to his self.

"Yeah I'm bout to fuck these niggas up and I'm finna flood this bitch wit this coke too these niggas ain't finna be able to fuck wit me!" he said to himself. He quickly looked up when the front door opened.

"Who you talking to?" Tammy asked as she walked into the apartment and closed the door.

"Nobody, why you say that?" Shah asked.

"Cause I heard you talking when I put the key in the door," Tammy said.

"Oh, I was doing the math on this shit," Shah said as he pointed to all the shit he had stacked up on the table.

"Damn Shah don't you think that's too much?" she asked as she looked at all the bricks of boy and coke stacked up neatly on top of the table. Shah started laughing "It ain't no such thing as too much money," he said.

"Well I guess when you put it like that," Tammy quickly said.

"Oh, I got something for you!" Shah quickly said then walked over to the couch and grabbed the McM book bag and handed it to her. Tammy started laughing "So giving me my book bag back is what you got for me? You funny ass hell," She said Shah started laughing.

"Naw it's in the bag!" he said. Tammy unzipped the book bag and pulled out a big ass stack of twenty-dollar bills wrapped in rubber bands.

"That's your cut," Shah said as he watched Tammy unwrap the rubber bands and fan through the money.

"This shit a whole lot better than my job," she said as she laughed. Shah's phone started to ring so he rushed back to the table to answer it.

"What up cuz?" he asked as he answered.

"Aye I'll be up there at six at the park and ride, make sure you on point. I aint tryna be out there lacking," Lil Ant said. Shah started laughing "Man cuz this White-consin, you ain't gotta worry about lackin but I'ma make sure I'm there," he said.

"Tight bet," Lil Ant said and ended the call. Shah looked at the time on his phone. "Damn it's 5:40pm, I need to get up out of here. Aye Tammy, put this shit back in the bag for me and put it in the closet in the other room," Shah said.

"Alright," Tammy said as Shah hurried and left the apartment.

(6:00pm)

Lil Ant sat in the back of the Van Galder bus looking out the window as they exited onto Stoughton Rd. Wisconsin felt so foreign to him as he looked around the bus at all the white faces. He felt out of place. He wasn't used to this type of scene, back home he rarely if ever seen any white people and when he did, they stayed far away from him. But the white people in Wisconsin was different. They actually spoke to you as you passed by, and in a weird way that made him even more uncomfortable. The bus came to a complete stop in front of an Arbys and a gas station that were connected. The interior lights came on and the bus door opened.

"You have reached the Park and Ride," the bus driver said over the intercom.

"Damn this the Park and Ride?" Lil Ant said to his self as he looked out the window. He hadn't seen Shah in years and had no idea what kind of car he was in. He got up and walked to the front of the bus and got off. He stood there for a moment looking around as he pulled his phone from his pocket. Shah came walking out of Arbys and seen lil Ant standing on the sidewalk in front of the bus.

"Aye nigga where you from?" Shah said in a deep voice. Lil Ant looked in the direction of where the voice came from and saw Shah standing in front of Arbys and started laughing as he walked toward him.

"I was finna get on yo ass!" Lil Ant said as he shook Shah's hand.

"Nigga you was shook, you thought you got caught lackin," Shah said.

"Naw, naw. It's good to see you though cuz!" Lil Ant said.

"Hell yeah! It's good to see you too. Ever since Shawn got locked up I been feeling like I'm out here by myself. Now I got some family out here we finna fuck this city up!" Shah said as they walked back over to his car.

"It's official let's fuck this bitch up then!" Lil Ant said as they got into Shah's car. Shah pulled out of Arbys parking lot and made a right onto Stoughton rd and jumped on the beltline headed west.   Shah tossed a half ounce of kush into Lil Ant's lap. "Man, cuz roll some of that shit I ain't been able to smoke all day I'm tryna get high," Shah said.

"Tight I see you smoking out the bag this the shit I like," Lil Ant said as he reached to the cup holder and grabbed the box of cigarillos.

"Aye cuz what you fucking wit up here?" Lil Ant asked. Shah looked over at Lil Ant then back to the road. "I been fucking wit the boy, but I just got some coke in and I need you to work the coke line I'm tryna set up. That way we fuck the town up on both sides of the board. This shit I got gone take the city by storm when we put this shit out there," Shah said with confidence.

"Tight so what you gone need me to do?" Lil Ant asked as he twisted up the cigarillo.

"My man's nem got this block they hustling on and I wanna open up shop in one of the buildings over there. I'ma need you to work that mafucka until we build up the clientele then we can pay somebody to work it while we sit back and collect," Shah said. Lil Ant pulled his lighter from his pocket and dried the blunt off then flamed it up. "Tight I'm wit it. But give me the run down, let me know what I'ma be pulling in off what I sell," Lil Ant said as he exhaled a big cloud of smoke and started coughing.

"Tight look, I already did the math on this shit. I got 15 bricks I paid $30,000 for each one. Now if we straight drop each one and bag up $1600 a zip, we make $57,600 a book. If we sell all 15 like that in bags, we gone blow all competition out the water. We gone pull in $864,000 off that. Now, I want the $450,000 I paid for them off the top. That'll leave us wit $414,000, and we just gone bust that down the middle. So, you a pull in $207,000 off this flip, then after this you can buy however many you want to buy wit yo cash and I'ma do the same and we just gone pay some lil niggas to work the line. You wit it?" Shah asked as he reached and grabbed the blunt. Lil Ant looked over at Shah with eyes wide, he was shocked to hear the numbers Shah threw at him. "Am I wit it? What kind of question is that! Cuz I just left a block where niggas killing over pennies. I ain't never seen a brick and you asking if I wanna help you wit 15 of em. Hell, yeah I'm wit it!" Lil Ant said.

"Good cause you would be a fool not to," Shah said as he inhaled the kush smoke. Shah pulled into the Zimmer's liquor store parking lot. "What you drink cuz?" he asked as he looked over at Lil Ant.

"Cuz I'm fucked up, I ain't got no cash," Lil Ant said.

"That ain't what I asked you. As a matter of a fact," Shah said reaching into the middle console. "Take this. Now let's go in here and grab something to drink on," Shah said as he handed Lil Ant three thousand dollars. Shah opened his door and jumped out of the car. Lil Ant sat there for a moment in shock. He wasn't used to this cause back in Chicago on his block his niggas was cut throat and fucked up and niggas like Shah was food to them niggas. He was now on the other side of things and knew this was a once in a lifetime chance for a nigga like him and he was going to be damned if he blew it.

"You coming in?" Shah asked as he stood in front of the car.

"Oh, yeah Skud. It's official," Lil Ant said as he stuffed the cash in his pocket and jumped out of the car.

Meanwhile

Tae G and X had been in traffic for hours and both lines had been going crazy and shit was starting to look like they was going to get rid of the rest of the bullshit coke they got from Kendall. X phone stated to ring, He looked down and saw that it was Honey.

"What up?" X asked as he answered.

"Damn, Xavier I been calling you all day. Why I gotta do all that just for you to answer the phone?" Honey asked with an attitude.

"Where you at?" X asked.

"Why Xavier? You didn't give a fuck about where I was or what I wanted when you sent all my calls to the voice mail. Now did you?" Honey asked.

"Man get dressed I'm finna come scoop you. Call yo friend Asia too, cause bro wit me," X said. Honey smacked her lips.

"Naw, what you on?" she asked

"Bitch just do it!" X said frustrated

"I'ma pull up in a minute so be ready. You hungry?" he asked.

"Yeah," Honey said

"Tight, we finna go out to eat somewhere so get dressed," X said.

"Ok. well we gone see y'all when y'all get here. I love you," Honey said.

"Yeah! I love me too,"X quickly said then ended the call.

"Damn I love that bitch!" X said to himself as he put his phone down in his lap.

"Where we finna go?" Tae G asked as he ended his call.

"Scoop the lil bitch Asia and Honey and go grab something to eat," X said.

"Dude right off the highway on Oklahoma said he got $2500! We gotta catch that like now!" Tae G said.

"Damn that's Eric Dawg. Call him back and tell him if he waits I'ma do something extra for him," X said as he turned the radio down.

"Tight," Tae G said and picked his phone. X drove down to 60th and Brown Deer and made a right. As he continued to drive, he started to reflect back on his life. The hand he'd been dealt was fucked up from jump. His mother was out there bad running the streets since he was seven years old. His father was nowhere to be found which forced him into the streets because he was tired of getting the ass end of everything in life.

"Man, I gotta get this money!" he said to himself. After a long drive he finally made it to Honey's block on 22nd and Cherry. He pulled out his phone and texted Honey letting her know he was outside. His phone started to ring, and he quickly answered.

"Yo" X said as he answered the phone.

"Hey, it's Kelly, I got 80 for you," she said

"Tight give me twenty minutes," X said and ended the call. He parked behind Honey's Kia and honked the horn. Minutes later, Honey and Asia both came walking out the house. Honey was what you called a "yellow bone." She was 5'7 a 160 pounds with a slim waist, a fat ass, and 32D breasts. She was beautiful and low-key, X had feelings for her from the moment he first met her, but he struggled with trust issues. He figured it was best to just stand on her. Asia and Honey both were college students attending UWM. Asia was an athlete. She played volleyball for the UWM Panthers. She was 5'9 and 160 pounds with a petite body frame. Asia was a chocolate beauty.

"Damn I might have to double back on her!" X thought to his self as he watched Asia coming down the stairs behind Honey.

"She valid bro!" Tae G said as he looked over at X. Tae G opened his door and got out allowing Honey to sit in the front seat, plus he wanted to get closer to Asia. He opened the door so she could get in then walked around in got in the car behind X.

"Hey boo" Honey said as X put his pistol and work in her purse and pulled off.

"What up," X responded. Honey pulled her iPhone out and plugged it into the USB. "Xavier don't cut my music off," Honey said before she pressed play. Musiq Soul child's song "Love" poured through the speaker's X looked over at Honey.

"I could see myself settling down with her and being a family man one day, but right now I gotta focus on getting my bag right. Maybe in my next life I could wife her," X thought to his self. He made a left on 27th and Burleigh then drove all the way up to 85th and Burleigh then made a right and pulled over. He turned the radio down some and called Kelly.

"I'm outside," X said.

"Ok here I come," Kelly said.

"Tight," X said and ended the call. Two minutes later, Kelly came rushing out the house and ran up to the car. X rolled down his window and Kelly tossed the $80 dollars on his lap. X grabbed it and made sure it was $80 dollars before he handed her the work.

"Thanks," Kelly said and turned and ran back to her house. X laughed then rolled his window back up and pulled off.

"Is this what y'all do all day?" Asia asked X.

"Yeah! why you ask that?" X asked.

"No real reason. It just look easy that's all," Asia said. Tae G started laughing "It's a whole lot harder than what it look!" he said cutting into the conversation.

"A whole lot harder than what it look," X added as he looked through the rearview mirror at Asia. While looking back, X noticed the same black early 2000's model A-6 Audi that he had seen earlier that day and the other day behind him.

"I been over here a thousand times I ain't never seen that car over here." He made a right turn on 85th and Chambers then another right up the block on 84th and then a left on to Burleigh and shot down to 76st and made a left. The Audi was nowhere in sight, so he waved it off.

"Damn this gas got me trippin!" X thought to his self, then turned the music back up and put his hand on Honey's thigh. He looked into his rearview mirror to see if Tae G was on Asia and noticed the Audi was behind him again. He reached over and grabbed Honey's purse and pulled out his glock .40 and held it in his hand as he kept checking the mirrors.

"What up bro?" Tae G asked sensing something was going on by X's body movements. X rolled down his window then blew through the stop light on 76th and Capital then abruptly stopped in the middle of the street with his gun in hand ready to shoot. The Audi whipped around him and sped by as cars in the intersection honked their horns.

"What the fuck bro?" Tae G yelled out.

"Is everything okay?" Asia asked.

"Yeah my bad I was trippin!" X said as he pulled off.

"Bro you want me to drive?" Tae G asked.

"Naw, I got it bro," X said.

"Tight! Don't forget that $2500 on the South side," Tae G said as he wondered what the hell X was just on.

"I'm on my way now," X said as he turned around and headed toward the South side.

Meanwhile

Keisha had brought her friends Emily and Samantha out with her to the bowling alley with Shah, his cousin Lil Ant, and Lil Jerry. Shah had made a bet with Keisha that he could bowl a higher score than she could. Keisha sat across the table from Shah as Samantha and Lil Jerry took there turns bowling. Shah sat there eating a slice of pizza as his phone lit up it started ringing. Keisha looked down at his phone and seen a picture that said Wifey. Shah picked up his phone and answered it.

"What up Cinderella?" Shah asked as he looked Keisha directly in the eyes.

"What you doing?" Audrey asked.

"Shit at the bowling alley. My cousin just got down here today I'm tryna show him a good time," Shah said.

"Oh ok, well is you coming home tonight?" she asked.

"Naw not tonight I wanna get him settled somewhere before I come home," Shah said.

"Why you don't bring him out here?" Audrey asked curious.

"You know I don't want nobody to know where we stay that's our safe spot," Shah said.

"Well you need to get him settled somewhere fast cause I ain't move all the way out here to be here by myself in this big ass house Shah," Audrey said.

"Your turn to bowl Shah!" Lil Jerry yelled out to Shah.

"Tight give me a second," Shah yelled back.

"But I'ma get him settled in and I'll be home tomorrow," Shah said.

"Ok. And you better not be up there with no bitches," Audrey said. Shah started laughing as he took another bite from his pizza.

"Naw we aint" he said.

"Yeah ok, don't get fucked up Shah. But I'ma let you go, I love you baby," Audrey said.

"I love you too! I'ma see you tomorrow," Shah said.

"Okay," she said.

"Ok," Shah said and ended the call and looked back over to Keisha who sat there pissed that Shah had the nerve to have a full conversation with another woman while she sat right there.

"What?" Shah asked as Keisha sat there staring at him.

"Really Shah? You just gone talk to this bitch in my face like I ain't here!" Keisha said.

"Look we gone get this shit straight right now. You ain't gone never disrepect her again. I like you and I enjoy hanging out with you, but that's my woman and I ain't putting her second to no one. So, if you wanna fuck wit me you gone have to understand that if she call and I'm wit you I'ma answer it. And if you don't like it, then maybe we shouldn't fuck around," Shah said. Keisha sat there shocked at what just came out of Shah's mouth. She stood up from the table and walked off toward the bathroom. Emily sat at the table next to the table Keisha and Shah sat at and saw the look on Keisha's face as she walked off. Emily jumped up from the table and followed Keisha to the bathroom. She walked into the bathroom and found Keisha at the sink looking in the mirror.

"You ok?" Emily asked.

"I don't know. I'm really feeling him, but I just found out he got a girl," Keisha said.

"Ok, well fuck him then girl," Emily said.

"I wish it was that easy. I like being around him, and girl he fucked the shit out of me last night I don't wanna let that dick go," Keisha said as she laughed. Emily started laughing "Well if it's the dick you want make y'all relationship based solely on sex don't get caught up in yo feelings cause you know he got a girl," Emily said.

"Yeah you right. That's what I'm going to do!" Keisha said.

"Okay so bitch fix your face and let's go out here and continue looking cute and enjoy ourselves. Cause I wanna put this pussy on his cousin, girl he fine as hell," Emily said.

"Bitch we some hoes!" Keisha said. They both started laughing and walked out of the bathroom. Emily and Keisha turned the corner and found everyone they were withstanding at the counter giving their bowling shoes back while Shah paid for their bowling time.

"Y'all done already?" Emily asked.

"Yeah. But if y'all want to we can slide to a bar and have a few drinks," Shah said.

"Ok I'm down," Keisha said as she grabbed her shoes from Samantha and took off her bowling shoes.

"Tight well we finna hit one of these bars then," Lil Jerry said as he put his arm around Samantha and started walking to the exit. Lil Ant could tell Emily was on his heels cause she kept finding ways to spark up conversations with him. He wasn't one hundred percent sure because he never hung out with a white girl before. His mind started to wonder as he thought about the possibility of being with a white girl. Emily was a 5'3, 125 pounds petite, with strawberry blonde hair. She had a nice ass for a white girl. Lil Ant stared at the way her ass looked in her leggings. The group walked outside to the parking lot. Keisha, Emily, and Samantha all walked over to their cars. Shah, Lil Ant, and Lil Jerry walked over to Shah's car and stood outside the car talking shit. Emily pulled up next to where Shah was parked in her 2017 BMW x6 and rolled her window down. "Lil Ant, you wanna ride wit me?" she asked. Lil Ant looked over at Shah and laughed a little. It sounded funny hearing a white person say his name.

"Yeah, she on my heels, I'm finna fuck the shit out this white bitch," he thought to his self and looked over at Emily "Yeah I'll ride wit you," he said and walked over to her truck and got in with her. Lil Jerry and Shah jumped in Shah's car and pulled out of the parking spot. Lil Jerry rolled down his window. "Follow us!" he yelled out to the the line of cars behind them as Shah pulled off. They drove off from the bowling alley in search of a bar to go to.

Chapter Twelve

*L*il Ant woke up to Emily giving him some head. He looked down and she was looking right at him, he was mesmerized by her light blue eyes. She had her strawberry blonde hair pulled back into a ponytail.

"Damn you sexy ass hell!" he said as he watched Emily slowly suck his dick with her back arched and ass up in the air. Emily wanted to make sure she put on a show for Lil Ant now that she had his full attention. Emily twirled her tongue around the tip of his dick never looking away from him. Then she slowly took him into her mouth until he was in her throat. Lil Ant's whole body stiffened up when he felt her throat muscles wrap around his dick tightly. Emily felt Lil Ant's body stiffen and she knew just what to do to drive him crazy. Emily had plans to keep Lil Ant around and she was willing to do whatever it took to keep him around. Emily kept forcing him deeper and deeper into her throat as she watched Lil Ant's reaction. She continued to use every trick she knew while she sucked his dick until he finally bust. Emily jumped out of the king size bed and walked to the bathroom in her master bedroom. Lil Ant laid there looking around the room, it was huge, and he'd never been in a house as nice as this. It was so clean; he could only assume she had just moved in a few weeks ago. He reached over and grabbed the remote off the nightstand and turned on the 72"in flat screen that was mounted to a huge Tv stand in front of the bed. Emily came walking out of the bathroom with a towel for Lil Ant while she was brushing her teeth. She gave Lil Ant the towel then walked back into the bathroom. Lil Ant jumped out of the bed and walked to the bathroom with her,

Emily stood there watching Lil Ant wash his self-off as she brushed her teeth.

"Damn I love his light brown skin, and that slim muscular body filled with all those tattoos. And those dreads are so sexy. I gotta have him to myself," Emily thought to herself as she watched him. Lil Ant finished washing his dick off and walked back into the bedroom and put his clothes on. Emily came out of the bathroom full of energy.

"Would you like something to eat?" she asked him.

"Naw, I'm good," Lil Ant quickly said.

"Are you sure? I don't mind making you some breakfast," Emily said.

"Yeah I'm sure. Where we at?" Lil Ant asked.

"Verona," Emily said as she walked out of the room. Lil Ant got off the bed and followed her down the hall. "Damn this a nice ass crib," he thought to his self as they walked down the long hall and down the stairs.

"You live here by yourself?" he asked.

"Yeah, I live here alone," Emily said as she walked through the dining room and into the kitchen.

"This a nice ass house!" Lil Ant said as he looked around the kitchen.

"Thanks. My dad brought it for me a few years ago for my 19th birthday," Emily said.

"How long you been in Wisconsin?" Emily asked.

"I just got down here yesterday from Chicago. I needed a change of scenery," Lil Ant said.

"How old are you?" Emily asked curiously.

"I'm twenty. How old are you?" Lil Ant asked.

"I'm twenty-two," Emily said. Lil Ant's phone started to ring in his pocket. He pulled it out and saw that it was Shah and quickly answered.

"What up Skud?" Lil Ant said.

"Where you at?" Shah asked.

"I'm at Emily crib," Lil Ant replied.

"Tight, tell her you got some shit you gotta do and have her drop you off on Russit," Shah said.

"Tight. You said Russit right?" Lil Ant asked.

"Yeah Russit," Shah said.

"Tight Skud!" Lil Ant said and ended the call.

"Aye Emily I got something to do and I need you to drop me off on Russit," Lil Ant said.

"I'm kind of tired. How bout you take my Cadillac truck I barely drive it," Emily said using her truck as a way of being able to make sure she see Lil Ant again. Lil Ant sat there silent not sure what to say. "She don't even know me like that and she gone let me drive her shit," he thought to his self as he sat there. Emily walked out of the kitchen and walked to the living room, then walked back into the kitchen. She sat the truck keys on the counter.

"It's in the garage, I'll call you after I get off work," Emily said as she pointed to a door that led to the garage. She reached into the fridge and pulled out some fruit yogurt then walked out of the kitchen.

"Make sure you let the garage door down when you leave. The garage door opener is on the sun visor," she yelled out as she walked back up to her bedroom. Lil Ant grabbed the keys and walked to the door in the kitchen that lead to the garage. He opened the door and saw a candy apple red 2017 Cadillac truck parked next to her BMW x6.

"Damn I had to have been lit last night cause I ain't see this mafucka," he said as he walked to the truck and opened the door and jumped in. The new car air freshener lingered in the air. Lil Ant hurried and dialed Shahs number back.

"What up?" Shah asked as he answered.

"Aye Skud, she ain't wanna drive so she gave me her truck to take. Skud white people here super friendly this shit scary," Lil Ant said. Shah started laughing.

"You must have fucked the shit out of her for her to let you take the BMW after the first night," Shah said.

"Na Skud this bitch got a 2017 Lac truck too. She forced this mafucka on me," Lil Ant said.

"Oh yeah? She tryna keep you around. It sound like she on top of her shit and her lil white ass sexy. That's a good look for you cuz," Shah said.

"Yeah she official. Skud you know all this type of shit new to me, especially white bitches, but look I don't know how to get where you at, so I need a address to put in my GPS," Lil Ant said.

"Damn I don't know a address for Russit. Fuck it just put this address in and I'ma meet you there. 2318 A-l-l-I-e-d drive," Shah slowly said.

"Tight I got it skud. I'm finna leave now," Lil Ant said.

"Tight cuz" Shah said and ended the call. Lil Ant started the truck and hit the garage door opener. He waited for the door to open all the way up and put his seat belt on and backed out of the garage. He closed the garage door as he backed out onto the street then he pulled off.

Meanwhile

Shah stood in the parking lot on Allied with two crack heads. He'd just gave them both a sample and told them he wasn't doing nothing on the phone. Shah looked up and saw the sun shining off the wet candy apple red paint job on the Cadillac truck pulling into the lot. Lil Ant pulled into a parking space and parked.

"Damn that bitch nice!" Shah said to Lil Ant as he jumped out of the truck. "That bitch brand new!" Lil Ant said as he walked up to Shah and shook his hand.

"Let's get up out of here. We gotta get over here to Russit and pass out these samples and get the word out here," Shah said.

"Tight," Lil Ant said. They both jumped back into their cars. Lil Ant waited for Shah to pull out so he could follow him. He trailed Shah over to Cameron and parked behind him. Shah lead the way around the corner to Russit.

"This the block I was telling you bout," Shah said as they walked down Russit. The block was packed with niggas and bitches everywhere. Lil Ant looked around at the different groups of people that was standing on both sides of the street.

"Damn this bitch bussin!" Lil Ant said as they walked down Russit.

"Yeah this bitch is bussin today for some reason. But its about to be a lot of cash out here," Shah said as he scanned the crowds. He looked across the street and seen Tonya his old co-worker. He hadn't seen Tonya since he got fired. "Aye Tonya" Shah yelled out to her. Tonya looked up and seen Shah and started laughing. "Shah what up?" She yelled out then ran across the street. Tonya gave Shah a hug, she was excited to see him. Tonya and Shah used to hang out and talk shit at work all the time.

"Damn what you doing over here?" Shah asked.

"I live over here now," Tonya said.

"When you move over here?" Shah asked.

"I moved in three days ago in those blue buildings over there, but I stay on the front side on Raymond," Tonya said.

"Oh ok. That's what's up. How the job been going?" Shah asked.

"Boy I quit! They got to doing the most, I couldn't take it no more. I'm looking for something new right now. What about you? Where you working now?" Tonya asked. Shah started laughing

"I ain't even working right now. But I'm doing a whole lot better than I was when I was working. So, I don't think I'll be working no time soon," Shah said. Lil Ant stood there looking around while Shah was talking to Tonya. He noticed a grey Mazda had rode past them twice since they been standing there and the dude in the passenger seat was looking at them real hard which gave him a bad feeling.

"Aye Skud, you know these niggas in this grey car coming up the street?" Lil Ant asked as the Mazda was coming down the block for the third time. Shah and Tonya both looked to the street to see what Lil Ant was talking about. The Mazda rode past real slow and both the driver and the passenger was looking at them. Shah caught eye contact with the passenger, and they locked eyes the passenger turned his head and looked back at Shah as they rode past.

"Na I don't know them niggas. But they looking hard as hell," Shah said.

"I don't know them either," Tonya said as they watched the car continue to drive up the block.

"Them niggas on bull shit Skud. They drove by three times looking crazy like that," Lil Ant said.

"Fuck them niggas cuz they ain't on shit!" Shah quickly said. Lil Ant stood there quiet, but he had a bad feeling in his stomach. He knew some shady shit when he seen it cause he grew up around sharks. He could sense when a nigga was about to try and bite off eye contact alone.

"Tight Skud. I'ma take your word for it, but I can smell bullshit from a mile away," Lil Ant said.

"We in White-consin, these niggas know better!" Shah said.

"Tight," Lil Ant said. Shah turned back to Tonya and continued talking. He wasn't worried about what Lil Ant was talking about. He knew Lil Ant just left a war zone and he had to realize this ain't Chicago.

"You tryna make some money?" Shah asked Tonya.

"It depends on what you talking about," Tonya said.

"Tight, look I need a safe spot to keep some shit at. I'ma pay you five G's a month and I'll pay the rent. Now all you gotta do is make sure you don't let nothing happen to the shit," Shah said.

"Yeah I want some of that money!" Tonya quickly said.

"Tight I'ma need a set of keys for me and cuz. We gone be the only ones to come over cause I wanna make sure we keep the spot low key," Shah said.

"Ok, when you tryna do this?" Tonya asked.

"Today!" Shah said then reached in his pocket and pulled out a roll of cash and peeled off a twenty-dollar bill and handed it to Tonya.

"Use this to get us a set of keys then call me and I'ma come over to your crib so I know where it's at," Shah said.

"Tight. yo number still the same?" she asked.

"Yeah it's still the same," Shah said.

"Alright well I'm finna go do this right now and I'll call you when I'm done," Tonya said and walked off. Lil Ant and Shah started walking up the block to Tamara's building. Shah wanted to hurry up and pass out the samples so they could get to business.

Meanwhile

Blue Dini pulled over and parked on Sunny Mead. He looked out his rearview mirror and saw Jeff coming down the hill from Capital View. Jeff had a good clientele but would never grab more than a hundred grams at a time even though he knew he was going to run through them in four days. Blue Dini would try to get him to buy more than a hundred grams, so he didn't have to keep pulling up on him every four days. Jeff would always say, "The goal is to stack the cash not the grams." It really didn't make much sense to Blue Dini, so he stopped trying to get him to upgrade. Jeff was set in his ways and Blue Dini knew, so he was happy with the ten G's every four days. Blue Dini unlocked his car door and let Jeff in.

"What up big bro?" Jeff asked as he got in and closed the door.

"Shit!" Blue Dini said as he tossed the grams on Jeff's lap. Jeff picked it up and flipped it around in his hands as he inspected them. "Is it the same shit from last time? My people loving that shit," Jeff said.

"Yeah that's the same shit. I was gone tax you $120 a grit like I been taxing everybody else. But I fucks wit you so I can't do you like that," Blue Dini said. Jeff went into his pocket and pulled out ten thousand dollars and handed it to Blue Dini.

"This the whole ten?" Blue asked.

"Damn big bro that's how you do me?" Jeff asked in shock.

"You know what that's on me, you do come correct. My bad lil bro," Blue Dini said.

"Tight, it's all love big bro," Jeff said and shook Blue Dini's hand and jumped out the car. Blue Dini pulled off headed toward the trailer park. He pulled into the trailer park and parked behind Lil Lord's truck. Lil Lord was pissed Blue Dini had him waiting there for twenty minutes. Lil Lord jumped out the truck and walked up to Blue Dini's car and got in.

"Damn bro, why you got me sitting here like a hype?" Lil Lord asked as he closed the door.

"My bad bro, you know how this shit be," Blue Dini said. He opened the middle console and pulled out two hundred grams and handed them to Lil Lord.

"Damn bro this ain't five hunnit," Lil Lord said as he looked at Blue Dini.

"That's the last two. But I'ma be ready for you with the other three in two hours," Blue Dini said.

"Damn bro, I needed the whole five," Lil Lord said.

"Shit I figured two was better than nothing," Blue Dini said. Lil Lord shook his head as he counted off twenty thousand and handed it to Blue Dini. "Bro call me when you get back straight. The new shit gone be like this? Cause my people eating this shit right here up," Lil Lord said.

"Yeah it should be the same quality. I'ma hit you as soon as I get good lil bro," Blue Dini said.

"Bet," Lil Lord said then jumped out the car and walked back to his truck. Blue Dini pulled out his phone and called Shah as he drove down Badger Rd.

"What up big bro?" Shah asked as he answered.

"Same shit. Check it out though, I need five whole ones lil bro," Blue Dini said.

"Tight," Shah quickly replied.

"How long?" Blue Dini asked.

"Twenty minutes," Shah said.

"Tight look I gotta make a stop and grab my gym shorts real quick just meet me at the Princeton club out west," Blue Dini said.

"Say no more," Shah said.

"Tight," Blue Dini said and ended the call.

Later That Evening

Audrey and Tammy sat in Audrey's living room talking about work and school as they enjoyed a bottle of Rosé.

"So how you like living out here?" Tammy asked Audrey.

"It's nice cause this my first time ever actually living in a house. But girl, Shah be running the streets all the time I be here lonely as hell," Audrey said. Tammy took a sip from her glass and sat it down on the coffee table.

"Well you know you always welcome to come to my apartment and stay there the days Shah gone be away," Tammy said as she pulled her hair back and put it in a ponytail. Tammy was starting to feel a little tipsy from the few glasses of Rosé she had, it was slowly creeping up on her.

"Yeah I know. Now that I got this house in order, I'm about to start doing that," Audrey said. They both looked toward the front as they heard the door open and close. Tammy looked over at Audrey and took a sip from her drink.

"Well bitch he home tonight!" Tammy whispered and they both started laughing. Shah walked into the living room holding a duffle bag. "What's so funny I wanna laugh too," he said.

"You!" they both said simultaneously. Audrey quickly got up and walked over to Shah and gave him a hug and a kiss. Shah held Audrey for a moment before letting her go, then she turned around Shah smacked her on the ass.

"What up Tammy?" Shah asked her as he gave her a look letting her know he wanted her.

"Hey Shah," Tammy said and quickly looked away and took a sip from her drink.

"This Rosé running through me," she said to Audrey as she sat her drink down and got up to go use the bathroom. Shah watched as Tammy walked to the bathroom. He wanted to fuck her badly, his eyes were fixated on her ass in the white Prada jeans she had on. Shah watched Tammy walk all the way down the hall to the bathroom. Audrey watched Shah as he watched Tammy walking down the hall. Audrey knew Shah wanted Tammy and she wasn't mad at him cause she wanted Tammy too. She had never been with another woman or had a threesome before. Audrey always imagined Tammy being a part of her first experience in both situations if she ever decided to try. Shah turned to Audrey and noticed she was already staring at him. "I'm finna go get in this shower," Shah quickly said as he panicked and tried to hurry and get out of the situation.

"Ok make sure you ready," Audrey said with a seductive look in her eyes.

"Ready for what?" Shah asked.

"Lil mama!" Audrey said as she licked the rim of her glass.

"You know I love it when lil mama stop by!" Shah said as he turned and walked out of the living room.

"Lil mama already here, she might have a friend come over too!" Audrey yelled out to Shah as he walked off. Shah stopped in his tracks and turned around.

"Who, Tammy?" he mouthed trying not to be loud. Audrey laughed and shrugged her shoulders leaving Shah with something to think about. Tammy came walking back into the living room and sat down on the couch. Shah turned and walked out of the living room.

"So, what's up with you and Xavier?" Audrey asked.

"Every time I call him, he acts like he's super busy. I like him but I don't wanna be wit him. He can get some of this pussy on occasions cause bitch he fucked the shit out me the last time I was with him!" Tammy said.

"I know that's right!" Audrey said, then leaned over and gave Tammy a high five as they both laughed.

Thirty minutes later Shah walked out of his bedroom; he could hear music coming from downstairs. The whole time he was in the shower he couldn't stop thinking about fucking Audrey and Tammy together. He walked downstairs and into the living room. Audrey and Tammy were both clearly drunk because they were loud. Shah looked to the empty Rosé bottle on the coffee table and saw a bottle of Patron next to it.

"Damn y'all in this bitch lit!" Shah said as he sat down on the couch and flamed up his blunt.

"We not drunk!" Tammy said, then started laughing. "Yeah iight!" Shah quickly said. Shah looked over at Audrey as she sat there with a real seductive look on her face.

"What y'all was just talking bout? Cause Audrey looking sneaky over there," Shah said as he took another hit from his blunt. Tammy started laughing and looked over at Audrey.

"You can ask him girl!" Audrey said to Tammy.

"No! Girl I was just joking," Tammy said.

"No, you wasn't! go ahead and ask him!" Audrey said again.

Tammy started laughing "No bitch I'm good!" she said as she continued to laugh.

"Ask me what?" Shah asked confused. Tammy got quiet and looked over at Audrey.

"Come here!" Audrey said as she looked over at Shah. Shah took another hit from his blunt, then got up and walked over to the couch Audrey and Tammy was sitting on. Audrey stood up and set her cup down on the coffee table. Audrey reached and grabbed Shah's waist band with one hand and reached into his sweatpants and boxer briefs with the other hand and pulled out his dick. Tammy looked than quickly covered her eye's.

"Oh my god! Girl you crazy!" she said as she laughed. Shah stood there shocked that Audrey was doing this. He couldn't believe it, but he was liking it. His dick grew harder and harder in her hand as he continued to take hits from his blunt.

"No bitch take your hands off your face. You said you wanted to see it. It's big ain't it?" Audrey asked as she reached and grabbed Tammy's hand and pulled it away from her eyes. "Was I lying or not bitch?" Audrey asked Tammy. Tammy opened her eyes and looked.

"Ok! Ok bitch you wasn't lying, now put it back" she said as she watched Audrey stroke his dick up and down. Shah grew even harder when he heard those words come from Tammy's mouth. Audrey pulled Shah closer to the couch and sat down.

"Girl you gotta feel it," Audrey said as she pulled Tammy's hand toward Shah's dick. Tammy quickly pulled her hand back and started laughing. "No bitch! Yo ass is a freak!" she said as she felt her body temperature quickly start to raise and her pussy began to feel moist.

"Bitch stop acting like you don't wanna touch it," Audrey said as she pulled Tammy's hand to Shah's dick. Tammy slowly grabbed ahold of it as Audrey held her wrist and moved it back and forth helping her stroke him slowly. Audrey started to kiss and lick on Shah's dick before she took him in her mouth never letting go of Tammy's wrist as she continued to stroke him. Shah stood there blunt in hand as he looked back and forth from Audrey to Tammy. He was overly excited and couldn't wait to get a piece of Tammy. Audrey let go of Tammy's wrist and reached for her pant's button and tried to unbutton it. Tammy couldn't believe what was happening as she continued to stroke Shah's dick while Audrey sucked it. Shah reached over and helped Audrey unbutton Tammy's pants. Tammy let go of Shah's dick and stood up then pulled her pants off. Shah pulled her closer to him and started kissing her as he grabbed ahold of her ass cheek. Audrey let out a soft moan before she stood up and told Shah to sit down on the couch. She turned to Tammy and started kissing her. Tammy wrapped her arms around Audrey and pulled her closer as they kissed. Shah sat there marveled at the two beautiful women standing in front of him.

"How bout we take this upstairs," Shah said as he took another hit from his blunt and stood up. Audrey and Tammy broke from their kiss and walked out of the living room headed up stairs. Shah grabbed the Patron bottle off the coffee table and took a few big gulps from it and sat it back down.

"I'm bout to fuck the shit out of both of them!" Shah said to his self as he walked out of the living room. Shah walked into the bedroom and found Audrey and Tammy wasted no time. Tammy laid on her back in the middle of their king size bed while Audrey was on her hands and knees with her face buried in between Tammy's legs eating her pussy. Shah quickly snatched off his clothes and walked to the edge of the bed and got in. He started eating Audrey's pussy from the back, hearing Audrey and Tammy both moaning at the same time turned him on even more.

"Oh my god Audrey, oh my god I'm about to cum!" Tammy yelled out as she grabbed the back of Audrey's head and pulled her closer. Audrey and Tammy both came one after another. Audrey rolled over and told Shah to lay down as she and Tammy both made room and sat on opposite sides of him. Audrey took Shah's dick into her mouth and started sucking it until it was completely hard.

"Get on top of this big dick!" Audrey directed Tammy. Tammy straddled on top of Shah. Audrey slowly guided Shah's dick into Tammy's pussy.

"Oh my god!" Tammy said as she leaned forward and laid chest to chest with Shah.

"Damn this pussy feel so good!" Shah whispered in Tammy's ear. He'd been dying to fuck her ever since he seen her in that yellow dress. Tammy slowly began to rock back and forth on top of Shah dick as it filled her completely. She quickly began to love the feeling of Shah inside of her. Shah gripped her ass cheeks and controlled her motions. The fact that she was laying chest to chest as Shah held her in his arms gave her a sense of comfort and security that she had never felt with no man.

Tammy was in complete bliss as Audrey laid next to them playing with her pussy. She was enjoying the site of her best friend and her man fucking, it turned her on like never before. The three of them shared a bond like no other and this act brought them that much more closer. Shah wrapped his arms around Tammy and began to pound her pussy as he held her tightly to his chest.

"Oh my god Shah! Fuck meeee, Oh yes just like that!" Tammy yelled out. The sound of Tammy screaming Shah's name forced Audrey into an orgasm and Tammy followed not soon after her. Tammy got up and Audrey took her place. She straddled him reverse cowgirl just how he liked and began riding Shah bouncing her ass up and down. Tammy sat on Shah's face and swayed her hips side to side as he ate her pussy. They went on and on for hours switching from position to position until they all collapsed and fell asleep. Shah rolled over the next morning hoping to find Audrey and Tammy still in bed with him. He was disappointed to find that neither of them was in bed with him. Shah looked over at the clock on the wall across the room and seen that it was 9:30am.

"Fuck I gotta get up!" he said to his self and slowly rolled over and got out of bed. He grabbed his sweatpants from the floor and put them on. He walked downstairs and as he reached the bottom step, he could smell breakfast being cooked. Shah walked to the kitchen and found Tammy standing in front of the stove cooking. She looked back over her shoulder when she heard Shah walk into the kitchen.

"Heyy Shah," she said and turned back to finish cooking.

"What up? Where Audrey at?" he asked.

"Oh, she went to the store to grab some more milk and jelly. You know she won't eat the toast without her jelly," Tammy said.

"Yeah, I know she don't fuck around when it comes to her jelly," Shah said laughing.

"Yeah. But Shah I already talked to Audrey and I wanna talk to you too. I hope what happened last night don't affect our friendship. I still want us to be able to be friends and hang out," she said.

"Na, we good. But hold on do that mean we can't do it again?" Shah asked.

Tammy started laughing. "Boy you don't play no games! I mean if y'all want to, I'm wit it," she said.

"I'm talking bout me and you!" Shah said. Tammy started laughing and turned around to face Shah.

"If Audrey cool wit it. I mean, I enjoyed myself last night or whatever," she said as she smiled.

"Tight! I'ma need some alone time with you so I can put you thru it without no interruptions," Shah said.

"Put me thru it huh? I like how that sound," she said as she laughed

"Good, cause you gone love how it feel!" he said and stood up.

"I already do!" Tammy whispered to herself.

"But I gotta get up out of here I need to go get dressed. Oh yeah it's a Cardi B concert in Beloit on November 17th you wanna go?" Shah asked.

"Yeah I wanna go! That's my bitch," Tammy responded.

"Tight let Audrey know. I wanna make sure we fuck V.I.P up so everything on me," Shah said.

"Everything? Outfits and hair?" Tammy asked.

"Yeah I got y'all" Shah said as he walked out of the kitchen.

(2:00pm)

"That lil bitch Asia one hunnit!" Tae G said to X as they walked into Boushards clothing store on 76th and Capital.

"Yeah, so she fucking wit you tough huh? What you finna cuff her up?" X asked. He was barely paying attention to the conversation. His mind was stuck on the cash they could be making if they wasn't out shopping. Plus, he could sense some turbulence in the near future and would prefer to at least be ready when it comes.

"X, Bro you good?" Tae G asked.

"Yeah, I'm good bro," X said as he snapped out of deep thought.

"You been acting weird lately bro. You sure you good?" Tae G asked again.

"Yeah bro I'm good," X said and walked over to the other side of the store and started looking at some True Religion jeans. Tae G walked up and tapped X as he clutched his heat.

"Aye bro you know Dawg over there he keep looking this way." X turned around to see who Tae G was talking bout. "Oh yeah I know Dawg that's bro from Madison. Ole girl people I was telling you about, Bro cool," X said as he walked over there.

"Shah, What's hannin bro?" X said.

"X, I thought that was you. I ain't on shit tryna grab some shit to wear," Shah said.

"How long you finna be down here?" X asked.

"Ain't no telling!" Shah said.

"Man, bro after you grab yo shit let's jump in traffic and smoke some of this bag," X said.

"I'm wit it. I got an eighth of some moon rocks in the car we can put that shit in the air," Shah said as he walked to the register. Tae G stood their eyeing Shah as he paid for his clothes. He pulled X to the side.

"Bro you trust Dawg?" Tae G asked.

"He cool bro. Plus I'm tryna network nigga we need to find some better coke. I can't keep fucking wit that nigga Kendall," X said. Tae G stood there. He hated when new niggas came around, but he knew X was right. The nigga Kendall was playing the fuck out of them and it was time to find a different source.

"I was gone grab this True fit but fuck it I'ma save my cheese!" X said. Tae G phone started to ring so he walked off. X walked to the counter where Shah was, he peeped the roll of hundreds Shah held in his hand.

"Damn Dawg playing wit some cash that's about thirty right there," X thought to his self.

"What Tammy been up too? I ain't had the time to hit her up in a few days. I know she probably think I'm on bull shit," X said.

"Oh, she been chilling bro. She work most the time so I hardly be seeing her myself," Shah said as he looked away trying to avoid the awkwardness of the conversation. Tae G rushed over and interrupted X and Shah.

"Aye bro we got some action online," Tae G said.

"Tight let's catch that," X said and looked over at Shah. "Aye bro you still tryna ride? We got a few moves to bust we can blow this gas while we riding," he said.

"Yeah, I'm wit it let me put this shit in the car and grab that eighth," Shah said as they walked to the door and left out the store.

Meanwhile

Lil Ant stood in the lobby of Tamara's building on Russit with five hypes. The word had got out fast about them having big twenty-dollar bags of straight drop. He had been up all night and couldn't believe how sweet it was in Wisconsin. The money was pouring in nonstop and Lil Ant was determined not to miss a dollar. He counted the money in his hand then handed one guy three bags.

"Tight want you want?" he asked the next person. Lil Jerry came walking down the stairs with Cortez and noticed Lil Ant directing traffic. He had a small line of hypes standing in the hallway.

"Damn bro you been going crazy all night," Lil Jerry said as he and Cortez stood at the top of the stairs watching.

"It's official Skud!" Lil Ant said to Lil Jerry.

"Tight everybody got what they need y'all can all leave out together," Lil Ant said to the hypes and watched them leave out the building. He checked to make sure the door closed all the way behind them so no one could run in on them.

"You ain't seen that nigga Cory?" Lil Jerry asked Cortez.

"Hell, naw'll I ain't seen him since he dropped me off in Saddle Ridge," Cortez said.

"Damn, What the fuck this nigga on! I ain't got no more smoke and I'm missing cash left and right. His phone been going straight to the voicemail," Lil Jerry said as he walked down the rest of the stairs and over to the door. Lil Jerry's phone started to beep in his hand, so he looked down at it and noticed he had a Facebook notification from Special_Kaaae.

"Damn this Lil bitch keep liking all my pictures and inboxing me. I don't even know this bitch," Lil Jerry said.

"Shidd what's that bitch name?" Cortez quickly asked and jumped the half flight of stairs and walked over to Lil Jerry.

"A Lil redbone bitch name Special_Kaae," Lil Jerry said.

"Let me see what she look like! I probably already took her down, I been fucking a lot of bitches off the book lately," Cortez said. Lil Jerry started laughing and handed Cortez the phone. Cortez looked at the picture of Special_Kaaae.

"Hell, yeah I seen shorty a few times before. She be on Thurston," Cortez said.

"Tight, iight I might have to take a look at her then. I thought she was a mafucka playing with one of them fake pages," Lil Jerry said.

"On Bd she one of my friends on Facebook. Her nigga was one of them niggas that got killed over there on Thurston matter of a fact!" Cortez said.

"Yeah? These hoe's ain't shit. The nigga ain't been dead a month and she tryna bust that mafucka open for a nigga already. That's why I be treating these hoes," Lil Jerry said.

"Look if you don't want the pussy I'ma take it. Shit I'ma shoot my shot right now!" Cortez said.

"I might have to see what's to this bitch then I'ma pass her yo way," Lil Jerry said as he laughed.

"Yeah do that cause that lil bitch bad and she got a fat ass!" Cortez said.

"I see!" Lil Jerry said as he scrolled through her profile pics. Lil Ant stood there listening to Lil Jerry and Cortez as he looked out the window to see if there were any more hypes coming. He wanted to finish the rest of what he had before he went and sat down for a while at Tonya's crib.

Meanwhile

Tae G sat behind X and let Shah sit in the passenger seat. Tae G didn't like letting niggas he didn't trust sit behind him. As X drove down Capital, Shah sat in the passenger seat filling up a Swisher with as much weed as he could. X looked in the rearview mirror at Tae G and laughed in his mind cause he knew why he chose to sit in the back seat. Shah turned around and handed Tae G a Swisher and the weed.

"Bro stuff that bitch as much as you can I like smoking big boys!" Shah said as he turned back around to finish rolling his blunt.

"Dawg a real smoker," Tae G said to X. Tae G had heard of moon rocks but had never smoked none. X phone started to ring as he drove, and he knew by the ring tone it was his trapper.

"Man, I love that sound!" X said out loud. Tae G started laughing cause he knew why he loved that sound, it was money calling. X quickly answered

"What up?" he asked calmly.

"I got two dollars over here," Sarah quickly said.

"Tight where you at doe?" X asked.

"I'm at my house, you remember where it's at right?" Sarah asked.

"Yeah I remember where it's at. I'll be there in 15," X said.

"Ok baby! But don't have me waiting all day like last time," Sarah said.

"I ain't I'm on my way right now," X said.

"Ok baby!" Sarah said and ended the call. Shah couldn't help but overhear X's conversation and quickly put two and two together and knew he was hustling. Shah was looking for a way to get rid of some more bricks and X just might be his way of being able to flood a whole different city. Shah flamed up his blunt and hit it a few times before he passed it to X.

"Who you finna pull up on?" Tae G asked X.

"Sarah! Why you ask that?" X asked him.

"Cause Tom and Greg still waiting on me," Tae G said.

"Iight we gone hit them next," X said as he exhaled a big cloud of smoke and passed the blunt back to Tae G.

"Say no more!" Tae G said then hit the blunt and inhaled a big cloud of smoke and started coughing. His cough quickly turned into him choking, X and Shah both started laughing.

"You good?" Shah asked Tae G.

"Yeah.... but, but this shit strong!" Tae G said as he tried to catch his breath in between words. X made a left turn at the light on 60th. He looked back at Tae G as he coughed his lungs up.

"Pass Dawg the gas, fo you kill yoself" X said as he laughed and made a right onto Hampton. Shah reached back and grabbed the blunt from Tae G.

"Yeah that's that gas," Tae G said still tryna catch his breath. X made a right on 57th and drove halfway up the block and pulled over and parked. He quickly called Sarah.

"I'm outside!" he said as soon as she answered.

"Ok" she said and hung up.

"Man, I love seeing niggas get money!" Shah said as he inhaled a cloud of smoke.

"Hell yeah! This light doe," X said as he flipped through Facebook.

"What y'all be fucking wit?" Shah asked as he handed X the blunt. X looked over at Shah as he processed the question.

"We jammin on the hard, why you ask that?" X said hoping his conversation lead to a good outcome for him. Sarah walked up and jumped in the back seat with Tae G and closed the door.

"Hey loves!" Sarah said, then handed Tae G the money. Tae G hurried and counted the money.

"It's $180 bro," Tae G said to X.

"Man, Sarah I thought you said two dollars," X said.

"I know baby I had to get me some cigarettes. You can take me to the ATM or I'll just give you extra next time," Sarah said.

"Just make sure you got it next time," X said as he reached back and handed Sarah the bags.

"Ok baby," Sarah said and jumped out of the car and closed the door. X pulled off and as he drove up the street Shah sat there shocked.

"Damn bro she young as a bitch smoking crack," Shah said. Tae G and X both started laughing

"Bro she like 45 years old," X said as he passed the blunt back to Tae G.

"Never!" Shah said.

"No bullshit she is," Tae G said as he made sure he hit the blunt lightly this time.

"Oh, if she wasn't no smoker, I would have slid on her, she valid to be 45," Shah said.

"Thank you! Bro I been saying that shit to X and he think I'm trippin!" Tae G said excited.

"Y'all trippin!" X said.

"Yeah iight! Make sure you slide on Tom and Greg," Tae G said.

"I know I'm bout to," X said.

"Y'all ain't never thought about fucking wit the boy?" Shah asked.

"Yeah something like that. I just never really knew a mafucka that was plugged with that shit. Plus, I been doing good fucking wit the hard," X said. Shah nodded his head as he broke down another Swisher.

"Man, bro the boy is where the real money at. Think about your best day ever fucking with the hard. That'll be what you'll make on your worst day fucking with the boy. Only reason I said something is cause I like y'all niggas and I think we could do some business together," Shah said. Tae G flamed up the blunt he rolled and hit it a few times "Our best day would be our worst day," Tae G thought as he exhaled the smoke.

"Business like what?" X asked.

"I can turn y'all onto this heroin money. I can plug y'all wit some of the best shit Milwaukee has ever seen. I guarantee this shit will sell itself," Shah said trying his hardest to sell them on his vision. Tae G reached up and handed Shah the blunt.

"I don't know bro. Let me get yo number I need to think on it I'ma hit yo line and let you know!" X said.

"Tight that's cool bro. Just think on it, but remember this shit is everyday consistent money. They need this shit EVERYDAY!" Shah said. Shah's phone started to ring, and he looked at it and saw that it was TJ so he quickly answered it.

"What up bro?" Shah asked

"Shit tryna link up wit you!" TJ said.

"I'm in the Mill right now but give me two hours I'ma be back in town," Shah said.

"Tight just hit my line when you touchdown," TJ said.

"I got you bro," Shah said then ended the call.

"Aye after y'all make this stop, drop me back off at my whip. I need to get back to Madison," Shah said as he passed the blunt to X.

"Tight, let me get yo line so I could hit you," X said.

"Tight," Shah said then gave X his number.

Meanwhile

"Aye cuz said he wit it as long as we cut him in," Magic said to Kay as they drove down Hammersly.

"Tight so when he tryna do it?" Kay asked.

"When he get ready to re-up," Magic said.

"So, when that's gone be?" Kay asked impatiently.

"He ain't say," Magic said as he made a left on Theresa.

"Man, cuz be acting scary as hell. We should rob his bitch ass," Kay said. Magic started laughing as he pulled into the driveway. Kay and Magic were known jack boys and if they didn't fuck wit you they would strip you for every dollar you had. Every nigga in Madison that was checking a bag made sure they stayed far away from them. The females in Madison loved Kay and Magic because there was something intriguing about them. When they walked into a room every nigga in the room would be on edge, they literally but the fear of God in niggas. They were known as the Terror Twins cause everywhere; they went they terrorized someone.

(2hrs Later)

Shah made a left off Thurston onto Rosenberry. He quickly took the blunt from his mouth when he noticed the police car parked in the middle of the block. Shah turned the A/C on to try clearing the smoke from the car before he rode past the police car. He noticed it was Officer Olsen as he got closer.

"Damn he finna flag me," Shah said to himself after he and Officer Olsen made eye contact. Shah looked in his rearview mirror after he passed him to see what Officer Olsen was doing. He noticed Officer Olsen put his car into drive and pulled off, then quickly made a left into a driveway.

"Fuck he on me!" Shah said as sped up and made a quick right. He could see Officer Olsen speeding down Rosenberry, Shah hurried and made a left onto Allied then a right into the first parking lot he seen. He quickly threw his car into park and tried to jump out, but Officer Olsen was already pulling into the lot with his lights on. Olsen jumped out of his car gun in hand as he pointed it at Shah.

"Put your hands-on top of the car!" he yelled out to Shah. Shah put his hands in the air and walked back to the car.

"What's the probable cause for you pulling me over!" Shah yelled back as he put his hands-on top of the car.

"You failed to use your turning signals," Officer Olsen said as he walked up to Shah. He put his gun back in its holster and quickly began to pat Shah down for any weapons.

"Man, why you always fucking wit me?" Shah asked.

"I'm not fucking with you I'm doing my job! Do you have anything sharp on you that would cut me if I go in your pockets?" Olsen asked.

"Man, I ain't got nothing!" Shah said as he looked down to make sure Olsen wasn't planting nothing on him.

"So, whose car is this?" Olsen asked as he began digging in his pockets.

"This my car," Shah quickly said. Officer Olsen pulled out a big stack of cash from Shah's pocket.

"I see you been real busy!" Officer Olsen said as he put the money on the roof of the car.

"Man, that's my girl school money!" Shah said. Olsen looked over to the driver door that was still open and could see the weed smoke still coming out of the car.

"Smell like you just got done smoking!" Olsen said.

"Man, I don't even smoke!" Shah said.

"That's funny cause there's a lot of smoke coming out of your car. I'ma need you to place your hands behind your back," Officer Olsen said.

"What I'm under arrest for?" Shah asked.

"You're not, I just have to detain you while I search your car," he said. Shah put his hands behind his back as Officer Olsen quickly cuffed him up and walked him to the back of the car. Olsen walked back over to the driver side door and quickly started searching the vehicle. Shah could hear his iPhone and his trap phones ringing while Olsen searched his car. He watched as Olsen did a detailed search of his car. He had every door open. Ten minutes later, Olsen popped his head out of the car disappointed. He picked the cash up off the roof of the car and started counting it.

"Where did you say this money came from?" Olsen asked again.

"That's my girl money! Half is for her new car and the other half is her financial aid money," Shah said as it was the first thing that popped in his head.

"Twenty-five thousand dollars! Why do you have it?" Officer Olsen asked.

"Cause! She bad with money. She'll spend it on something she not supposed to," Shah said.

"Ok, well tell her to bring a receipt when she come pick it up from the station," Officer Olsen said.

"Man, what you mean? How you figure you can just take it from me!" Shah asked.

"If you have proof of where it came from on you then I'll give it back. If not, she needs to come down with proof that it's hers," Officer Olsen said again as he took the cuffs off Shah.

"Alright well we finna be on our way down there!" Shah said.

"Good," Officer Olsen said as he walked back to his car. Shah walked around his car and closed all his doors back.

"Damn, his bitch ass just got me for twenty-five bands!" Shah said to his self as he got back into his car. He picked up his trap phone from the cup holder and called TJ.

"What up bro?" TJ said as he answered.

"Shit I'm back around what's the word?" Shah asked.

"Same shit," TJ said.

"Alright meet me at Toppers on PD in twenty minutes," Shah said.

"Tight," TJ said. Shah ended the call. He knew he just took a loss, but the fact TJ was grabbing a whole brick made him feel a lot better. Shah pulled out of the parking lot and headed toward Tammy's crib.

Chapter Thirteen

3 DAYS LATER

 continued to run as he struggled to catch his breath, He knew if he stopped it was over with for him. He held his pistol tight in his hand as he ran.

"I ain't going!" he said to his self as he ducked behind a garage. He looked up and noticed it was a flat top roof and quickly jumped up and grabbed the side gutters and pulled himself up. Just as he laid down, he could hear footsteps, then they quickly stopped.

"Officer Luke stop! He's somewhere around here," one officer yelled out to his partner. X laid completely still, making sure he didn't make a sound. He could hear the Officer radio and saw the reflection of his flashlight as he looked around.

"Suspect headed East on foot North of Greenfield," the man on the other end of the radio said. "10-4," the Officer said then took off running toward Greenfield. X let out a sigh of relief when he heard the Officer run off.

"Damn Tae G. Don't get caught bro," he thought to his self as he laid there. He could feel his phone vibrating in his pocket, but he knew it was too soon to move so he laid there. Fifteen minutes later, X rolled over and pulled his phone from his pocket, He had two missed calls and two text messages from Tammy. "Perfect timing," he said to his self when he saw her number. He had plans to meet with Tammy. X pulled out his phone and called her back.

"Hello?" Tammy said as she answered the phone sounding a little irritated.

"Where you at?" X asked in a low whisper. Tammy could sense something wasn't right by the tone of his voice.

"I'm on Bender at Tiffany house. You okay?" she immediately asked.

"Naw I'm in a lil situation and I need a ride. I need you to meet me on 45th and National. I need you to try and get here as fast as you can," X whispered.

"Okay, we on our way now," she quickly said.

"Tight," X said, then ended the call.

Meanwhile

Magic and Kay sat outside of Dave and Busters in the back seat of Magic's minivan waiting on Lil C to pull in. Kay grew more and more frustrated as every second went by. They'd been waiting on Lil C for over an hour.

"Man, I think this scary ass nigga spinning us!" Kay said to Magic. Magic sat there unsure what to think or say. He knew Kay was impatient, but he also knew Lil C was scary and might back out because of the fear of what could blow back on him.

"Be patient bro, He ain't finna spin us. He know we gone get on his ass if he do!" Magic said in an attempt to calm Kay down. Kay looked up ten minutes later and saw Lil C's car pulling into the parking lot.

"There his bitch ass go right there!" Kay said as he adjusted himself in his seat. His adrenaline began to rush as he watched Lil C pull across the parking lot. Lil C got out of his car and jumped into the passenger seat of a black 2015 Chevy Traverse with tinted windows.

"That's him right there! When he pull out trail him" Kay said as he watched closely. His heart was pounding in his chest as Magic sat there calmly waiting on Lil C to get out so he could go to work. As soon as Lil C got out of the black Traverse, it pulled off. Magic quickly jumped into the driver seat and pulled off making sure to keep a distance and keep the Traverse in eyesight.

Meanwhile

"You ok? Girl turn the heat up," Tammy said to Tiffany as X sat in the back-seat shivering.

"Yeah, I'm good now," X said as he pulled his phone out of his pocket.

"Where we going?" Tammy asked X. X's phone started to vibrate in his hand. He looked and saw it was Tae G and immediately answered it.

"You good bro?" X asked.

"Hell naw'll. I'm hiding in somebody shed and they got this mafucka surrounded. Bro get that bail money together and come get me asap!" Tae G said.

"Tight, I got you bro," X said.

"Tight! Love bro!" Tae G said, then ended the call. X sat there stuck with the phone still to his ear as he drifted off into deep thought.

"Who the fuck was that!" he thought to his self as he replayed what happened in his mind.

X and Tae G were parked at the Burger King on Lisbon and Appleton. They sat there waiting for Tae G's people to bring the food out. X's iPhone started vibrating in his lap, so he looked down then picked it up and answered it.

"You on Bolivar, still right? I'm finna pull up in thirty minutes," X said and quickly hung up.

"Tae bro we gone I got something online," X said.

"Hold on bro, she coming out right now," Tae G said.

"Tight, but let me drive," X said as he opened his door and got out. Tae G opened his door and got out of the car and switched seats with X.

Denise came out of Burger King with two bags of food in her hands. She walked up to the passenger side window.

"I'ma see y'all tonight when I get off work," she said to Tae G as he rolled down the window.

"Yeah, we ona move doe, good looking," Tae G said as he grabbed the food from Denise. X pulled off and turned onto Lisbon.

"So, what you think about switching up and fuckin wit the boy full time?" X asked Tae G as he sped down Lisbon.

"I'm wit it. I been thinking bout what bro said and I know that's where the real money at. But where we gone get our action from?" Tae G asked.

"I got something lined up for us. Fuck this inner-city shit, we finna go OT wit this shit. Trust me we finna take off we just gotta finish this shit first!" X said. Tae G nodded his head in approval to what he just heard. He strolled through his iPhone and played his favorite song from Team East side. X started to laugh.

"He love playing this old ass shit," X thought to his self as he crossed National on Miller Parkway to the South side of Milwaukee. X sat back nodding his head to the music when his iPhone started to vibrate in his lap. He turned the music down and answered.

"What up? I told you I'm ona way," X said.

"Okay, okay.... I-I-I'm just making sure," E said.

"Tight!" X said then ended the call. Ten minutes later, X pulled in front of E's house and parked. He picked up his phone to call E to let him know he was outside but put it back in his lap when he saw E coming out of the house. E walked up to the car and got in the back seat and closed the door.

"What up nephew, Man you look just like yo moma. How she doing?"

"Here you go, I got $150 for you," he said as he handed X the money.

"Yopp" X said as he grabbed the money from E. He knew E would go on and on about his moma if he let him, so he avoided his question. He quickly handed E his bags trying to get him to get out the car before he started talking his ear off.

"Man, you need to gone fuck wit my lil nephew nem on them cars. You know they got auctioneer license and all types of shit. They eating GOOD!" E said.

"Yeah. So, what you tryna say we ain't eating unc?" X asked as he quickly looked back at E. Tae G started laughing.

"Naw, lil buddie I'm just saying this shit ain't forever! Gone take that next step while you can ya hear me!" E said.

"I feel you," X said as he looked out the back window and saw the black Audi he had been seeing. "Damn that's that Audi again!" he thought to his self and seconds later shots started to ring out.

"Shit!" Tae G yelled out as the glass from the back windshield flew around the inside of the car. He quickly ducked down in his seat. X threw the car in drive and sped off. E opened his door and jumped out of the car.

"Shoot nigga!" X yelled to Tae G as he smashed on the gas trying to get away from the Audi as it followed them letting off more shots. X could hear the shots hitting the back of the car as he ducked down trying not to get hit in the head. Tae G let his seat all the way back and rolled over on his stomach. He lifted up and let off a few shots out the back window. X weaved through the streets of the South side suburbs as they exchanged shots back and forth. He made it to Greenfield and Miller Parkway and made a sharp left and lost control on the car. X hit his head on the steering wheel knocking his self out as the car flipped and rolled a few times.

"X! X! X! X!" Tae G yelled out as he pulled X from the car. X began to gain consciousness, but everything was spinning as he was finally able to focus his eyes.

"The Jakes coming Run!" Tae G said. X couldn't hear him, but he sure read "Run" come from his mouth. He managed to get to his feet. Still dizzy, he stumbled over to the car and grabbed his pistol and took off running. He was a few steps away from the car when he realized he left his phone and turned back around to go get it.

"Bro you trippin come on!" Tae G yelled as he turned and started running up Greenfield toward West Allis. X grabbed his phone and took off running in a different direction into a residential neighborhood.

"I aint going!" he said as sirens rang out from behind him. He ducked behind a garage.

"X, Hey X!" Tammy yelled and snapped X out of his trance.

"Where you tryna go?" she asked him again.

"Damn my bad. Take me on Bender," X said.

"Can you at least tell me what happened?" Tammy asked concerned. X was acting weird and she wanted to make sure he wasn't involving her in some bullshit. X looked at her then looked away.

"It's a long ass story. But I do appreciate you saving my ass," X said trying to give Tammy enough to satisfy her curiosity. He sat back and closed his eyes and within minutes of the drive he fell asleep. Tammy pulled up in front of Tiffany's apartment building on Bender and parked. She turned the music down and reached back to wake X up. He quickly jumped and grabbed a hold of his gun.

"Boy you ok?" Tammy asked as she jumped back startled by X's reaction. X quickly looked around and realized where he was and calmed down.

"Girl you got too much going on with this nigga!" Tiffany said then opened her door and got out of the car.

"My bad!" X said to Tammy, then looked around outside the car. X got out of the car and stretched as Tammy got out of the car and started walking to Tiffany's apartment building.

"I'm finna run down here to my spot real quick and grab my hoodie. I'ma be right back," X said.

Tammy looked back at X like he was crazy because the way he was acting was throwing her completely off. "Tight," she said as she walked up the stairs.

X walked up the street to his building thinking about everything that just happened. He walked up to the building and reached into his pocket and pulled out his keys and opened the building door. X walked up the stairs and turned the corner. His heart immediately dropped into his stomach as he got closer. He could see the door was open.

Pieces of the door laid on the floor outside the apartment, X quickly reached and pulled out his pistol and pushed the door open. He slowly walked in as his heart began to pound in his chest, then he noticed his spot had been ram sacked. "Fuck!" he said to himself as he rushed to the kitchen. "Damn the Cheese!" he thought as he kicked the kitchen table out the way and ran over to the refrigerator. Everything that was in the cabinets, refrigerator, and freezer was now all over the floor. X started moving shit out of his way as he looked for the waffle box.

"There it go!" he said as he reached down and grabbed it.

"What the fuck!" he yelled as he felt the box and it was empty. He threw the box and started kicking shit that was on the floor out of his way as he rushed out of the apartment.

Meanwhile

Magic watched as the black Traverse turned off Gammon onto Flower Lane and into the Wexford Ridge apartment complex. Magic slowed up a little putting some space in between him and the black Traverse before he turned into the apartment complex.

"This nigga sweet! And he pulling all the way to the back. When he stops, I'ma jump out with the K and you jump in and strip his ass. Take them phones and his car," Kay said.

"Tight but slow up let's make sure he not meeting somebody else back here before we get on his ass," Magic said.

"Tight!" Kay said as he grabbed the AK off the seat next to him and unlocked the sliding door.

Magic watched as the Traverse pulled over and parked, He pulled into the back lot and parked two cars down from the Traverse on the driver side. Kay impatiently watched the Traverse as he held the K in his hand. After a minute, Kay realized he was meeting somebody else back there because he hadn't got out yet.

"He finna meet somebody. When they get in, I want you to take the driver and I'ma take the passenger. I'ma take the car just trail me around the corner," Magic said.

"Iight!" Kay said.

"Aww shit I think he finna meet that nigga Trell. Yeah, this bitch ass nigga holding if he serving Trell," Kay said as he watched Trell come out of the building and look around before he walked toward the Traverse. Trell walked up to the truck and got in the passenger seat and closed the door. Magic and Kay quickly opened their doors and crept to the back of the minivan.

"If they reach, we kill em! But grab that cash!" Kay said.

"Let's get this cash!" Magic said as he ducked behind the car next to them. Kay watched as Magic ducked and crept to the passenger side of the truck. Then he quickly rushed the driver door and pulled it open. He grabbed Shah by the collar and snatched him out the truck and threw him to the ground.

"Nigga if you move I'ma blow yo mafucking head off!" Kay said to Shah as he pointed the K to the back of his head

"Iight, iight!" Shah said scared shitless. Magic was on the passenger side with his pistol in Trell's face. He quickly patted him down then emptied his pockets and pulled him out the car then walked him around to the driver side and made him lay next to Shah.

"You hit his pockets?" Magic asked Kay.

"Naw!" Kay said. Magic quickly hit Shah's pockets and tossed the cash into the truck and reached over to the passenger side and closed the door. He closed the driver door and reversed out of the parking spot and pulled off.

"If anyone of you bitch ass niggas move before, I get in this car, I'ma make sure you catch a few of these K shells!" Kay said as he laughed and slowly walked backwards to the minivan. He jumped in and hurried and pulled off. He trailed Magic to a nearby side street and pulled over. Kay jumped out the minivan and ran up to the Traverse and jumped into the back seat. Magic had already found most of the shit as he drove. Kay quickly looked around the back of the truck, but it was empty, so he checked under the seats while Magic checked the glove box. It was empty was well. Magic stuffed Trell's and Shah's cell phones with the cash he got off them into the book bag he grabbed off the back seat and zipped it up.

"I got everything let's go!" Magic said as he jumped out and ran back to the minivan and jumped into the driver seat. Kay jumped out the truck and ran to the minivan and jumped in. Magic quickly pulled off.

"On Bd that was just a sweet stain!" Kay said as Magic made a right turn on Gammon headed toward Middleton. He grabbed the book bag and unzipped it and looked inside it.

"Yeah that was a stain!" Magic said as he drove. "See how much we got and throw them phones out the window," he said to Kay. Kay grabbed the three phones out the bag and rolled down the window and tossed them out the car. He pulled two bricks of boy out the book bag and sat them on the floor.

"Well we both got a brick of D so far!" Kay said, then he pulled the stacks of cash from the bag and started counting it. A few minutes later Kay looked over at Magic.

"Look bro I think we should just say fuck Lil C and bust this shit down the middle," he said

"How much is it?" Magic asked.

"$258,000" Kay said.

"You bullshitting!" Magic quickly said.

"On shorty I ain't playin!" Kay said.

"Oh yeah, fuck that nigga Lil C! We gone bust that down the middle," Magic said.

"Let's strip his bitch ass too!" Kay said.

"Man, hell naw'll that's our cousin!" Magic said.

"On our daddy side! Fuck that nigga!" Kay said aggressively. Magic couldn't help but laugh.

"Bro yo ass cut!" Magic said.

"I know, that's why I'm Kay! That's why I do what I do. Either you gone strip him wit me or I'm doing it myself either way it's gone happen," Kay said. Magic sat there for a minute quietly thinking. He knew Kay was cutthroat and he meant every word he just said. He didn't agree with it, but there wasn't no way he was letting him do it alone.

"Fuck it we finna call him," Magic said.

"On Shorty, say no more let's strip his ass! He holding too, we finna make his ass open that safe," Kay said.

"Tight call him and tell him we got his cut then we gone strip his bitch ass," Magic said. Kay got excited and started laughing. This shit was right up his alley.

"Tight," Kay said as he grabbed his phone and dialed Lil C's number.

Meanwhile

Shah and Trell stood in the living room pissed. Shah was waiting for Lil Jerry and Lil Ant to pull up on him.

"I'm finna kill them bitch ass niggas when I catch them!" Trell said as he paced back and forth.

"Who the fuck was that?" Shah asked.

"Them bitch ass niggas Kay and Magic. They tried to get down on me last year, but I got out that jam! Them niggas robbed damn near the whole town!" Trell said.

"Them bitch ass niggas just hit me for two books and $98,000. I'm finna make sure they die wit that shit. I'm finna drop a bag on they head!" Shah said.

"I'm wit you on that! Them niggas gotta die" Trell said.

"That number y'all called just called back!" Trell's lil sister LaToya said as she walked from the back and handed Shah the phone. As soon as Shah grabbed the phone it started ringing again so he answered it.

"Y'all out there? he asked.

"Yeah bro come out!" Lil Jerry said.

"Tight I'm on my way now!" Shah said and ended the call.

"I'm finna get on top of this shit right now I can't have no niggas taking shit from me!" Shah said as he handed Trell LaToya's phone.

"Tight, but I still need two of them. I can't afford to lose no more cash. I just lost a $160,000. I gotta get my shit up and running," Trell said.

"Them niggas got the keys to my spot I gotta get my shit together real quick. I'ma call LaToya phone when I get shit together," Shah said.

"Tight bro!" Trell said as Shah opened the door and left out the apartment.

Meanwhile

X walked back down the street back to Tiffany's apartment building without a clue as to what the hell he was finna do. He texted Tammy and told her to meet him in the hallway. He paced back and forth in the hall wondering if the same niggas that just shot at him were the niggas that hit his spot. Either way, it was too much shit going on and he needed to get the fuck out of Milwaukee until he could wrap his mind around this shit. Tammy walked out of Tiffany's apartment and saw X standing at the end of the hall looking out the window.

"What's going on? You acting real strange," Tammy asked as she walked down the hall. X turned around with a look of devastation on his face.

"Today been a real fucked up day. Niggas just got done shooting at me, my man's just got locked up, and somebody broke in my spot and hit me for all my cheese! I know you just drove all the way down here to see me, but I gotta get up out of Milwaukee until I figure out what's going on," X said.

"Ok, so where you finna go?" Tammy asked.

"Shit, right now I don't kno I just know I gotta move around for a lil while," X said.

"You can come to Madison until you figure it out. I mean only if you want to," Tammy said.

"I'm wit it, but I'm tryna get up out of here right now," X said.

"Alright, that's cool. Let me grab my purse and say goodbye to my cousin," Tammy said.

"Iight," X said as Tammy turned and walked back to Tiffany's apartment.

Meanwhile

Lil Ant looked back at Shah in the back seat.

"Man, what the fuck happened Skud?" he asked Shah as Lil Jerry drove down Gammon Road.

"Man cuz, all I know is after the nigga Trell got in the truck and handed me the cash, I reached back to try and grab the bricks, but my door popped open and a nigga snatched me out the car and pointed a AK at me and made me get on the ground. Then another nigga walked Trell over to the driver side and made him lay next to me, then hit my pockets and jumped in my truck and pulled off. The nigga wit the K jumped in a blue minivan and pulled off behind my truck!" Shah said.

"You don't know who it was?" Lil Jerry asked as he drove.

"Yeah the nigga Trell said the niggas names was Kay and Magic!" Shah said.

"Damn you say Kay and Magic?" Lil Jerry asked.

"Yeah! What you know them niggas?" Shah asked.

"Yeah them niggas be fucking wit my big homies off my block. Them niggas super savage's bro!" Lil Jerry said.

"I don't give no fuck what them niggas is me and my niggas do this shit for fun skud!" Lil Ant said.

"You ain't got no poles up here?" Lil Ant asked Shah.

"Naw bro, I ain't never needed none!" Shah said.

"Skud you up here getting all this money and you ain't got no guns? Cuz you sweet!" Lil Ant said. He couldn't believe Shah ain't own not one gun.

"Bro I got all type of shit!" Lil Jerry said letting Lil Ant know he wasn't sweet! Shah sat there feeling stupid that he'd never thought about buying some weapons, but now it was necessary.

"Skud them niggas can't get away with that. I'm finna have my niggas come up here. Them niggas gotta pay for that shit," Lil Ant said.

"I got fifty bands. I want them niggas did something nasty!" Shah said. "As a matter of a fact Lil Jerry bro let me buy some of them joints from you," Shah said.

"Tight I got you!" Lil Jerry said as he turned onto Hammersly Road.

Meanwhile

Magic pulled in front of Lil C's house and parked. Kay hit the blunt and passed it over to Magic.

"Call that nigga and see if he coming out or if he want us to come in," Kay said as he looked out the window at Lil C's house.

"Bro why you be acting like you can't never call the nigga?" Magic asked as he dialed Lil C's number.

"Cause he fucks wit you more than he fuck wit me. His bitch ass scared of me," Kay said. Magic started laughing "Bro you a fool!" he said knowing it was true.

"Hello? Aye cuz you coming out or you want us to come in? Magic asked Lil C.

"Come in cuz I got my daughter right now," Lil C said.

"Tight," Magic said then ended the call. Magic looked over at Kay who was still looking out the window. "Aye bro, I don't think we should do this tonight!" Magic said. Kay quickly turned and looked at Magic. "What you mean?" Kay asked.

"The nigga said he got his daughter in their wit him," Magic said.

"Man don't tell me you finna bitch up on me! Fuck that lil girl! Plus, I left all the bread at your crib what we gone give him?" Kay asked. Magic shook his head in disbelief. He looked over at Lil C's house and noticed the porch lights turned on.

"Bro you a grimy ass nigga! Come on. This nigga got the door open for us," Magic said as he opened his door.

"Aye bro I am who I am and that which I am not I will never be. When have you known me to give a fuck about anybody but you?" Kay asked. Magic stood there looking at Kay. He couldn't disagree with what he said because Kay was always Kay and he knew that.

"We ain't doing nothing in front of his daughter! Grab that bag we in here!" Magic said as he closed the door and walked toward Lil C's house. Kay grabbed the book bag off the back seat and got out of the car and followed Magic up to Lil C's house. Lil C opened the screen door and let Magic and Kay into the house and closed the door.

"So, what up cuz?" Lil C asked as he led the way into the living room.

"Shit where lil cuz bad ass at? I ain't seen her in a while!" Magic asked.

"Man, her lil ass upstairs sleep," Lil C said. Magic and Kay both looked at each other then sat down on the couch. Kay sat the book bag in between his legs.

"You wanna hit this shit?" Magic asked Lil C as he tried to pass him the blunt.

"Na I'm good cuz I gave that smoking shit up. I was spending too much bread on that shit," Lil C said.

"Thats fucked up!" Kay said as reached and grabbed the blunt from Magic and hit it.

"But good looking on that stain. Dude was sweet. I got your cut right here!" Kay said as he held the bag up then sat it back in between his legs. Kay unzipped the bag and reached in. Lil C stood up and walked closer to the coffee table. Kay quickly stood up holding the book bag in one hand with his other hand inside of the book bag.

"This you right here!" Kay said as he pulled out his Glock 19 and pointed it at Lil C. Lil C turned and tried to run. Magic sprung up from his seat and jumped over the coffee table and on to Lil C's back pulling him to the ground. Kay started laughing as he walked around the coffee table and over to Magic and Lil C.

"Cuz you a real-life bitch!" Kay said as he put the pistol to the back of Lil C's head and grabbed the back of his shirt collar.

"Grab this blunt!" Kay said to Magic as he held it between his lips. Magic got up off Lil C's back and grabbed the blunt from Kay's mouth.

"Man, what y'all on?" Lil C asked nervously.

"It's real simple! We came for the stash. You got two options: you can give it up and live or don't give it up and we kill you and Lil cuz upstairs. What you choose?" Kay calmly said. Lil C laid face down on the ground with Kay's pistol to the back of his head.

"Fuck man we blood!" Lil C said.

"Time ain't on your side. I got some pussy online. Make you decision before I make it for you and leave your thoughts all over this nice ass carpet! Kay said as he pressed his pistol harder into the back of his head.

"Man, the safe in the basement behind the washing machine. Use the crowbar on the shelf to pull back the dry wall. The combination is 13-20-16," Lil C said.

"My nigga! Good choice" Kay said as Magic stood up against the wall smoking and shaking his head. He knew Kay was just being Kay, but this shit was getting out of hand.

"You gone take care of that or you want me to?" Kay asked Magic.

"Naw I got it" Magic said as he started walking toward the basement.

"Hold on, hold on. Let me hit that weed!" Kay said as he as put his foot on Lil C's back. Magic stopped in his tracks and started laughing and passed Kay the blunt and walked to the basement. Kay stood there with one foot on Lil C's back as he pointed the gun down at him as he inhaled a cloud of smoke.

"Cuz I remember when we was shorties. You used to act like a real bitch. Yo hoe ass used to stand in front of the TV so we couldn't watch yo shit! You used to act like a bitch wit yo Nintendo and yo toys. I grew to hate your bitch ass. The moment I seen you getting money down here, I wanted to strip yo bitch ass. Maybe if you would have been a playa back then I would've been a playa and gave you yo cut. You know this shit ain't bout the money, this shit personal. I might just put a bullet in yo head anyway!" Kay said as he ashed his blunt on Lil C's back.

"Kay I was kid!" Lil C said.

"Bitch ass nigga keep my name out yo mouth before I-----" Before Kay could finish what he was about to say, Magic came around the corner with a white crash bag and some rope in his hands.

"I got the cash! Tie him up and let's get up out of here," Magic said as he tossed Kay the rope.

"Put yo hands behind you back, hoe nigga!" Kay said. Lil C quickly put his hands behind his back and Kay tied them together then tied his feet together. Magic opened the door and left out the house. Kay walked over to the coffee table and grabbed his book bag then walked back over to Lil C and kicked him in his ribs.

"Bitch ass nigga, you was sweeter than the nigga you put us on! Good lookin cuz!" Kay said as he laughed and walked out the door.

Chapter Fourteen

(9:45AM)

*L*il Ant pulled into the Park and Ride at the same time the Van Galder pulled in. He was excited to have his guys in town. With niggas of his caliber surrounding him, he knew Madison had some problems on its hands. Lil Ant pulled in front of Arby's and parked. He sat there looking at the bus waiting for Mook and Rell to get off. Rell and Mook both got off the bus looking like immigrants fresh off the boat from Jamaica. Lil Ant quickly opened the door and jumped out the truck.

"Aye Skud!" Lil Ant yelled out to Mook and Rell.

"What's good!" Mook said as they started walking toward Lil Ant.

"I'm good skud!" Lil Ant said as he shook Mook and Rell's hand.

"This shit look crazy!" Rell said to Lil Ant as he looked around.

"I know that's the same shit I said when I got up here. But this shit ain't bad it's a gold mine up here skud!" Lil Ant said. Mook jumped into the passenger seat of the truck and Rell jumped in behind him.

"Who shit this is?" Mook asked as he looked around the inside of the truck.

"This lil white bitch I been fuckin wit skud. I been driving this bitch since my second day down here. It's sweet down here and we bout to take this city by storm just follow my lead I got a plan," Lil Ant said.

"I'm wit it," Rell said from the back seat.

"Ain't no question if I'm wit it," Mook said as he looked out the window eyeing the city.

"Good cause we got some work to put in. A nigga robbed my cousin last night and cuz got fifty bands on them niggas head and we gone collect that!" Lil Ant said as he drove away from Arby's.

"Yeah it's official!" Rell said.

"After we handle that I'ma need y'all to help me with this line. I got a line on one of these blocks and it's been nonstop traffic. I sold three bricks in bags in the past five days. I ain't been able to do shit but take quick naps its been so crazy skud!" Lil Ant said.

"Damn you say three bricks? You up here doing it like that already?" Mook asked.

"Cuz up here having his way! that's why I said we finna take this city by storm. I'm telling y'all skud just follow my lead!" Lil Ant said. Mook and Rell sat back, quiet and ready to see if this town was as sweet as Lil Ant said it was.

Meanwhile

"Damn I forgot all about dude!" X said as he jumped up from the bed and walked across the Hotel Suite Tammy had taken him to and picked up his phone off the desk. He quickly dialed the number.

"Hello?" Andy said as he answered not recognizing the number that called him.

"This Jay, Andy," X said.

"Dude what the fuck man, I saw your fucking car on the news flipped over and shit. You alright bro?" Andy asked.

"Yeah I'm good!" X quickly said.

"Dude I been looking for some shit all night I been getting garbage. I got $75 can I come to you right now?" Andy asked. X laughed a little cause he knew if he not been in this situation, Andy would be pissing him off.

"Hell naw. I ain't call you for that Andy. I aint fucking around like that no mo," X said.

"Fuck bro, what up?" Andy asked.

"You remember you was telling me about yo family up North?" X asked.

"Yeah, I remember," Andy said.

"Well I need you to put me in contact with them asap. Can you do that?" X asked.

"Fuckin A dude, I'll do it right now on three way," Andy said excited.

"Naw, naw. I want you to give me their number and tell them what's up and I got you," X said.

"No problem bro, but you know they live in Fondu lac, they were only down here for a second," Andy said.

"Man don't worry bout all that Andy. Just make that happen like Asap. Like Now!" X said then ended the call.

"Fuck" X said as he contemplated his next move. X knew everything could go smooth or horribly wrong in a second, so he had to be careful. X phone chimed in his hands. He looked at it and saw it was a text from Andy.

"Dude call them asap, they're waiting on you. (920-933-0176)" the text read.

"Yup!" X said to his self. He quickly dialed the number Andy just gave him.

"Hello?"

"This Jay Andy guy," X said.

"Oh, ok how's it going? I'm Travis. If your uh uh around I can drive to you," Travis said.

"Naw I ain't around but check it out. I need to get some shit together I'ma call you I want you to come down and pick me up. I'ma hit you wit something to show me around town for a few days. That's cool?" X asked.

"Yes, sir I'll be waiting on the call," Travis said.

"Bet," X said then ended the call. He sat there and brainstormed on his next move.

(12:30pm)

Shah sat inside his rental car at the Speedway gas station on Verona Rd. He had just left the AT&T store buying a new phone. Yesterday was a fucked-up day for him, but he was ready for anything today. Shah got out of the car and walked inside the gas station.

"Tia, how you doing?" Shah asked as he walked up to the register.

"I'm doing fine. how you doing today Shah?" Tia asked.

'I'm good! Let me get $30 on pump 2," Shah said as he handed Tia the $30 dollars.

"Oh, no cigarillos today?" Tia asked.

"Naw I ain't smoking today I got some shit to handle today. I need to have a clear head," Shah said.

"Well that's good!" Tia said. Shah stood there for a moment just looking at Tia.

"What time you get off today?" Shah asked.

"I get off at 3pm. Why? You finna give me a ride home?" Tia asked.

"I wanna do more than just give you a ride home," Shah said seriously. Tia started laughing

"Shah, baby, I don't think you can handle me. You might wanna stick wit yo lil girlfriend," Tia said and smiled.

"I'ma be here at 3 to pick you up. I'ma show you what I can and can't handle," Shah said. Tia started laughing again

"Ok Shah, I'll see you at 3."

"Good!" Shah said as he walked off. He walked outside the store and over to his car and started pumping his gas. His phone started ringing in his pocket he reached in and pulled it out. Noticing it was a 414-area code, he debated on answering.

"Who dis?" Shah asked as he answered the phone.

"What up bro? Dis X."

"Oh X, what's good bro?" Shah asked.

"Shit down here in Madison right now I was tryna get up wit you so I could holla at you," X said.

"Tight so where you at?" Shah asked.

"I'm at the Grand Magnuson Hotel," X said.

"Tight, give me an hour I'ma pull up on you," Shah said as he finished pumping his gas.

"Tight bro," X said then ended the call.

Meanwhile

Lil Jerry pulled on Thurston and parked. He reached under his seat and grabbed his pistol and tucked it in his waist band. He had gotten off the phone with Special_Kaae an hour ago She wanted him to come over and smoke with her. He could tell by the tone of her voice that he was going to do more than smoke with her. Lil Jerry grabbed his cigarillos and weed and put them in his hoodie pocket then jumped out of his car. As he walked up the street, he pulled his phone out and called her.

"I'm outside," Lil Jerry said as she answered the phone.

"You at the door right now?" she asked.

"I'm walking up to it right now!" Lil Jerry said.

"Ok, I'm finna buzz you in!" she said.

"Tight," Lil Jerry said as the door started to buzz. Lil Jerry walked into the building as he ended the call. He heard a door open up stairs, so he walked up the stairs. Special_Kaaae stepped into the hall and motioned for Lil Jerry to come in. He walked over to the apartment and stepped in.

"Damn you look a whole lot better in person," she said as she closed the door behind him. She walked past Lil Jerry and went and sat down on the couch. Lil Jerry stood at the door as he scanned the apartment.

"You can sit down I won't bite you!" she said as she looked at Lil Jerry while he stood by the door.

"Oh ok. So, what's your real name?" Lil Jerry asked as he walked around the couch and pulled the weed and cigarillos from his pocket and sat down.

"My real name is Alexis," she said as she laughed.

"Alexis! I like that name," Lil Jerry said.

"Thank you," Alexis said as she grabbed a blunt, she had already rolled from the ash tray on the coffee table.

"So, do you have a woman?" Alexis asked.

"What's that? Na, I'm fucking wit you. I don't do those. I like living life," Lil Jerry said.

"Well at least you honest I can respect that cause I like living life. I wanna be able to do me cause life is too short," Alexis said as she flamed up her blunt.

"I probably could help you do you. But I wanna be able to watch that ass move while I'm doing it," Lil Jerry said. Alexis instantly started laughing.

"That sounds like reverse cowgirl to me!" Alexis said. Lil Jerry dumped his tobacco into the ash tray and looked over at Alexis. "Shit…doggy style, from the side while you on your side, or any position I could see that ass jiggle!" Lil Jerry said.

"I like that!" Alexis said as she reached to pass Lil Jerry the blunt.

"No disrespect but if I don't see it rolled, I don't smoke it," Lil Jerry said Alexis sat back with a disappointed look on her face.

"Well I can't argue wit that!" Alexis said as she hit the blunt again.

Meanwhile

Shah pulled into the Grand Magnuson Hotel parking lot and called X. He pulled in front of the Hotel's entrance and parked. He reached into the back seat and pulled his book bag from the back seat. X's phone rang and rang, then went to the voicemail. Shah hung up and called him back.

"What's good bro?" X asked as he answered on the first ring.

"I'm outside," Shah said.

"Tight I'm on my way down," X said.

"Yep!" Shah said and ended the call. Shah unzipped the book bag to make sure he didn't leave his scale at Tammy's apartment. He looked in and saw the scale, then hurried and zipped it back up and tossed it back on the back seat. Shah looked up and saw X walking through the lobby. He unlocked the car door as X walked up to the car.

"What's good bro?" Shah said as X got in and closed the door.

"Shit bro, I did a lot of thinking last night about what you said about fucking wit the boy. I want in on that shit!" X said as Shah pulled off.

"Tight, I can help you wit that. What you tryna do?" Shah asked.

"I had plans on coming wit twenty bands, but a nigga ran in my spot and hit me for some cheese I had put up. But right now, I ain't got shit but $2500 to my name. But I got some people up north that's gone grab whatever I come wit for three hunnit a grit. So, if you can fuck wit me wit this lil $2500 I'ma come back wit more cheese next time," X said. Shah's phone started ring. He'd been waiting on Trell to call him back. Shah quickly answered it.

"What up bro?" Shah asked.

"Shit I'm ready! Where you need me at?" Trell asked.

"Shit right now I'm out south where you at?" Shah asked.

"I'm south too. I'm on Park street," Trell said.

"Tight meet me at wing stop on Regent. I'ma be there in ten," Shah said.

"Say no mo bro and be on point too!" Trell said.

"Oh, I'm on point today!" Shah said.

"Tight!" Trell said then hung up. Shah checked his mirrors to make sure he wasn't being followed. "You say yo people gone pay $300 a grit?" Shah asked as he passed the Monona Rd exit.

"Yeah, they gone pay that," X said.

"Tight, this what I'ma do. I want you to hold on to yo cash if that's all you got. I'ma front you a hunnit grits just bring me back ten bands when you done," Shah said. X sat there nodding his head as he did the math on that shit. "Tight I can do that!" X said.

"Bet," Shah said as he reached into the middle console and pulled out a box of cigarellos.

"You wanna roll some of this gas?" Shah asked. "Hell yeah I aint have no bag all night and Tammy acted like she couldn't find none," X said.

Shah started laughing. "She ain't want you to smoke. She hate that shit," Shah said.

"I knew she was on some bull shit," X said as he broke down a cigarello. Shah pulled into the Wing Stop parking lot and parked. Trell walked out of Wing Stop and walked over to his car and grabbed a black bookbag from his passenger seat, then walked over to Shah's car and jumped into the back seat.

"What's good bro?" Shah asked.

"Shit I'm tryna get back in business my people been going crazy," Trell said.

"My bad bro! I went and laid down after that shit. I took a nice lost behind that shit but it's small shit to a giant," Shah said. Trell unzipped his bookbag and pulled out two stacks of cash both in $80,000 bundles and tossed them up to Shah. X's antennas quickly went up when he saw the cash hit Shah's lap. Shah reached in the back and grabbed the bookbag that was on the back seat and unzipped it. He put the cash in the bag and pulled out two bricks and passed them back to Trell. Trell grabbed the bricks and stuffed them into his bag.

"Aye do you be fucking wit that nigga Lil C?" Trell asked.

"Yeah. Why you ask that?" Shah asked.

"I was just wondering cause Kay and Magic his cousins. My mans told me fool be putting them niggas on stains," Trell said. Shah instantly started thinking about yesterday, He remembered meeting Lil C before he met Trell. Shah knew what Trell was saying was true cause how them niggas know what he was riding in and where to hit him.

"Yeah that bitch ass nigga put them on us. I met him right before I met you. I'm on his ass!" Shah said as he began to grow furious.

"Don't trip my people gone handle it. He hit me for $160,000 and I need that back!" Trell said. X passed the blunt over to Shah and sat there as he listened to Shah and Trell go back and forth. The numbers he heard them throwing around made him mad, but at the same time gave him some motivation. X figured as long as he fucked with Shah, he had the opportunity to get his cash all the way up.

"Tight bro," Trell said, then got out of Shah's car and walked back over to his car. Shah pulled out of Wing Stop and made a left on to Regent Street. He reached in his bag and pulled out a hundred grits and handed it to X.

"I wanted to bend a few corner wit you bro, but I got some important shit to take care of now. That's a hunnit grits. Just hit my line when you done," Shah said.

"Tight I got you bro. I'ma be back asap!" X said as Shah drove down Park Street.

Meanwhile

Lil Jerry sat on the couch while Alexis knelt down on her knees in between his legs with her forearms on his knees.

"So, can I show you?" Alexis asked.

"Hell yeah you can show me!" Lil Jerry said.

"This bitch too bad to be this thirsty!" he thought to his self as he unzipped his hoodie and pulled his pistol from his waist and sat it next to him on the couch. He stood up and pulled his pants down to his ankles then sat back down. Alexis walked to the back and opened the hall closet and grabbed a bath towel and walked back into the living room.

"Here sit on this. I don't wanna mess my couch up," Alexis said as she handed Lil Jerry the towel. Lil Jerry stood up and laid the towel down on the couch cushions and sat back down. Alexis knelt down in between Lil Jerry's legs. She grabbed ahold of his dick with both hands and slowly began to lick the tip as she took him into her mouth. Lil Jerry's phone started to ring, so he started to reach for it but stopped. Alexis took his dick from her mouth and looked up at him.

"Answer it!" she said as she went right back to sucking his dick. Lil Jerry pulled his phone from his hoodie pocket and answered it.

"Damn! Wha, What's up?" Lil Jerry forced out as Alexis started to deep throat his dick.

"Where you at bro?" Shah asked.

"Ummm I-I-I'm out west," Lil Jerry said.

"Aye I need them joints asap!" Shah said.

"Tight give me a min, a minute and I'ma meet you on Russit," Lil Jerry said.

"Say no more!" Shah said and ended the call.

Lil Jerry set the phone down next to him and watched Alexis as she continued to use every trick she knew to prove her point. Lil Jerry reached and grabbed the back of Alexis head, forcing her to go deeper as his body stiffened up. He held her head down as he exploded into her throat. Alexis continued to suck as Lil Jerry began to relax then she looked up at him and started laughing as his legs begin to shake.

"Yeah I think you see what I mean!" Alexis said as she stood up and started walking to the bathroom.

"Yeah you did dat! But look I got some shit I gotta do real quick. What you on tonight?" Lil Jerry asked as he pulled his pants up and put his pistol back on his hip.

"I'll be here all day you should came back so we can finish where we left off," Alexis said as she walked out of the bathroom.

"Tight I'ma call you when I'm done wit this shit," Lil Jerry said as he walked toward the door.

"Ok!" Alexis said as she walked past Lil Jerry to unlock the door.

"Yeah I gotta see that ass bounce!" Lil Jerry said as he reached and grabbed Alexis's ass.

"Make sure you come back!" Alexis said as she laughed.

"Yeah, I will," Lil Jerry said as he walked past her and out the door.

Meanwhile

Kay and Magic sat in the living room of Magic's house on Maywood Rd in Middleton counting the money they got from Lil C last night.

"Aye bro you going to the reunion tomorrow?" Kay asked as he set a stack of hundreds on the floor. Magic looked over at Kay and finished counting the money in his hands.

"Hell yeah! Last year I missed it. I gotta go this year and flex!" Magic said.

"This a $160,000 right here!" Kay said and stood up.

"Tight this $75,000 right here. So that's like $117,500 each," Magic said.

"Yeah that was an easy half a million we hit they ass for. I ain't running through this shit like I did when we hit them Mexicans!" Kay said.

"Yeah don't blow this shit like you did when we hit them. Yo ass was fucked up in a week!" Magic said. Kay started laughing

"On Bd I was in KOD tryna keep up wit cuz nem I blew a hunnit that night!" Kay said.

"I ain't looking back after this stain. This robbing shit starting to get old," Magic said.

"What you gone do? We can't get no money down here, ain't none of these niggas gone fuck wit us we did too much dirt!" Kay said.

"Yeah I know. I been fucking on this white bitch that be up North in Fondu Lac and she say it's sweet up there. After the reunion I'm going up there wit that brick and see what I can do," Magic said.

"You know me, I ain't wit the hustling shit. I'ma let a nigga do all the stacking and I'ma jack him!" Kay said and started laughing.

"Well let me get that brick. I got fifty bands for it," Magic quickly said.

"Bet!" Kay said.

"Tight. Take off that $40,000 you owe, and I got $10,000 for you right now," Magic said.

"Man, hell naw'll! If that's the case, I want $70,000. Take off yo $40,000 and just give me $30,000" Kay said.

"I got $20,000 for you right now!" Magic said.

"Tight I'ma take that dub!" Kay said and started laughing. Magic quickly handed Kay the twenty thousand.

"Let me put these bricks up so we can hit this highway and get the fuck out of here for a while," Magic said.

"Say no more!" Kay said as he stuffed his $266,500 dollars into his bookbag.

Meanwhile

Shah and Lil Jerry met up with Lil Ant, Mook, and Rell in Tamara's building on Russit.

"What's good Skud. This my mans Mook and Rell" Lil Ant said to Shah.

"What up!" Shah said to Mook and Rell.

"I figured out one of the niggas I was serving put them niggas on me. I know where he live at I want y'all to slide through tonight," Shah said to Lil Ant.

"Tight but what the nigga look like? We gotta make sure we get the right person. We don't do blind missions skud!" Lil Ant said.

"I would never send you on a blind mission cuz. I got a picture of the nigga right here," Shah said and flipped through Facebook until he found the picture and passed it to Lil Ant. Lil Ant grabbed the phone and looked at the picture and passed it to Mook.

"I'ma show y'all where he live at and what kind of car he drive. I thought about calling him and having him link wit me but that might give it up. Plus, the element of surprise is a mafucka!" Shah said.

"Tight look skud all you gotta do is show us where he live and the car. We gone handle the rest, so just get us the tools," Lil Ant said.

"You got those?" Shah asked as he looked at Lil Jerry. "Yeah, I got em hold on," Lil Jerry said, then started walking downstairs to the basement. Lil Ant looked out the building door and saw Hustle Man walking up to the door.

"What you need?" Lil Ant asked Hustle Man as he opened the door. Shah looked toward the door and saw Hustle Man.

"He good! He here for me," Shah said to Lil Ant.

"Oh iight!" Lil Ant said as he let Hustle Man in the building. Hustle Man walked up to Shah then looked around at Rell and Mook.

"I need to holla at you," Hustle Man said.

"These my people, they good!" Shah said letting Hustle Man know it was cool to talk around them.

"Alright. Well I'm done," Hustle Man said as he pulled out $12,000 from his coat pocket and handed it to Shah.

"This the whole thing?" Shah asked.

"Yeah, it's all their nephew," Hustle Man said. Lil Jerry came walking up the stairs with a blue bookbag and noticed Hustle Man standing next to Shah.

"This ugly ass nigga right here!" Lil Jerry said and started laughing. Hustle Man turned around and saw Lil Jerry.

"Yo skinny ass can't call nobody ugly. You ain't got no hoes. I got more hoe's then you do nigga!" Hustle Man said.

"Man, them ain't hoes them hypes! All you doing is dope dating," Lil Jerry said. Hustle Man started laughing. "As long as I get the pussy lil nigga!" he said. Shah reached into his bookbag and pulled out a hundred grams and handed it to Hustle Man.

"Get at me when you done. We got some shit we need to handle I'ma holla at you later," Shah said.

"Tight I'ma call you when I'm done," Hustle Man said as he stuffed the grams into his underwear, then walked toward the door. Lil Ant opened the door and let him out and quickly closed it.

"Look this three Glock 40's. It's two drums and a thirty clip in here," Lil Jerry said as he handed the book bag to Shah.

"Tight what you want for this?" Shah asked.

"Just give me a band," Lil Jerry said. Shah peeled a thousand off the money he just got from Hustle Man and handed it to him. Mook stood there watching Shah. He could tell by his body language that he was sweet. Lil Ant was his mans and Shah was Lil Ant's cousin, so Mook stayed in his lane.

"Here you go cuz," Shah said as he handed the bag to Lil Ant. "You should take them bitches over to Tonya crib," Shah added.

"Skud speaking of Tonya, I went over there a few days ago to chill for a lil while. The lil bitch must not have known I was there. She came walking out the bathroom asshole naked. I fucked the shit out of her on shorty!" Lil Ant said.

"Yeah? Do she got some good pussy?" Shah asked because he thought about tryna fuck Tonya but decided against it.

"It's iight. I had that bitch top me for like an hour straight. She a monster on the neck skud!" Lil Ant said.

Shah started laughing "Oh yeah I'ma have to see what's too that neck," Shah said. Mook handed Shah his phone back.

"Good looking," Shah said as he looked at his phone and saw it was 2:45pm

"Damn I gotta get up out of here I got some shit I gotta do. I'ma slide back on y'all in two hours and take y'all past dude crib," Shah said.

"Hold on! I was just getting some of the best top I ever had, and I cut that shit short cause you made this shit sound like an emergency!" Lil Jerry said. Shah started laughing

"My bad I needed to make sure cuz nem got them tools asap. But I got some pussy online I gotta get to. I'ma catch y'all later," Shah said as he walked over to the door and left the building.

Meanwhile

Shah pulled into Speedway five minutes early, so he parked on the side of the gas station and pulled out his phone. He flipped through Facebook checking his notifications. He had over five hundred likes on the picture he posted on the V.I.P Cardi B tickets. He strolled through the comments and noticed almost everybody asked where they could buy some tickets from.

"My bad I ain't been on here in a minute, but the number for the tickets is (608-213-3321). Call asap before they all gone," Shah responded to the comments. He checked his messages and instantly started laughing when he saw he had a message from Lisa Stone.

"This bitch be thirsty!" he said to his self as he logged out of Facebook. Shah looked up as Tia came walking out of the store. He couldn't believe she was about to give him a chance. Tia walked up to the passenger door and got into the car.

"You sexy ass hell!" Shah said as Tia closed the door.

"Aww thank you" Tia said as she buckled her seat belt.

"So, where you stay at now?" Shah asked.

"I stay on McKee," Tia said.

"Oh, that's where you been hiding at!" Shah said as he pulled out of the gas station.

"I wasn't hiding you just wasn't looking hard enough!" Tia said as she shifted her body so that she was facing Shah.

"Maybe I wasn't looking hard enough, but now that I found you I'ma show you how much I grew since you stayed next door to us," Shah said. He figured Tia was the kind of female that looked for a nigga with money to save her from all her problems and he knew she was a certified sack chaser. Shah knew she heard he was the man now, and that's the reason why she was being so flirtatious with him. He was cool with that cause he wanted the pussy. Tia started laughing

"Shah, I don't think you could handle me if I put this pussy on you. I might make you leave that Asian girl alone in a heartbeat!" she said. Shah looked over at her as he drove past Walgreens on Raymond Rd and started laughing.

"As a matter of a fact let me see how big yo dick is," Tia said as she reached across and grabbed his belt buckle.

"Go ahead!" Shah said as he leaned his seat back and gave her room to unbuckle his pants. Tia unbuckled his belt and reached into his pants; Shah's dick instantly got hard as Tia grabbed ahold of his dick. This was a childhood fantasy coming true. Tia pulled Shah's dick from his pants and was shocked to see it was a whole lot bigger than what she thought it would be.

"Oh ok! I can't be calling you a baby wit a dick like this!" Tia said as she stroked up and down on his dick.

"I ain't one to brag but that's what I been telling you," Shah said as he glanced over at Tia. Her eyes were locked on his dick as she played with it.

"Where you stay at on McKee?" Shah asked as he approached the intersection of Raymond and McKee.

"I stay in the first lot behind the bank in them town houses," Tia said as she put Shah's dick back into his pants. Shah made a left on McKee and a quick right into Tia's parking lot.

"The last one on the left," Tia said as she pointed to her garage. Shah pulled in front of her garage and parked. Tia quickly got out of the car, so Shah jumped out behind her and followed her to the door. Tia unlocked the door and walked into her house as Shah followed behind her.

"Make yourself at home. The remote over there, and food and drinks in the fridge if you want anything. I'm finna get in the shower" Tia said as she walked away. Shah looked around before walking over to the couch. He grabbed the remote and turned the TV on as he flipped through a few channels, Almundo popped in mind.

"Damn I'm bogus!" he said to his self as he pulled his phone from his pocket and dialed Almundo's number.

"Hello?" Almundo said as he answered the phone.

"What up brother? This Shah!" he said. The tone in Almundo's voice went from being dry and dull to overly excited.

"My main man. Where you been?" Almundo asked.

"I been busy brother. But I got something for you," Shah said.

"Good cause I been dealing with the other guy and he don't look out. I been waiting for your call," Almundo said.

"That's my bad! From now on call this number," Shah said.

"I'm in the middle of something I'm going to call you back when I'm done," Shah said.

"Okay just give me a call," Almundo said.

"Tight," Shah said and ended the call. Shah sat there thinking of a lot of Hot Boi's clientele and he knew every last number by hard. He quickly started storing their numbers in his phone. He remembered how much he was pulling in off that line and decided he was going to undercut Hot Boi and swipe his whole clientele. His phone started to ring as he held it.

"Damn TJ," Shah said to his self before answering the phone.

"What up bro?" Shah asked.

"I ain't on shit I'm tryna link up wit you!" TJ said.

"Tight what's the word?" Shah asked.

"Shit sum light like a hunnit!" TJ said.

"Tight, shit I'm on McKee. Call me when you get this way," Shah said.

"Tight bro," TJ said and hung up. Shah stood up from the couch and walked into the kitchen, he opened the fridge to see what was in it. He reached in and grabbed a bottle of water then walked back to the living room and sat down.

"Damn I'm trippin!" he thought to his self. He stood up and walked over to the stairs and walked up. He made his way to the bathroom and opened the door. Tia pulled the curtain back some and looked out at Shah.

"You told me to make myself at home, so I think I wanna shower too," Shah said.

Tia started laughing "Well you're too late! I'm on my way out," She said as she grabbed her towel and wrapped it around herself and got out. Shah stood there looking at Tia as she got out the shower. She reminded him of Kelly Rowland. Tia was what you called slim thick she was slim and thick in all the right places.

"Damn!" Shah said as Tia walked past him and headed to her bedroom. Tia looked back at Shah before walking into her room.

"Don't wait too late to come in my room!" she said and smiled as she walked into the room. Shah hurried and walked into Tia's room. She stood at her dresser looking back at Shah through the mirror. Shah walked up and pulled the towel from around her body and tossed it to the floor.

"Don't be scared!" Tia said as she stood there in anticipation of Shah's touch. He walked closer and wrapped his arms around Tia grabbing her breast. His dick pressed against her ass and quickly hardened as he kissed her neck and shoulders. Tia let out a soft moan pushing her ass back harder against Shah's dick.

"Fuck me with that big dick Shah!" Tia whispered and bent over the dresser as he kissed the back of her neck. Shah really couldn't believe he was about to fuck Tia. He looked up and looked her in her eyes as she looked at him through the mirror. Tia reached over and opened the drawer next to her and pulled out some condoms and sat them on the dresser. Shah unbuckled his belt and pulled his pants and boxers down to his feet. He reached over and grabbed a condom and opened it and put it on. Tia spread her legs as Shah reached down and started playing with her pussy then he slowly slid into her.

"Oooh shit!" Tia said as she reached back and put her hand on Shah's hip keeping him from going any deeper. Shah laughed a little as he looked at Tia through the mirror then moved her hand and pulled her closer to him.

"Oh my god Shah!" Tia said as he slowly began to thrust in and out of her. Shah could feel his self-getting harder and harder as he watched Tia's facial expression through the mirror. He couldn't believe he was actually fucking Tia.

"I'm finna fuck the shit out this bitch!" Shah thought to himself as he picked up his pace. "Sha- Shaa - Shah, Oh my god it's in my stomach!" Tia yelled out as he fucked her with force. Tia tried her hardest to put some space between herself and Shah as he fucked her at a rapid pace, but the more she fought the harder he fucked her.

"Ohh shit, Ooh shit I'm cumming!" Tia yelled out and Shah began to pound her harder and harder making sure he left his imprint in her mind! "Oh my god!" Tia yelled out as she looked back at Shah through the mirror.

"Let's take this to the bed!" Tia said out of breath.

"Tight" Shah said as he laughed and backed away from the dresser allowing Tia to walk over to the bed. Shah's phone started to ring in his pocket, he reached down and pulled his phone from his pocket and answered it.

"What up bro?" Shah said as he answered.

"I'm on McKee. Where you at?" TJ asked.

"I'm in them town houses in the first lot behind the bank," Shah said.

"Tight come out I'm finna pull in right now," TJ said.

"Tight!" Shah said and ended the call. He quickly snatched the condom off and pulled his pants up and walked out the room. Tia laid in the bed in disbelief, Shah had fucked her better than a lot of niggas twice his age and she couldn't wait to get some more. TJ got out the car and started walking toward Shah when he seen him walk outside.

"I see you in their wit Tia!" TJ said and laughed.

"You know how this shit go," Shah said as he opened his car door and got in. He unlocked the door for TJ, so he could get in. TJ jumped in the car and handed Shah eight thousand dollars. Shah reached in the back seat and grabbed his book bag and unzipped it. He reached in and pulled out a hundred grams and handed it to TJ.

"Tight I'ma let you get back to it. Make sure you get some of that neck she a beast," TJ said as he got out of the car. Shah stuffed the cash in his bag and got out the car. "Say no more," Shah said as he put the book bag on his shoulder and walked back into Tia's house.

Chapter Fithteen

LATER THAT EVENING

S hah turned on to Pennwall Street with Lil Ant, Mook, and Rell in the car with him.

"You see that brown house over there?" Shah asked as he point to a house in the middle of the block.

"Yeah the one on the left?" Lil Ant asked.

"Yeah that one! That's his crib and that's his black Malibu in the driveway. He in there right now," Shah said as they drove past his house.

"Drop us off around the corner we finna go in that bitch right now!" Mook said from the back seat.

"Naw skud we gone come back after we drop cuz off," Lil Ant said.

"Fuck that he might be gone when we get back let's get him now," Rell said.

"I agree wit them cuz let's get him now. But I wanna kill him myself!" Shah said. Lil Ant looked at Shah unsure what to think.

"You sure Skud?" Lil Ant asked Shah.

"Yeah I'm sure. But somebody gotta stay in the car," Shah said. Mook and Rell both looked at each other "Man you got me fucked up!" Rell said to Mook.

"I got the best shot out of all of us. It ain't no way in hell I'm staying in the car," Mook said to Rell.

"Skud y'all trippin! Rell you stay wit the car, Mook you comin in," Lil Ant said. Shah turned off Pennwall Street and drove a few houses up and parked. Rell handed Shah his pistol. Shah pulled his hoodie over his head and got out of the car. Lil Ant and Mook got out and followed him around the corner.

Meanwhile

Lil Jerry stood on the side of the couch smoking a blunt while Alexis sat on the couch sipping a glass of Hennessey.

"You want something to drink?" Alexis asked Lil Jerry.

"What you drinking?" he asked.

"Hennessey," she said as she took another sip from her glass.

"Yeah, I can drink wit you," Lil Jerry said as he exhaled the weed smoke.

"The cups in the cabinet and the Hennessey in the freezer," Alexis said. Lil Jerry handed Alexis the blunt and walked into the kitchen.

"So, you from Madison!" Lil Jerry asked Alexis as he opened the cabinet and grabbed a cup.

"No, I'm from Detroit," Alexis said as she inhaled the weed smoke. Lil Jerry opened the freezer and pulled out the Hennessey and poured a cup.

"Oh, you from the D? Why you come to Wisconsin?" he asked as he put the bottle back in the freezer.

"Cause it wasn't much up there and I needed a fresh start so I left. I moved to Chicago and fell in love with this nigga then he wanted to move up here. Not too long after we moved up here, he caught a federal case and they gave him 30yrs. I just decided to stay. That's my life story," Alexis said. Lil Jerry walked out the kitchen and back into the living room. He sat down on the couch across from Alexis. She hit the blunt again and handed it to him.

"So how you end up in Madison?" Alexis asked. Lil Jerry took a sip from his cup and sat it down on the coffee table.

"My cousin came to Chicago and we smoked a few blunts. I fell asleep and when I woke up, I was in Madison. I been back and forth ever since," he said as he hit the blunt again.

Meanwhile

Shah, Lil Ant, and Mook knelt down on the side of Lil C's house. Shah looked into a window he could see it was the kitchen. He knelt back down and whispered to Lil Ant.

"That's the kitchen I can't see shit else. How we finna get in?" he asked. Lil Ant looked over at Mook "You ready?" Lil Ant asked Mook.

"Tight," Mook said as he stood up and walked around to the front of the house. Lil Ant looked back at Shah. "Aye skud just follow my lead," he said. Mook walked up the stairs on the porch. He looked around then rang the doorbell three times and opened the screen door.

"Who the fuck is it!" Lil C yelled and snatched the door open.

"Aye my car just died you think I can get a jump?" Mook asked. Lil C looked up the street then back at Mook. "Where yo shit at?" Lil C asked.

"Right over there," Mook said and pointed to a car up the street. Lil C looked in the direction Mook pointed then back to Mook. He was caught off guard when he saw the pistol in Mook's hand. Mook grabbed Lil C by his collar and forced him back into the house.

"Who else in here nigga?" Mook asked as Lil Ant and Shah rushed from the side of the house into the front door.

"Nobody!" Lil C said as he held his hands in the air. Shah closed the door and turned and looked at Lil C. "What up fool?" Shah said as he walked up on Lil C. Lil C eyes opened wide when he saw Shah.

"Ma- Man Shah, I ain't have shit to do wit that. Them niggas robbed me too," Lil C said. Shah reached over and smacked Lil C with his pistol then grabbed him and threw him to the floor.

"Bitch ass nigga you think I'm stupid huh? Where the fuck my money at?" Shah asked.

"Shah I'm telling you them niggas robbed me too last night. They took me for everything I own," Lil C said.

"Man gone put two and his top and let's get up out of here!" Mook said to Shah.

"Hold on, hold on Shah. Man, I'll tell you whatever you wanna know bout them niggas. I promise I ain't have shit to do wit that shit," Lil C begged. Mook stepped in front of Shah and put two in Lil C's face and looked over at Shah

"Now let's get the fuck up out of here!" he said then ran to the door. Lil Ant followed right behind him. Shah stood there for a second frozem before he snapped out of it when Lil Ant grabbed his arm.

"Skud you trippin" Lil Ant said as he pulled him toward the door.

Meanwhile

Lil Jerry finished his drink and sat the cup down on the coffee table. Alexis stood up and turned some music on.

"Aww that's my shit!" she said as Cardi B's song Money flowed through the speakers. She walked up to Lil Jerry and started twerking, then sat on his lap facing him and leaned in and whispered.

"I ride his dick and some big tall heels!" Lil Jerry reached around and grabbed both of Alexis ass cheeks and held them in his hand. "Damn yo ass soft ass hell!" he said as he looked into her eyes.

"I could get used to being in your arms," Alexis said as she let out a soft moan into his ear. "Yeah?" Lil Jerry asked before he started to feel a little faint. The room quickly started spinning "I need some water!" Lil Jerry said as he tried to move Alexis off his lap. Alexis reached for Lil Jerry's hip and grabbed his pistol. He quickly grabbed her wrist.

"What the fuck you doing?" Lil Jerry said as the room started to spin faster and faster. Alexis snatched away from his loose grip and jumped up from his lap.

"Stupid ass nigga!" Alexis said as she backed away from the couch with his gun in her hand.

"Bitch what the fuck you do to me?" Lil Jerry asked as he stood up and lunged toward her. Alexis stepped to the side and watched as Lil Jerry fell headfirst into the wall knocking his self completely out. Alexis sat the gun down on the couch and walked over to him and rolled him over on his back.

"Damn I wanted to fuck you first!" Alexis said as she grabbed him by the arms and dragged him down the hall to the extra bedroom. She hog tied him and duck taped his eyes and mouth shut and locked him in the room.

(10:00am)

Audrey and Tammy stood at the front counter in the schmidts tow yard. Audrey got a call from the Madison police department and they informed her that the truck she reported stolen had been recovered.

"Girl I can't believe they just charged me a hundred and ninety dollars for a tow," Audrey said.

"I know they need to hurry up cause I'm tired and I have to be at work in a few hours," Tammy said as she stood there looking across the tow yard.

"Here they come!" Tammy said as she watched the truck pull out the back lot.

"About time!" Audrey said as she walked out to the gate. The tow truck guy pulled up to Audrey and Tammy and parked.

"Here you go ma'am," the guy said as he handed Audrey the keys.

"Thank you," Audrey said as she walked up to the driver door. "Follow me to drop this truck off to Shah," Audrey yelled out to Tammy. Tammy nodded her head as she walked over to her car and got in. Audrey got into the truck and started it, then pulled off.

Meanwhile

Lil Jerry struggled to free his hands from the rope while he laid on his side. He wiggled and pulled for over an hour until he finally got one arm free. Lil Jerry quickly snatched the duct tape from his mouth and eyes then untied the rope from around his legs. After a minute he managed to free his legs and quickly snatched the rope from his other arm.

Lil Jerry jumped to his feet and rushed over to the door and tried to open it, but it was locked. He quickly started searching the room to see what he could find. He looked in the closet and found a stun gun on the shelf. He quickly rushed over to the window when he heard voices outside. Peeking through the blinds he could see Brittany and Alexis standing in front of Brittany's car.

"These bitches think I'm sweet!" he said to his self-realizing what was happening. Lil Jerry walked over to the door and continually kicked the door until it split down the middle. He kicked a big hole through the wooden door and climbed out the room and instantly started searching the house for his gun. Lil Jerry searched Alexis's room and found his gun and hers in her dresser drawer.

"Yeah I'm finna kill these bitches!" he said as he checked the clips for bullets. Lil Jerry rushed back to the other room and peeked out the window he could see Alexis and Brittany walking back toward the building. He quickly ran into the living room and hid behind the front door with a pistol in each hand. He could hear Alexis and Brittany laughing as they walked up to the door.

Alexis put the key in the door and unlocked it. She walked in with Brittany right behind her as Brittany started closing the door Lil Jerry stepped from behind the door and smacked her in her face with his gun knocking her over the couch. He instantly pushed the door closed and pointed his gun at Alexis.

"So, you bitches thought y'all was gone kill me huh?" Lil Jerry asked as he rushed over to Alexis. Alexis stood there stuck she was in shock. She couldn't believe he got out.

"Wait! I-- I wasn't going to kill you," Alexis said as she slowly started walking away from him. Brittany laid on the floor knocked out as blood poured from her forehead. Lil Jerry put one gun on his hip and grabbed Alexis by the shirt. She snatched away and tried to rush toward the door, but Lil Jerry tripped her then smacked her on the back of her head with his gun knocking her out.

(10:35am)

Audrey and Tammy pulled over and parked on Raymond rd in front of Shah and Lil Ant.

"Damn that's yo bitch?" Lil Ant asked Shah.

"Yeah that's Wifey!" Shah said before he walked over to the driver door and opened it. Audrey stepped out of the truck and gave Shah a hug and a kiss.

"Damn you smell good!" Shah said as he held her in his arms.

"Thank you," Audrey said. Tammy got out of her car and walked over to Shah and Audrey in the street. "You better not let nobody else steal yo car!" Tammy said to Shah. "Oh, trust me it won't happen again," Shah said as he leaned over and gave Tammy a hug.

"Aye this my cousin Ant," Shah said as he walked back onto the sidewalk. "Hey how you doing," they both said as they walked out of the street. "This my Wifey Audrey and my other wife Tammy!" Shah said and laughed as he put his arms around both of them.

"Wait a minute! Well where the hell our rings at?" Audrey said jokingly.

"Cause you gotta put a ring on it before you think it's yours!" Tammy said.

"They on lay-away y'all know I'm fucked," Shah said.

Lil Ant started laughing. "Well either way, how y'all doing?" he said.

"So, when we going shopping for this Cardi B concert? you know its in eight days," Audrey said looking over at Shah.

"Shit right now I'm waist deep in these streets, but y'all can go shopping for all of us," Shah said.

"Ok good cause I'm off this weekend and I wanna go shopping in Chicago," Tammy said.

"Tight I got y'all," Shah said before his phone started ringing. He reached into his pocket and pulled out his phone.

"Damn Almundo!" Shah said realizing he forgot to call him back yesterday.

"Damn my bad, I forgot," Shah quickly said once he answered.

"I see brother!" Almundo said.

"Just come meet me on Russit right now," Shah said.

"Ok I'm on my way," Almundo quickly said.

"Tight," Shah said and ended the call.

"Man, cuz I forgot to tell you I got some new action for you. We gone put them on the phone cause they heavy hittas," Shah said.

"It's official," Lil Ant said, not too comfortable talking business in front of Audrey and Tammy.

"Well baby we gotta go. She gotta be at work in a few hours, so I'ma be at her house if you need me," Audrey said as she walked up to Shah and gave him a kiss.

"Tight love you," Shah said.

"I love you too," Audrey said as she turned and walked away.

"It was nice to meet you Ant," she said before getting into Tammy's car.

"Let's slide up to Tonya crib real quick," Shah said to Lil Ant as Tammy and Audrey drove off.

Meanwhile

Lil Jerry tied Alexis and Brittany up and dragged both of them in the back room. He walked into the kitchen and grabbed a pitcher of water and walked back into the room and threw it on her. Lil Jerry smacked her a few times and woke her up. Brittany looked around, still dazed as he grabbed her by her hair.

"I'm right here bitch!" he said as he turned her face in his direction.

"You set this shit up huh?" he asked.

"No, I swear!" Brittany managed to say.

"Well why the fuck is you here?" he asked.

"This shit was her idea. She killed Cory and she was about to kill you too," Brittany said.

"Why?" he asked. Brittany laid there breathing heavily her eyes gazed at the floor cause she knew the answer to this question would only dig her deeper into a hole. Lil Jerry grabbed her hair tighter in his grip and pulled her head back.

"Bitch if you don't tell me what I wanna know I'ma burn you hoes alive," he said in a real aggressive low pitch tone. Brittany looked him directly in his eye. "Please, promise me if I tell you you won't kill me!" Brittany said.

"Tight! But bitch if you lie or I think you lying yo ass dead!" he said.

"Ok, ok. So, what you wanna know?" Brittany asked.

"Where the fuck is his body at?" Lil Jerry asked.

"We waited until it was dark and took him up the street and buried him in the park," Brittany said.

"Tight. Good lookin!" he said then let go of her hair and walked back to the kitchen. He searched the kitchen until he found a bottle of lighter fluid under the sink.

"I'm finna burn these hoes alive for you cuz!" he said to his self as he walked back to the room and stood there. He grabbed the duct tape and put it over Brittany's mouth and eyes then did the same to Alexis. "Ok Brittany I think you lying!" he said as he began to pour lighter fluid on top of her then Alexis. He grabbed some clothes from the closet and tossed them on top of both of them and emptied the rest of the lighter fluid on top of the clothes.

"This for you cuz!" he said as he lit a piece of paper and tossed it on top of them. He stood there for a moment and watched as they were engulfed in flames, then he hurried and rushed out the apartment.

Meanwhile

Shah walked back into Tonya's apartment after meeting Almundo. Lil Ant sat on the couch next to Tonya. He was happy he was finally able to sit down and relax. He wasted no time putting Mook and Rell to work running the dope line in Tamara's building. Shah had already called all of Hot Boi's people and told them not to call the old number and gave them a new number to call. Shah walked into the kitchen and grabbed a bottle of water from the fridge.

"Aye cuz I gave your number to all the new action I was telling you about. They gone call, just make sure you stay on top of shit cause they gone come with that bread at all kinds of hours," Shah said as he opened up the bottle of water and took a sip.

"I'm on it!" Lil Ant said before he leaned over and whispered into Tonya's ear.

"They used to buying half a gram for $50 that's a easy $2800 a zip" Shah said. Tonya started laughing at what Lil Ant just whispered in her ear then got up and walked to her room.

"So, you want me to whip this shit like the last shit?" Lil Ant asked.

"Yeah bro, don't let this distract you!" Shah said as he walked out the kitchen and pointed to Tonya in the back.

"I'm focus skud," Lil Ant said.

"Tight," Shah said as he nodded his head. His phone started to ring in his pocket, so he quickly pulled it out and answered it.

"What up bro?" Shah said.

"Aye bro it's stupid action up here I'm finna be back tonight!" X said.

"Damn already?" Shah asked.

"Bro I gotta holla at you in person," X said.

"Tight just hit me when you touch!" Shah said.

"Tight bro love," X said then ended the call.

(1:00pm)

Blue Dini pulled into the Walgreen's parking lot on PD and parked. He picked his phone up from his lap and dialed Shah's number.

"Yeah I'm up here!" Blue Dini said as Shah answered.

"Tight I'm pulling in right now," Shah said.

"I see you," Blue Dini said and ended the call. Shah pulled next to Blue Dini and parked as Blue Dini got out of his car. He jumped into the car with Shah and closed the door.

"What up?" Shah said as he shook Blue Dini hand.

"Shit. fuck you been up too lil bro?" Blue Dini asked as he tossed a book bag on the back seat with $350,000 in it.

"That's $350,000!" Blue Dini said.

"Tight. But I need you to show me how to re-rock this shit!" Shah said.

"When you tryna do it?" Blue Dini asked.

"I got a play coming from out of town I'm tryna do it right now if you ain't busy!" Shah said.

"Damn lil bro you picked a perfect time to ask when we got all this shit on us."

"I had you meet me right here cause my bitch buddy stay up the street you can show me how to do it over there," Shah said.

"Tight I'ma show you how to do it wit out the compressor so you can be ready for yo people. Next time we gone hit my spot and I'ma show you how to do it wit the compressor," Blue Dini said.

"Bet!" Shah said.

"Look, run in there and grab a baby blinder. Matter fact fuck it I'ma come in wit you and show you what you need," Blue Dini said.

"Tight," Shah said and turned his car off and jumped out of his truck. Shah and Blue Dini walked out of Walgreen's fifteen minutes later with a bag full of stuff Shah was going to need. They jumped in Shah's car and pulled around the corner to Tammy's crib and went upstairs. Shah unlocked the door and walked into the apartment and closed the door behind Blue Dini.

"Audrey what up? how you doing?" Blue Dini asked.

"Heyy Blue! How you been?" Audrey asked.

"I been chillin!" Blue Dini said.

"That's good," Audrey responded. Blue Dini followed Shah into the kitchen and sat down at the table. Shah sat the bag on the kitchen table then started pulling everything from the bag and sat it on the counter. He took his bookbag off and sat it on the table and unzipped it. He pulled out a brick and handed the bookbag to Blue Dini.

"That's yo five," Shah said. Blue Dini looked in the bag and zipped it back up then sat it on the floor.

"Grab a big pot and fill it up with some water," Blue Dini said. Shah walked over to the cabinet and pulled out the biggest pot he could find and started filling it up with water. Blue Dini stood up and opened the blender box and pulled it out.

"How many you tryna do?" Blue Dini asked.

"I'm tryna give him five hunnit grams," Shah said.

"Tight. Put the pot on the stove and let it boil," Blue Dini said. Shah put the pot on the stove and turned the gas on. He walked over to the table and watched as Blue Dini got the biggest bullet and connected it to the blender.

"You got a scale in here?" Blue Dini asked.

"Yeah," Shah said.

"Tight grab it and grab something to break the brick down," Blue Dini said.

"Tight," Shah said as he walked over to the drawer and grabbed the scale and hammer out and walked back over to the table.

"Tight now break off 250 and put them in this," Blue Dini said as he handed Shah the bullet.

"Tight," Shah said. He grabbed the brick and walked over to the counter and used the hammer to break the brick and weighed up 250 grams and put them into the bullet.

"Now what?" Shah asked.

"Grab those pills. Now normally, I wouldn't use these, but we in a rush, so pour five of those bottles in with that," Blue Dini said. Shah quickly did as directed. "Tight now blend it all up til its dust," Blue Dini said. Shah did just that and Blue Dini checked to see if everything was good.

"Now grab that mask and put it on," Blue Dini said as he put on one of the masks. Blue Dini grabbed the toothbrush from off the table and opened it. He walked over to the blinder and took the bullet off of it.

"Just watch, so you can see what to do!" Blue Dini said to Shah. Shah stood there and watched as Blue Dini did the next few steps. Blue Dini tossed it into the bowling water.

"Now let it sit there for thirty minutes then toss it in the freezer for thirty minutes. When you unwrap it its gone be rock solid," Blue Dini said.

"Tight and that's that?" Shah asked.

"Yeah that's it lil bro," Blue Dini said. Shah stood there watching as it boiled in the pot. Blue Dini's phone started to ring.

"That's the sound of money!" he said then answered the phone.

"What's up?" Blue Dini said.

"Same shit big homie, I need you to pull up on me," Jeff said.

"Damn already, I just slid through last night," Blue Dini said shocked that Jeff ran through that shit that fast.

"Hell, yeah big homie I told you they loving that shit. I'ma take yo advice and up it to three of em," Jeff said.

"Tight give me an hour and I'ma pull up on you," Blue Dini said.

"Tight I'm here," Jeff said.

"Yep," Blue Dini said then ended the call. Blue Dini looked over at Shah who was standing there looking at the pot fascinated with how Blue Dini just did what he did.

"Aye lil bro, Have Audrey watch that real quick, I got some shit lined up I need you to take me back to my car," Blue Dini said as he grabbed the bookbag off the floor and put it on his shoulder.

"Say no more," Shah said, snapping out of his trance.

"All you gotta do is make sure you don't let all the water boil out, then toss it in the freezer. Remember thirty minutes in the pot and thirty minutes in the freezer," Blue Dini said.

"Tight I got it!" Shah said as he walked into the living room.

"Aye Cinderella, I need you to watch that pot for me. Make sure all the water don't boil out of it. I'm finna run up the street I'll be back in five minutes," Shah said to Audrey.

"Ok baby!" Audrey said.

"It was nice to see you again Audrey," Blue Dini said as he walked over to the front door.

"Nice seeing you too," Audrey said never looking away from her phone.

"Make sure that water don't boil out!" Shah said again as he grabbed his phone and car keys and opened the door.

"Boy bye" Audrey said.

"Tight keep playing!" Shah said as he walked out and closed the door.

(3:30pm)

Blue Dini drove up Badger Rd past the Saddle Ridge Apartments. He had a bad feeling in the pit of his stomach. He wasn't sure if it was the pizza he ate or if he was nervous about Jeff getting three hundred grams.

"What if this nigga tryna jam me up? Naw bro wouldn't do that I'm trippin I been knowing fool since he was in diapers. But niggas tell on they own momma don't be no fool. Fuck it, I'm finna see what up," Blue Dini spoke out loud to his self as he went back and forth debating on what he should do he turned into the trailer park. "Fuck it I'm finna catch this cash," he said to his self as he drove through the trailer park taking the back way to Sunny Mead. He pulled over and parked on Sunny Mead and picked up his phone and called Jeff.

"What up?" Jeff said as he answered the phone.

"I'm out here," Blue Dini said.

"I'm on my way out now," Jeff said. Blue Dini sat there quiet, trying his hardest to listen to the background, but Jeff hung up too fast. Blue Dini sat there nervous. He looked all around trying to see if he seen anything that was out of place. He watched as Jeff came walking down the hill from Capital view, Jeff walked up to the car and got in.

"What up big homie?" Jeff asked as he closed the door.

"Same shit different day," Blue Dini said as he looked out the windows and rearview mirror. Jeff went into his pocket and pulled out thirty thousand and handed it to Blue Dini. He looked down at the cash then opened the middle console and pulled out the grams wrapped in a white plastic store bag and handed it to Jeff.

"Good lookin," Jeff said then quickly jumped out the car. Blue Dini pulled off and drove the back streets toward Penn Park as he drove his heart began to beat extremely fast. He watched through the rearview mirror as he drove. His nerves started to calm as he drove under the viaduct and passed Baird St. Blue Dini reached over and grabbed his cigarettes as he drove up the hill. His heart dropped when he reached the top of the hill and saw a black Ford Explorer police truck at the stop sign on Fisher. He quickly made a right onto Fisher so he couldn't get behind him. He lit his cigarette as he drove down the hill on Fisher. He looked into the rearview mirror and noticed the Ford Explorer police truck was now behind him.

"Fuck!" he said out loud as he slowed down at the stop sign. He slowly reached down and grabbed the money he just got from Jeff and put it in his hoodie pocket. Blue Dini made a complete stop at the stop sign then hit his left turning signal and made a left turn. Just as he turned the Police hit their lights.

"This bitch ass nigga!" Blue Dini yelled out as he stomped on the gas and flew up the street. He made a hard-left turn blowing through the stop sign and flew up Bell Street and tried to make another left turn on Bram Street but lost control of the car and hit the curb flying through a parking lot. He crashed into a parked car. Blue Dini quickly jumped out of the car and took off running through the apartment complex. He ran past a dumpster and tossed his phone in it and shot across Fisher Street, running in between two houses and into a back yard. As he panicked, he noticed a doghouse in the yard to his left he hopped the fence and ran to the dog house and tosses the cash in it then took off running to his right trying to put as much space between him and the money. After running through several yards Blue Dini stopped in between two houses. He could hear police cars nearby so he hid under a side porch.

"He's right here, He's right here!" a woman yelled from across the street as she ran in his direction with two police officers. Blue Dini crawled from under the porch but just as he got to his feet an officer jumped on his back and tackled him to the ground.

"Stop resisting. Stop resisting!" the officer yelled out as other officers approached him and helped subdue Blue Dini and put him into cuffs.

(Later that Evening)

Shah sat at Keisha's house at the dinner table eating chicken and french fries. Shah enjoyed fried chicken and French fries.

"Shah its not that serious!" Keisha said as she took small bites from her chicken.

"I got a lot of shit I gotta do!" Shah said with a mouth full of food.

"You need to slow down and take some time out for yourself Shah!" Keisha said.

"I do take time out for myself. I just got a schedule to keep. Plus, I got a nigga up the street waiting on me," Shah said right before his phone started to ring.

"What up? You out there?" Shah quickly said as he answered.

"Yeah you said Vernon right?" X asked.

"Yeah," Shah said.

"Tight I'm walking down Vernon now," X said.

"I'm on my way out now," Shah said and ended the call. He jumped up from his seat and took a few big gulps of his cool aid and put the cup down.

"I gotta go," Shah said as he rushed toward the door. Keisha looked over at Shah disappointed as she watched him rush out the door. She wanted to spend some time with him, but understood he was busy. Shah ran down the stairs and out the building. He hurried and jumped in his car and pulled out of the lot. On his way up Vernon, he noticed X walking up the street. He slowed down and pulled over in front of him. X stood there looking at Shah's truck crazy until Shah rolled the window down.

"Aye X," Shah yelled out. X started walking up to the car. Once he realized it was Shah, he quickly jumped in and closed the door.

"Damn bro why you walking?" Shah asked.

"I ain't got no wheels. I had my people bring me down here and I didn't wanna pull up on you wit them in the car," X said.

"Yeah you right. You gotta grab you some wheels asap," Shah said.

"I am. But bro its crazy up North. They ate that shit up fast it was already sold before I got there and once they got it, they went crazy!" X said. He reached in his hoodie and pulled out $30,000 and handed it to Shah.

"What's this?" Shah asked.

"That's 30 G's! 10 of it is yo cheese the other 20 is for two hunnit more," X said. Shah counted off $10,000 and handed the rest back to X.

"Look bro I wanna see you eat. Stack yo extras and I'ma front you this shit every time just as long as you bring my bread back correct I'ma flood you wit this shit," Shah said.

"Tight!" X said as he stuffed his cash back in his hoodie. Shah reached over and grabbed a brown paper bag from behind the passenger seat. "Look bro, this time I'ma hit you wit five hunnit since you ran through that shit so fast. Just bring me back $50,000" Shah said.

"I can do that!" X said.

"Tight," Shah said then tossed the bag to X.

"Let me get to this cheese. I'ma hit you when I'm done," X said.

"Hold on before you go. Next week it's a Cardi B concert in Beloit. You should slide through and fuck wit us. It's gone be a lot of bitches down there!" Shah said.

"If shit keep going this good, I'm there," X said as he got out the car.

"Tight bro, drive safe and buy a car!" Shah said. "Tight love bro," X said then closed the door and started walking up the street. Shah pulled off and headed West to bust his next move.

Chapter Sixteen

NOVEMBER 16ᵀᴴ

*H*ot Boi was pissed he had just found out Shah had stole his people from off his phone. He had been wondering why his bag line wasn't ringing. He called all his people and they told him that his guy called them and told them not to call the old number no more. Hot Boi flew over to Balsam and parked. He grabbed his 9mm and tucked it in his beltline. He took his phones and sat them on the passenger seat then jumped out the truck. He walked across Raymond Road and onto Russit.

"This nigga think I'm a bitch!" he said to his self as he walked up Russit. It was one thing he wasn't gone tolerate and that was a nigga taking anything he worked hard for from him. Shah sat in the passenger seat of his Traverse as Lil Ant drove. Lil Ant turned off Whitney Way onto Russit. As they drove down Russit, Shah spotted Hot Boi walking up the block.

"Fuck he doing over here!" Shah said to his self. Lil Ant looked over at Shah "Who you talking bout skud?" he asked.

"That nigga right there!" Shah said as he pointed at Hot Boi. "I used to get money wit fool, all that new action I put on the phone I took them from him," Shah said.

"Oh, well you know why he over here!" Lil Ant said as he turned on to Cameron and pulled over and parked. Lil Ant reached under the seat and pulled out his Glock .40 and handed it to Shah.

"You better handle that before he get at you skud. Niggas kill over that bread. I know I would," Lil Ant said. Shah sat there with the pistol in his hand not sure if he wanted to kill Hot Boi. Lil Ant could tell by looking at Shah that he was scared.

"Look cuz, we finna walk around here and see what he on," Lil Ant said as he grabbed the pistol out of Shah's hands and tucked it on his waist. Lil Ant and Shah got out the car and walked around the corner. Hot Boi stood in the middle of the block waiting and ready for the moment he ran into Shah. He looked up the block to his left and saw Shah walking with a dude he never seen before. He quickly made a bee line in his direction.

"So, you taking cash out my pockets after I put you on?" Hot Boi asked as he walked up on Shah.

"This business! You don't own them nigga!" Shah said as he walked in Hot Boi's face. Hot Boi hit Shah with a quick left-handed punch knocking him to the ground. "Bitch ass nigga!" Hot Boi said as he stood over Shah. Lil Ant quickly upped and pointed his gun at Hot Boi.

"We aint finna do that skud! Gone move around before I lay yo ass down!" he said as he walked toward Hot Boi. Hot Boi put his hands up and started laughing as he backed up. "Tight, iight y'all got that. This shit ain't over Shah!" Hot Boi said and walked off.

"Man, cuz you let this bitch ass nigga put you on yo ass! You ain't acting like my cousin!" Lil Ant said as he helped Shah to his feet.

"I was finna kick his ass!" Shah said as he held his chin.

"Skud, it didn't look like that was about to happen," Lil Ant said as he laughed.

"Man fuck you!" Shah said as they walked up Russit. Hot Boi walked back across Raymond Road and over to Balsam and got back into his truck and grabbed his phone.

Meanwhile

Quantay sat at his kitchen table counting the money he made so far from the concert tickets. His phone started to ring, so he picked it up and answered it

"What up cuz?" he asked.

"I got a situation I'ma need yo help wit," Hot Boi said.

"You know I'm in. Slide on me so we can talk in person," Quantay said.

"I'ma be down there tonight! I sold them tickets you gave me too that bitch finna be bussin!" Hot Boi said.

"Hell yeah! It's at capacity right now if every person that brought a ticket come," Quantay said.

"I'm finna come down there and flex! I'm tryna fuck Terry, Alesha, and Kayla together," Hot Boi said

"Man, that ain't nothing, you got that! Them hoes wit it," Quantay said.

"I'm finna slide to my crib and grab my shit then I'm finna come down there," Hot Boi said.

"Tight I'm down here!" Quantay said.

"Yep!" Hot Boi said and ended the call.

Meanwhile

Lil Jerry took some time to lay low at his aunt crib on 69th and Emerald while the heat cooled off from Alexis and Brittany's murder. He sat there smoking a backwood thinking about what he was going to do as far as a connect since Cory was dead. He heard the back door open and quickly stood up and walked toward the kitchen to see who it was.

"Damn cuz when you get back down here?" Skrew head said to Lil Jerry as he walked into the kitchen.

"I been down here for about five days. Where the fuck you been at?" Lil Jerry said.

"I been fucking around in Harvey," Skrew head said as he walked into the living room. Lil Jerry walked into the living room and sat down on the couch. Skrew head looked around the crib.

"Where my og at?" Skrew head asked Lil Jerry.

"She left wit my og bout five minutes ago," Lil Jerry said.

"Oh, iight let me tell these niggas to come in for a minute," Skrew head said as he walked back to the kitchen. Lil Jerry inhaled then exhaled a big cloud of smoke and picked up his phone from the couch.

"I need some top!" he said to his self as he flipped through his contacts tryna see who he was finna call. He heard Skrew and some more niggas coming through the back door as he dialed Kendra's number. Skrew head walked into the living room with two other dudes and they sat down on the couch across from Lil Jerry. Lil Jerry was shocked when he looked up and seen Kay and Magic sitting across from him.

"Hello?" Kendra said as she answered.

"What up shorty?" Lil Jerry asked her as he looked over at Kay and Magic and watched as they rolled up their weed.

"Shit, in the house bored," Kendra said.

"Iight, gone throw some shit on and come down to my Aunty crib," Lil Jerry said. Kendra sat on the phone quiet for a moment before responding.

"Alright, I'm finna be on my way," she said.

"Iight I'm waiting on you," Lil Jerry said then ended the call.

"What up lil folks?" Magic said as he reached over and shook Lil Jerry's hand.

"What's good B!" Lil Jerry said as he shook Magic hand then shook Kay hand.

"You be fucking around over there on Russit?" Kay asked as he dried off his blunt.

"Yeah I be over there. Why y'all don't ever slide through and grab some of that gas I be having?" Lil Jerry asked.

"Cause we come up there wit our own bag that way we ain't gotta deal wit niggas," Kay said.

"I understand that," Lil Jerry said as he stood up and passed his backwood to Skrew and walked to the bathroom and closed the door. Lil Jerry quickly dialed Shah's number.

"What up fool?" Shah said as he answered the phone.

"Aye Kay and Magic right here right now!" Lil Jerry said.

"Where? Where you at?" Shah quickly said.

"I'm in city! I told you them niggas be fucking wit my cousin. They at my people crib right now!" Lil Jerry said.

"Damn I thought you was up here. Them niggas gone be gone by the time a mafucka get down there. Just play it cool wit them niggas and get they number we gone get on they ass another time," Shah said.

"You sure? Cause for that price I would handle that!" Lil Jerry said.

"Naw its cool bro. I'ma let my people handle it."

"When you coming back?" Shah asked.

"Man, I don't know!" Lil Jerry said disappointed in Shah's answer.

"You know it's a Cardi B concert in Beloit tomorrow and its finna go down. I know it's about to be plenty of bitches there," Shah said.

"Damn I forgot about that" Lil Jerry said.

"I still got this ticket for you! We finna fuck V.I.P up" Shah said.

"I'm coming up there tomorrow. You ain't got no extra tickets?" Lil Jerry asked.

"Shit I got two extra tickets now that Blue Dini locked up," Shah said.

"Damn what fool get locked up for?" Lil Jerry asked.

"They say some nigga he was fuckin wit jammed him up. They saying he got a controlled buy for three hunnit grits," Shah said.

"Damn who got down on him?" Lil Jerry asked.

"Some nigga. I don't know the nigga," Shah said. Lil Jerry's other line started to ring he looked and seen that it was Kendra calling.

"Aye look, I'ma be up that way tomorrow. I got this bitch on the other line. I'ma hit you when I'm on my way up there make sure you save those tickets," Lil Jerry said.

"I got you" Shah said. Lil Jerry quickly clicked over to answer for Kendra.

"What up?" Lil Jerry said as he walked out the bathroom.

"I'm outside come open the door," Kendra said.

"Iight," Lil Jerry said as he walked toward the door to open it.

Meanwhile

Audrey drove down Verona Road while Tammy trailed behind her. She was exhausted after shopping all morning, then having to drive halfway across Chicago to pick up Shah's new truck. Audrey picked up her phone and called Shah.

"What up Cinderella?" Shah asked as he answered the phone.

"Where you at?" Audrey said.

"I'm on Raymond. Why you sound like that? You good?" Shah asked.

"Sound like what?" Audrey asked.

"I don't know like you mad," Shah said.

"Oh no I'm fine! I'm just tired I had a long day," Audrey said.

"Oh! Now you see how I feel being in the mall with you all day!" Shah said.

"Boy stop! I don't be in there all day!" Audrey quickly said.

"Yeah iight!" Shah said.

"Well I'm about to pull up. You at that building over there?" Audrey asked.

"Yeah, I'm finna come outside right now" Shah said.

"Ok I'm coming down Raymond right now," Audrey said.

"Tight," Shah said.

"Alright," Audrey said then ended the call. Shah grabbed his new Glock 19 off the counter and put it on his waistline and left Tonya's apartment. He walked downstairs and out the building onto Raymond.

"Damn I'm finna fuck these niggas up," Shah said to his self as Audrey pulled up in his new 2018 Jaguar F-pace Portfolio truck. The Royal blue paint job shined as Audrey came to a complete stop. Shah walked over to the truck and stood there looking at it. "This bitch look a whole lot better in person," Shah said. He opened the passenger door and got in. His body instantly soaked into the luxury leather seats. Shah looked over at Audrey as she looked at him smiling.

"This bitch nice," he said as he ran his hands across the glossed figured ebony veneer.

"Yeah it's nice. I like it cause it drives smooth and its fast," Audrey said. Tammy got out of her car and walked up to Shah's truck and opened the passenger door. Shah quickly looked over at Tammy.

"This a nice truck and y'all look cute together in it," Tammy said.

"Yess bitch thank you!" Audrey said and started laughing.

"So, what y'all get me to wear?" Shah asked.

"Well you know I'm the one with all the style, so I got you some Balmain jeans, a Gucci polo, some Gucci shoes, and a Gucci belt," Tammy said.

"Ok, ok, I like that," Shah said.

"We finna have so much tomorrow!" Audrey said.

"Yes, I can't wait," Tammy said. Shah phone started to ring in his pocket he quickly reached in his pocket and pulled it out it was his cousin Lil Ant calling.

"What up cuz?" Shah said as he answered.

"Aye skud fool nem just called me and said they done and I'm dead too," Lil Ant said.

"Tight I'm at the spot. Grab the bread and slide through," Shah said.

"I'm finna leave from out here in a few minutes. I'm finna have fool nem meet you at the spot right now," Lil Ant said.

"Say no mo!" Shah said and ended the call. Shah turned and looked at Audrey. "Did y'all grab the clothes for fool nem too?" he asked.

"Yeah. that's what took all day. We had to shop for all y'all," Audrey said.

"How much did all that shit cost?" Shah asked.

"$30,000" Tammy quickly said.

"Damn y'all spent $30,000 on clothes?" Shah asked as he looked back and forth at both of them.

"Your outfit cost $7,000, your cousin's cost $5,000, the other two was $3,000 each, and ours was $6,000 each," Audrey said.

"Well how much of that $100,000 I gave y'all was left over," Shah asked.

"$2,000. This truck came out to $67,000 with registration and her hair cost a $1,000" Audrey said.

"Damn yo hair cost a$1,000 Tammy?" Shah asked as he looked over at her.

"Boy don't do me! And stop being so cheap. You said everything was on you and it costs to look this good!" Tammy said.

"So that's the hair you just bought on yo head right now?" Shah asked. Tammy reached into the truck and hit Shah on his shoulder. "Ok now! You got jokes? I'ma kick yo ass, I'm finna go get my hair done tonight," Tammy said.

"Shit I don't know I'm just asking!" Shah said as he laughed.

"But naw, I got some shit I gotta take care of I'ma call y'all in a minute. What y'all finna do?" Shah asked.

"I'm finna go with her to get her hair done," Audrey said.

"Tight," Shah said.

"So, do you want your truck, or you want me to take it?" Audrey asked.

"Naw you gone head and fuck the town up. I like the way you look in the driver seat. I gotta grab you one too," Shah said.

"Yeah we need to get both of us a new truck!" Tammy said.

"Yes! Bitch we gotta do that!" Audrey said as they both started laughing.

"Tight I got y'all!" Shah said.

"Ok but do you want they clothes?" Audrey asked.

"Yeah let me grab that shit. take mine to Tammy crib," Shah said. Audrey reached in the back and grabbed two big bags and handed them to Shah.

"Tight let me get up out of here," Shah said then leaned over and kissed Audrey and jumped out the truck.

"Tight Tammy!" Shah said as he gave her a hug and grabbed her ass. "You gone let me get some of that pussy tomorrow?" he asked as he whispered in her ear.

"Maybe!" Tammy said then laughed as she broke away from his hug and walked back to her car.

Meanwhile

Hot Boi pulled into Quantay's driveway and parked. He pulled out his phone and started texting Jamie.

"Aye, I'm in town hit me when you get off work." He put his phone back into his pocket and jumped out of his truck. He walked up to the porch and knocked on the door then hit the doorbell. Quantay peeked out the window on the door then opened it.

"What up cuz!" Quantay said as Hot Boi walked into the house.

"I need you to take care of something for me," Hot Boi said.

"Iight what up?" Quantay said as he closed the door and followed Hot Boi into the living room.

"It's this ass nigga I grew up wit! I let the nigga work my phones while I was down here laying low. Shit was cool when I got back but then the nigga found a different connect and started fucking wit the boy and got big headed. I just found out today the nigga stole all my people off my phone. Now I wanna take his life for playing wit my cash!" Hot Boi said as he looked Quantay directly into his eyes.

Quantay sat there for a second scratching his beard. "Iight do you know where he be?" Quantay asked.

"Yeah!" Hot Boi responded

"Iight look, this what we gone do. Saturday, we gone slide up there and I'ma get him out the way. But for right now we gotta get this bread together from this concert and get ready to fuck the city up tomorrow," Quantay said.

"Iight you right let's get this money straight. I got the bread from them tickets you gave me," Hot Boi said as he reached in his pocket and pulled the cash out and sat it on the coffee table.

"That's $12,500 for the 50 V.I.P and 150 regular admission tickets," Hot Boi said.

"Ok, so we pulled in $110,000 altogether. Minus the $50,000 we gave shorty, that mean we made $30,000 each," Quantay said.

"That's $27,500 cause you forgot the $5,000 for the venue," Hot Boi said.

"Oh, damn you right! $27,500 ain't bad," Quantay said.

"It's profit. Ain't no such thing as a bad profit! We gotta do this more often," Hot Boi said.

"Nicole pissed she gotta work tomorrow night. She been talking shit all week, talking bout she gone quit. I had to talk her ass out of quitting.

I'm glad she gotta work cause I got some hoes coming up from Rockford and I ain't gotta worry bout her being all on my heels," Quantay said.

Hot Boi started laughing

"Man, cuz just make sure Nicole don't get wind that you had some hoes up here cause she gone kick both our ass," he said.

"Yeah iight!" Quantay said as he laughed, but he knew deep down Nicole didn't fuck around.

Meanwhile

"These Balmain jeans bussin!" Mook said to Rell as he set the jeans back down on the couch.

"Yeah them bitches is bussin," Rell said as he looked to the kitchen where Shah and Lil Ant was. He looked back at Mook

"Aye Skud?" Rell said with his eyes wide. Mook looked up and instantly recognized the look in Rell's eyes.

"What up?" Mook whispered.

"How much cash you think that is in there on that table?" Rell whispered. Mook started shaking his head because he knew where the conversation was headed.

"Look fool, that's skud cousin we aint on that!" Mook said in a low tone as he looked toward the kitchen.

"Man, you trippin, I'm just asking how much cash you think that is," Rell said trying to convince Mook that he wasn't on bull shit.

"Yeah iight skud! But it's bout $800,000," Mook said, letting Rell know he was far from stupid. They both sat there in an awkward silence as Rell scratched his beard.

"Aye Skud!" Lil Ant yelled out from the kitchen.

"What up?" Rell yelled back as he looked at Mook not sure if they heard their conversation.

"Check it out," Lil Ant yelled out. Mook and Rell got up and walked into the kitchen. Shah was sitting on one side of the table while Lil Ant sat on the other side.

"What up Skud!" Mook asked as he looked at Lil Ant then to the money on the table which was separated in five different piles with most of the money on Shah's side of the table.

"Y'all my niggas so y'all know I gotta break bread wit y'all. This $50,000 a piece" Lil Ant said and pushed the two piles of cash toward Mook and Rell as he smiled. He knew neither one of the three of them had ever seen this much cash, so he was happy to be the one to introduce his niggas to the next stage in life. Mook and Rell both walked up to the table and grabbed their cash. "Yeah it's official!" Rell said as he reached and shook Lil Ant's hand.

"This just the beginning!" Shah said and tossed Mook and Rell both $10,000 each.

"That's for the mission we went on," Shah said. Mook looked over at Lil Ant then back over at Shah. "Good looking fool!" Mook said as he grabbed the cash off the table and put it with the rest of the cash he had in his hands.

Shah started dumping the rest of the cash on his side of the table in a duffle bag. Rell stood there, eyes wide as he watched Shah push so much cash in that bag it made their stacks look like crumbs.

"You good?" Lil Ant asked Rell breaking him out of his trance. "Yeah, I'm good. I'm just shocked at how fast a nigga can come up in Wisconsin," Rell said as he looked down at the cash in his hands then back at Lil Ant.

"Yeah this shit real skud!" Lil Ant said.

"I see!" Rell quickly responded. Lil Ant stacked a pile of cash together and handed it to Shah. "That's $90,000. You know what I need," Lil Ant said. Shah grabbed the cash and tossed it into the duffle bag.

"Tight I got you, I'ma get up wit y'all tomorrow. Make sure y'all ready for this concert, we finna go down here and act an ass!" Shah said as he put the duffle bag strap on his shoulder and walked out the kitchen.

"We stay ready!" Lil Ant said as he grabbed his $38,000 off the table. He looked over at Mook and Rell and smiled.

"Aye skud, my lil white bitch tryna go out and kick it tonight. She got two of her buddies they thirsty to kick it wit us. Let's go get cut up and shit so we be ready for tomorrow," Lil Ant said.

"Lock the door!" Shah yelled out then left the apartment.

Meanwhile

X picked up his phone and dialed Shah's number. He was happy things had been moving at a fast pace for him in Fond du Lac cause he was now in a comfortable position and was finally able to relax. As the phone continued to ring X counted a stack of twenty-dollar bills.

"What up bro?" Shah said as he answered the phone.

"What's hannin bro, I'ma be down there in a minute, I'm ready for you," X said as he continued to count the money in his hands.

"I'm dead until tomorrow bro, but you should still come down and kick it wit us at this Cardi B concert tomorrow night," Shah said as he switched lanes.

"Damn bro, I forgot all about that. I gotta go back to the Mil and grab some shit to wear. But I'ma be down there tomorrow bro," X said.

"Tight," Shah said.

"I'ma hit you tomorrow," X said.

"Tight bro do that," Shah said.

"Love fool" X said and quickly ended the call. X clicked over and dialed Honey's number. She was the only person he knew that would rent him a car, plus he low-key wanted to see her.

"Hey Xavier," Honey said as she answered the phone. X could hear it in her voice that she was happy to hear from him.

"What you been up too?" X asked.

"I been busy doing all this damn schoolwork. What you been doing? Why haven't I heard from you?" Honey asked.

"Shit was all bad for me down there, I had to take some time to get my shit together. But look, I need you to do me a favor and reserve me a rental car for tomorrow and I need you to come pick me up from Fond du lac," X said.

"Alright Xavier. Give me some time to take care of a few things then I'm going to pick Asia up and come up there. Text me an address so I know where to come to," Honey said.

"Tight I'm finna text you right now. Call me when you leave," X said.

"Alright, I will. love you" Honey said.

"Tight love you too," X said then ended the call.

(One Hour Later)

Shah pulled into his driveway and parked. He reached into the back seat and grabbed the duffle bag and hurried and got out the car. As Shah walked up the stairs, he remembered he was supposed to go visit his brother Shawn in Green Bay.

"Damn I know bro finna be pissed," he said to his self as he unlocked the door and walked into his house. He quickly locked the door then walked upstairs to his office. Shah walked over to his desk and sat the duffle bag down.

"Let me get this cash together," Shah thought to his self he walked over to his safe and opened it.

"Ok, so I know it's $1,439,000 right there," Shah said to his self as he looked in his safe. He then walked back over to his desk and grabbed a calculator.

"Alright, so minus Berto's $800,000 that leaves me wit $639,000, plus X still owe me $30,000. Matter of a fact I ain't even going to count that, I'm finna blow that tomorrow," Shah said, then looked over at the duffle bag on the desk.

"Tight that's $658,000 if I add that wit my shit that's $1,297,000. Shit that make me a millionaire," he said to his self as he walked around his desk and sat down.

"Ok so cuz gave me $90,000 for 3 bricks. I might as well just grab the same 15 bricks for $300,000 and give cuz his 3 and keep 12. I can stash the million in the safe and put $210,000 wit cuz and $90,000 for the coke. Shit that leaves me wit $87,000 to play wit," Shah said to his self then hurried and reached into his pocket and dialed Alberto's number.

"Damn I just made my first million dollars!" Shah said to his self as he waited for Alberto to answer.

"How you doing brother?" Alberto asked when he answered the phone.

"All is well brother, I'll be to see you tomorrow if that's fine," Shah said.

"Yeah that's fine," Alberto said.

"Ok I'll be there first thing in the morning," Shah said.

"Ok brother," Alberto said.

"Tight," Shah said and ended the call. Shah got up from his desk and walked over to his safe and pulled $439,000 out of it and closed it back up. He walked over to his desk with the money he pulled out the safe and counted off $87,000 and put it to the side. He tossed the rest of the cash into the duffle bag and sat the bag under his desk.

Chapter Seventeen

FRIDAY
NOVEMBER 17TH
(12:30 PM)

L il Jerry jumped into the back seat of Kendra's car and closed the door.

"Heyy Jerry" Angelic said as she looked back from the passenger seat.

"What up Shorty!" Lil Jerry said as he looked over at Kendra. Angelic and Kendra were best friends, but they both had been secretly fucking Lil Jerry. Lil Jerry planned to make tonight the night he fucked them both together.

"So, we going to Beloit?" Kendra asked.

"Yeah in Wisconsin. But did y'all get that case of patron?" Lil Jerry asked.

"We got it," Angelic quickly said.

"Kendra you got that address to the hotel?" Lil Jerry asked.

"Yeah, it's in my GPS already," Kendra said as she started the car.

"Tight, let's get up out of here and make sure you don't be speeding and shit cause I'm dirty!" Lil Jerry said as he laid across the back seat.

"It sound like Wisconsin lame as hell," Angelic said as she looked over at Kendra and turned the radio up some. Kendra looked over at Angelic then back to the road. "It sounds lame, but it's not. Yo ass going to have a nice time! You might not wanna come back," Kendra said as she drove down Emerald. Lil Jerry reached into his hoodie pocket and pulled out an ounce of weed and tossed it up to Angelic.

"Roll that shit up!" he said as he laid low and set his pistol on the floor and pulled out his phone. He flipped through his phone call log and found Shah's number then dialed it.

"What's good!" Shah said as he answered.

"You still got them other two tickets for me, right?" Lil Jerry asked.

"Yeah, I got em bro," Shah said.

"Tight I'm on my way up there now I'm just going to get a room in Beloit," Lil Jerry said.

"Tight we gone link up in Beloit so we can all slide through together," Shah said.

"Say no more, I'ma hit you when I touch," Lil Jerry said.

"Tight," Shah said.

"Yep!" Lil Jerry said and ended the call.

(12:45pm)

Shah pressed the end button on his phone and set it down on the table. He stood up and walked to the fridge and opened it. He reached in and grabbed a bottle of Gatorade and closed it. Shah opened the Gatorade bottle then leaned up against the stove as he looked over at the forty bricks of boy and the fifteen bricks of coke that sat on the table. He felt like there was nothing that could stop him. He was having his way and all the pieces to his puzzle were falling right into place. Tammy walked out of her bedroom and into the living room.

"I know he didn't leave this shit out like this," Tammy said out loud as she looked at the kitchen table.

"What you ---"

"Ooohh shit!" Tammy yelled before Shah could finish what he was about to say. Shah started laughing as he walked toward the table.

"You scared the shit out of me!" Tammy said as she held her hands over her chest.

"My bad" Shah said as he laughed.

"It's not funny! I was about to curse you out for leaving all this shit on the table," Tammy said as she walked into the kitchen. Shah stood and looked at her from head to toe, he loved the way she looked.

"Damn them thighs looking good as hell!" Shah said as he looked at Tammy's legs.

"Boy stop!" Tammy said as she laughed. She loved hearing the compliments from Shah. Tammy turned and walked out of the kitchen.

"I ain't playin! So, what up wit what I asked you yesterday?" Shah asked.

"I don't remember what you asked me," she said as she continued to laugh and walked back to her room.

"Yeah, she think I'm playing," Shah said to his self as he walked out the kitchen and walked to Tammy's room. Shah walked into her room and seen she was sitting on the edge of the bed flipping through the channels on her Tv.

"So, you finna act like you don't remember what I asked you?" Shah asked as he looked at Tammy. She started laughing then looked back over her shoulder at him and smiled.

"I don't remember, ask me again," She said as she looked at him. Shah started laughing then walked over to Tammy and spread her legs apart and stood in between them.

"I think we both already know the answer to my question," Shah said as he leaned in and kissed her on the neck. Tammy started to breathe heavy as she reached and grabbed the back of Shah's head as he kissed her. Shah laid her all the way back on the bed as he began to run his hands up her thighs. He reached and grabbed the waist band to her shorts and panties. Tammy lifted her hips up allowing Shah to pull her shorts and panties off. Tammy had thought time and time again about the threesome she had with him and Audrey and she'd been dying to have sex with him alone. She pulled her shirt over her head and tossed it on the floor. Shah stood in between her legs and slowly ran his fingertips down the middle of her stomach. His touch felt heavenly to her as she let out a soft moan.

"Damn, you beautiful!" Shah said softly as he leaned in and began kissing her stomach. Tammy quickly arched her back as every kiss sent chills through her body. She reached down and ran her hands over his head as he continued to kiss lower and lower. Shah slowly ran his hand over her pussy before he leaned in and kissed it.

"Ooh Shah" She said as she tried to catch her breath. For some reason every touch of his hand against her skin made her experience feelings she'd never felt from anyone. Shah lifted both legs and squatted down and started licking and sucking on her clit.

"Oh my god Shah I lov----" Tammy quickly caught herself and stopped in mid-sentence. She reached over and grabbed a pillow and put it over her face and bit it as she held it tightly.

"Oh my god!" she said as the pillow muffled her sound. Shah stopped and started playing with her clit as he looked up at Tammy and laughed a little before reaching up with his other hand and grabbing the pillow pulling it from her face.

"I wanna hear it!" he said, then went back down and kissed her pussy. "And I love you too!" he said as he stared back licking her pussy. Tammy laid there in complete ecstasy as Shah brought her to her first climax with a series of orgasms following.

"Oooohhh! Fuuucck!" Tammy yelled out as she tried to push Shah's head away. The harder she tried to push him away the harder he fought against her and sucked her clit harder.

"Sha- Shah! Please," she managed to force out of her mouth as she tried to breathe. Shah stood up and wiped her juices from his face then took off his shirt and tossed it on the floor. He kicked his shoes off as he watched Tammy struggle to catch her breath. He took his pants and underwear off then walked back in between her legs.

"Hold on!" Tammy said as she sat up and put her hands on his chest pushing him back a little. She stood up and grabbed the back of Shah's neck and kissed him.

"Sit down!" she said as she broke away from their kiss. She then turned and faced Shah as he sat on the bed. She walked in between his legs and ran her hands across his chest.

"Shah, I love you!" she said as she reached down and grabbed ahold of his dick and started stroking it as she kissed him again. Tammy pushed him back on the bed and kissed across his waistline, then she started twirling her tongue around the tip of his dick as she continued to stroke him. Shah laid there looking up at the ceiling. He couldn't believe she was actually doing this.

"Damn!" he said as she took him into her mouth and began sucking his dick. Shah closed his eyes and laid there enjoying the moment. Tammy grabbed a hold of his dick with both hands and started twisting them as she stroked and sucked his dick at the same time.

"Damn Tammy!" Shah said as he opened his eyes and leaned up on his elbows. The sensation felt so good he had to see what she was doing. Tammy moaned as she picked up the pace. Shah sat there and watched as she began to show out. She grabbed ahold of his balls with one hand and started playing with them without slowing her pace. Shah started to think about other shit as he watched her, trying his hardest not to bust too fast, but he couldn't control it. Tammy let out a soft moan then looked up at Shah directly in his eyes. The site sent Shah over the edge. "Fuucckk!" Shah said as he grabbed ahold of the sheets and started to lift up from the bed. Tammy quickly pulled his dick from her mouth and continued to stroke him and play with his balls as he exploded in her hands.

"Damn!" Shah said as he began to sit back on the bed breathing heavy.

"That was fast!" Tammy said as she stood up. She looked at Shah then walked to the bathroom. Shah laid there thinking about what she just said. She walked back into the room with a towel and grabbed ahold of Shah's dick and wiped it clean. She tossed the towel on the dresser and went right back to sucking his dick.

Within a few seconds Shah was rock hard again. "You don't fuck around!" Shah said.

Tammy stood up and started laughing as she got on the bed and straddled on top of him.

"Hold on!" Shah said as he pulled her closer to him then stood up. He turned around and laid her on her back, he felt he had something to prove after that comment she made. Shah grabbed her thighs with one arm and held both her ankles in the air with one hand and slowly slid into her pussy. Tammy moaned as she reached to Shah's waist pulling him closer and allowing him to go deeper. He slowly thrust in and out of her with each stroke feeling better than the last one. After a few minutes, he began to pick up his pace pounding her harder and harder with each stroke.

"Yes! Fuck me Shah!" she yelled out as he continued to give her just what she asked for. "Don't stop! Don't stop! I'm about to cuummm!" Tammy yelled out as she grabbed ahold of the sheets. Shah started pounding harder and harder as Tammy began to have an orgasm. Her eyes rolled in the back of her head as she began to have multiple orgasms.

"Yeah I'm finna fuck the shit out this pussy!" Shah thought to his self as he pounded harder and harder. After about fifteen minutes he pulled out. "Let's get all the way in the bed," Shah said. Tammy worked her way to the middle of the bed and Shah climbed in bed with her.

"Let me get this pussy from the back, I wanna see that ass," Shah said. Tammy turned over into the doggy style position and arched her back and put her ass up, then she looked back at Shah. He grabbed one of her ass cheeks and quickly guided his dick into her pussy. Shah grabbed ahold of her other ass cheek and watched his dick slowly slide in and out of her pussy then he picked up his pace, pounding harder and harder. He was shocked when Tammy raised up and started throwing her ass back at him helping him go deeper. Shah let go of her ass cheeks and watched as they bounce with every stroke. Tammy started throwing her ass back harder and harder and within minutes Shah stiffened up and fell on top of Tammy forcing her to lay all the way on her stomach.

Tammy and Shah both laid there breathing heavy before Shah pulled his dick from her pussy then got up and walked to the bathroom. Tammy followed him into the bathroom as Shah stood at the sink. She walked to the shower and turned it on then sat down on the toilet. Shah quickly washed his self-off and walked back into Tammy's room and put his clothes back on. Shah walked back out of her room and saw that she was in the shower. Shah walked back to the kitchen and picked his phone up and saw that it was 1:40pm.

"Damn let me call this nigga Ant!" he said to his self as he dialed his number.

"What up skud?" Lil Ant said as he answered the phone.

"Aye where you at?" Shah asked.

"I'm over here at Tonya crib. Why? What up?" Lil Ant asked.

"I need you to meet me at the Walgreen's off PD," Shah said.

"Tight, I'm on my way now," Lil Ant said.

"Tight, call me when you pull in, I'm around the corner," Shah said.

"Say no more skud," Lil Ant said then hung up. Shah pressed the end button on his phone and set it down on the table. He grabbed the duffle bag off the floor and started stuffing the bricks of coke in it then zipped it up.

(1:50pm)

Lil Ant pulled into the Walgreen's and parked. He reached and grabbed his phone and just as he picked it up it started to ring.

"What up skud?" Lil Ant asked as he answered.

"Aye cuz pull out of Walgreen's and make a left. Then make a right on that first street. I'm sitting over here," Shah said.

"Tight skud," Lil Ant said as he drove through the parking lot and made his way back to the exit. He made a left out of the lot then a quick right. He could see Shah's truck halfway up the block. Lil Ant drove up the block and parked across the street from Shah. Shah jumped out of his truck and walked across the street to Lil Ant's driver door. Lil Ant rolled his window down.

"What up skud?" Lil Ant asked as he looked at Shah.

"Shit I got that for you. I forgot you was driving this loud ass truck. I want you to take this shit over to Tonya's crib. We gone switch cars. It's fifteen bricks in the duffle bag on the back seat. I got some shit I gotta do. I'ma meet you over there in a hour," Shah said.

"Tight skud," Lil Ant said as he opened the truck door and got out. Shah jumped in the truck then closed the door. "Be careful cuz," Shah said.

"You know dat," Lil Ant said as he walked across the street and jumped in Shah's truck and pulled off.

(2:15 pm)

Quantay drove down Prairie on his way to meet Hot Boi. He had just left from meeting up with the DJ to make sure he had all the local acts song and their time slots. Quantay invested a lot of time and money into this and wanted to make sure everything went as planned. His name and reputation were on the line and he wasn't willing to compromise either one. He knew if tonight was a success there was more money to come.

Quantay made a left into Jamie's driveway and parked. He got out and walked to the back door and opened it, then walked up the stairs to the kitchen. Jamie was standing at the stove cooking.

"Ok, big booty Judy, I see you got the ass cheeks hanging out the bottom of them shorts," he said and laughed. Jamie started laughing and looked back at Quantay and grabbed ahold of her ass cheek. "You know you like it! And I see yo bald head ass just keep busting in my back door whenever you feel like it," she said. Quantay laughed and ran his hand over his head. "You know you like it!" he said as he laughed harder and walked past her and went into the living room.

"Boy yo ass stupid!" Jamie said as she laughed. Quantay walked over and sat on the couch next to Hot Boi. "I see you got Wifey in the kitchen," Quantay said loud enough for Jamie to hear him then started laughing. Jamie walked to the living room and stood in the doorway and gave Quantay a hard stare.

"Yo ass bout to get kicked out already!" Jamie said as she pointed her spatula at him.

"Ok, ok my bad! That's crazy, I thought we was family. You said we was family, right? Y'all bought me these new clothes and this game!" Quantay and Hot Boi both started laughing. Jamie couldn't hold it back and started laughing.

"Quantay you get on my nerves!" she said and walked back to the kitchen laughing.

"Cuz yo ass funny as hell!" Hot Boi said as he laughed. "But what's good? Everything lined up for tonight?" he asked.

"Yeah everything ready. I talked to Cardi B's manager earlier and she'll be here as planned. I went by the club and made sure everything was good on they end, and I got security set up. The DJ on deck now all we gotta do is wait for tonight. I'ma slide to the club at nine and make sure the DJ get set up and get the security crew together," Quantay said.

"Tight. Shit after tonight we gotta bring somebody else down here," Hot Boi said as he picked up the remote and changed the channel.

"Quantay you want some of these tacos?" Jamie asked as she walked into the doorway. "Hell yeah! let me get three," he quickly said.

"How many you want Hot Boi?" Jamie asked.

"Bring me three of em," he said.

"Alright," Jamie said as she walked off.

Quantay looked over at Hot Boi and whispered, "Aye we going to Rockford tonight. Shorty and her buddies ready." Hot Boi started laughing "Why you whispering?" he asked.

"I aint want yo Wifey to hear me," Quantay said and started laughing. Hot Boi jumped up from the couch and put Quantay in a head lock.

"Iight iight!" Quantay said as he laughed. Hot Boi let go of him and walked off to the kitchen.

(3:00pm)

As X drove down Capital, he was satisfied with the way things had been going for him. He had went shopping immediately after Honey got him the rental car this morning. He was ready for the concert, but he really couldn't wait to get some more boy and shoot back to Fond du lac. As he drove, he remembered that Kendall got a cousin that they all grew up with that's been hustling in Fond du lac for years.

"Damn I need to get in tune wit that nigga," he thought to his self. "Man, I don't wanna call this bitch ass nigga Kendall. Fuck it I'm chasing a bag right now," he said to his self as he picked up his phone and dialed Kendall's number.

"What it do fool?" Kendall asked as he answered.

"Shit my nigga tryna get back!" X said.

"Man, I heard Dawg. I talked to Tae G, he said he good on that high speed and the shooting, but his dumb ass forgot he had ten bags in his fuckin pocket......idiot!" Kendall said.

"Yeah?" X asked shocked.

"Hell yeah, you know all he got is the case for getting caught wit the work, so they want some type of time out him. But I sent em a lil I-care and some cheese. Aww speakin' of cheese, he said you had something for him," Kendall said.

"Man look that shit dead, I'm - I mean we fucked up. Niggas hit the crib and took all that shit. We back to square one, that's why I'm calling you right n----" before X could finish Kendall cut him off.

"I knew it! I'm finna have my lil bitch drop a line and some work on you all you gotta ------"

"Whoa, slow down!" X said cutting Kendall off. "I was calling to see if you still fuck wit Vince?" X said.

"You talking bout cuz in Fondy?" Kendall asked.

"Yeah, send me his line. I know some hoes up there and I think they got some cheese. I'm tryna finesse a come up out one of these hoes you hear me?" X asked.

"Yeah, yeah," Kendall said, not buying the story X was tryna sell him.

"I know bro, he know his way around that mafucka. Plus, I need to move around from down here anyway," X said.

"Well shit..... um I'ma text it to you just let me know if you need something," Kendall said.

"You a love dat!" X mumbled.

"What?" Kendall asked.

"I said love bro," X said then ended the call. A few minutes later his phone chimed with a text from Kendall.

"(920-254-5671) #catchup #FreeGrits"

"Lame ass nigga!" X said to his self as he pressed the numbers into his phone and called Vince.

"Vince, what's hannin?" X asked as Vince answered.

"Who dis?" Vince asked aggressively.

"This lil X bro!" X said.

"Mannn what it do lil nigga? I ain't seen yo ass in a minute. I heard y'all was all grown doing y'all and shit. What up doe lil cuz you good?" Vince asked.

"Yeah I'm straight. I been up that way where you at a few times. I'm in the mil right now, but I'll be back up that way tomorrow. I need you to show me what's what and who's who up there," X said.

"Iight, iight say no more it's done. Just hit me when you touch down lil cuz," Vince said.

"Iight love cuz," X said.

"You know it's love," Vince said.

"Bet!" X said then ended the call.

"Man, that's what I need now I just need to make sure Dawg back online," X said to his self and quickly flipped through his call log and found Shah's number and dialed it.

"X what up bro?" Shah said as he answered.

"Shit bro tryna see if everything good?" X asked.

"Oh yeah shit good. You still sliding through, right?" Shah asked.

"Hell yeah, what time it start?" X asked.

"It starts at 11 but we gone slide through at 12. We gone link up in Beloit then slide through together," Shah said.

"Iight bro I'ma meet y'all down there," X said.

"Iight bro we gone be down there at about 11:30, 11:45" Shah said.

"Say no more, I'ma call you when I get there," X said.

"Iight love bro," Shah said.

"Love," X said, then ended the call and tossed his phone in the cup holder.

(3:40pm)

Lil Jerry sat in the back seat of Kendra's car in the Quality Inn parking lot in Beloit while Kendra and Angelic checked in. He was nervous about being in Wisconsin even though the police said they had no suspects at the time, but he believed it was better to be safe than sorry.

Lil Jerry's phone started to ring as he looked around the parking lot nervously. He noticed it was Kendra, so he answered it.

"Yeah," he said.

"You staying in the car or you gone come in?" she asked.

"Oh, y'all checked in already?" he asked.

"Yeah we in room 215," Kendra quickly responded.

"Tight I'm on my way up there!" Lil Jerry said then hung up. He reached down and grabbed his pistol off the car floor, but then he quickly set it back down and slid it under the driver seat. Lil Jerry reached up and grabbed the keys out the ignition then jumped out of the car. He looked around not sure what to expect being that this was his first time in Beloit. He quickly made his way into the hotel and up the stairs he walked down the hall until he found room 215. As he stood at the door, he could hear Angelic talking to Kendra.

"Girl why he only get one bed?" Angelic asked Kendra.

"Bitch quit acting slow!" Kendra quickly said. Lil Jerry started laughing, then knocked on the door. The door quickly swung open and Angelic stood there with her hands on her hips.

"What's wrong wit you?" Lil Jerry asked acting like he didn't know what was going on.

"Why you only get one bed?" Angelic asked with a smirk on her face. Lil Jerry started laughing as he walked past her and into the room.

"I got one bed cause after this concert tonight I'm finna fuck the shit out of both of y'all. Plus, its big enough for the three of us," he said as he sat down on the couch.

"So, you just sure that's what's finna happen?" Angelic asked trying to act like she wasn't down. Kendra quickly jumped into the conversation. "Bitch don't act like yo pussy ain't get wet at the thought of being naked in the bed wit us!" she said.

"It didn't bitch!" Angelic said with a big ass smile on her face.

"Now you know that's a lie! I wanna see for myself!" Kendra said. Angelic started laughing "Yeah y'all doing the most I'm finna go get my bag out the car!" Angelic said as she started walking toward the door.

"Well bitch hurry up cause I'ma need you to help me suck his dick!" Kendra said, then burst out in laughter. Angelic stopped in her tracks and turned around.

"Yeah bitch you a hoe!" Angelic said then turned and walked out the door.

"I like how that sound, we gotta make that happen!" Lil Jerry said as he looked at Kendra.

"I don't think you ready for both of us together!" Kendra said and licked her lips.

"You got me fucked up! I'ma put this mafucka on both y'all!" Lil Jerry said.

"Well I guess we gone find out if yo actions match yo words tonight!" Kendra said and walked into the bathroom.

(4:15pm)

Shah stood in the living room talking shit with Lil Ant, Mook, Rell, and Tonya.

"Hold on, hold on real quick!" Shah said as his phone started to ring.

"What up fool?" Shah asked as he answered the phone.

"I'm down in Beloit right now. I'm tryna see what time y'all coming down here?" Lil Jerry asked.

"We a be down there around 11:30 or 12," Shah said.

"Tight," Lil Jerry said.

"Matter of a fact we gone link at the Citgo on Cranston and Prairie at 11:30, it's right down the street from the club," Shah said.

"Tight. Cranston and Prairie. Say no mo I'ma catch y'all at 11:30," Lil Jerry said.

"Tight," Shah said and ended the call.

Shah turned and walked back into the living room. Mook was standing by the window smoking a blunt and Lil Ant and Rell were sitting on the couch laughing at the story Mook was telling them.

"So, the bitch got down on her knees and started sucking my balls, I was standing ther---"

"Hold on, hold on what I miss?" Shah asked as he cut Mook off.

"I'm telling these niggas about the white bitch I fucked last night," Mook said as he hit the blunt. "But listen, let me finish. So, I'm standing there thinking to myself this bitch a freak. I looked down and the bitch had her eyes closed while she was sucking my balls while my dick was sitting on her face," Mook said then paused for a second and started laughing. "Aye, Aye! I reached for my phone cause I'm like fool nem ain't gone believe me I gotta record this shit. Man, when I started recording the flash from the camera came on and the bitch opened her eyes. She took my balls out her mouth and was like. "Oh, fuck no dude. Delete that shit!" I started laughing loud as hell cause her voice sounded funny as hell. But I told her I was going to delete that shit. She stood up and was like, "Dude you're a fucking jerk I'm out of here!" The bitch grabbed her coat and left the hotel room," Mook said and started laughing. "Fool the bitch left me standing their ass hole naked wit just my socks and shoes on," Mook said and continued to laugh.

"Yo first time wit a white bitch and you fucked it up," Lil Ant said as they all laughed.

"Man, the nigga said he aint have shit on but his socks and shoes!" Rell said as they all continued to laugh.

Chapter Eighteen

BELOIT
(11:25PM)

hah was speeding down Prairie feeling his self. He had already drunk a fifth of patron with Lil Ant nem earlier. Now he was drinking Grey Goose with Audrey and Tammy.

"Slow down some Shah!" Tammy said trying to yell over the music from the back seat.

"What you say?" Shah asked as he turned the music down and continued to speed.

"Slow down some! And you leaving your cousin nem," Tammy said. Shah looked out the rearview mirror and noticed there was a nice distance between him and Lil Ant, so he slowed down some.

"This mafucka so smooth it don't even feel like we going that fast!" Shah said. Audrey turned the music all the way down and looked back at Tammy. "You got some gum in your purse?" Audrey asked. Tammy set her cup in the cup holder and started looking through her purse for some gum.

"Nope, I left it," Tammy said.

"We bout to meet fool nem at the gas station y'all can grab some then," Shah said. His phone started to ring in his lap he reached down and noticed it was X.

"What up bro?" Shah asked as he answered.

"Aye bro you said citgo on Cranston and Prairie, right?" X asked.

"Yeah!" Shah said.

"Tight well I'm up here bro," X said.

"I'm finna pull up I'm right down the street," Shah said.

"Tight bro," X said then hung up the phone. Shah sat his phone back down in his lap and hit his right turning signal and switched lanes as he approached the gas station. He could see two cars sitting in the gas station as he pulled in. Shah pulled next to a black Infiniti and jumped out his truck then Lil Jerry jumped out the back of the Infiniti.

"Damn bro, that's yo shit!" Lil Jerry asked.

"Hell yeah, I bought this bitch yesterday," Shah said in a cocky voice.

"Damn yo bitch ass just went crazy! I see you shot through the roof real quick. You gone have to cut me in on some of that shit now!" Lil Jerry said.

"You know I got you bro!" Shah said.

As he and Lil Jerry stood there talking, Audrey and Tammy jumped out of the truck and walked into the gas station. X noticed Shah through his rearview mirror and got out the car and walked up to him and Lil Jerry.

"What up bro!" X said to Shah.

"What up bro!" Shah said then shook X hand.

"This my mans X, X this my mans Lil Jerry" Shah said.

"What up fool!" Lil Jerry said.

"What up bro!" X said. Shah reached in his pocket and pulled out the tickets and handed Lil Jerry three of them then handed X one.

"Aye we finna go in here and fuck the scene up!" Shah said.

"Shit I'm wit it" X said. Lil Ant, Mook, and Rell jumped out of their truck and walked up to Shah, Lil Jerry, and X. Lil Jerry shook all their hands and Shah introduced them to X.

"You brought them hittas?" Shah asked X.

"Hell yeah!" X said as he reached into his pocket and pulled out a bag of ecstasy pills.

"On BD let me get one of them!" Rell quickly said as X handed the bag of pills to Shah. Shah started laughing and handed Rell a pill.

"Y'all fucking around?" Shah asked Lil Ant, Mook, and Lil Jerry. "Hell yeah!" They all said at the same time.

"Let me get another one for my lil hoes!" Lil Jerry said. Shah passed out the pills and thought about Audrey and Tammy. He knew he was going to have to talk them into taking one after they got drunk.

"Let me holla at you bro," X said to Shah as he started walking back toward his car.

"What up bro?" Shah asked as he followed X to his car. X opened his car door and pulled out a stack of cash from the middle console and handed it to Shah.

"That's the cheese I owe you," X said.

"Tight. We gone handle business tomorrow. I'ma give you a whole book, just bring me back $80,000 when you done," Shah said.

"Bet! Love too bro," X said.

"You know dat!" Shah said.

"Let's go to the club!" Audrey yelled out to Shah as she and Tammy came walking out the store.

"Tight here I come!" Shah said as they walked back to the truck. "Let's get up out of here!" Shah yelled out to Lil Jerry and Lil Ant nem as he walked back to his truck.

Meanwhile

The club was packed from wall to wall with dope dealing niggas and money hungry bitches. To Quantay's surprise, the club was turnt off the local acts alone. There was so much talent in the building you would have sworn that everybody who hit the stage was a signed artist already.

Hot Boi stood in the middle of three bitches. He had one dancing on him while he held his arms in the air holding a bottle of Grey goose in one hand and a Rosé bottle in the other hand. Most the niggas from Beloit were showing Hot Boi a lot of love off the strength he was Quantay's cousin and the bitches were choosing left and right. Hot Boi was feeling his self, he looked to the bar and saw Quantay nodding his head to the music with $60,000 dollars to his ear like he was on a cell phone. Hot Boi started laughing "I'ma be right back!" he whispered to the female dancing on him then walked over to the bar where Quantay was at.

"I see you over here flexing!" Hot Boi said.

"Man, cuz I'm tryna live life!" Quantay said.

"I most definitely feel you cuz! But what up wit the bitch Cardi B? I'm tryna see what that ass look like in person!" Hot Boi said as he took a sip from his Grey goose bottle.

"They gone be here at one. We gone meet up wit her and her manager before she go on at 1:15. You know they want the rest of that bread!" Quantay said.

"Tight I'm finna step outside and smoke some of this gas!" Hot Boi said.

"You ain't gotta step outside we can step in the back. I'm tryna get high too!" Quantay said as they started walking to the back of the club.

(12:15am)

Shah stepped in the club feeling like the man. He was dripping in designer from head to toe. He had a Gucci book bag on his shoulder with $116,000 in cash in it. He had his arm around Audrey's shoulder, and she was killing almost every bitch in the club in her skintight Fendi dress and six-inch Fendi heels to match. Shah lead the group through the crowd over to the bar.

"What can I get you?" the bartender asked Shah as he stood there. Shah looked toward Lil Ant nem. "What y'all drinking?" he asked.

"Same shit we was drinking earlier!" Lil Ant yelled over the music.

"Tight," Shah said then turned back to the bartender. "Let me get 10 bottles of Rosé Moet, 5 bottles of Patron, a bottle of Grey Goose, and 10 bottles of water," Shah said as he sat his bookbag on the bar.

"Ok I'll be right back!" the bartender said and walked over to another bartender and had her follow her to the back. Shah reached in his book bag and pulled out the $30,000 X just gave him, then zipped his book bag back up. He turned around and started nodding his head to the music. Lil baby's song "I'm straight" turnt the club up. Shah scanned the crowd, then looked over at Lil Jerry. "This bitch packed!" he yelled over the music. "Hell yeah!" Lil Jerry said as he looked around the club shocked at how many bad bitches were there. He was beginning to wish he came alone. He was excited about the threesome he had lined up, but nothing is more exciting than some new pussy.

X stood next to Tammy sizing her up. She stood there looking good as hell in a gold Yves Saint Larant dress that hugged every curve on her body. Her black Jimmy Choo heels made her look a lot taller than what she was. X walked a little closer to her and wrapped his arms around her waist and pulled her closer to him.

"Damn you sexy as hell!" he whispered into her ear. Tammy smiled as she looked up at X. "Thank you!" she said as she tried not to seem so distant cause she felt uncomfortable being around him after what happened with Shah earlier. She was feeling X but her feelings were caught up in what she had going on with Shah.

Three bartenders walked out the back with all the bottles and set them on the bar. The first bartender walked over to the cooler and grabbed the water bottles. The original bartender walked over to the cash register then walked back over to Shah.

"That'll be $2,166," she said. Shah counted off $3,000 and handed it to her. As she stood there counting the money Shah grabbed the bottles and started passing them back.

"Can I get four cups?" Shah asked the bartender.

"Yes," she said and quickly handed him four cups. Shah passed Audrey, Tammy, Kendra, and Angelic a cup. He popped open his Grey Goose and poured Audrey and Tammy a cup.

"Y'all want some of this Goose? or y'all fucking wit the Patron?" he asked Kendra and Angelic. They both looked at each other before saying they wanted Patron.Lil Jerry poured them both a cup from his bottle. "Aye we finna move through this bitch!" Lil Ant said to Shah then him Mook and Rell made their way through the crowd. Lil Jerry wrapped his arms around Kendra and Angelic and looked over at Shah. "We finna mingle around this bitch too. Hopefully we can catch something new to take back to the room wit us tonight!" he said then walked off. Shah started laughing then took a sip from his Rosé. "You wanna take this pill wit me?" he whispered to Audrey. She quickly looked him directly into his eyes. "You for real? What kind of pill?" she asked. Shah started laughing at her reaction. "It's an ecstasy pill. I don't want to take it by myself, I want you to take it wit me," he said then reached into his pocket and pulled out the bag of pills. Audrey looked down at the pills and thought about it for a second, she wasn't sure if she wanted to. She had never messed around with any drug before, but she trusted Shah so she opened her hand for him to give her one. Shah had already taken one but wasn't feeling it so he handed Audrey one and took another one. Shah turned to Tammy and handed her one "Take it!" he said. Tammy looked down at it and quickly handed it back. "No Shah I'm not taking that!" she said

"Bitch take it!" Audrey said as she popped her pill. "No bitch y'all can do it I'm good," Tammy said. X stood there laughing. He had already popped two pills and was feeling good. He took a sip from his patron then scanned the club. Quantay and Hot Boi walked from the back of the club and ran into Trouble G standing in the middle of a crowd of females.

"What up bro?" Quantay asked as he walked up on Trouble G.

"Man, I'm good. I'm ready to hit that stage and set that bitch on fire wit this heat I got," Trouble G said.

"Tight! Make sure you do that! You gotta put on for Porter Ave!" Quantay said.

"I do that everywhere I go. I am Porter Ave you know dat!" Trouble G said.

"Yeah I know that, but these other niggas don't! It's a nigga from Madison name Cash Moody, he finna go up then you on after him so be ready!" Quantay said.

"I stay ready!" Trouble G said.

"Say no mo. Let me get over here and make sure my hoes straight. I'ma catch you before you go on!" Quantay said.

"Bet!" Trouble G said.

Quantay looked over to the V.I.P section. Hot Boi was dancing with Kelly, Rachel, and Kimi. He moved through the crowd and showed love to all the niggas and bitches he knew as he headed to the V.I.P section. Quantay walked in the V.I.P section and grabbed Kimi and started dancing with her. Shah still hadn't gone to the V.I.P section. He was too busy moving through the club dancing with Audrey and Tammy and taking pictures. The concert was lit and everybody was having a nice time, the pills had finally kicked in and had Shah turnt to a whole different level. Shah went crazy when he heard Cash Moody start performing. He reached in his bookbag and pulled out $20,000 dollars and started throwing money in the air.

"I Get Money! Broke Ass Niggas!" he yelled out as he continued to throw money. The bitches around him started going crazy jumping and grabbing money as it fell out the air. The niggas around him felt highly offended as money rain down on top of them.

"This next Artist is one of our own. Straight from Porter Ave. Y'all show some love for Trouble G," the DJ yelled out.

"Stand the fuck up Beloit!" Trouble G yelled out as he walked out on the stage. The crowd went crazy when the beat dropped, and Trouble G started rapping. Hot Boi stood there nodding his head as he listened hard to the lyrics Trouble was spitting.

"Both sides I don't play that I can't stand when a nigga do that, I was yelling East side Porter Ave when they was scared to represent true fact, Trouble G gang but you been knew that Beloit Wisconsin where the crew at, I got niggas banging Almighty, Folks, Stones, Kings too on stand, I'll kill a nigga if a nigga try me then get his mans whacked for a band, I got money wrapped in rubber bands my shoes cost about a band, real niggas only in my band for a feature I'ma need a couple bands."

As Hot Boi listened to the song he noticed a lot of pushing and shoving over by the bar area. He looked closer and saw Shah throwing money in the air.

"This bitch ass nigga!" he said to his self then quickly walked out of V.I.P and made his way through the crowd. He headed straight toward Shah with every intention of getting on bullshit wit him. He walked up on Shah and bumped him then pushed him.

"Bitch ass nigga watch out," Hot Boi said. And before Shah had a chance to turn around to see who pushed him X pushed Hot Boi.

"Fuck you think this is Dawg!" X said. Several of Quantay's guys noticed what was going on and stepped in between Hot Boi, Shah, and X.

"Y'all ain't finna do shit to fool!" one of them said as they stepped up to Shah and X. Lil Ant was standing on the side of Quantay's guys and instantly smacked one of them with his Rosé bottle knocking him out cold. Hot Boi quickly punched Lil Ant knocking him to the floor.

The club went up into an all-out brawl. It was every nigga from Beloit against Shah, Lil Ant, Lil Jerry, X, Mook, and Rell. Lil Ant balled up on the floor as ten niggas stomped him out. Lil Jerry and X bounced around throwing punches and getting punched. Rell was knocking niggas out left and right as Quantay and Hot Boi jumped on Shah.

Mook dodged a few punches then pulled his pistol out and shot the closest nigga to him in the chest. The crowd instantly scattered when they heard the first shot go off. Mook started shooting every nigga he didn't know. He rushed over to Lil Ant and helped him to his feet as he waved is pistol around.

"Let's get the fuck up out of here!" Mook yelled out to Shah.

Shah looked around for his bookbag and quickly picked it up. "Go get the car," Shah yelled out to Audrey and Tammy as he tossed Audrey the keys. Audrey and Tammy rushed to the door. Shah looked around making sure everybody he came wit was with them before they left. He could see niggas and bitches laid out on the ground everywhere. They rushed over to the exit and as soon as they stepped outside shots went off. They all ducked and took off running toward their cars as Mook quickly sent shots back.

Lil Jerry made it to the car and grabbed his gun and ran in between two cars and opened up on some niggas across the parking lot.

"Get in the car!" Kendra yelled out as she pulled up behind him. He rushed and jumped in the car as Shah and nem hauled ass out of the parking lot. Kendra quickly sped off driving off the curb and on to the street as niggas ran behind them shooting. She followed behind Lil Ant's truck as they sped down Cranston.

Back in Madison
(2:30am)

Audrey pulled into the BP gas station on Park Street. X pulled in behind her as Lil Ant pulled in behind him and Kendra behind them. Shah got out of the truck laughing, the pills he took had him through the roof. He rushed over to Lil Ant's truck. Lil Ant rolled the window down and a cloud of smoke came flying out. He looked at Lil Ant's face. He had a lot of knots and scratches on his face.

"Let me hit that shit!" Shah asked then grabbed the blunt Lil Ant passed him. He took a hit from the blunt and laughed as he exhaled a cloud of smoke.

"Them niggas just tried to beat the shit out of us!" Shah said.

"Shit tried Skud? Them bitch ass niggas stomped the shit out me," Lil Ant said then laughed.

"That's gone be the last time a few of them niggas every put they hands on a mafucka!" Mook said from the back seat and started laughing. Lil Ant and Rell both started laughing

"On Bd!" Rell said as he inhaled a cloud of smoke.

X got out of his car and walked up to Lil Ant's truck. "Let me hit that shit bro!" X said to Shah then reached for the blunt. "Bro one of them bitch ass niggas punched the shit out of me in the back of my head," X said as he rubbed the back of his head. Lil Jerry laid low in the back seat of Kendra's car. Angelic was pissed she lost a heel in the club, then had to leave her clothes at the hotel. Kendra hit the blunt, then passed it back to Lil Jerry.

"Pull up next to fool nem real quick," he said to Kendra.

"Ok," Kendra said then put the car in drive and pulled up to the pump next to Lil Ant's truck. Lil Jerry rolled his window down then raised up from the back seat so Shah could see him.

"Y'all be smooth I'm finna get up out of here!" Lil Jerry said as he took a hit from his blunt.

"Let me buy some of that," Shah said as he walked up to Kendra's car.

"Tight," Lil Jerry said then pulled the baggie from his pocket and untied it. He reached in the bag and pulled out a hand full of buds and handed them to Shah.

"What you want for this?" Shah asked.

"Shit bro, I'm smoking this shit anyway," Lil Jerry said.

"Tight love bro!" Shah said.

"Love fool," Lil Jerry said and rolled the window up and sat back. Kendra pulled off and pulled out of the gas station making a right onto Park Street.

"Yeah skud we bout to get up out of here too. We gone link wit you tomorrow so we can get back to the cash!" Lil Ant said to Shah.

"Tight cuz I'm finna take my ass to the crib these hittas got me on one!" Shah said.

"You need one of these poles before we get up out of here?" Lil Ant asked.

"Naw I got one in the truck," Shah said.

"Tight we up out of here skud!" Lil Ant said.

"Tight cuz," Shah said.

Lil Ant pulled off and made a right turn onto Park Street. Shah and X walked back over to Shah's truck. Shah got back into the passenger seat and closed the door. Tammy opened her door and got out the truck.

"Bitch call me tomorrow," Tammy said as she reached back into the truck and grabbed her cup of Grey Goose.

"Girl you already drunk as hell!" Audrey said as she looked back at Tammy.

"So, what! Call me tomorrow," Tammy said and closed the door. Shah rolled his window down

"Tight bro I'ma hit you in the AM!" Shah said to X.

"Tight bro," X said and turned and walked toward his car. Shah looked back at Tammy as she started walking to X car.

"Aye Tammy check it out real quick" Shah said. Tammy stopped and turned around and walked up to Shah's window.

"What you want Shah?" she asked drunk. It was clear to Shah that she was drunk as hell and he wanted to make sure she remembered not to take him to her crib.

"You got some money on you?" Shah asked.

"Yeah I do why you ask that?" she asked.

"Cause I was gone pay for yo hotel room tonight. You know I don't want dude at the crib," Shah said.

"Oh Damn! I forgot. Yeah you can pay for my room," she said and started laughing.

"Yeah bitch you drunk as hell, you sure you don't wanna come with us?" Audrey asked then licked her lips and smiled. Tammy started laughing then leaned her head all the way into Shah's window.

"Bitch I ain't that drunk! I don't think Shah could handle both of us tonight anyway," she said as she ran her hand over his crotch area.

"Yeah iight!" Shah immediately said. Audrey and Tammy both started laughing as Shah pulled out some money from his pocket and handed it to Tammy.

"I'ma show you want I can and can't handle!" Shah said.

"Yesss tell her baby!" Audrey said.

"I see those pills got y'all in there on some freaky shit! Y'all have fun and call me tomorrow bitch!" Tammy said and walked away from the truck.

"Bye bitch!" Audrey yelled out as she pulled off and made a right onto Park Street.

(2:45am)

Tammy and X walked down the hall of the Hilton Hotel until they reached their room. Tammy slid the key card through the lock and opened the door then walked in. X walked in and closed and locked the door. Tammy walked over to the table and sat her clutch and the money Shah gave her for the room on it. She stumbled over to the bed and laid down. The Grey goose hit her all at once and the room started spinning as she laid there.

"You straight?" X asked.

"Yeah I'm fine!" she mumbled.

"You sure?" he asked.

"Yes!" she said lower than her last answer.

"Iight!" X said as he turned the Tv on. He could see Tammy was drunk as hell and judging from the sound of her voice, he knew he wasn't getting no pussy. X looked back at her and saw she had her eyes closed, so he knew she would be sleep soon.

"Aye Tammy, what happened to your crib?" he asked.

"Nothing," she mumbled.

"Why we always getting rooms if you got a crib?" he asked.

"Because sha---" she mumbled as she fell asleep. X walked over to the bed and sat down he reached over and took her heels off.

"Yeah you drunk as hell!" X said as he stood up. He knew she was asleep when she didn't respond, so he cut the lights off then turned the heat up and laid down next to her.

Chapter Nineteen

NOVEMBER 18TH
(9AM)

S hah laid next to Audrey half asleep. He could hear his phone ringing but was too tired to move. Shah and Audrey made it home at 3:15am and the very second, they made it through the door, Audrey started ripping his clothes off. Shah had never seen Audrey so horny, but he loved every minute of it. They fucked until the sun rose and when he finally bust, she literally sucked him to sleep.

Shah's phone continued to ring and ring until he finally said fuck it and jumped out of bed and picked it up.

"Who the fuck is this?" he said to his self as he flipped it over.

"What up fool?" he said dry as hell as he answered.

"Wake yo ass up fool! I need you," TJ said.

"Shidd nigga I'm up now, what's the word?" Shah asked.

"The whole demo," TJ said letting Shah know he wasn't blowing him up for no reason.

"Tight.... Let me get my shit together real quick. I'ma be down there in a hour. I'ma link wit you somewhere out west," Shah said as he wiped the sleep from his eyes.

"Tight fool, I'm out here," TJ said.

"Say no mo," Shah said then ended the call.

Shah looked at the time and notices it was only 9:05am. "Damn it's early!" he said to his self. He'd only had two hours of sleep and he was still high off the pills he took last night. Shah looked over at Audrey as she laid ass hole naked on her stomach, then walked back over to the bed.

"Why you up so early?" Audrey asked as she rolled over and looked at him.

"Business!" Shah quickly said.

"Ok," Audrey said. "I love you," she added.

"I love you too!" Shah said as he bent down to grab his boxer briefs.

"Hold on baby! let me give you some head before you leave!" Audrey said. Shah instantly started laughing at her. "Damn lil mama on some freaky shit early! But you know I ain't about to turn it down!" Shah said as he climbed back into bed.

(10:30am)

Shah was in a great mood. As he walked into Tammy's building, he flipped through the pictures from last night in his phone as he walked up the stairs. He walked down the hall to her apartment and his heart fell to his feet when he looked and seen the door was wide open. He rushed into the apartment running straight to Audrey's old bedroom and looked under the bed.

"What tha Fuck! Fuck!" he yelled out when he didn't see the duffle bag. His heart started pounding in his chest as he rushed to the closet to check and see if he left it there. Shah ran into Tammy's room and checked under her bed then her closet.

Shah put his hands over his head as he tried his hardest to catch his breath. Thoughts of what Berto might do if he didn't have the cash in time ran through his mind. Shah started taking deep breaths. "1.6 million, 1.6 million" he said to his self as he thought about what he owed Alberto. "Ok, ok it's cool.... I'm straight. You good Shah you got a million put up. Alright, iight I got 13 bricks I need to make $600,000 and I'm straight!" Shah said as he talked himself out of a panic attack, but his stomach started hurting and his mouth became super wet. He rushed to the bathroom but before he could reach the toilet he vomited everywhere.

"Shit!" he said as he breathed heavily. He leaned over to the sink and turned the cold water on then rinsed his mouth out and threw water over his face. He looked up at his self in the mirror.

"Shah you got this!" he said to his self and stood up straight. He pulled his phone from his pocket and dialed Tammy's number.

(10:45am)

The hotel phone started ringing as Tammy and X laid in bed sleep. Tammy's phone started to ring inside her clutch. X reached over and grabbed the hotel phone and answered it.

"Hello," he said still asleep.

"Hi Mr. Young. I'm calling to inform you that you have fifteen minutes until check out," the woman from the from desk said.

"Iight," X said.

"Thank you," the woman said. X quickly hung the phone up and looked over at Tammy who was still knocked out. X shook her and woke her up.

"Tammy!" X said as he shook her.

"Whaaat!" Tammy said still tired.

"Yo phone keep ringing and it's fifteen minutes until check out," X said. Tammy yawned and stretched, then slowly rolled over and sat up. She noticed she was fully dressed, and she realized she fell asleep on him. She got up and walked over to the table and opened her clutch and pulled her phone out.

"Damn four missed calls from Shah," she said to herself before her phone started to ring again.

"Hello," she said still tired.

"Where the hell you at? I been blowing your shit up!" Shah said aggressively.

"Shah, I'm not Audrey, so don't talk to me like that!" she quickly snapped back at him.

"Man fuck all that! A mafucka broke in the crib and took all my shit!" Shah said pissed.

"What!!!" Tammy said shocked. "Somebody broke into my house?" she asked.

"Hell yeah!" Shah said.

"Oh my God! I'm about to leave this room right now, I'm on my way," Tammy said. Shah immediately ended the call. Tammy turned around and grabbed her heels.

"I need you to take me home somebody broke into my apartment," She quickly said to X as he laid in bed.

"What?" X said as he quickly jumped out the bed and put his shoes on. Tammy rushed over to the bathroom and grabbed a towel and washed her face.

(11:20am)

Shah ended the call with TJ just as Tammy and X walked through the door. Shah looked up and shook his head. Tammy examined the door and realized it was kick off the hinges.

"I can't believe this! And didn't nobody hear this shit or call the police!" Tammy said as she walked away from the door.

"You can't! Shit I can't I just got hit for forty bricks!" Shah said. X looked over at Shah with his eyes buck wide. "Damn bro forty bricks?" X asked.

"Hell yeah! Shit finna be dead on my end for a few weeks. I can't even fill yo order fool!" Shah said defeated.

"Damn Dawg, I just got my line up and running... Damn I gotta figure something out," X said as he sat down on the couch.

"I don't think shit else missing, but you might wanna check. I'ma send somebody over here to fix the door. I'm finna get up out of here," Shah said to Tammy then looked over at X.

"I'ma hit you when I'm back online!" Shah said, then picked up his phone from the coffee table. Shah knew he ain't have no time to waste he needed to make Alberto's cash asap so he could get back in business. Shah quickly dialed Lil Ant's number as he left Tammy's apartment.

(11:30am)

Nicole opened the door for Hot Boi and gave him a look that could kill.

"He in the living room," she said as she walked off. Hot Boi stood in the doorway not sure if he really wanted to come in. He knew Quantay was pissed about last night. It fucked up his plans to throw parties in the future and he had to deal with hours of questioning from the police. Hot Boi slowly walked into the house and closed the door.

"What up cuz?" Hot Boi asked as he walked into the living room. Quantay sat on the couch watching Tv he looked over at Hot Boi then back to the Tv.

"What up cuz?" Quantay said.

"Man, cuz that's on me. That's my bad," Hot Boi said.

"Cuz all you had to do was wait. I told you we was gone get the nigga. Now that shit got my name out here bad, ain't nobody gone want to rent they shit out to me. The law all on my heels cause these niggas got killed at my party," Quantay said as he looked at Hot Boi pissed. Hot Boi sat there with nothing to say cause he knew he was in the wrong and he fucked up. Quantay reached and grabbed the blunt he rolled earlier out of the ash tray and lit it.

"Look, five of my niggas died last night behind that shit," Quantay said as he exhaled the smoke. "Now I gotta help pay for five funerals. But that ain't my point. I can't let them niggas get away wit that shit. We going down to Madison tonight and we finna kill all them niggas!" Quantay said.

"Tight, I'm wit it and I'ma pay for all they funeral's that's the least I can do since the shit was on the account of me," Hot Boi said.

"Tight! You know exactly where them niggas be at?" Quantay asked.

"Yeah I know where they be. But the nigga that was shooting, I don't know him. I ain't never seen him before," Hot Boi said.

"Tight, well the rest of them niggas gone pay for it then!" Quantay said.

"You know dat!" Hot Boi said cause he was more than ready to put a hole in Shah's head. But first he wanted to strip the nigga of every dollar he was worth, and he knew just how to do it.

(3:30pm)

Shah and Lil Ant had been in traffic since 1pm catching every dollar that called the phone. Shah filled Lil Ant in on how much cash he had for Alberto and how much he needed to make so he could hurry and pay him his money and get some more product.

Lil Ant knew Shah was holding but he didn't know the dollar amount and now that he was all the way in, he planned to take full advantage of the situation. He filled Mook and Rell in on what was going on and had them working the building. Lil Ant let them know that after Alberto was paid, Shah was going to get eighty bricks and that they were going to split the profits four ways.

Shah and Lil Ant drove down East Washington smoking as they headed to catch some cash. Shah's phone started to vibrate in his lap he looked and noticed it was Keisha. Shah hadn't heard from her, so he quickly answered the phone.

"What up Keisha?" Shah asked as he answered.

"Heyy how you been stranger?" Keisha asked.

"I'm living! How you been?" Shah asked.

"I been doing fine. Thinking about you a lot lately," Keisha said.

"I been busy as hell! My bad I ain't called in a while shit been crazy!" Shah said.

"Oh, I'm sorry to hear that!" Keisha said.

"It's cool it ain't nothing I can't handle. You know small shit to a giant. But what up tho?" Shah asked.

"Nothing much. I just got off work and wanted to see you tonight if you not too busy!" Keisha said.

"Tight we can make that happen. I'ma slide through there tonight when I finish taking care of this shit," Shah said.

"Ok well make sure you do cause I miss you and I wanna see you," Keisha said.

"I won't forget I'ma be there tonight cause I miss you too!" Shah said.

"Ok," Keisha said.

"Tight!" Shah said and ended the call. Shah put his phone back down on his lap and grabbed the blunt Lil Ant was passing him.

"Who that the lil chick Keisha?" Lil Ant asked.

"Hell yeah!" Shah said as he sat back onto the leather seat and enjoyed the luxury of his new Jaguar F-Pace as he sped through the streets of Madison on a mission.

(7:00pm)

As X drove up the Interstate headed to Fond du lac, he picked up his phone to call Vince. He reached and turned down the music while he waited for Vince to answer.

"Yeah what up?" Vince said as he answered.

"I'm on my way dawg," X said.

"Tight where you coming from?" Vince asked.

"It don't even matter it's where I'm going you hear me!" X said. Vince started laughing.

"Ok talk that shit den, let me know when you get here," Vince said.

"Shit my GPS say I'm twenty minutes away cuz," X said.

"Tight..... Aw yeah we in apt 4," Vince said.

"Yup, say no more," X said then ended the call. He sat his phone down in his lap. As he drove, he started to reflect back on what happened last night.

X pulled into Tammy's lot and looked around for Shah's truck before he pulled into the closest parking space in front of her building. He looked at his phone and seen that it was 3:35am. He wanted to make this as quick as possible. He picked up the keys to her apartment he took from her clutch and jumped out the car and ran to her building.

X made his way up the stairs and down the hall to her apartment. He unlocked the door and opened it slowly. He peeked his head in to see if anybody was there before he walked in. When he didn't see anyone, he walked in and closed the door. X quietly crept through the apartment as he checked both rooms making sure no one was there. After realizing no was there, he immediately started looking for a safe.

He searched Tammy's room top to bottom. He didn't want to make a mess just in case he was mistaken and read too much into what she was about to say. He walked over to the next bedroom and checked the closet, then the dresser drawers then under the mattress. X looked under the bed and his heart started pounding when he seen a duffle bag. He quickly pulled the bag from under the bed and opened it. He was shocked when he saw it was stuffed full of bricks of boy. X immediately zipped the bag and rushed out of the apartment. He ran to the car and popped the trunk and tossed the bag in and closed it. X jumped in the car and was about to pull off when he realized he didn't lock the door.

He quickly decided he needed to make it look like somebody kicked the door in, so he jumped out of the car and ran back into the building. X rushed up stairs to Tammy's apartment and locked the door then kicked it off the hinges and ran out the building. X hurried and rushed back to the hotel before Tammy could realize he left.

"Exit right!" his GPS said interrupting his thought. X got geeked once he knew he finally made it. He quickly exited the freeway and made a left on Pioneer Road. He instantly made a conscious effort to calm his nerves.

"I ain't made a penny yet let me calm my nerves" he said to his self. He noticed he was coming up on a gas station and decided to pull in. X pulled in front of the gas station and parked. He pulled the duffle bag off the backseat and stuffed it on the floor behind the passenger seat and got out and walked into the gas station. X walked straight to the back cooler and grabbed a bottle of water and a red bull. He was still feeling the pills he took last night and needed to hydrate his self. He walked up to the register and sat the water bottle and red bull on the counter.

"Can I get a pack of Newport 100's?" he asked the clerk. She reached and pulled down a pack of Newport's and sat them on the counter as she rung up his stuff.

"That'll be $11.95," she said to X who was too busy watching his car making sure no one went in it. "$11.95," she said again louder. X looked over at the clerk "Oh my bad!" he said then reached into his pocket and pulled out a fifty-dollar bill and handed it to her. He grabbed his cigarettes, red bull, and water bottle off the counter and started walking off.

"Sir, sir your change!" the clerk quickly said when she noticed he was about to leave.

"Damn I'm trippin! Thanks," X said as he grabbed his change and quickly walked out the store. He jumped into his car and called Travis. As he waited for Travis to answer he packed his cigarettes then pulled one out and lit it.

"Hey what's up?" Travis asked as he answered the phone.

"It's all good Trav, check it out. I want you to get all y'all funds together and I'ma get at you in like an hour," X said.

"Okay, I got something right now if you wanna meet me somewhere really quick," Travis said.

"Naw, I'ma let you know when it's time. I ain't even there yet. I'm just calling so y'all can be ready when I get there," X said.

"Oh, me and my guys always have money so it's always a go, so you know," Travis said.

"Tight say no more see y'all in an hour," X said then quickly ended the call. X cracked his window and opened his red bull then took a sip, he looked out his rearview mirror then reversed out his parking space. He pulled out the same way he came in and made a right on Pioneer Road.

"In three hundred feet turn right" the GPS said. X made a right into an apartment complex and drove through the lot.

"Your destination is on your left" the GPS said. X pulled over in front of Vince's building and parked. X reached behind the passenger seat and grabbed the duffle bag and pulled it into the passenger seat. He unzipped the bag and pulled out a brick and sat it on the passenger side floor then zipped the bag back up.

Vince was always known for getting money, but X wasn't too sure what Vince been up too he hadn't seen or heard from him in years. X reached into the back seat and grabbed his pull over hoodie and put it on, he reached over to the passenger side floor and grabbed the brick and stuffed it in the front of his pants then pulled his hoodie and shirt down. X grabbed his glock .40 from under his seat with his left hand and pulled his hoodie sleeve over his hand and the gun. X wanted to be ready for whatever, now that he had his mill ticket the only way he was parting ways from it was if he was dead. And before death he was gone make sure he gave a mafucka hell cause he refused to die alone. X turned the car off and popped the trunk, he grabbed the duffle bag off the passenger seat, and got out the car. He tossed it in the trunk and closed it. X made sure he locked the car doors before walking up to Vince's building.

(1:50am)
Present Day!

"Look man I got $80,000 in the truck on the back seat y'all can take it!" Shah said as he held his hands in the air.

"Shut yo bitch ass up!" Rell said as he pressed his glock harder against the back of Shah's head.

"Skud we came to break the bank!" Mook said as he picked Shah's car keys up off the ground.

"Put his bitch as in the back seat! let's go for a ride!" Mook said to Rell.

"Iight!" Rell said as he pulled Shah backwards by the back of his hoodie to the back door and opened it then forced Shah into the back seat. He held his pistol to the back of Shah's head as he sat next to him in the back seat. Mook got into the driver seat and started the car and pulled out of the parking lot.

"Man look y'all ain't gotta do this!" Shah begged.

"Shut the fuck up!" Mook said as he pulled his phone out to make a call. Shah was trying his hardest to think of who this was robbing him because the voices sounded familiar.

"I got him! You wanna talk to him! Iight, iight hold on," Mook said, then reached back with the phone.

"The phone for you!" Mook said to Shah.

"What?" Shah asked.

"Bitch ass nigga grab the phone!" Rell said to Shah. Shah reached up and grabbed the phone.

"Hello?" Shah asked confused.

"What up Skud! Look I'm out here wit Audrey. I need that combination," Lil Ant said calmly.

"Damn cuz this how you gone get down on me?" Shah asked when it finally dawned on him that Lil Ant was behind this hit.

"Look cuz, don't take it personal but you a fish and I'ma shark! It's in my DNA to attack when it's blood in the water. So I'm doing what I do," Lil Ant said. Shah held the phone to his ear shocked and speechless.

"Look skud I'ma ask you one more time and if you hesitate or stall, I'ma just shoot this bitch in the head! Now what's the fucking combination to the safe?" Lil Ant said.

"Iight, iight it's 30-3-23" Shah quickly said.

"Okay let's see if that's the truth!" Lil Ant said as he walked Audrey over to the safe and pushed her to the floor.

"Bitch open it! 30-3-23" Lil Ant said to Audrey. Shah held the phone to his ear listening to what was happening.

"Shah skud you sweet. I don't know how you lasted this long," Mook said as he continued to drive. Shah listened closely as Audrey opened the safe. Lil Ant pushed Audrey out the way as he looked into the safe.

"Ok skud! Now put it in here!" Lil Ant said to Audrey, as he tossed her the duffle bag he took from the side of Shah's desk. Audrey immediately started filling up the bag as she panicked.

"Please don't hurt me!" Audrey asked.

"Bitch shut the fuck up!" Lil Ant quickly said.

"Aye cuz you know I love you right!" Lil Ant said to Shah then started laughing.

"Man fuck you!" Shah said.

"Put Mook back on the phone," Lil Ant said.

"You got what you wanted just let her go!" Shah said.

"You ain't running shit no more cuz. Put Mook on the before I change my mind and kill this pretty ass bitch of yours!" Lil Ant said. Shah tossed the phone back into the front to Mook.

"What up skud?" Mook asked.

"I got it skud! Go ahead and handle him and I'ma take care of this over here. Meet me at Tonya's crib," Lil Ant said.

"Tight!" Mook said and ended the call.

"What's up?" Rell asked Mook.

"Skud said we gone let him go he got the cash!" Mook said.

"Tight!" Rell said, then started laughing.

"Take his phone!" Mook said to Rell.

"Tight!" Rell said as he reached into Shah's pocket and took his cash and his phone. Rell looked around outside the truck then looked back up to Mook.

"This street look good enough!" Rell said. Mook quickly pulled over and looked back.

"Tight get yo bitch ass out!" Mook said as Rell pushed Shah closer to the rear passenger door.

"Just know I'm coming for yall!" Shah said as he opened the door and stepped out of the truck.

"No you ain't pussy!" Rell said then he shot Shah in the back of his head and shot him three more times before Mook pulled off into the darkness of the night!

To be continued!!!!!!!

Also Available by Bagz of Money Content

Live by It, Die by It (By: Ice Money)

Mercenary (By: Ice Money)

The Ruler of the Red Ruler (By: Kutta)

Block Boyz (By: Juvi)

Team Savage (By Ace Boogie)

Team Savage 2 (By Ace Boogie)

Available at Bagzofmoneycontent.com and most major bookstores.